# MOUNTAIN LION BLUES

## ADAM GREENFIELD

Pelekinesis

*Mountain Lion Blues* by Adam Greenfield
978-1-949790-83-2 Paperback
978-1-949790-84-9 Ebook

Library of Congress Control Number: 2023943691
Cover artwork by Abby Weintraub
Cover photograph: Jena Ardell/Moment via Getty Images
Layout and book design by Mark Givens
First Pelekinesis Printing 2023

For information:
Pelekinesis, 112 Harvard Ave #65, Claremont, CA 91711 USA

www.pelekinesis.com

# MOUNTAIN LION BLUES

Adam Greenfield

For Ellen

# CONTENTS

Joke: What's the difference between a violin and viola?

Answer: A viola burns longer.

# CHAPTER 1

If you'd told me on Friday, when I drove deep into Koreatown to the address Lydia gave me, my newly washed jeans and shirt giving off the Florida-fake smell of dryer sheets, my face stinging winterly from the aftershave I'd slapped on as the cherry on top, that things could go so wrong and so right at the same time, and that both could feel true and warm in their own impeccable ways, I'd still have taken her out that first night and fallen in love with her.

Lydia lived with her mother in a five-story shipwreck of a building in a run-down part of Los Angeles that was flanked by long-abandoned vacant lots. The ground sprouted long, willowy strands of weeds, concrete, and rebar from its depths — evidence of earthquake epicenters and ancient civilizations that existed here long before us.

I parked, rolled down my window and felt grateful for the warm breeze — I didn't even care that it was the exhaust of passing cars. Someone in the building was playing a Chet Baker record from an open window, and I could hear the bumps and scratches as Chet made his case for either a woman or a narcotic he wanted but couldn't have.

All along the sidewalk, bits of broken glass glittered garishly in the headlights of passing cars, giving the impression that there was something valuable here, but that it was fleeting, a state of mind. A meter maid bobbed by me, flitting from meter to meter like a bee, pollinating misfortune as she went.

"Am I safe?" I asked her, nodding at my car.

"Are any of us?" she replied with a smile. I gave her a shrug as a courtesy, letting her know she had stumped me in the best way possible.

As I got closer to Lydia's building, I saw the chaotic and overwhelming network of cracks that ran the length of the building. They were busted capillaries describing the rich social life of a broken-down grande dame who had known how to have a good time in her day and hadn't stopped until it was too late. I approached the front steps just as an old Korean woman was trying to lug up a small shopping cart filled to the brim with the most vivid assortment of the freshest fruits and vegetables I'd ever seen.

"Let me help you," I said, grabbing the cart and pulling it up. I couldn't believe how beautiful the produce was. This wasn't white-people-with-disposable-income produce; it was food for people in the know. Deep-state nutrition.

Fridays usually meant very little to me, but tonight I felt positively giddy. Though I had no close friends, I had acquaintances — regulars at the nearby Hollywood Tennis Club bar who knew me as well as anyone could know anyone in a place with cottage cheese ceilings. Joining the Club was one of the few extravagances I allowed myself once I made VP at the investment banking firm McGiven, Loam & Cank. I had no intention of ever learning to play tennis and took my exercise in the form of the other indulgence I allowed myself once I started to make a little bit of money; a waterbed which took the abs of a god to get out of every morning.

"I'll take the stairs," I said to no one in particular as the old lady went through the elevator doors. I bounded up two steps at a time, essentially throwing myself towards the fifth floor. Once I arrived, the hallway seemed to summon the spirits of all the doomed dandies who had doubtlessly called this place home at one time or another. I whistled something grating and optimistic for company as I walked down the hall, found the apartment and loudly knocked. I straightened an imaginary tie and waited for everything to start. No one answered and I was about to knock again, when, instead of the voice of my future, I heard a scream.

I always wondered how I'd react if ever called upon to perform some spontaneous feat of bravery. I realized they're not exactly complementary, spontaneity and bravery. The former is more of a state of mind and the latter a quirk of nature, like double-jointedness or near-sightedness. But still, faced with the opportunity, what would I do?

I opened Lydia's door just enough to get my head through and was immediately assaulted by a succession of odors coming at me, one after another, like a gang initiation: fish sticks, stale cigarette smoke, generic vitamins, a life story told in increments of barely getting by.

"Hello?" I called out, somehow expecting my voice to echo back as though I'd just discovered the hidden entrance to another dimension. Nothing greeted me but the ground-up static coming from a TV somewhere.

I squeezed my way in and tip-toed down a long hallway towards the only light I could see, a wedge of pale yellow hatcheting its way under a door at the far end of the hallway. I walked past what I assumed were framed family pictures, but really, they could have been anything — torture-porn Polaroids, relatives in blackface. My imagination was getting away from me. Where just a minute or so ago, the building had been a charming old wreck of a place, I now imagined row after row of apartments filled with boa constrictors coiled in toilet bowls and sink water that caught fire if you held a match to it. And Chet Baker wasn't a recording; someone had him tied up and was forcing him to sing torch songs to their taxidermied mother. Beneath my feet the wooden floor moaned, heartbroken, with every cautious step I took.

"Duncan? Is that you?"

"Hello? Lydia?" I asked cautiously, as though waiting for a trap to be sprung on me.

"Yes, Duncan! It's me. Can you come back here, please?" She was still yelling, but not quite as loudly. "I need your help."

As I opened the bathroom door, mist swirled around the room in cartoonish spirals and a coat of steam covered the mirror above the sink. Lydia sat on the side of the tub, her arm plunged into the soapy water, holding the hand of one of the fattest people I'd ever seen in my life.

Lydia smiled at me. "This is my mother, Martha. Mom, this is Duncan." From the water, she began to extract her hand, which I quickly realized was joined to her mother's. "Mom is stuck…" said Lydia as she slowly stood, still trying to gently pull her hand away. But her mother held on tightly. "Well, not stuck exactly, but she won't get out of the tub unless I get the neighbor to come down and coax her out. Would you mind holding her hand while I run downstairs?"

She managed to get free and was already joining my hand with her mother's. "I know this is really weird," she said, and I had the distinct sense that this was not her first obese-woman-stuck-in-a-tub rodeo, "but Mom's got a lot of…problems…I hope you don't mind. I promise I'll be right back," she said, already moving down the hallway. "I'll make it up to you, Duncan," she half-yelled as I took a seat on the edge of the tub and tried to tactfully avert my eyes.

As I took Martha's hand in mine, I felt a quick pulse of irrational fear that she was gone forever, that I'd be stuck here, tethered to Martha for all eternity, a willing recipient of an ancient curse that everyone in the civilized world but me knew all about. Martha's small blue eyes were fixed rigidly on my face, searching for something, it seemed; answers in the abstract sense, and more specifi-cally, proof beyond the shadow of a doubt that helplessness might just be the new biological imperative. I grinned and turned away, but her grip tightened and my hand began to throb. The bare lightbulb above the mirror was coated in a film of condensation, blurring the light in the room so that everything appeared submerged, drowning in a pool of Vaseline. Beneath everything I noticed the sweet smell of women's soap, fragrant and hopeful, and wondered just how the hell I'd gotten myself into this mess.

Around the room was a gloomy combination of girlish ephemera and nursing home necessities. A Barbie doll was stuck in a spare roll of toilet paper, its badly knitted pink dress overflowing to keep the offending paper out of sight, and on the wall was a crocheted picture of a smiling mermaid. Like a legion of good little soldiers, rows of prescription bottles, vitamins and supplements stood at strict attention. Behind those, the serious shit: diabetes medicine, stuff for gout, and ancient medicines besides, cures and salts I could only guess the use of. That was all not to mention an interminable supply of antibiotics for infections past, present, and future. In my mind I nicknamed her 'Big Pharma' and decided that she was either the sickest person I'd ever laid eyes on or the best prepared, which, when considered in a certain light, was a horrible kind of sickness all on its own.

Water dripped into the bath, slowly, and I saw it was coming from the ceiling right above the tub where a brown semi-circle of plaster was shitting out marble-sized drops of water that hit the surface of the tub with a dull *plop*, a singular hollow sound that echoed throughout the room, but that also reverberated, centerless, within me, a subtle tintinnabulation that was the perfect accompaniment to the mounting dread I felt that I'd been left here for good.

"Lydia isn't always that nice to me." Martha whispered.

"Oh," I replied, and then teetering on the edge of trying to decide how involved I wanted to get, I asked, "What do you mean?"

"Sometimes she yells at me." Her fingers wiggled like startled leeches.

"Well," I said, trying to put a positive spin on things, "we all lose our patience sometimes. She must love you very much." I looked around the room taking in the lavender towels, the shell-shaped hand soap. If this wasn't love I didn't know what was. "In fact," I went on with a shred of confidence, "I'm sure that she loves you."

Martha made a little noise like a machine being turned off.

"Mrs. Kim told me that I have an animal spirit. Did you know that?" She nodded her head, and without waiting for an answer said, "And every night I dream I'm an animal. Sometimes it's a bird, and sometimes it's a skunk. But do you know what I mostly am?"

I shook my head, curious despite myself.

"Mostly I'm a big, beautiful mountain lion that has black circles around its eyes and tan fur and I'm strong and I can run as fast as anything God ever made," she said, genuinely in awe of herself. "I can just plop down and lick my paws, and yawn and stretch, and no one bothers me. You know why?"

"Why?" I asked, genuinely interested.

"Because I'm a mountain lion!" She burped up a little laugh which made me laugh too.

"But then in my dreams, Lydia always shows up. She starts petting me and sometimes she's trying to feed me something. But no matter what she does, I always do the same thing. I leap up," she picked her arms out of the water, our hands still joined, "and I jump on top of her and I tear her apart!" She let her hands fall back in the water as chills waltzed down my arms. "And that's not even the end of it. I wish it was, but it goes on and pretty soon I'm ripping her apart, and I can feel my claws slashing her skin, my teeth going into the meat of her, and it's so easy…it's so easy to tear her apart. And when I wake up," her voice suddenly sheared off into a whisper, "I can still taste Lydia's blood."

I didn't know what to say. I'd had dreams of being more powerful than I really was, of being victorious despite the odds. Why shouldn't it make sense then that some people had dreams in which they were animals, dreams in which they preened in their plumage and reveled in metaphors that were more real than the real them?

Before I could answer, though, the front door squeaked open and Martha looked at me, wide-eyed with panic. "Don't tell, okay?"

"I won't," I said, feeling like we should do a pinkie swear or something to cement our doleful understanding. But there was no need, I told myself as she gripped my hand even tighter, her eyes wider than the night. I was already in way too deep.

# CHAPTER 2

Lydia hurried back into the room, trailed by the old Korean lady I'd seen when I came into the building.

"Mrs. Kim is here, Mom, but you have to promise me you're not going to do this anymore. Do you understand? Can you say 'I promise I won't stay in the tub when Lydia tells me it's time to get out'?"

Martha, her eyes still searching my face - maybe for a nod that I wouldn't reveal her secret dream or maybe just because she didn't want to look at Lydia - gave no indication that she'd heard a word her daughter said.

"Jesus Christ!" Lydia screamed as she reached down into the water to separate our hands. I felt her double down on her grip, and I was surprised at how strong she was. Whatever she was, she wasn't a sick woman. Sick women couldn't crush hands like that - sick women knew how to hurt in other ways.

"Mom, let go!"

Mrs. Kim walked to where Martha's head was and, kneeling next to her, began whispering in her ear. I couldn't hear what she was saying, whether it was in Korean or English. Maybe it was just the tone of her voice, a noise I imagined as being soothing, sing-songy and silken, but I felt Martha's grip begin to loosen.

I looked over at Lydia, who bore the expression of someone who was no stranger to defeat. In fact, it looked good on her, the way grief made some women look more exotic. Whatever it was, it was another secret I would never tell her.

Christ, I thought, the secrets were really piling up.

Finally, Martha turned to Mrs. Kim and nodded. She began to try and get out of the tub, all of our hands hoisting parts of her, pulling, pulling, pulling. I didn't even bother looking away. We were way past modesty by this point. On to bigger and better things: exploration, survival, climate change -- I was making a fucking difference.

Martha leaned on all of us as she struggled out of the tub, one foot and then the other, a little slip and the whole thing would come crashing down. I felt terrible for her as I caught a glimpse of her gigantic pink breasts hanging heavily from her chest. Rolls of fat rippled as she moved and it almost looked like she occupied many dimensions at once, one where she was and the other where her body lagged behind slightly in another space and time.

Mrs. Kim draped a towel around Martha's shoulders, led her slowly into the bedroom, and gently closed the door. Whatever was happening in there was being done in silence. As Lydia and I stood in the middle of the bathroom, staring at one another, each of us out of words but for very different reasons, the only sound we heard was the last of the water being sucked down the drain with a lecherous slurp that almost made me blush.

"Lydia," I started to say, but she began sobbing heavily into my ear. I plied her with glass after glass of cold water, patted her back, and said "Shh" in the most uncondescending way I could. Nothing terrified me more than seeing a woman cry. It was a horrifying sight: the red, puffy eyes and heaving, collapsing breaths, the short-circuiting tremor that ran through them like wildfire. I was suddenly reminded of a movie we saw in high school biology class that showed the time-lapsed decomposition of a rabbit carcass — how the dead thing twitched as it was devoured by insects and then by the earth itself. I wasn't sure what else to do but wait it out and hope there'd still be a trace of her when it was done.

In her mother's old room, stacks of romance novels teetered to precarious heights like offerings to the gods of love and hoarding. Along one wall were a number of open suitcases spilling out their guts of bikinis and Stevie Nicks scarves. An old exercise bike rusted in the corner, looking more like farming equipment or an iron lung than anything that could ever possibly be good for you. Added together, it was what was left of a lifetime of New Year's resolutions, spineless good intentions to which I could all too easily relate.

I saw that Lydia was watching me with something like hope.

"Thanks," she said, the last of her sniffles trailing off.

"For what?" I asked.

"For not telling me that 'everything is going to be okay'. I hate that."

"Oh," I said, "I'd never say that."

"Wanna put some music on?" She pointed at an old boom box with a stack of cassettes lined up next to it. I scanned the tapes with a million questions burning in my mind.

"How about the Smiths?"

"Ugh!" she shouted. "I am SO sick of Morrissey telling me what to do! What is it...25 years of that little snake making me feel bad about having a uterus? I'm so over it."

I laughed. "These are your tapes, not mine."

"I know, I know," she said, walking over to where I was standing. When she reached down to run her fingers along the row of tapes, her arm brushed mine.

"I've got it!" she said, grabbing a tape and jamming it into the player without letting me see what it was.

The first couple twisting guitar notes of something only vaguely familiar snaked their way out of the tinny speakers, followed by a sax, and then percussion that was as tropical as it was drugged out.

"Steely Dan," I said, tapping my chin knowingly. "Interesting choice."

"Felt like the right thing to do," she said, as matter-of-factly as if she'd just given someone CPR. "Who doesn't like Steely Dan?"

I thought about it for a minute.

"I don't know if anyone really likes Steely Dan. It's more like a cry for help."

"But a very funky cry for help."

I had a million questions for her, and I could feel the feral words scrolling back and forth across my skull, things I needed to know about her life, answers I felt that I deserved. Lydia turned down the stereo, sat on the edge of the bed, and patted the spot next to her. I sat and folded my hands in my lap.

"Relax," Lydia said, laughing and taking one of my hands in hers. Normally, there was nothing I hated more than being told to relax. When she said it, though, it was different.

We stared at the rug, searching its swirling purple and red patterns for answers to questions that were too embarrassing to actually say out loud, let alone admit to ourselves. I leaned over and inhaled. She smelled good. Sweet. She was the smell of flowers after the flowers had been taken away and all that was left was the lingering scent, a fading memory of beauty.

"If I were to tell you," she began, her voice barely more than a whisper, like an animal poking its head out of a warm winter cave, "that my mother was once a beautiful woman, would you believe me?"

Thinking about her mother, the mountain lion, who could dream extra folds in time and space, I nodded without hesitation. I decided on the spot that I would start believing everything people told me, that I would be a sponge of faith from that point forward. When the right person came along, my heart would sing out, unbidden. *I've been waiting my whole life to be lied to by a woman like you!*

I wanted to be tricked, I realized, to be lied to and lovingly toyed with, to worship little disappointments as a cornerstone of my faith, which, up until that point, was a lifelong membership in the Unholy Church of Going Through the Motions.

"Sure, I believe it," I said. She didn't know her mother dreamed of ripping her from limb to limb, of devouring her and licking the blood off her hands, and I certainly wasn't going to be the one to tell her. "Why wouldn't I?"

"Thanks," she said as her eyes tumbled bashfully away from mine.

"For what?"

"For not asking me any questions."

"Oh, that," I said. "I'm naturally uncurious. I come from a long line of conformists and capitulators. If you put my DNA under a microscope you'd see it goose-stepping." As the words left my mouth I wondered how long my bad jokes would keep her entertained.

She smiled and walked over to the dresser. "What are you looking for, Duncan? Can I ask you that?"

I chuckled. "I think we're beyond personal," I answered thinking of her mother. "We're downright gynecological at this point. Besides, I'm an open book. It's called *The Reluctant Human*. It's the one that has a picture of a crying FBI profiler on the cover. Ever hear of it?"

She laughed. "Well, how about it?"

I thought for a moment. "If I was to say a Jewish girl who does German things, does that ring any bells?"

She laughed again. Making her laugh felt like getting to the top of a low mountain or swatting a particularly annoying mosquito, a small, shallow victory I could write on my resumé to prove that there was more to being human than a waterbed and a signature beverage at Starbucks.

"I'm serious, Duncan."

*You*, I wanted to say. *This place.* And it surprised me to think those things, surprised me to want something when, for so long, I didn't even know what it was I was supposed to want, let alone actually desire it.

"I don't know," I confessed, scared to ask her the same question.

"I've got an idea," she said, snapping her fingers with the thrill of mischief lighting up her eyes. "Go wait in the hall. I want to show you something."

"What?" I asked, letting her push me out into the hall and then close the door in my face with a girly squeal.

I pressed my ear against the door for a moment, trying to get a clue as to what odd nightcap she might have in store for me, but all I could hear was the beaded curtain of sound that was Steely Dan, sincere as all get-out about someone or something named Kid Charlemagne, so I took it as a cue to wait for as long as she needed me to. Waiting was the easy part.

# CHAPTER 3

It was hard to fathom that we'd only met a few days earlier, at a Starbucks in the lobby of the building where I worked. Since I was still only a vice president at the firm, I took only quick breaks from my desk. As I gleaned from my peers, all of whom were hell-bent on advancement, being seen at the job was almost as important as the job itself. The firm was a place of unlimited mobility if you were willing to put in your time, the next level up a closely guarded secret accessed only by those willing to blindly sacrifice everything for the sake of the 'greater good.' That term was thrown around pretty liberally, I thought, for a place that made its employees rich beyond all common decency by acting as middle men while moving money from one organization to another, sloughing off bits and pieces of commissions that, when added up together at the end of the day, were nothing short of obscene.

The line at the Starbucks was longer than usual. I tapped my loafer impatiently as I suffered through one slow customer after another. It was the most profound series of convoluted coffee orders I'd ever witnessed in my consumer life, each more complicated than the last.

I noticed the woman ahead of me crossing and uncrossing her arms at each new curveball thrown at the minimum-wage staff, vexing flavor profiles that were the equivalent of culinary Sanskrit, growing angrier and angrier by the moment. "Jesus Fucking Christ," she muttered, just loud enough for everyone within a three-block radius to hear. "You've got to be fucking kidding me."

Her sandy brown hair was pulled up in a high ponytail, and she had on a Mötley Crüe tour t-shirt and jeans that were too tight for a real day job. This probably meant she was in the building for a session with a psychologist or some equivalent extraneous doctor appointment like Rolfing or accu-hypnosis or one of those other things on the directory I could never quite intuit, and besides, wasn't medicine supposed to be the opposite of esoteric?

There was just one guy in front of her, his shirt hung low exposing back hair that looked as though it'd been combed and parted. "The croissant…,"he said., "What exactly is your definition of savory?" she spun around on her axis of psychic desperation and beseeched me, with the saddest eyes I'd ever seen, "Kill me. Please."

Her face was vivid and suffused with brightness, and the smile she flashed washed over me like sunshine coming over a transom.

"Maybe not quite yet. At least not until we get to know one another a little better," she said, smiling.

"That seems reasonable," I said, giving her a smile of my own. "I appreciate that in a woman."

"What? Reason?"

"That and wanting to wait until at least the second date for homicide. Shows prudence."

She laughed, and I felt proud that I'd entertained her. It was important to me, for some reason I couldn't quite put my finger on, that she liked me. She had that effect. Even later, when it was all over, the desire to please her never really left me — an unconscious need that sometimes felt more like creeping dread compelling me to make sure she was happy and comfortable.

At first, I found it part of her irresistibility, this immediate sense of calm it gave me to be near someone I wanted to unconditionally care for. Later, it became a burden, as everyone's qualities we once thought unimpeachable eventually do.

It was her turn to order and, before she could tell the shell-shocked barista what she wanted, I leaned in closer to her than I should have and whispered, "Make it quick." She laughed and turned around, and our faces were suddenly only a couple of inches apart, close enough to smell her sweet breath, to see the fine blonde hairs on her upper lip, the blush of pale freckles pollinating her cheeks.

When the barista asked her name she said, "Lydia," in a voice loud enough for me to hear. And then she added, "310-467-8907."

She hung around the counter as I placed my order. "Duncan Beldon," I said, turning towards Lydia. She smiled and pretended not to be listening.

As I paid, I saw her walking out the door with her coffee. I considered going after her, but thought better of it. I had her number, and besides, I worried that going after her would just annoy her.

I went back upstairs and pushed some more papers around, added up a few more columns, and waited for two other VP's to leave, packed up my stuff and headed for the car. There were rules about leaving the office. Leaving first was like playing Russian Roulette with a fully loaded gun. Second was as low as I would go. Usually I liked to be fifth or later, but I was eager to get home and call Lydia.

I called her around 9 and we wound up talking for almost an hour. She told me she used to be a fashion buyer but that now she cared for her mom, a job she found infinitely more rewarding. "Yeah, right," she mocked herself, and I caught more than a hint of bitterness. But I didn't mind it. My parents had died before it ever got to that stage with them and I sometimes wondered whether or not I'd have had the patience to be their caretaker; feed them, drive them around to their appointments, or, god forbid, bathe them. To be honest, it sounded like a fucking nightmare. I didn't consider myself a selfish person, but didn't the nature versus-nurture thing kind of exempt me? I mean, clearly they hadn't raised me to do that kind of thing otherwise I'd have had that inclination. "In a way," I told her, "I see myself as fulfilling their parenting philosophy by not feeling like I needed to be there. My neglect of them would have been the icing on their parenting cake. I only wish they could have lived long enough to see what a selfish piece of shit I've become."

She laughed and it was even sweeter than I remembered.

I opened the fridge and took out a sweaty beer, clutching the phone between my neck and shoulder as I twisted off the cap, pitching it into the garbage.

"Do you mind if I ask…what's wrong with your mom?"

There was a silence, and I wondered if I had overstepped.

"Oh, this and that. A lot of things." And then. "It's a long story."

"Got it," I said to her, trying to let her know that it was okay with me if she didn't want to talk about it.

"Anyway…" she said in that way that said it was time for me to put up or shut up.

So, I asked her for a date.

As I waited for Lydia outside the room, I wandered down the hallway leading back to the kitchen — a minefield trapped with little creaks and groans. It seemed like every other step set off a moan from the floor, a low painful "euthanize me now" structural plea for release with which I could wholly sympathize.

Walking further and further from the only illumination in the apartment, the twin slices of light bleeding out from under each of the bedroom doorways, I stuck my arms out and let my hands feel around for a light switch. I knew that straight ahead was the kitchen because I could hear the hum of the fridge and the ticking of a wall clock, two sounds that, when blended together, were the very articulation of home, what the sound of a heavy breather was to anonymous phone calls or the crashing of waves and screams of gulls were to the beach.

In the kitchen, a man's cardigan lay draped over a chair, a bottle of Men's Centrum vitamins sat covered in a fine layer of dust on the counter next to the toaster, and a pair of rimless readers rested on the window sill. Added together, these felt more like evidence than reminders, as though there'd been a heinous crime committed years ago and the police had told Lydia and Martha not to touch anything, but then never came back to tag it and bag it.

I bent to read a grocery list still taped to the fridge. It was a reminder to buy celery, chicken stock, carrots and parsley; someone had planned to make soup and I wondered if they ever went through with it or if that's when everything had gone to shit making the idea of soup not just untenable, but utterly unimaginable.

I slipped on the old brown cardigan, which fit almost perfectly. I inhaled the scent of it and it was that perfect balance of damp wool and one of those old-fashioned colognes that was supposed to make white-collar schlubs smell like merchant marines, olfactory-inspired delusions of grandeur that launched a thousand extra-marital affairs and that many more unaffordable sports car purchases. And it only took me a minute of inhaling that scent, of the come-hither silence I was suddenly enveloped within, to make me realize that this was what I wanted. All of it. The secrets, the stillness, moments that were black holes of meaning.

"Duncan?" Lydia called out.

I walked down the hall and, trying the door handle, found it locked.

"Lydia," I said, sticking my hands into the sweater pockets and finding a cigarette butt. I didn't have to look at it to know it was a Winston, the same brand my dad smoked, "open the door."

"Only if you promise me something."

"Sure," I answered her, and, if I was being honest with myself there was nothing she might want me to do that I wouldn't say yes to. I was stuck in a moment I could see myself living in until the end of time, growing old within the confines of its perfect shape. These were broken people who didn't try to hide their damaged parts, and I felt at home among them.

"Okay," she answered, and I could just about hear the smile that lurched to her lips, like the sound of the hammer of a gun being pulled back, something loaded and dangerous. "Before I open the door I want you to promise me that this doesn't count as a first date. This isn't what I wanted it to be."

"Absolutely," I said. "Not a first date. Not by a long shot." I tried to find the exact word that would let her know I understood, that I saw purpose everywhere I looked. "This is something else. But Lydia, I wanted to ask, what happened to your dad?"

I heard her sigh and then a bump which I guessed was her leaning her forehead against the door. I tried the handle again. Still locked.

"I'll give you a hint; fathers either leave or die. Guess which mine did."

"I don't want to guess," I said, recognizing a no-win situation when I saw one. "But you don't have to tell me."

The door was still locked and I wondered what she was waiting for.

"Ly-di-a," I sang to her, hoping it would be close enough to the password she was looking for to let me in.

"Oh, fuck it," she finally muttered, which, coincidentally, were my three favorite words in the English language. The lock clicked and the door opened just a crack, enough to let me know that I could come in if that was what I wanted.

# CHAPTER 4

When I was in college, I had a different girlfriend for each of the four years, matriculating from one to the next as though it were part of the curriculum. Senior year's girl was a stunning redhead from one of those soft states in the middle of the country – Nebraska, Oklahoma – I couldn't remember which one exactly. One night, we were going back to her place after a long study session in the library. While we'd been inside, an ice storm had come and gone, lacquering the entire campus in an even coating of dazzling glass. Everything, from the buildings to the trees, sparkled maniacally as the lights on campus sent off cartwheeling vapor trails of cartoonish wealth in every direction, infecting the air itself with a sense that we had struck the motherlode and would all soon be rich.

"Isn't it beautiful, Duncan?" she asked, all wide-eyed, and I admitted, somewhat begrudgingly, that it was. Graduation was just around the corner, and I couldn't decide what to do about our relationship. It wasn't an unpleasant thing, our being together — in fact, of all four of my girlfriends throughout college, she was definitely the one I liked the best. She was that perfect combination of sexual curiosity and common-sense that men over 30 would kill to discover. But at 20, I was genetically predisposed to not know a good thing when I saw it. She was edging closer to something permanent as I was simultaneously trying to figure out the next iteration that life had in store for me. I didn't yet know what I was going to do about "us" until she took her head off my shoulder and stared at me with eyes that had plainly gone loopy with romance.

"What are we, Duncan?"

"I'm not sure what you mean."

She bit her lower lip as she continued to smile. She was a pre-vet major, and I imagined a dog or a horse being put at ease by her sweetness and the optimism that attached itself to everything she said.

"I mean, let's say I got pregnant. I'm not saying I am, but let's say that I was. And say I decided that I wouldn't get an abortion. What would you do?"

I looked into her eyes and said with as much sincerity as I could muster, "Kill myself."

That's what I was thinking about when Lydia finally opened the door, and, judging by the look on her shallow grave of a face, I must have nailed her dad pretty closely because she just stood there staring at me, her lips slightly ajar, poised to scream, or yell, or do some other similar sort of freeform, panicked war cry. I was overcome with relief when they came together in an exquisite smile.

"I wasn't expecting that," she said, lightly touching the sweater, her voice barely more than a whisper. While I was locked out of the room, Lydia had dressed herself up in what I had to imagine were her mother's old clothes. She nervously smoothed down the folds of a brown, mid-length, starchy skirt and then pulled at the sleeves of a nondescript white blouse.

Her hair was swept up in a dramatic pile bringing to mind one of those rock piles hikers cleverly stacked up on trails to indicate they'd been there. They always made me kind of scratch my head, because I thought the purpose of going out into nature was to make yourself feel insignificant, not prove you existed. You could prove that anywhere: Whole Foods, a doctor's waiting room, your neighborhood Starbucks. The world was a smorgasbord of meaninglessness.

"Guess what my father did for a living," she said, still admiring my disguise.

Her make-up – bright red lipstick, rogue, some sort of body glitter that made her shimmer like a land-locked mermaid – was a real distraction, but I was loving every minute of it. I've always loved how women dressed in the mid-sixties. It was that moment where they were coming out of the conservatism of the fifties, but hadn't yet fully entered the lubed gates of the sexual revolution – let's call it the eternal limbo of want.

"He made wrecking balls. Can you believe that? You've got nowhere to go but up after finding out something like that. Except that's not exactly true, is it? There's always more down, don't you think?"

We looked at one another for a second, neither of us sure of what came next. We'd long ago jumped the rails of a normal first date (and besides, I'd already promised her that this didn't count as one) and were now wading into territory where 'courtship ritual' and 'satanic ritual' rubbed up against one another with all too much familiarity.

"What do we do now?" I asked her.

"I don't know," she said, sounding genuinely mystified. "I hadn't planned on…" she paused and cracked her knuckles with the easy menace of a professional bouncer, "…this."

"Fair enough," I said, not being a huge fan of role-playing even under the best of circumstances.

She looked at me and asked, "What are you thinking about right now?"

"All the terrible things I want to do to you," I said, without giving myself the chance to figure out if this was a good idea or not.

She smiled and blushed. "That's the sweetest thing anyone's ever said to me."

Romance was in the air; brutal and blushing, we were becoming undone by it.

She put a finger in her mouth and chewed on a nail. She said, "I owe you for what you did for my mom."

"You don't owe me anything."

"No," she insisted, "I do. I want to do something no one's ever done for you before."

"Okay," I said, submitting to her little whims as though they were direct messages from God. "I can't think of anything."

"Really?" She looked at me a little mystified and a little disappointed. "Nothing?"

"All I can think about is kissing you? Is that too ordinary?" I hoped it wasn't, but I couldn't be too sure. Need had a funny way of making tenderness seem unimportant.

The sex came as inevitably and wonderfully as I'd hoped it would and when I came inside of her, I immediately pulled out, giving her a look usually reserved for minor traffic accidents and bounced checks.

"Don't worry," she laughed. "I've been fixed."

"Oh, good," I replied, not sure what, exactly, that meant.

Feeling suddenly exhausted, I pulled the covers over us and she immediately clamped on to me with all of her limbs, reminding me of the way loggers have to strap themselves bodily to a gigantic tree in order to shimmy up the side. Hook, line and sinker, I was hers.

As I drifted off to sleep, a thought came into my head, a sentence I didn't want to be there, but couldn't help thinking as hard as I tried to push it out of my head. Over and over I thought, *Please don't need me too much.* I searched for the switch to shut the words out, but it was somewhere outside of me. It was a thing I did sometimes, an old gambler's trick, of saying a thing but in reality hoping for the opposite. It didn't ever work, but it sometimes cushioned the disappointment of not getting what I wanted.

When we woke up again, I glanced at the clock. 2:17 a.m. Lydia was propped up on her elbow staring down at me. I smiled weakly at her and she smiled back.

"You were mumbling in your sleep," she said. "Something about 'needing me too much.' What was that all about?"

"I don't know," I lied.

"If you're worried about me getting too attached, don't. I'm not a 17-year-old idiot."

"I know that. And besides, if you were I'd have to kill you," I joked, hoping she'd think it was funny. "You know, to save myself from the statutory…"

"I get it," she cut in. "Do me a favor, okay?" she asked, and I dreaded what she was going to say next, because whatever it was it would require a level of sincerity I wasn't sure I was ready for. I was of the firm belief that Faustian bargains, which I considered sincerity to be the chief modern-day example of, were usually more of a second to third date thing, sandwiched discreetly in between discussions about food allergies and experimenting with S&M. "Don't ever ask me to save you, okay? I'm done with all that."

"You happen to be in luck," I told her, a grin spreading mold-like across my face, "because I might be the only guy in town that has no interest in ever being saved."

"Good," she said, exhaling. "We're going to get along great."

I nodded in agreement and added, "At least at the beginning."

"Right," she said. "I love beginnings."

# CHAPTER 5

I always felt amazed watching women as they dressed — the deftness of it, the degree of skill and fluidity, all of it is a true marvel to behold. I watched her as she stretched her way into a pair of skinny jeans, pulled a Guns n' Roses t-shirt over her head, and then twisted her hair up and back, fastening it with a green elastic thing, all of it in one motion.

"We could have our date now," she suggested.

It was just after 2:30 a.m. and I fretted about what could possibly be out there for us, a little intimidated if I was to be honest, about whether or not I could cook up something interesting enough to not only occupy our time, but to satisfy the fairy-tale expectations I knew were sometimes placed on first dates.

"Hmmm," I said, thinking as quickly as I could.

"It doesn't have to be anything special. Let's just take a walk."

I'd heard those words before. They were the very definition of "doomed to fail." But when she said them, I believed her.

On our way out we passed her mom's bedroom and I stopped for a second to listen as what sounded like a lullaby was being whisper-sung from inside.

"It's Korean," Lydia said, pulling me away gently as if she knew all too well how it could just hold you there, how, in a way, it could be the answer to everything you ever wanted.

There was something about walking around Los Angeles at 2:30 in the morning that made me feel like I was being held underwater, submerged as cars swam slowly down the street. Sounds, too, were damp things at that hour, hushed as much for the sake of intergalactic decorum as for the atmospheric pressure that sat heavily atop it, a fact of life as pure as any other.

I wondered if she felt it, too, but just as I looked over at her, the trance was broken by an old burgundy (why did they bother even selling it another color?) Coupe DeVille driving slowly by, bumping "Regulator" by Warren G., a song that, under the right circumstances, could very well be the next national anthem. And then, in the very next moment, we rounded the corner and came face to face with a middle-aged Mexican man, neatly shaved and wearing a short-sleeved shirt and tie, screaming about Jesus, using a hand-held megaphone to amplify his unbearable joy.

"I've gotta get out of here," I said, holding down a wave of fear that was rising up in me.

"Get a hold of yourself," she shot back, and I couldn't tell for sure if she was joking or not. And then, softer, she said, "Tell me something about your mother." She grabbed my hand and began to rhythmically squeeze it, in time to who knows what, but it did its job, calming me.

"I thought you were going to tell me about yours."

"I will," she said. "I just thought it would help if you told me something first. To get your mind off of whatever it is that's bothering you."

"I don't know if that's going to do the trick," I said, "but if it'll make you happy…"

"Oh, shit," she said, letting go of my hand, "don't say that. I *hate it* when people say that."

"Sorry."

She grinned at me. "That's okay. It's just one of those things people say when they really mean to say something else. I hate it."

"I know what you mean," I answered her. "The guys I work with do this thing where they start sentences by saying, 'With all due respect…', and it's just so obvious that whatever they say next is going to be hugely insulting. 'With all due respect, I wish your mother and father had never met.'"

"I like that," she laughed. "I'm going to start using it."

"Fine by me," I said, "but with all due respect, I hope you choke on your fucking tongue the first time you try it."

She laughed some more.

"Fine," she countered back, joining in on the fun, "but with all due respect, you still haven't told me anything about your mother."

"She's dead," I said simply, not sure if we were still playing a game or if she just needed me to warm her up before she told me her own story.

"What about something from when she was alive?"

"Fine. Let me think," I shoved my hands into my pockets and noticed we were now walking down Pico Boulevard, where dense puddles of Korean men and women were pooling up in neon clots along the sidewalk, shrouded in massive plumes of smoke outside the karaoke bars and coffee shops that lined the street.

"My mother smoked the whole time she was pregnant with me," I said.

"What else?"

"I once asked my mother what she craved when she was pregnant with me and she told me 'a divorce'."

"Getting better. I think I would have liked your mom."

"She was the kind of person who wouldn't go anywhere unless she could be assured they had Splenda. You know what I mean?"

"I want you to tell me something *good*," she said and I suddenly understood what she meant.

"Okay, I don't want you to take this the wrong way, and I've never really thought about it like this before, but you know what her best attribute was?"

"What?" Lydia asked.

"This is going to sound crazy," I said, laughing a little at myself, "but it was putting in the dog's eye drops."

"What?" she almost screamed at me.

"I know I know, it sounds horrible, but we had this old dog that used to just walk around the house shitting and pissing wherever it went. He was blind, but I think he just did it to be a dick..."

"Dogs can't be dicks," she interrupted me.

I looked at her with pity.

"You're so wrong. Dogs are some of the biggest dicks in nature. They'll eat your food if you turn your back, rip up your favorite shirt...Ever fall down and hurt yourself in front of a dog? They just look at you, smiling, probably wishing you'd gotten hurt worse than you did so they could sniff your ass and raid your pockets while you're down. It's all about manipulation with them. They know."

"So, Moe," I continued, "that was the dog's name. Moe had glaucoma and apparently it's really painful for the animal because of all the pressure that builds up behind their eyes so the vet had to do this thing where they put him under and kill the eye, which is essentially deadening it with a needle, so the dog doesn't feel pain from it anymore, but it also loses its sight. Anyway, Moe needed these eye drops every day for the rest of his life, in the morning and at night. He'd squirm at just the moment when you'd manage to squeeze just one drop out and the thing would land on his face, or he'd start crying. Pissing. Shitting. All of it. He acted like someone was trying to kill him. Real dick move."

She snorted.

"But my mom, man, she was amazing," I went on, thinking about her stalking across the kitchen with the bottle of eye drops in her hand, poking her head around corners looking for him, wanting to do right by him. "She'd pet him a few times, talk to him in this funny baby voice she used with him; '*Who's my good boy? Who's the best boy in the world?*' And he'd just kind of relax

– you'd see his whole body not go limp exactly, but just mellow out – and then she'd take him by the snout, tilt his head up, and wham, put the drops in like she was closing the fridge.

"And it wasn't just that she was good with animals. Because she wasn't. It was just this thing she was good at. It was this thing she had with him."

Lydia smiled.

"That's sweet," she said. "That's the kind of thing I was talking about." She stuck her hands in my coat pocket and pulled out a pack of orange Tic-Tacs I had never seen before, and popped two into her mouth.

"It's hard for me to talk about my mom, to tell this story," Lydia continued, "because I never know how to start, and after that, to tell the next part and then the part after that, because it's everything, every piece of it is as big as the whole, and to leave any of it out would make the rest of it make no sense at all. Am I…" her words trailed off into a horizon of exhaustion. I knew exactly what she meant, and I wanted to tell her that, but I also sensed that empathy wasn't on her agenda.

Her mom, she said, had been a Pan Am stewardess in the sixties and she'd worn a uniform with the short skirt and pillbox hat.

"Legs for days," Lydia said dreamily, conjuring an image of her mom up in her mind, and I tried to do the same, tried to reconcile the Martha I'd seen in the tub with the Martha that Lydia was describing, a woman who'd been the prototype for free love, who embodied everything the next decade had in store. "I learned all this later, after my mother had her accident. I'll get to that in a bit," she went on. "A friend of hers from those days came to visit and she told me all this stuff I'd never known about my mom before. In one afternoon I learned more about my mom than I had in the 30 years prior."

I nodded.

"Anyway, her friend told me that there was this flight they were working, and a guy got really sick on the plane. Nobody knew if he was going to die or what, and there was no doctor aboard to help him. They were pretty sure he had a heart attack so my mom just sat there with him and stroked his hand. It was a long flight - I think they were going to Turkey or something – and apparently my mom never moved once. She just sat there holding this guy's hand, and knowing my mom, I know exactly what she was thinking."

"What was that?" I asked.

"That if she let go he would die. She's been that way my whole life." New details came to Lydia in flashes and she jumped around excitedly with the spark of them, each new clue a piece of a puzzle she'd never had the energy to try and put together before. She went on with the story, about how her mom found a deeper meaning in what happened to her on the plane, how she became convinced of her ability to heal people; maybe not literally, but close enough that most of her old friends began to distance themselves from her, giving themselves over to the me-ness of the late sixties and consequently having little time for this friend who'd found some version of God while trapped in an airplane at 35,000 feet. So when Woodstock came along and her friends had tried to get her to go with them, Lydia's mom solemnly refused. She would stay behind in Philadelphia, where they were on a layover.

"That Friday night she went by herself to a bar, ordered a ginger ale, and within five minutes was talking to my father, who was there waiting for some friends. He was wearing brown corduroys and a button-down shirt with this crazy pattern and a big collar that's still in the back of her closet, hanging there like a holy relic. He was wearing aviator glasses and his hair was parted to the left. He was drinking a gin and tonic. She remembered every detail. And do you know what her pick up line was?"

I shook my head.

"She asked him what Jack Nicholson was doing in a place like this."

I laughed.

"I know. Can you believe it? So cheesy. Anyway, they talked and went out on a proper date the next night, where, I like to say, she started one of the most epic games of doctor of all time."

"What do you mean?"

"There's this mental illness called Munchausen by Proxy. It's when someone induces an illness, either real or imagined, in a loved one, so that the sick person becomes dependent on the poisoner. It's a way to guarantee that someone's going to need, and if you're lucky, love you for the rest of your life. It's the equivalent of a drug dealer giving little kids their first taste for free. Really evil shit, not to mention a hell of a first date. Do you know how I found out she was crazy?"

"Tell me," I said.

"Well, I would go to school with all these crazy hypochondriacal facts stuck in my head...imagine trying to use an atlas of Germany to get around Downtown LA. I would tell my friends some of the things my mom had told me and they'd look at me like I was fucking nuts."

"Like what?"

"Like, my mom told me to never sit on the ground because worms would crawl up my butt and lay eggs in my stomach." She tried to suppress a smile. "Imagine never being able to sit with your friends in the yard because you were afraid of becoming infested with ass worms. I was terrified all the time."

"Jesus," I sighed. "The worst thing my mother ever told me was to never trust anyone wearing transition glasses."

She looked at me for a second and then nodded sagely, as if she'd given the matter a Talmudic level of consideration.

"You're a good listener," she said, kissing me, a kiss that felt like the life was being pulled out of me in the best way possible.

When we started walking again, I asked her if her mom was really poisoning her dad.

"No, not really. I mean she wasn't giving him little traces of cyanide every day. Instead, she'd constantly give him these little ambiguous jabs. Things like 'you look kind of peaked, are you feeling ok?' or 'Have you been losing weight?' Nothing real, but enough to get him thinking. I come from a long line of people who are susceptible to suggestions."

"Death by a thousand imaginary cuts. Classic."

"We'd fight over him, too," she said. "Like, I'd want him to come read me *Lord of the Rings* before bed and my mom would want him with her, and when I went in to look for him, they'd be in bed browsing though the *DSM* like they were a newlywed couple picking out their starter furniture from a Sears catalog." She shook her head.

"Do you think the same person wrote all three of these things?" I asked her, stifling a yawn and observing the graffiti below us: a shaky swastika inscribed in the sidewalk, something vague about the devil, and, in extra-large writing, a heart with the formula 'TA+WB' in it.

"Duncan! Are you with me?"

"I'm listening," I replied, reciting the words back to her. "Mom. Munchausen. Dad. *Lord of the Rings*. A thousand imaginary cuts. Does that about cover it?"

This cruel part of me bubbles up now and again. We all have wrecking balls inside of us, I guess, swinging around, hungry for damage, but that's what it was to be human. To want to tear down what we've just built.

"How did your dad die?" I asked.

"Heart attack," she said matter-of-factly, as though it couldn't be any other way. "A widow-maker."

"What's that?" I asked, intrigued to learn about a new thing I could add to my long and ever-growing list of ailments to be on the lookout for.

"He had no history of anything cardiac. Never. He was just walking the dog one day and BOOM," she clapped her hands together.

"There are so many things that can kill you out of the blue. Airplanes, lightning, pets, mountain lions. It's not surprising your heart can kill you, too."

She stopped and touched my arm.

"Why did you say 'mountain lions'?"

"What?" I asked, stalling for time as I thought of how to answer.

"I said," she spoke slowly, "why did you say 'mountain lions'?"

"It just popped into my head. Why?"

"It's just weird, because I was just about to tell you that after my dad died, my mom and I got close for awhile, the kind of close I always wanted to be with her. A closeness that was equal for once, a clean slate. Neither of us wanted to remember anything, and we let each other have that blankness. Oblivion. Whatever you want to call it, it's one of the greatest gifts you can give someone. One day, we were hiking up in Bronson Canyon, past the Batcave," I nodded. I knew the spot well. It was the spot where they filmed the Batmobile coming out of the Batcave in the old *Batman* TV series.

"So, we were up there one day, walking around, not planning on going very far. Just walking. And we came around a bend and there was like this flash of beige coming down at us from the hill. I thought it was a dog at first, but it was a mountain lion. It leapt on my mom's back and..." she started to cry a little, something that, for some reason, I hadn't imagined she was capable of, "...I started screaming, but no one came, and I had to run away to get help. I had to leave her there to save her life, and it was terrible. It was the worst thing I've ever had to do. When I got back a few minutes later with some people I found on the trail, the thing was gone, but her back," she paused as if summoning the image of it could only be done in silence, "her back was in shreds. Ribbons of skin…pools of blood."

I held her and felt her warm tears sear my chest.

"I don't want to ever have to save anyone again, okay? Do you understand? Never again."

"Perfect," I told her, putting my hand on her back. "That works just fine."

The next morning, I awoke in my waterbed at some ambiguous hour deep in the bowels of the afternoon. I searched in vain in the kitchen for something to put in my mouth while I contemplated the ultimate expression of nihilism, which was venturing out to the great gastric rat race known as brunch. I honestly didn't know if I had it in me. Food as a cultural phenomenon was always a problematic proposition for me, scarred as I was by parents who fetishized the Macaroni Grill and Cheesecake Factory to such an extent that I worried I'd be written out of their will in favor of the Cheesecake Factory's meatloaf plate, which my father used to refer to as "the son he never had."

I grabbed my phone and was pleased to see that the only message waiting for me was a text from Lydia.

*Thanks for a great night. Same time next Friday?*

I smiled as I wrote her back that I'd be there with bells on.

# CHAPTER 6

Knee-deep in a game of Minesweeper, my nearly-blind albino secretary, Deedee, had her white face pressed up against the enormous custom monitor the firm had bought for her as part of her disability requirements. She clicked haphazardly at the game's squares, starting over every few seconds as though the object of the game wasn't to clear the board, but to die and begin again.

"Duncan, is that you?" she asked, not bothering to look.

"Good morning, Deedee. How's everything in Minesweeper land?"

"Fine," she said earnestly, clicking away. "Dutch wants to see you in his office."

"Huh," I said, not knowing exactly how to respond. Technically Dutch wasn't my superior so he had no right to summon me to his office.

"What's that mean?" she asked, turning her face to look at me with her red eyes. She was justifiably wary of me ever since I once insensitively asked her if she could see in the dark, conflating her condition with the superpower of a comic book character I'd followed as a kid.

"It means…" I thought about what it meant. "It means I'm going into my office for a little bit."

"What should I say if he calls back?" she asked.

"Tell him we talked about it and that if I find myself near the paper shredder that I'll think about stopping by."

"Okay," she said, either not sensing the sarcasm or not caring.

My night with Lydia had taught me that if you wanted to, you could just let yourself slip into a fissure of pleasure, with a head full of heartbeats and the skin on your arm prickled from the tender nuances of friction, and drift. I must have made some happy noise because when I looked at Deedee again she was staring at me with her eyes all scrunched up.

"Don't mind me, Deedee," I said, backing into my office, enjoying, in a visceral way, the gentle swoosh sound of the door scraping along the low gray carpet.

"If you're going to have a nervous breakdown in there," she said, shaking her head and then turning back to her game, "please use the can of air freshener I left in your bottom left drawer."

I knew I wasn't like the other Vice Presidents at the firm, but then again, she wasn't like the other assistants, most of whom had, at one time or another, been out for various lengths of "medical leave" which was shorthand for an extended panic attack they'd suffered at the hands of their tyrannical bosses. I'd heard stories of edible arrangements going to bulimic assistants, middle-of-the-night demands for Chipotle – knowing full well Chipotle closed at 10 p.m. – and, in one case, an assistant being asked to sit at the bedside of her boss' terminally ill parent where she was asked to "do the hand stroking thing" and to call her boss when it looked like it was getting close to "go time." Deedee had had to endure none of that from me. High expectations, I'd realized early on, were a slippery slope and I knew better than to set myself up for a lifetime of disappointment in people.

At my desk I jiggled my mouse and, while I waited for the monitor to crackle to life, I leaned back, laced my fingers behind my head, and stared up at the giant rain cloud that floated in the middle of my office. Each Vice President was given a budget with which to decorate their office, and I'd found the thing on one of these men's lifestyle websites. I tried at first to get into watches. Then into whiskey. Then it was these knives that were carved out of mammoth bone. None of it really stuck, though, not as an aesthetic point of view and even less so as a lifestyle. The things just sat in a kind of dark-arts tableau on my kitchen table, the sordid artifacts of a serial killer's origin story.

I'd just about given up on the hope of finding a lifestyle when I found it; my cloud. It was about two feet by four feet and hung from the ceiling of my office by a piece of invisible fishing wire. When turned on, it thundered and lightning'ed and the sound was perfect, the rumbling of the thunder beginning back behind you a million miles and coming up fast, the very progeny of inevitability, and the light that accompanied it was just subtle enough that sometimes I felt I was either having a stroke or else plugging into the same pleasure centers it took Buddhist monks lifetimes of celibacy to locate. My cloud was a shortcut to Nirvana. It was possible to activate the lightning without the thunder, but I'd never found the occasion where I wanted one without the other. Maybe one day it would become apparent, but until then I'd continue to be a full-on glutton for the gloomy ambience I'd adopted as a lifestyle.

I pressed a button on the remote and Mikey Dredd's music oozed from the cloud's built-in speaker. Thick shrouds of bass vibrated around my head and without thinking I swatted lazily at them and relaxed into the cool parasitic beat of it. I closed my eyes and imagined a haze of yellow radiation that was everywhere and nowhere at once, stuck to every surface in the office, including the skin on my face where it settled sickly and humid, grime where there was no dirt, but alive and deeply reminiscent of an invigorating feeling I'd had once as a kid when I became convinced for several weeks that I was the only real person in the world and that everyone else was a robot there to interact with and observe me. It was a feeling I deeply loved, and I found myself wanting to call

Lydia and ask her if she ever felt the same, if she ever yearned to be invisible from the inside out.

When I opened my eyes, I was greeted by the picture of my grandfather, my mother's father, that was my computer desktop wallpaper. There were few people I'd ever loved as much as I loved him, and, in the picture I had of him on my computer, he had on that sly smile I still tried to emulate, a hairline crack in something ancient, and cornflower blue eyes patiently waiting beneath an avalanche of snow-white hair. He was wearing a red velour shirt and I could still feel the soft crush of it against my cheek when I hugged him, the smell of some long-defunct aftershave clinging richly to his skin.

Strangely, he was also the reason I originally became interested in finance. Not because he himself was a wealthy man or particularly interested in money, so to speak (although he did buy me my first stock; one share of IBM given to me as a Bar Mitzvah present, the certificate for which hung in a frame on the wall behind my desk), but because he died on a Saturday in October, 1987, and his funeral, which was two days later, fell on Black Monday, the day the stock market fell 22% in a single afternoon.

My mother and grandmother began crying the moment we stepped into the funeral home and were led back to view his body. My mom told me I didn't need to look, but I felt like I had to, that if I didn't, I'd miss seeing him for the last time. But that wasn't him in the casket. Where was the velour shirt? Why was his skin a shiny piece of rubber? And where were his glasses?

My grandmother, wailing so loudly it sounded like a song, leaned into the coffin and, for an awful minute, I thought she was going to get in there with him. But she only wanted to kiss him, to touch his face, to mutter his name again and again like a wish, a deal you made with God on your way over a cliff.

I instant messaged Deedee. It was easier than shouting at her through the door, or, God forbid, actually picking up the phone and speaking with her.

*Deedee, can you please get me a cup of coffee?*

There was a short pause before she wrote back.

*Now?*

*If that works for you.*

Another pause.

*You're the boss,* she typed back to me, followed by a knife emoji.

I was just starting to read my email when another text from Deedee appeared on the screen.

*Dutch is asking for you again.*

"Fuck," I whispered. I was growing weary of the bullshit and closed my eyes, surprised to see an animal there waiting for me in the darkness. I wasn't sure exactly what it was, but I knew it had enormous power lurking under its sleek brown fur and when it turned to look at me all light fell away from us and I was frozen beneath the starry yellow of its eyes and the sharp dead stench of its breath. It opened its mouth and fangs the size of princely dowries dripped glistening teardrops of saliva at my feet. Whether it was planning to devour me or speak to me, or if it was simply yawning the careless yawn of an apex predator, of an animal that knew no danger but the slow ticking clock of its own perfect mortality, I wouldn't know because, in a panic, I opened my eyes.

Everything in my office was in its place. The cloud was manufacturing its thunder and lightning and the music was still leaping to the rescue with stoned undertones, and peeking from behind the open browser window on my computer I could see my grandfather's puff of white hair. I could have had my eyes closed for 15 seconds or 15 minutes. It was hard to say for sure.

All that I knew was that I'd been visited by something that needed me as much as I needed it. But when I closed my eyes again, ready to face the thing that had been trying to greet me, the animal was gone.

# CHAPTER 7

In theory, I knew Dutch was a redhead. I had sat across from him at a million meetings, nursed drinks with him in bars I was mortally ashamed to be sitting in, listened to his repulsive sex stories all while trying to avoid looking in his eyes. It was one thing to conjure an image of him in my mind, but it was another thing to see him and his red hair.

At the door to his office, I knocked weakly and heard his bright voice from the other side instantly invite me to "entrée." I looked back at his assistant, Evelyn, a woman I knew to be broken because there was no other way for her to be, and we pitied one another with sad smiles before I turned the knob and went in.

There he was, behind his desk, smiling wildly at me, his left hand compulsively and rhythmically squeezing some sort of stress relieving device he probably didn't even realize he was handling.

"Duncan, Duncan, Duncan," he said, continuing to stare and smile at me. He put his hands on his hips and shook his head in the awestruck way one did when appreciating the Grand Canyon.

"Dutch, Dutch, Dutch," I said back to him. Fuck it, two could play at this idiotic game.

"Sit. Dude. Please. Can I get you something? Water? Kombucha?"

I didn't point out to him that I was already sitting. He looked redder than usual today, but I think it was because of how gray his office was. The walls and sofa were charcoal, and the chairs, which were ultra-modern and promoted scoliosis, were also the color of neutral space.

You couldn't help but pity the furniture. The chair I'd chosen was a piece of skinny modern sculpture that, if you squinted at it just right, looked like a frightened man transformed into a chair by an evil sorcerer; his arms flung open wide and his head a beseeching oval of misery. I liked sitting in it.

"What is it?" he asked me, confused. "Why are you squinting?"

"I'm not," I said, even though I was.

"Hmm," he said, picking up the pace of his squeezing. "Whatever you say, hombre."

"I'm actually glad you asked me in here today, because I wanted to ask you how the concert was. Did The Eagles play 'Hotel California'?"

He looked aghast.

"Of course they played...oh, you're joking," he shook a finger at me, letting me know that he knew I was naughty and that it was okay with him. "That's funny, dude. Did they play 'Hotel California'? Ha! I mean, can you imagine if they didn't?"

"Bedlam?" I suggested, coyly.

"Yes! Totally! People would lose their fucking minds! By the way," he said, plunking himself down in a minimalist desk chair that would make Barbie feel like she had a fat ass, "I'm totally not mad that you didn't let me cut the line at Starbucks the other day. I get it. I honor your integrity. I actually kind of respect you for standing your ground. Your conviction is..." he paused as he sniffed the air for the right word. "...gnarly. Everyone knows it, and we all respect you for it. All of us. The team."

The fact that he was speaking for the company as a whole raised several red flags for me at once. Nothing good ever happened in the name of the team.

I nodded my chin at the only personal effect in the office, a picture of his wife, nine months pregnant at the time, jokingly lifting a bottle of Jack Daniels to her filler-inflated lips. Beneath the picture someone had lamely tried to make a joke by adding the inscription "Rounding Error."

"You guys gonna have another one?" I asked, completely uninterested in the answer.

"Oh, hell no, my man. One and done."

"Right," I said. "Good plan. But do you ever wonder if there's anything to the theory that people have more than one kid in case one of them dies. You know, so they'll still have another one to carry on the name and pass the genes along and all that. Like, a spare?"

He stopped squeezing the ball.

"That is a really good question, my man. That's just the kind of thinking I'm going to need when I'm running this department and precisely the reason I asked you to come talk to me today."

*What? Running the department?* I must have looked at him like he had two heads because he started in again on the ball and gave me this tight-lipped grin that made it look as if his face was flat lining.

"Well, Dutch. I appreciate that. I really do. Your faith in me is… everything."

I worried for a second that he'd be able to sense I was full of shit, but then relaxed as I reminded myself that the part of him that could detect sarcasm had most likely been absorbed in utero, like an underdeveloped twin. It was quite possibly his first hostile takeover, whetting his appetite for a lifetime of rapacious conquests.

"Please don't tell me you're thinking of supporting Les for this. A guy like that, a guy who wears his heart on his sleeve," he leaned across the desk, and I instinctively pulled back, worried he was about to launch himself at me to prove a point about human frailty. "He'd get eaten the fuck alive."

Les Oberdick, Dutch and I had all joined the firm about the same time. Les and Dutch came from the same business school, where it seemed they must have been friendly, because there was a lot of horsing around between the two of them at first. Their cubicles were near one another and I used to hear them giggling and high fiving all day long. Then there was the relentless playing of "Jump Around" every day at five o'clock, as if life were just another keg ready to be tapped. The good times began to fray, though, after Les got married and had his first kid. We were all promoted and got our own offices, and I noticed that Les and Dutch were spending less and less time together. I chalked it up to simple bro-on-bro resentment at first, but then Les' marriage fell apart at what felt like celebrity speed. His wife simply walked out one day while he was at work, taking his kid and credit cards with her. "Classic" was how Dutch described it.

A few days later word began to spread (by way of Dutch, who was still listed as Les' emergency contact) that Les had tried to asphyxiate himself by shoving a towel under his bedroom door and lighting the family's charcoal barbecue, and he had been saved at the last minute by a process server who was waiting at the front door to hit him with divorce papers. Granted, it would have been a weird way to go, and it certainly may have been a cry for help, but at the very least, it gave Les a depth I never knew he had, a flare for the dramatic that was sorely missing from my life.

Dutch, though, seized upon it as a demonstration of weakness, the last bit of proof he needed that Les had gone permanently soft. When Les finally came back, still a little puffy from the carbon monoxide he'd inhaled, Dutch began a merciless campaign to tear him down whenever and however he could. The form it took most often were the almost nearly constant subtle references he made about barbecues whenever Les was around. The most egregious example was when Dutch named his son Coleman, a living reminder to Les of his rock bottom and something he swore he'd never forgive.

"I don't know, Dutch," I said, still pretending I knew what he was talking about, "the guy is pretty good at what he does. And that whole suicide thing gives him a kind of vulnerability that's been missing at the top, you know?"

"Duncan, my man," he stood up and walked around the desk. "You and I both know the guy isn't stable enough. Do you want someone steering the ship who might wake up one day and say, 'You know what? I think I'm going to skip that big meeting today so I can stay home and choke down a couple dozen Xanax instead?' Is that who you want deciding your fate, buddy? Because I've gotta tell you something." He walked behind me, and I braced myself for what was to come, "that's not cool with me. You deserve more than that."

*Here it comes,* I thought, and braced myself just as he put his hands on me and began to give me one of his patented "bro-massages," guaranteed to make anyone want to peel the skin off their living body and launch themselves through the nearest window.

I stood up and pretended to examine the picture of his wife.

"Rounding error," he said, hooking his thumbs in his pockets. "Get it, because…"

"Because she's pregnant in the picture and her stomach is round. Gets me every time."

He sat back down and I was on my way out when I stopped and turned around.

"Let me ask you something, Dutch, if that's okay."

"Dude. Are you kidding? Anything for you."

"When you were a little kid, what did you want to be when you grew up?"

The question seemed to short-circuit something in him and for just a second, his smile slid away, and he looked at me with a hurt expression on his face, the look of someone who'd been wronged deeply and inexorably. I felt a little twinge of excitement as I watched him squirm, but it was only a moment, because it melted away almost immediately and he forced the grin back up on his face and commenced squeezing the ball again, compressing it like he was trying to bring the thing back to life.

"This," he said, nodding his head sagely.

I looked around, thinking maybe I'd missed something in his office. I saw his desk, his computer, the picture of his wife with the stupid quote. I saw the furniture performing its sleepy calisthenics, the chair frozen in mid-scream.

"What do you mean, 'this'?" I asked, knowing full well I was risking life and limb by forcing him into a psychological corner he might have no choice but to bite and scratch his way out of.

"All this," he said with a proud look on his face.

"Okay," I said, opening the door. "You know, who's to say I might not throw my hat in the ring for this thing. Wouldn't be the craziest idea in the world, right?"

I had no intention of putting myself up for any promotion. I wasn't even sure what this new job was, and I seriously doubted whether Dutch did either.

He stood and put his hands on his hips and I could have sworn I saw his freckles began to move, slowly and subtly, but they were definitely in motion, and I took it as a sign that I'd better get out while the getting was good, lest he continue to morph and become something I might genuinely fear.

"By the way," I said, trying to change the subject, "it wouldn't hurt you to come down to my office once in a while. You're not my boss yet."

"Okay, buddy," he said, sitting down again. He was already back tapping wildly on his computer and as I started to leave he called out to me one more time.

"By the way," he said, with no trace of irony in his voice, "some of us have been wondering for awhile, and I hope you don't mind me asking you this," he went on and I braced myself for what was to come, "but are you a Christian?"

"What?" I heard myself say before I even knew what I was doing. "No. Why?"

"Huh," he said, already expending his concentration on something on his monitor, some careful equilibrium of facts and figures that might finally fill the void in his life he neither knew nor cared was there. "Nothing."

# CHAPTER 8

As if I needed any more proof that I was on the wrong side of history, a freezing blade of cold air came down on me like the business end of a guillotine from an air conditioning duct as I walked back to my office. I was in the land of the barely getting by, the cubicle forest, and I felt a thousand pairs of eyes watching me as I tried to walk like a person with some dignity might walk, like a person who was not just accused of being a Christian, which, as everyone knew, was really code for *strange in a way that was not socially acceptable.*

Clenching my fists, I speed-walked back down the long hallway, trying not to notice the gaudy stares of the support staff who thrived on situations like this; conflict between the bosses was their real Christmas bonus, and I resisted the urge to snarl back at them like some crazed madman, feeding the cheap thrill machine that was the real perpetual motion engine of any office. But as soon as I turned to face them they'd be gone, disappeared behind a wall of Dodgers bobblehead dolls and cheap Vornado fans that were the end product of the Industrial Revolution. I needed a reason to scream, a way to let them know I was still in control, if not exactly in charge. So I dragged my feet along the carpet for a few yards, letting myself get lost in the pattern that always reminded me of my father's EKG as he lay dying in a hospital of COPD, and then touched the metal wall of some poor asshole's cubicle, giving myself a static shock, the zap of which could be heard down in the mail room. "GOD DAMNIT!" I screamed and had the immense satisfaction of seeing the tops of 50 heads pop up as the entire floor of casualty vampires jumped in their seats. That'll teach you to be voyeurs, I thought, and then instantly regretted having done it, because who among us didn't like to watch?

Back at my office, Deedee was right where I left her, engaged in primal battle with 1024×768 worth of resolution, a struggle against myopic dissonance she was doomed to lose. For about 30 seconds, as she clicked madly, her eyes going through a Sisyphean gymnastics routine of focusing, losing focus, focusing again, getting close, losing it, and then trying again, she was my hero.

"So," she said, without looking up, "I hear Dutch thinks you're a Christian."

"Jesus," I gave her the gift of my being impressed, "news travels fast."

"We are nothing if we're not in the know."

"Can you believe the nerve of that guy to accuse me of something like that. Fucking asshole," I went on, crossing my arms and looking off in the distance, trying a little too hard to strike a pose like one of those old Eastern European statues celebrating the heroic actions of some beefy, mustachioed sadist who made a whole village of Romani disappear without even breaking a sweat.

She raised her eyebrows at me, and I couldn't help but feel like I was staring into the dilated buttholes of two adjacent house cats.

"There are worse things."

Shit, I thought, hoping I hadn't stuck my foot in it. But she seemed unperturbed and changed the subject.

"Do you want to have lunch with Les?" she asked me.

"Why? Are you trying to set us up?"

"I wouldn't dream of it," she came back, deadpan. "He called me when he saw you go into Dutch's office. He probably wants to ask you about the promotion," she said.

"You knew about that, too?"

"Of course, everyone knows about it. Old news."

"Old news," I repeated dumbly.

"Last to know..." she said, leaving it hanging in the air.

"First to go."

Deedee smiled. "Exactly."

"Deedee, has there been any talk about..."

Without even letting me complete the thought, though, she barged in.

"About you for the job? Duncan," she looked up at me with something like pity, "you didn't even know about the job until 15 minutes ago. What's that tell you, sweetie?"

It was one of the universe's most understood laws that when your day turned to shit, it became an irredeemable thing. I wasn't a fatalist, but I also wasn't a masochist. At least not yet. It was hard to fathom that little less than an hour ago I was sitting at my desk with my eyes closed, inhabited by the spirit of an animal I neither recognized nor could make reappear. He was still crouched there, though, sated from the filling meal it had made of my insides, resting now in my head and licking its massive claws, biding its time until it could do it all over again, secure in the fact that, above all else, routine was the natural order of things, that too much change got you nothing but dead.

On my way to the elevator, I ducked into a janitorial closet and leaned against the mop sink. There was a heaviness on my chest the likes of which I'd never felt before, and I struggled to take a deep breath. I squeezed my eyes shut as hard as I could and felt the blinding spike of a migraine stabbing its way into my skull, trying its damndest to slice me in half, starting at the top and, slowly but surely, working its way down to the bottom, until I was nothing but two halves of an aggravated whole.

"FUCK!" I shouted, worried for a minute that someone might come in and find me like that and call the paramedics, and I'd have to explain that I wasn't having a heart attack, but that I was trying to trap the jungle cat in my head, the one that was currently having a nap before it made another meal of my pride. Luckily, no one came, so I went on searching for it, that enormous cat, and when a mop slipped, falling into me, I reached out and grabbed it without thinking and began to wrestle with its thin wooden pole, imagining it was some prey I'd gotten my claws on, and I did everything I could to snap the thing in two, including putting it in my mouth and trying to bite it in half, snarling and grunting all the while, trying desperately to conjure the Cat, because, well, I needed it. I needed the rush of relief as the wood gave way, the snapping and popping sounds it would make as it splintered into thin fragments of itself, and then all the dangers those new sharp pieces threatened, the endlessness of it, every action the elongated shadow of the one that came before it. I needed all that in much the same way I needed to know when my life had gone from then to now, when I'd crossed the barrier from want and wandered naively into the land of regret. I used to think of that moment as a clearly delineated line, some kind of magical barrier between being a child and feeling like an adult, but as I continued to strain against the wood, finally getting to the bend of it, the soft way of saying the beginning of the end, I began to reconsider. Maybe this line had nothing to do with becoming an adult. Maybe I actually hadn't yet crossed it at all.

Grunting and sweating, I brought the mop handle down over my knee and the relief I imagined I'd feel came rushing into me all at once. The raining sound of the wood splintering, the obscene gash it left in my pants, and even the little worm of blood that started to wriggle down my thigh, all of it, every millimeter of pain was perfect. Electrified with this feeling, I looked for more stuff to break. My hands landed on a container of Windex, which I dropped to the ground and stomped on as hard as I could. A popping sound, like the single confident shot of a trained assassin, was followed by a wash of chemical-scented liquid I could feel soak the cuffs of my pants and my socks, some of it dripping down into my shoes where it coated my feet and made me as flammable as I felt. Was this how Martha felt when she dreamt of long claws and steel jaws? Were these the words she wanted to say when words wouldn't come to her? When all there was was the helium feeling in her heart that she loved her daughter too much for it to be true?

When I was done I straightened my tie, opened the door to the closet, and walked to the elevator with my eyes stitched to the ground. If I couldn't see them then they couldn't see me.

# CHAPTER 9

Although they were unable to be measured precisely, the proportions of an out-of-body experience bore more than a passing resemblance to those of the perfect kiss; wet, lingering, struggling through depthlessness. Both experiences approximated magic, and it was thus, under the twin spells of romance and disassociation, that I left the building upon formless feet and floated two blocks over to Sparkles, a strip club with a better-than-adequate buffet where we always ate when it was just me and Les having lunch. That he chose to always meet me at such a dubious location affirmed to me that he didn't give a fuck about what I thought about him, and I appreciated him for that vote of confidence, his tip of the hat to my flexibility which we both knew was actually a cover-up for the heartfelt apathy that throbbed within me when it came time to decide things like where to eat or what to do on a Friday night.

Inside the club, the darkness felt good, caked on, layer upon layer of distraction I wanted to pull over my head like a kid in his bed during a particularly bad thunderstorm. Mottled neon tubes along the floorboards wheezed trace elements of radioactive pheromones, a smear of purple meant to light the way to the dance floor one way, to the buffet another, an atlas of false hopes I wanted to tattoo on my skin for fear of ever losing my way again. The air was clotted with the thick and hopeless music of Nine Inch Nails, which I thought of as the national anthem of venereal diseases, and, everywhere I looked, businessmen like myself sat in parties of one, hunched over their plates of fried food and pizza, their ties loosened in an approximation of relaxation.

I spotted Les at a table near the stage conveying something limp and damp from his plate to his mouth. I assumed it was pizza, but you could never be too sure.

"What did I tell you about finger foods in strip clubs," I said, slapping him on the back.

He turned to me and, patting the seat next to him for me to sit down, let loose a booming laugh that was almost certainly a gateway to hell.

"Jesus," he said, looking me up and down, "are you bleeding?" And then he sniffed the air. "Is that Windex?"

The lighting in Sparkles was such that a careful examination was impossible, a frequency meant to focus you on the women and the booze. Anywhere else you looked you were met with blurry, washed-out pastels, blank spaces that grew larger and larger as the days wore holes in them.

I sat next to him and took a gigantic breath of acrid air. "I think I'm in love," I blurted out just as he licked the last of what I hoped was blue cheese dressing from his fingers. He looked at me calmly, then at the stage, where a platinum blonde in a day-glo green bikini was eating a taquito while simultaneously smoking a cigarette from her vagina.

He shrugged. "I can see that."

"Not her," I said.

He looked around, confused. "Who then?"

I pitied any elevated levels of consciousness that had him as one its champions, but I let it slide, because tangents were the natural predators of progress, and I was all about moving forward today, not back.

"Lemme back up," I said, grabbing the half-eaten slice of pizza off his plate and shoved the whole thing down my throat before he even had a second to process what was happening.

"Hey," he said, hurt-sounding. "I was eating that,"

"I'm sorry, but it's a buffet right? You can get some more. I just got so hungry all of a sudden."

"Growing pains," he said, and started laughing at his own joke that wasn't really a joke as much as it was something to say, an automatic response he'd been conditioned to utter given a certain set of circumstances, like an out-of-office auto reply. "So who's this girl?" he asked again.

"A woman I met in line at Starbucks. Lydia. We had the most incredible first date…"

"Wait a minute," he put his cup down and wiped his mouth. "You can't be in love after just one date, are you crazy?"

"Why not?" I knew better than to take relationship advice from someone who was voted 'Most Likely to Accidentally Summon the Devil' in high school, but I couldn't help myself. The Cat had me feeling particularly exposed, vulnerable in the worst possible ways, and I could feel him back there still, pacing its deliberate shapes as it waited for just the right moment to pounce.

"Give it until the second date to know whether or not you're in love. It's the least you can do for yourself. Wait," he burped gently as he scanned his plate for something else to shove in his mouth, "did you have sex with her?"

"Does that make a difference in the first date versus second date thing?"

"It can," he said. "Depends on how freaky it got. Freaky sex on a first date can go a long way toward cementing feelings."

I leaned in closer so I could hear him over one of those slow, drudgy, shit-stains of a song by AC/DC that mysteriously kept time with everyone within earshot's biological clocks. Strobe lights bounced off Les' face, wrecking it with a riot of soft colors.

"We did have sex, but it wasn't especially freaky. I mean it was, but in a kind of existential way. More psychic kinky than physical."

"What the hell does that mean?"

"Nothing weird happened with the mother. She…" I stopped and tried to think how to put it so he would understand. "Do you know what a spirit animal is?"

Les leaned back in his chair and let out a sigh loud enough for me to hear over the music.

"Man, I didn't know you were into all that LA woo-woo shit."

"Anyway," I went on when the moment seemed right, trying to keep the story as short as possible, both for his sake as well as mine, "her mother was sitting in this tub…and she's huge, okay… and she won't get out."

"What do you mean 'she's huge'?" He asked, his face all mashed together as he was trying to make a mental picture.

"She's, like, obese, okay? But that doesn't matter."

"I don't see how that doesn't matter."

"Listen. Please. Take your analytical hat off for a few minutes, will you? I just need you to listen. Can you do that?"

He shot me a nasty look and then made a motion with his hand that I should keep going.

"She was kind of stuck in this tub, and Lydia…that's the daughter… asked me to sit there with her so she could go get help to coax her out, because I guess this sort of thing has happened before. But anyway, she finally started talking to me, and she told me that she has a mountain lion inside her that she feels is just waiting to, like, bust out and maul her daughter to death. But I didn't get the impression she really wants to kill Lydia, or rip her apart or whatever. To me, it was more like…" I stopped, because I was on the verge of getting into some seriously corny territory that I wasn't sure he'd ever let me live down. But there was no way else to say it, and besides, I was already knee-deep in the story and to stop now would be even stranger than to just get it all out there, "She was saying she loved her, but she didn't know how to love her. That there was this animal inside of her that was pacing around, stalking back and forth, frothing at the mouth, all that animalistic shit. It was this creature that was all of her feelings for Lydia, and she didn't know how to let it out. Or, not that she didn't know how to let it out, but more that she didn't know what it would do once it was out. I don't know…" I sat back in my chair and took a deep breath. I realized I was sounding like a fucking lunatic.

Les turned his head to look up on the stage and I was worried that I'd lost him. But then he said, "I went through a phase in college where I was reading a little bit about spirit animals, which are these dreams we have, visions of the things that are inside of us." I didn't want to imagine the vile circumstances that led to his reading about spirit animals. "But what you're talking about is different. The way you're describing it the mom seemed helpless to do anything about it, like she's the animal's dream instead of the other way around. Is that it?"

A shock ran through me followed closely by a sick feeling, the creeping rise of cold nausea that Sparkles was all that was left of the world, that everything else that existed outside of these four sticky walls had, in the last half hour or so, fallen through a narrow crack in the universe, a crack of my own making.

"Huh?"

"Well, what you're talking about is the notion of ascribing the characteristics of a human soul onto an animal or a plant or even an inanimate object. That's Animism. This thing you're talking about is the opposite. You're talking about the idea of animals conferring our humanity on us. Dreaming us into existence in a way. Interesting."

"Wait a minute," I started to say without really thinking it through. "Do animals dream?"

"What do you mean?" he said, looking puzzled for the first time. "Are you fucking with me?"

"No," I said quickly, realizing how stupid the question had been. "How do you know all this stuff?"

He shrugged like it was no big deal, all this talk of Animism and the free will of animals, while at the next table a redhead was trying to get the lawyer in the beige suit to put down his slice and follow her into the Champagne Room.

"Did I ever tell you I lived in India for a while?"

This was a bald-faced lie. After he'd let it slip over the course of many conversation that he'd lived for a time in Egypt, China and Nigeria, among other places, I thought that maybe his parents had been in the Foreign Service or something exotic like that, but I could never get a clear answer out of him. He was always vague about the circumstances of his cosmopolitanism, and I got the feeling that he had something to hide, something I would find either horrifying or hysterical should I ever get him to spill his obfuscating guts – there could be no middle ground. And then recently, after his suicide attempt and after Shirley had taken their son and left him forever, we were having drinks and he must have had some kind of realization that being a chronic liar was bad for his immortal soul. He'd admitted to me that he'd done a Semester at Sea program as a junior at Arizona State and considered the experience somehow so incredibly enlightening that he felt justified in saying that he'd lived in all the places the boat would dock and he and his friends would disembark and get hammered without ever leaving the harbor area of whatever country they were visiting. The experience, therefore, had been a catalog of sites he'd missed seeing – the Great Wall, the Great Pyramids, everything "great", basically – and therefore his perspective had been formed in a literal negative space, opinions soundly cemented in the absence of real evidence, which was, the way he explained it. This nuance was somehow different than ignorance; ignorance being implicitly malicious. In subsequent conversations, he continued to cling to the notion that he'd lived all over the world, and I was so intrigued by his happy-go-lucky self-delusion that I never bothered to argue. In fact, it went further than that. I seriously doubted whether he knew the difference between Asia and Europe, but

I also understood that it didn't matter, that his chicanery was its own super-continent, a Pangea of delusion I could only hope to one day aspire.

I smiled at the India comment and fingered the rim of my glass of root beer.

"You have. That's amazing," I said, hoping the compliment would be sufficient to staunch the conversation as though it were a bleeding wound that, left untended, would drain the life out of me in no time flat. Besides, he'd given me enough to think about without adding in his massively uninformed ex-pat anecdotes that were nothing more than a mixture of hearsay and alcohol-induced hallucinations.

I looked at my watch and frowned. It was rude, I knew, to be ending lunch before he'd had a chance to talk to me about what it was he'd invited me to discuss, but I also knew he was going to want to know every little thing about my conversation with Dutch and I didn't really have anything interesting to tell him. However, there was currency in letting him believe I knew something important, something that could help him maneuver himself within the corporate structure, but was withholding for some mysterious reason, just as there was currency in letting him believe I had somewhere I needed to be, when, in fact, neither thing was true.

I stood and slid my coat on. He hurried to his feet and threw down some money on the table.

"Wait," he said, his tone suddenly changing into something more violent, more cop-like. "What happened with Dutch? What did he want to talk to you about?"

"Well…" I started to say when the waitress came over to us and asked if there was anything else she could get us.

Before I could tell her no, Les surprised us both by turning to her and shouting in a voice so loud it could be heard over the announcer who was in the middle of bringing out Delilah, who, "Gentlemen, will be the end of us all…"

"This is a time and a place!" He narrowed his eyes so he could read her name tag. "Brittany, there is a time and a place!"

I'd never seen him truly angry before, wasn't sure he actually had it in him past the petty gossip and idle threats that made up the better part of the time we'd spent together outside of the office. But there he was, cords standing out on his neck, a savage line of drool connecting top lip to lower lip, even his goofy fangs were bared, reflecting the stage lights so that it looked like he was full of a purple and green energy that was spilling up and out of him, on the verge of swallowing our world and all worlds yet to come.

Brittany let out a little whimper of fear, and I committed the worst faux pas that one could commit at Sparkles: I touched her shoulder. I was only trying to console her, to let her know that there was humanity here, amidst all the fried food and broken dreams that there was someone who knew the difference between right and wrong, but it didn't come off that way, because she threw my hand off and began to scream in a way that was both feral and mournful, the sound of an animal watching its habitat being destroyed by the venal greed of man. The lights in the place came on, and I saw the bouncer crane his fat neck around, and then, catching sight of us, start to weave his way over to where we were standing. I froze, imagining myself being used by this collector of souls as a mop for the men's room floor, my fate sealed as an absorbent penitent destined to swab the foul decks, be wrung out and used again for all time.

Before he could reach me, though, someone else began to scream and we all turned to see another waitress, her hands pressed to her mouth in horror, standing at the table with the lawyer in the beige suit who was banging on the table with one hand, the other struggling to dislodge something from his throat that was clearly choking him to death.

The bouncer, who was on his way over to manhandle me into oblivion, stopped and then hurried off in the other direction to help the choking litigator.

As if on cue the rest of the clientele scattered like roaches, embarrassed for ourselves, but more so, I thought, for someone who might die in a place that smelled like egg rolls and baby oil. I took one last look at the choking guy, and for the briefest of moments, we locked eyes. He was eerily calm, his finger down his throat trying to find the errant strand of mozzarella that had him hovering between this world and the next, and I wanted to call out to him over the din of the panic, tell him that everything was going to be okay, but before I could so much as utter a word, I was swept up in a mad rush of $2,500 gabardine suits, all headed to the exit at once. As they came pouring out of the club and running off in every direction, I thought of those old pictures I'd seen in a magazine of cops raiding gay clubs in the fifties and sixties, men escaping onto a bright sidewalk, cursed by sunlight, their hands in front of their faces, something real to lose, consequences worth mentioning, and not just the paranoia that self-aggrandizement could make any small problem seem actually significant.

I turned to run, to join them in their collective mitosis of cowardice, but Les caught my arm and he looked so sad, so crushed that he'd learned nothing of interest, because life to him was information. He gave me this weepy look – actually stuck out his lower lip and said, "Pweese," and oh shit, I just wanted to get out of there. Back to my office. Back to my cloud. My Deedee. The thing that prowled behind my eyes. It was all home now, all the same thing, nature and nurture and the giant softness that came from knowing perfectly one particular version of the future.

"Fine," I said, pulling my arm out of his hands. "I think he wants to be a chair."

"What?" Les gaped, his eyes doing this bugging out thing like he was physically choking on this gristly piece of esoterica.

"Yup," I said, sussing out escape routes, "I asked him what he wanted to be when he grew up and he pointed at his chair. And his couch. And maybe some artwork. You know that painting he has that's all white? I think he wants to be that, too."

At first Les just stood there, his face a shallow grave of apprehension, and then slowly, bit by creepy bit, a smile began to rise like something geological and impenetrable emerging from the horizon, and when it was at its zenith, and it looked like his face might split in half. He wagged a finger at me and said, like he knew exactly what I was talking about, like we were somehow complicit in one another's malfunctioning insights that we secretly hoped passed for mind games, but knew, somewhere deep down in our slack hearts, that insightfulness was something to suffer and not to capitalize upon, "You dirty dog. Oh, you dirty, dirty dog."

And before I could clarify the situation for him, before I could make him see that Dutch had his number, that his suicide attempt would forever be construed as a fatal flaw despite it only being a near-fatal act, he turned and left. That's right. He had the nerve to just leave like HE was done with ME. I took a few deep breaths to calm myself down and when that didn't work I silently wished him bon voyage and imagined him getting back on the boat that had been so transformative to him as a college junior. But this time, it would be a journey called Midlife Crisis Abroad, a transformative program for middle-aged men to see the world from the fetal position and then return home and extol the virtues of coming apart in foreign lands to their friends, who were otherwise on the verge of opting for Porsches and mistresses, newer models of older dreams.

The world outside the club was too bright, too thick with humidity to qualify as reality. It would take me years to readjust. All I wanted was to go back inside and tell Brittany that I was sorry for touching her, and that Les had no right to treat her the way he did. His truth, I would have told her, had nothing to do with our truth, and hopefully that would have been enough for her to understand that we weren't so different, she and I, that getting back on the pole and loosening the thing that wanted to christen me with its ferocious claws, were two sides of the same desperate coin.

# CHAPTER 10

I awoke in the middle of the night with a splitting headache. I looked at the clock. 3:14 a.m. I needed to piss but was too tired to leave my bed, so I compromised with myself by emptying the glass of water I had on my nightstand onto the floor, rolled over on my side and attempted to piss into it, hoping against hope that if I remained prone I'd spare myself the fate I'd just invented. It was shocking but not surprising how readily you'd buy into your own delusions at 3:14 in the morning, how much like the truth they seemed.

I filled the bottle and then some, sighing resignedly as my urine overflowed onto the floor. The acrid smell of it singed my nose hairs, but, at the same time, there was also this moment of peace that descended, this sense that everything was finally in its place and that if I fell asleep now my dreams would once again be my own and not the byproduct of a narcissistic feline's mission creep.

And then, just as I began to drift off, I heard the strangest thing. Birds just outside my bedroom window were chirping at one another, daytime songs in the perfect pitch black part of the night where sound had no right existing, where darkness was its own sound, a full-throated thrum that swaddled the world in a sensory-deprivation tank of bliss for a few hours a day, a sensation so enveloping it was reasonable at that hour to deny the daylight as an elaborate hoax, a feel-good heresy of the highest order.

But the truth of the matter was I needed my sleep, so I left my house and crept on tip-toes toward the tree with the nest in it and started to move the branches around, gently at first, using just the tips of my fingers, but then when they still didn't shut up,

I plunged both my hands into the dense and sharp foliage and started making growling sounds, not consciously at first, but once I realized what I was doing, I took them up whole-heartedly, channeling the Cat inside of me to do the thing it was born to do.

I must have been making a real racket, because after a few minutes I heard a neighbor's window slam open and a voice bellow out at me from the darkness.

"What the fuck is going on out there?! Would you shut the fuck up?!"

I pulled the robe tight around me and ran back into my apartment, closing the door gently behind me even though everything inside of me wanted to slam it as hard as I could; I wanted to make the building shake, bringing it down to the studs wouldn't be enough. I would settle for nothing less than total obliteration. I wanted every trace of it gone, this life, my stupid things, even the waterbed - I wanted it all reduced to a rumor, a scary story parents told their kids to make them go to sleep at night.

My hands were hurting from having jammed them into the tree and when I turned the light on in the bathroom I wasn't surprised to see that my hands and fingers were all sliced up. A slick stream of blood ran down my fingers where it would coalesce and hang for the briefest of moments, jewel-like, before dropping to the floor. It was mesmerizing to watch; the perfect little ruby spheres, worlds unto their own, and I had to force myself to blink and remind myself that it was my blood I was watching tick away. How long would it take to bleed to death in this way, to die drip by drip, moment by moment, instead of all at once?

The bathroom floor was beginning to look a little like a murder scene so I held my hands up in the air as I pondered what to do. Thin red lines of blood began to stream down my arm and after just a few seconds I looked like Carrie at her prom. The idea occurred to me to go back outside and start yowling at the moon. Instead, I opened up the medicine chest to see if I had anything I could use to clean off the wounds on my hands as well as the one on my leg, which, now that I was in the light I could see was turning various shades of red and purple and excreting something that was a bluish color, which I hoped was pus, but feared might actually be excess Windex.

There wasn't much in the medicine chest, which I think spoke more to my lack of self-care than it did to my generally decent health. There were a few half-empty bottles of various antidepressants that I'd started and abandoned over the past several years, an ointment for canker sores, some hydrogen peroxide, and a plastic bottle of rubbing alcohol. I knew that there were probably some cotton swabs and Band-Aids in the earthquake kit in my closet, so I fished it out, popped the seal and began to dig through it, more than a little surprised when I found, among the first aid items I'd been looking for, a small ax, a poncho, and a pair of white cotton gloves.

Between rubbing alcohol and hydrogen peroxide, I couldn't remember which one you were supposed to use on a fresh wound. I knew one would maybe sting a little and then fizz up and the other would make every nerve ending in my body scream. I could have easily looked up the right answer on the internet, but I wasn't thinking clearly. I had a cat in my head that was making me do crazy things, and I was covered in the blood and guts to prove it. I was falling in love with a woman and her mother at the same time. Under the circumstances, I was quite proud of myself for not making even worse decisions than the horrible ones I'd already made. I was ahead of the game, in some perverse sense of my understanding of how karma worked, and, so emboldened, I grabbed the rubbing alcohol off the shelf and poured some of it on to my poor thrashed hands.

Instantly, I was filled with electricity, not just in my hands, but throughout my whole body, as holistic a sensation as I've ever felt, like a spiritual awakening only in reverse. I opened my mouth to scream, maybe to roar, but it seemed that during my awakening my lungs had also evolved, replaced by a pair of quivering black holes, and instead of exhaling, I inadvertently inhaled, taking in God knows how many galaxies worth of air, and when I looked in the mirror, there it was again, a quick glimpse of the Cat, crouched, muscles tensed like bunches of coiled rope, ready to pounce, its tail up and swinging wildly from side to side, conducting nothing less than the tempo of my imminent eradication.

The sight of the thing sent me reeling and I stumbled back, tripping over the edge of the tub, and in that split second of falling, which is like a fairy tale in that anything was seemingly possible, the only real thought that crossed my mind before I hit my head on the shower wall was that I was finally going to be able to get some sleep.

It was in those few moments before daybreak that I came to and I laid there, afraid to move, not sure how hurt I was, because, in all honesty, I couldn't really feel anything; not my leg, my hands, or even my head. I knew that, at the very least, I had a concussion, because I was having trouble focusing my vision and felt mildly, and not entirely unpleasantly, nauseous. But I could move my fingers and toes, meaning I wasn't paralyzed, so I just stayed where I was for a moment, gazing out the window, waiting for the sun to make its dramatic appearance.

Somewhere down on the street a motorcycle gunned its engine as it hurtled past the building. In another five minutes, it'd be just another commuter, but in these, the last few trembling minutes before daybreak, it was a monstrous sound, a full-throated gin blossom on the face of the night, the devil on some doomed last-minute errand.

I touched the back of my head, felt the fresh blood grease my fingers, and winced, the pain reoccurring to me like a bad case of déjà vu. Sadly, though, I remembered exactly how I'd received every injury; I remembered what had happened to my hands, my head, my leg, every last scratch and gash was writ large across my mind's eye. But I couldn't shake the feeling that these wounds were not new, that they had existed somehow for years, in forms and shapes that I'd yet to comprehend, and the only reason they were occurring to me now was that there was someone suddenly sitting on my shoulder, smugly recounting for me the forgotten details of these lasting injuries.

I spent the next half hour or so patching myself up and then slowly got dressed. My hands had swollen up and looked like ugly pieces of homemade pottery. Before I left, I took one last look in the mirror and laughed. With the white gloves and bandage covering the back of my head I looked a bit like an eccentric billionaire, Howard Hughes on his way to his volcano lair. I wasn't sure what I was going to tell people - maybe that I was starting my own fashion line? The Cat must have found it funny, too, because I could hear it purring contentedly from somewhere deep within me, an uncharted zone I swore to get to one day, as though it were India or Antarctica, a bucket list destination and not a gray spot on my brain.

# CHAPTER 11

Out on the road, I sat calmly in my car as I let the morning commute come undone around me. Red brake lights burned through the early morning fog, tracing neurotic lines of transit off into the unseemly distance. It would have been comforting to try and find a pattern in it all, something familiar, but it was a couple of hours earlier than I usually headed into work and it might as well have been a completely different city for all I could get my head around it.

Everywhere around me, Los Angeles was busy putting away its nighttime habits. I sat at a red light and watched a pair of homeless men on the corner loading up their shopping carts and moving to the freeway overpass, because location, location, location. A dog with a cartoon-sized steak bone strutted down the sidewalk, its swishing tail a cocky affectation meant to show the world all the good that could come from dumpster diving if you didn't let pride get in the way. Next to me, an old Korean man wearing just a white tank top undershirt, driving a limousine, lit a cigarette and dropped the match out the window. It fell in what felt like slow motion, the smoke coming off it in a trickling arc of smog that lingered just long enough to be alluring. When I looked up again he was watching me with narrowed eyes. He took a drag off his cigarette, and I noticed a pinkie ring the size of an inoperable tumor on his finger. I smiled and for my troubles I got back a scowl fit for an ex-wife.

The traffic light changed, and a pigeon was illuminated in front of the circular green light, raising its head and stretching its wings as though it were about to start a burlesque act. I stared at the bird as I pondered how I might be able to get in touch with Martha before Friday night. She didn't seem like the kind of person who'd yet entered the digital age, and I certainly couldn't rule out telepathy. What did it really matter, though? The truth was I had so many questions to ask her that I didn't even know where I'd begin.

I must have been sitting at the light too long, marveling a little too soundly, because someone behind me in a massive truck started laying on their horn. I looked in the rearview mirror and saw that he was flipping me off with both hands, which left me curious as to how he was also hitting the horn. Oh well, it was truly a morning full of wonder. I made no move to insult him in return, though, because I knew what I could do to him if I wanted: I knew about claws and biting force per square inch, about laying in wait and the element of surprise; there was a power in knowing these things, a wisdom in recognizing the intrinsic value of instincts and the relative value of love. I gave him back a little wave, too tired to care anymore about it, and when I looked back up at the light the bird was gone.

It was still early when I got to work, so I was able to sneak into my office without running into anyone, saving myself from having to explain to anyone why I was covered in what felt like head-to-toe bandages. The office was far from empty, though; there was apparently an entire night or early-morning shift of workers who were busy performing all manner of tasks I'd never really given much thought to before. Reams of paper were being expertly moved around on bright red dollies, like the sports cars my colleagues drove. A cleaning lady pushed a space-age looking vacuum cleaner over the steel gray carpet that already looked spotless, her bent back curving seamlessly into the arc of the handle as though she were part of the appliance. A maintenance worker stood at the top of a ladder, being slowly eaten by the building itself, the upper half of his body swallowed up by an exposed part of the ceiling, which had a hunger I knew, from first hand experience, to be insatiable and merciless. All of this so we could take our long lunch breaks, collect our huge bonuses, and spend our office decorating allowances like good little boys and girls. The whole business reminded me how tired I was. I went straight to my office, turned on the cloud, and promptly fell asleep on the couch.

When I opened my eyes, Deedee's bright white face was peering down at me.

"What happened to you?" She asked, gently touching my hands and head.

I smiled, unsure exactly what to say. "I...I got attacked by a mountain lion," I said without really thinking about it. It just kind of popped out of me.

"What?!" She almost screamed and then, seeing my smile, she carefully batted my hands away. "No you didn't, you asshole."

"I'm just playing with you, Deedee." My voice was barely a thing, just a sliver of sound. "I fell down."

"Jesus Christ. You scared the shit out of me," she said in a fretting way that made her sound both concerned and annoyed at the same time. I never knew she had such range. "I'm going to get the first-aid kit from my desk. Don't move a muscle. Got me?"

"Got you," I agreed, but she'd already left the office, moving at a clip I didn't know she was capable of.

"Roll your pant leg up," she commanded when she reappeared. She opened the kit and, to my relief, she reached for a small bottle of hydrogen peroxide. She "tsk'ed" while she dabbed gently at the cut, and I let me eyes slide shut again, confident that I was in good hands.

"I kind of like this music," she said after a bit. "And the storm. I can see why you spend so much time in here. It makes me feel like I'm somewhere else, but in a subconscious way. In a way that doesn't feel like I need to be anywhere other than here."

"Like where?" I asked, curious about the dimensions of Deedee's bucket list.

"I don't know," she shrugged as a grin wormed its way onto her face. "Maine, maybe. The coast of Maine in a cabin." She closed her eyes and floated away on the breeze of a moment, a moment that, under different circumstances, might carry her away to that cabin, to the salty air and the childish shouts of sea birds, to the rocky shoreline and the solitude that was behind it all, the most well-intentioned of conspiracies.

"Can I tell you something, Deedee?" It felt perfectly natural to dive right in given the confessional-in-Ibiza atmosphere I'd created, and besides, I found myself desperate to tell someone what was happening with me, to speak aloud what had only been in my head up to that point, to test its resonance, the weight of it on my tongue and against my teeth. "I feel like I have this animal inside of me. Some kind of cat, a wild thing, and I'm not sure what it wants from me. But I'm worried that I might be a figment of its imagination, that I'm not really here at all but for it willing me into being."

"Are you saying you're someone else's spirit animal?" She asked. I blinked and inhaled the pale sounds that streaked the room, color that was music and thunder, hues that were invisible to the naked eye but that could be absorbed nonetheless. "That doesn't sound so bad to me," she said. "Sounds kind of wonderful, actually. To be dreamt about."

"Are your parents still alive, Deedee?"

"Huh," she said, as though it was something she was going to have to think about. "You've never asked me a personal question before."

"I haven't? I'm sorry. I didn't mean not to."

"To answer your question, yes, my folks are still alive. But they live in Phoenix so I don't see them that much. You know…the sun. How about you? Are your parents still around?"

"No," I said. "Both dead. They haven't been gone for very long, though. My dad died about seven years ago and my mom just last year. I inherited her house, the house I grew up in. It's in the Valley. I haven't been there since the funeral."

"I didn't know that," she said, and she sounded kind of guilty so I quickly told her, "Don't worry. I didn't talk about her much. In fact, I don't have that many memories about either of them, my mom or dad. I have vague recollections, like déjà vu kind of glimpses, but it's so hard to remember anything concrete. Like, I remember going bowling with my dad a bunch of times, but I don't remember any particular bowling stories."

"Maybe it's okay you don't remember the specific events," she said after thinking about it a minute, and I imagined her there, in the near dark, cataloging her own experiences, all of the moments that make up a whole picture you're not entitled to see just because it's yours, just because you lived it. "Because maybe it's the sum of those experiences that's important in the long run. The way they make you feel when you try to think of them. The way they make you feel even when you're not thinking of them. Isn't that the most we can hope for? That they become part of us. Anything more than that feels greedy to me," she said, and in my mind's eye, I could almost see each of those fragments of time as individual atoms, each one containing a blueprint for life that was as vital and genuine as any other, and all of them glittering in spite of themselves.

"I know I'm not the only one, but it seems more acute here, doesn't it? No one here really talks about their past. Ever. It's all about the now. The future. Plans and planning. That's all anyone ever does. They're trying to erase the past with every step they take forward. I don't want to be like that."

"Maybe that's what the cat is there for – to remind you. Maybe," her voice went to a high place and teetered there, on the verge of collapsing on top of me, burying me under a new way of looking at this thing, a perspective I hadn't yet considered, "the cat is there to stop you from forgetting."

I opened my eyes and searched for her in the darkness and there she was, instantly, the roundness of her pale face hovering above me like a beacon, a lighthouse on the coast of Maine somewhere, perhaps, a place of such beauty and isolation it ached to think of it.

"Can I ask you something personal and slightly offensive?" she asked.

"I thought you'd never ask," I fluttered my eyebrows and she laughed. "Of course," I said. The truth was I would have done anything for her in that moment, so that it was only a question she wanted made it feel like I was getting off easy.

"Do you think you might be having a nervous breakdown? Or a mid-life crisis? Is there a difference?"

"I'm not sure," I said, thinking about it. "I think one is an explosion and one is an implosion. And if you have both at the same time you go white-hot supernova, and they write country songs about you, the net result is the same, so in the long run, it probably doesn't matter which is which...Why are you asking me anyway? I thought you hated me?"

"Hate you? Really?" She sat forward at an interested angle. "Why?"

"I don't know, the whole thing with HR."

She waved her hand around like she was shooing away a fly.

"Come on, Duncan. That was years ago. I'm way over that now. I just thought it was important to set a precedent in our relationship."

"A precedent to stop me from being an idiot?"

"Yeah. Something like that. You're not so bad, really."

The effort of rolling on to my side sent a new swarm of stinging insects flying through my body, but I didn't argue with her. I was only too happy to have someone telling me what to do. I could get used to not making decisions, just following blindly. Maybe I should join a cult, I thought, fleetingly considering the nature of salvation.

God, I loved this woman. Reassuring me even when we both knew she was lying. It was the kind of deception that made your heart swell. I closed my eyes again and folded my hands over my chest.

"Of course," I said. "I wouldn't have it any other way, Deedee. Wouldn't change a thing."

I could feel her smile as she continued to dab at the back of my head. It felt so good, lying there, the cloud chiming in with intermittent dollops of thundering exuberance, Deedee's hands leafing through my hair as she cleaned the dried blood from my scalp. For a second, I had the urge to reach up and take her hands in mine and just hold them. She must have sensed it, too, because she pulled her hands away quickly and began to pack up the first aid kit.

"I've stopped the bleeding, but you need to go see a doctor. Otherwise, this is going to get infected, and we'll have to amputate your head." She made a motion like she was cutting her own head off and let her tongue loll to the side. I started laughing which only made the headache worse. "Will you do that? I'll clear your schedule and you can go right now."

"I wouldn't know where to go."

"Nowadays, everyone just goes to urgent care. How do you not know this stuff?"

"I'm not sure," I said.

I got up to leave.

"What about the evaluation form?" Deedee asked as I opened the door, letting the light of the real world flood in.

"You fill it out," I said as I grabbed my stuff.

"What do you want me to say? Who would you rather get the promotion?"

I shrugged. "You decide," I said. "I trust you."

"Okay," she said, as I walked out the door. "And Duncan?" I looked back, feeling in that moment that I'd do anything for her, "I don't want you to be afraid of me anymore. It's not a good feeling."

"No," I said as I pressed the button for the elevator, "it's not."

# CHAPTER 12

The doors to the elevator closed slowly around me as I slumped against the wall, glad to be alone once again. My eyelids began to drift closed, and I calculated the pros and cons of a two- or three-minute nap when, out of nowhere, someone thrust their arm between the elevator doors just in time for them to crash against it.

"Ow! Jesus!" I heard Dutch yell.

"Sorry," I mumbled as the door slowly slid back open, allowing him to enter.

"Didn't you hear me calling your name?" he asked me, rubbing his arm. "I was like, 'Yo, Duncan! Hold the door!' Didn't you hear that?"

"Guess not," I said. "What floor?"

"What?"

I pointed at the elevator buttons with a flourish and felt for the briefest of moments like a Fuller Brush Man. "What floor do you want me to push?"

"Oh," he said, "I'm not…I just wanted to talk to you. To have a word. Do you have a minute?"

"I guess," I said, as we began to descend. "I have until the garage."

"Client meeting?" he asked, genuinely interested.

"No," I replied, turning around so he could see the back of my head. "I'm going to the doctor. I had an accident."

"Jesus! Shit! That's disgusting!" He backed away as much as the elevator would accommodate, obeying an instinct, I could only guess, that told him retreat was the only acceptable option in the face of something that had even the slightest chance of being contagious. "What the fuck happened to you?"

Without hesitating I replied, "I was mauled by a mountain lion this morning."

His face went kind of lax, and I watched with no small amount of glee as his freckles all retreated from the tense center of his face like ants running for cover in the face of an incoming child's glob of spit. "No shit?" he asked in a whisper. This was currency to him, new information I was sure his brain was already trying to figure out how to exploit. "What the hell..."

"Yeah," I said, trying my best to not be distracted by the digital advertising screen on the wall of the elevator that was encouraging me to go to Disneyland this weekend, suggesting ever-so-discreetly that if I didn't, I might be a fucking monster. "I was jogging - five miles every morning - and it just kind of sprang out of the bushes. ROAR." When I did the 'ROAR' I held up my hands as though they were claws and made a move toward him, suggesting that I might not be above pouncing myself.

"Jesus," he said, and I felt his esteem for me growing, multiplying with cellular efficiency into a new organism that might soon be recognizable as envy. "How'd you get away?"

"I'm still not sure," I said. "I punched it, so I must have stunned it because I was able to get away."

"And you came to work instead of going to the hospital?"

"Mm-hmm," I said without hesitating. "The firm," I added, as if that explained everything.

"The firm," he repeated, and it was like we were making a toast on the eve of a monumental battle. "See, this is what we need. Loyalty, dedication, sacrifice," he was stabbing me in the chest with his index finger with every word and the pain brought on by the prodding radiated throughout my body and deep into my bones. I did everything I could to keep from throwing up. "This was what I wanted to talk to you about, Duncan," he went on, switching the conversation back to himself, "I want to know if I can count on your support as I make this move for upper management. I want you on my team. I want us to tear into this place with our claws and our teeth, I want to maul it, shred it, I want to…" his enthusiasm had him nearly to the point of hyperventilation and I was embarrassedly giddy at the prospect of witnessing my first heart attack, unsure whether or not I'd have the nerve, let alone the inclination, to use the defibrillator that hung on the elevator wall underneath the button panel. These defibrillators were everywhere throughout the building and I'd always kind of wanted to see one in action.

"I get it," I said, saving him the cardiac event, "you want to tear it all down. But can I ask you a serious question?"

He stood up straight and crossed his arms. A hulking platinum watch, the face of which was as large and expressionless as a corpse's, caught the elevator light and stung my eyes with a stain of light. Dutch laughed a throaty chuckle. "Sorry about that. It's so big." He put his hands in his pocket so as not to inflict more damage. "Anyway, of course you can ask me a question. Anything."

"Why?"

"Why what?" he asked.

"Why do you want it? The job, I mean. Why?"

The advertising screen had moved on from hocking Disneyland to now pimping the idea of taking a Catalina cruise. I'd been to Catalina as a child for Boy Scout camp, a week on an island surrounded by nothing but wild boars and child molesters, and to think of it now as a destination for families seemed as absurd to me as the expression of incomprehension to which I was being treated. Dutch let his arms go limp at his sides as he scrutinized me, at first with something like bewilderment, before suspicion took its place. The car shivered a little, just the tiniest fragment of velocity reminding me that we were in motion, a fact that had oddly slipped my mind.

"Why do you want to know?" he asked, and when he crossed his arms in his creaseless, crisp white shirt, I saw the outline of tense muscles and I knew he was getting irritated. I hadn't meant to piss him off. It was just a simple question and, frankly, I found it hard to believe I'd been the first to ask it.

"I don't know," I answered truthfully, "I'm just curious." The truth was that I didn't have an agenda other than better understanding his motivation for wanting the job, perhaps even a basic reassurance that he knew what the job he was applying for was. "What's wrong with wanting to know why someone wants something?"

"It's just strange. People don't usually…"

"Care?" I interrupted him.

"Jesus," he said, a look of marginal astonishment appeared on his face, "that's dark. I was going to say 'ask'. People don't usually ask. But since we're asking questions, let me ask you something. Why are you even here? You've never gone out of your way to hang out with any of us, in fact you avoid us at every turn. Wait a minute," he smiled, waving his finger at me. "Is this because I called you a Christian?"

"No, no," I said as the elevator door opened and stepped past him into the hollow wasteland of the parking garage. "Happens all the time. I have the face of a penitent. It's a family curse. For generations, my people have looked contrite, but in reality we're all reprobates. Every last one of us. Grandma Pearl, especially. What that woman could do with a pillowcase and a D battery would scar you. Inside."

"Funny," he said. "You're a really funny guy."

"Thanks," I was trying to focus on Dutch's red face and not the door that kept crashing into his shoulder, opening back up and crashing again - *SLIDE-CRASH-RUMBLE. SLIDE-CRASH-RUMBLE.* In my head, it was quickly becoming its own resonant mechanism, an essential function of the building's essence, and I wondered if things really adapted that quickly, if *SLIDE-CRASH-RUMBLE* wasn't already the new normal.

"Anyway," he went on, completely unaware of how badly I wanted to get away and for him to let the elevator doors close, "the form you got..." But before he could finish, I felt the Cat leap from its rocky perch and I lurched at Dutch and shoved him with both hands into the elevator, stunning him long enough for the doors to finally close, and I took a deep breath as I watched his face looking up at me with something between bewilderment and amazement.

"Sorry!" I yelled as the doors finally closed trapping me in the garage with the dense echo of my half-hearted regrets. After all, it wasn't me who'd shoved him back into the elevator, was it? Blame was a tricky game, I reasoned, and it was not uncommon for us to lose ourselves in one another's stories, to play stowaway in lives not exactly our own.

I must have been really out of it, because when a figure stepped out from behind the concrete stanchion next to my car a few minutes later I thought the world was coming to an end. The Cat reared and growled as I clutched my chest, wondering where the closest defibrillator was now that I finally need one. Les grabbed my shoulder and laughed.

"Sorry," he said, seemingly unaware of how close to death we both had just come, me by cardiac maleficence and him by feline disembowelment. "Didn't mean to scare you."

"You didn't mean to scare me?" I asked breathlessly as the garage rolled and pitched and a kaleidoscope of brightly colored dots bloomed in my vision, replicating with ruthless efficiency so that for a few moments everything looked as though it were under a microscope and that I was witnessing the birth of some kind of new disease. "What did you mean to do, exactly?"

"I just saw you walking and..." he paused, realizing how implausible this sounded, and put his hands in his pockets. "I followed you down here because I wanted to talk to you about something."

"You followed me because you saw me talking to Dutch and you wanted to know what was going on," I said, regaining my senses inch-by-inch as if they were the heavily contested city blocks of some city under siege.

"Fine," he said, taking his hands out of his pockets. He tried to touch my shoulder but before I could tell him to 'stop' the Cat snarled and swiped it away with a flick of its gigantic paw that was as much of a warning as it was blood sport, a natural inclination toward personal space I couldn't exactly argue with. Still, I hadn't meant to do it and I worried about how much control I was ceding in this arrangement and how long it would be before what I wanted no longer mattered, when I'd be nothing but instinct, one long raw nerve with a bone to pick. "Jesus, Duncan, you don't have to shame me." He looked so much like a little boy in that instant, his lower lip jutting out in a pouting curve of confusion.

"I'm sorry," I told him, slipping my hands into my pockets where I hoped they'd stay. "It's been one of those days. I was attacked by a mountain lion this morning."

"What?" he almost yelled, and the word ricocheted around the garage for what felt like hours.

"Yeah, it got my leg, my hands, and the back of my head," touching these parts of my body as I recited reminded me of that old game Simon Says. "I was lucky to get out of there with my life. I'm going to urgent care now."

"Did it…"

I interrupted. "Yup. Claws, teeth, the whole shebang."

"Wow. The whole shebang…" He reached in his breast pocket and took out a folded piece of paper. "I wanted to give you this to help you out. You know, save you a little bit of time."

I knew what the paper was even before I'd opened it, but I did him the kindness of unfolding it and reading the recommendation form he'd had the courtesy of filling out in advance. He didn't spare an ounce of praise for himself, not that I'd expected him to, noting specifically his "international perspective" and "universal likability," both of which he underlined twice with red ink. The form, which he'd filled out in pen, had a frantic appearance to it, jagged handwriting and emphatic sentences that wound their way up and down the margins of the page and made me feel like I was looking at the manifesto of some internet nutcase, the last words of a doomed ideologue. I folded the paper back up and handed it back to him.

"Thanks, but I can't turn this in. Besides, I haven't made up my mind yet."

"You haven't..." he stalled out and took a step backwards. I hadn't meant to kneecap him like that, but I didn't have it in me to be vague anymore — the Cat had seen to that. "You mean you'd support Dutch instead of me? You'd do that?"

I was about to answer him when someone chirped their alarm, which in the garage, sounded remarkably like the quick shriek of something being put out of its misery. I nearly jumped out of my skin, but Les didn't move a muscle.

"I'm not sure yet, Les. I was talking to Dutch about..."

"What'd he say?" Les spat, cutting me off.

"Well, I was getting there," I wasn't sure exactly why I was taking my time to explain this to him, but it seemed the simplest type of mercy to speak to him in this slow way, because I got the sense that just one out-of-place word, one misconstrued insinuation, could send him off the deep end. Les would never admit he was more sensitive than most, but he didn't need to; the smile on his face that was a captive animal, desperate to escape, and the way he kept crossing and uncrossing his arms, shifting his weight around, trying to find a way to be, because (due either to prolonged exposure to disappointment or just a general mistrust of his own skin) he'd been somehow desensitized a long time ago to feeling at ease; these and a thousand other unintentional gestures said it for him. "I asked him why he wanted the job and he had a hard time articulating his reasons." I paused to think of how I wanted to say this next part. "Actually, I got the feeling he thought I was somehow attacking him. I wasn't, though. I couldn't be the only one to ask, could I?" As soon as I said it, though, I knew without a doubt that I was.

"Of course, you're the only one," he said, and it comforted me in a strange way to be reassured about what I already suspected.

"So, you're saying because I'm not even entirely sure he knows what the job is, let alone why he wants it is immaterial? Or worse, that I'm being somehow cruel by asking?"

"No, not cruel…" he said, and he seemed to be almost pitying me now, speaking to me in the patient-but-patronizing way a parent teaches their child a lesson because it's their responsibility to do so, even though they know it won't sink in for at least a decade or more. "Does it really matter why you want a thing? Can't wanting be enough?"

I didn't know what to say, so I said nothing.

And the Cat purred.

"Anyway," he went on, "You don't have to ask me why I want the job," he went on, and before I could think of how I wanted to respond he shifted a little and his face was lost beneath an avalanche of shadows. "You know exactly why."

Whatever line in the sand he thought he'd drawn I had neither the interest nor the inclination to come up right against the edge of it, let alone cross it. Besides, my aches and pains were starting to hurt in a new way, not as acute now, but as reverberations of suffering that came in waves as if from distant places, from other bodies perhaps, a pain that was more a hint of what might still be to come and not necessarily a keepsake from the past.

Les started whistling a little tune that sounded a hell of a lot like a Christmas carol I hated, and I couldn't remember whether or not

I'd ever told him that I hated it or if it was just a lucky stab in the obnoxious dark. In any event, it was a strange power move, to set a tune like that free in the garage to bounce around endlessly from wall to wall and down through the rows of cars, granting it ever-lasting life, but in the way a ghost had ever-lasting life, that is, not life exactly, but permission to linger.

"Bye, Les," I said. I needed to go – to the doctor's, back home, find some nice gulag to curl up in and call my own. Anywhere but here.

"Okay," he said in that way people speak when they want you to know that you've probably just missed out on the best thing in the world, "but do the right thing, Duncan. You've been warned."

I was so sick of being warned.

Once I was in my car and out of the garage, where my phone could get the fresh air it needed to make a call, I immediately rang up the office.

"Deedee," I said, "you know that form I gave you to fill out before I left?"

"You mean the evaluation thing? Yeah, what about it?"

"Did you turn it in yet?"

"No. Why?"

"I want you to shred it."

She was quiet.

"What is it? What's wrong?" I asked.

"Nothing. It's just that you've never asked me to use the shredder before. I'm touched." She faked a sentimental sniffle and I laughed.

"Thanks, Deedee."

# CHAPTER 13

The urgent care was located in an old Cheesecake Factory, a place I knew well from going there for family dinners for years when I was younger. Inside and out, *Dr. Ibrahim's Urgent Care* had done very little to update the decor, opting instead to incorporate the insatiable *je ne sais quoi* of the dining experience into his medical practice. I'd never begrudge anyone their idea of elegance, so when I walked in and was greeted by the receptionist who stood behind the old hostess counter, I knew I was in for a real treat.

"How many in your party?" the young lady asked, pen poised over a piece of paper with the words *Waiting List* written at the top.

"Excuse me?" I asked.

"I said, 'How many in your party?'"

"One," I said, and had a sudden hot flash of humiliation at being alone, but then remembered that unless you had a conjoined twin, you were supposed to come to the doctor alone, that it wasn't something normally added to one's social calendar. "How long is the wait?"

She looked back into the restaurant, where I saw nurses walking briskly to and fro dressed in scrubs made to look like tuxedos, the old uniform of the Cheesecake Factory's wait staff.

"If you're just one I think I can squeeze you in in just a few minutes," she winked at me.

"Thanks," I said, wondering if it was appropriate to slip her a ten-spot.

She handed me a menu and asked me to take a seat, and when I opened it, I was a little surprised to see a listing of treatments and tests. At first blush it looked like you could order these things a la carte or Chinese Menu style, where you chose one from column A, one from column B, and so on. I briefly considered the "lunch special" - which included Botox, an enema, and a tetanus booster - when I heard my name called out in a thick Persian accent.

"Here," I said, and stood.

"Hello, Mr. Beldon," said a sad-faced attendant with a clipboard. "Follow me, please."

I followed her down a long hallway lined with small rooms where I thought I remembered the large booths being back in the old days.

I was disappointed to find that the examination room looked like any ordinary medical office. The nurse asked me the usual questions then took my vitals. Everything was normal, and I was amazed that she didn't ask me anything about the state of my head or legs or hands. There was a mirror on one of the walls in the overly bright room, and after she left, and I undressed to put on the examination gown, I was shocked at the scraped and bruised body that stood in front of me. I still looked like myself for the most part. Sure, I'd started to change a little in all the predictable ways as I rounded the corner into middle age. A little paunch grew out from my mid-section that made me look, not fat exactly, but certainly gassy. Also, my hairline appeared to be engaged in its own version of manifest destiny, desperate for some reason to get to the back of my head where I could only guess it had visions of a follicular utopia where scalp and strand would live in peace and harmony. And on my chest and back, hair ran as rampant as wildflowers, needing no specific season to bloom.

Dr. Ibrahim came in just in the nick of time as the zit on my thigh I'd begun to pick at started to bleed.

"Mr. Beldon," he announced my name with a confidence I didn't quite understand, "what seems to be the trouble today?"

He looked up from my chart and froze. I guessed the nurse hadn't written anything down about the fact that I was covered with scabs and dried blood, not to mention a head wound, which, were I a soldier in a war, would earn me a one-month furlough, minimum.

Christ, he was a handsome guy. Tall and thin with movie-star good looks, jet-black hair slicked back in a perfect wave. Tailored slacks and an expensive pair of Italian loafers extended out from the bottom of his white doctor's coat that had not a spot on it save for his name embroidered in bright blue thread over his breast pocket. It was hard to imagine this dreamboat as a med student with a blood-spattered pair of scrubs on, but I had to trust that he'd put his time in at some hellhole hospital or another, and that he was now enjoying the fruits of his labors, something I hadn't quite gotten the hang of yet.

Without a word, he put his clipboard down, rummaged through a cabinet, and took out a bag of bandages and disinfectant. He looked me over, shining a light in my eyes, ears and down my throat, and then prodded at my stomach and lymph nodes, stopping immediately when I winced from a cold jet of pain.

"Does that hurt?" he asked.

"It all hurts," I answered, and he nodded.

"You don't need stitches, but I'm pretty sure you have a concussion." He began cleaning my wounds himself, gently rubbing away the dried blood and dabbing on disinfectant. "Want to tell me what happened?" He was trying to be nonchalant about it, but I could tell he was worried, and there was a part of me that was proud to be making his day a little more interesting than his normal Botox emergencies.

"I fell," I said. "Down some stairs."

"Oh," he said, as he went on bandaging me. "I know those stairs."

I appreciated the fact that he wasn't pressing me, and I thought, in what passed for a tender moment these days, about telling him about the Cat, how everything that had happened to me, every scabby square inch of my battered body was a not-so-subtle reminder that I was no longer the sole owner of this corporal corporation, that my voting rights were *maybe 50* percent on a good day.

He worked on in silence, and I was careful not to let him catch me watching him and, when he was done ten or so minutes later, he stood back and looked at me, appraising his work like an art forger judging his brushwork to see if it'd pass for the real thing. Taking that as a sign that we were done, I started to get dressed, but he put a hand on my arm and stopped me.

"Are you depressed, Mr. Beldon?" he asked as I sat back down on the examination table.

"I don't know how to answer that," I said.

"Yes you do," he said, sitting down to face me. "Are you married?"

"No," I said, resisting the urge to giggle.

"Do you have a girlfriend?"

"Kind of," I said.

"Can you describe your bedroom for me?"

"My bedroom?" I had no idea where this was going. "Um, good-sized, I guess. I have a big TV on the wall and there's a big dent where I once punched the wall. Oh, yeah," I said, "talk about burying the lede. I also have a water-bed."

"Why did you punch the wall?"

"I was mad," I said, shrugging my shoulders.

"About what?"

"Oh, Christ, who can say? Could have been global warming or animal cruelty. Maybe human trafficking? I can't really remember. There's just so much injustice."

"Do you think punching your wall is a good way to deal with your anger?"

"Of course. I think it's an incredibly noble way to deal with anger."

"Why noble?"

"Think of all the other things I could be punching." I couldn't believe I had to explain this to someone with an advanced medical degree. "If this were Central Europe they'd pin a medal on my chest for denting a wall like that. They might even throw me a parade."

He ignored this. "I don't think it's a good idea for you to have all these fun things in your bedroom."

"No?" I asked.

"No. A bedroom isn't for fun and games. It's for sleep and sex and that is all. In fact, a bedroom should even be a little bit frightening. You should have things in your bedroom — maybe a picture of a clown or a pet tarantula — so that you won't want to spend too much time in there. Sleep. Sex. That is all. I want you scared of that room. Just a little." He held his thumb and index finger apart about an inch so I could see how much "a little" frightening was.

"Seems reasonable," I nodded. This mix of Western and ridiculous styles of medicine was something I could see really getting into.

Dr. Ibrahim looked at his watch; it was the same kind Dutch had almost blinded me with in the elevator, and said, "You smile a lot. You know that?"

"Do I?" I asked, feigning innocence. "Must be the concussion."

"Yes…" he said, writing in my chart. "Is there anything else I can do for you today, Mr. Beldon?"

"There actually is one more thing," I said.

"And what's that?"

"I was hoping you could take an X-ray of my body."

He stopped writing and looked up at me. "Excuse me?"

"I know it's kind of odd, but I would deeply appreciate it if you could, like, X-ray my entire body. Like, head to toe. Everything."

He put the tip of his pen between his teeth. "And why would we do that?"

"Because," I said, making it up as I went along, "it's been awhile and I'd like to know what's inside of me." How could I possibly tell him that I wanted to make positively sure that there was no big cat curled up inside of me like my fucking body was a window sill?

He regarded me with something like disgust for a few seconds before finally shrugging his shoulders. This wasn't a hill he was interested in dying on. Besides, as far as elective procedures went, at least this one was noninvasive. He wrote on a slip of paper and handed it to me.

"Imaging is right next door. I'm also prescribing you some painkillers for your…" he paused, "…body."

"Thanks, doc," I said, popping off the examination table.

"Take care of yourself, would you Mr. Beldon?" And then going off script a little, he put a hand on my shoulder. "I'm worried about you."

"That's sweet of you, doc. Really. But you don't have to worry. This has all been really helpful. And," I went on, doing my best to make him feel at ease, "this has been a real blast from the past for me. I used to come here for family dinners with my grandparents when I was younger."

"Uh-huh," was his answer. "Just keep your gown on and walk next door. You can come back later and get dressed."

"But," I said, puzzled, "I have to walk outside. Along Wilshire? Isn't that weird?"

"I don't know," he said. "Is it?"

A few minutes later I walked outside and stopped on Wilshire for a moment, feeling the hot, cursed air of the passing cars waft up and under my gown.

"Hold your breath," the technician called out to me from behind his little glass booth, and I heard the elegiac whirr of the camera as it started slowly scanning my torso. "Okay," he said, "you can let it out now." But I didn't want to. I wanted to stay like that forever, condensed and elongated, a sliver of myself, too narrow to accommodate the girth of malignant thoughts and visitors who didn't know when they'd worn out their welcome.

*Click. Whirr.* A fantastic sound! Because if the world wasn't just these noises we made, the ones in nature and the accidental ones, then we'd always have to believe our eyes, which were no more reliable than what we wished we were seeing. Footfalls, the wind outside churning up a witch's brew of pollen and allergies, birds sounding their relentless alarms from the dense green heaven of the treetops outside my window. Warnings, every last one of them, augurs that needed to be obeyed if I was ever going to get out of this mess alive.

"Wait a minute, you forgot these." I turned to see the receptionist holding out a doggie bag. "Your Percocet and your imaging."

"Thanks," I said sheepishly, as though she were handing me porn, and although I resisted the urge to peek in the bag before I was in the car, I could only hope the portions of painkillers were as big as portions they used to serve back when this was the Factory.

"Come again!"

# CHAPTER 14

On the sliding glass door in my living room, I reconstructed my body with the flimsy images and then stood back to admire my silhouette in the daylight. Starting at the feet and working my way upwards, I examined every square centimeter of my superstructure, scrutinizing it the way I imagined a ship builder looked for leaks in the hull of a new tanker. I looked for any signs of the Cat, and whenever I thought I saw something — say the brittle ends of its whiskers or the swish of a tail that may or may not have been a tumor — I circled it with a red pen. There were signs of him, I thought, but he was too smart to be just laying out there in the open. He was probably hiding out behind a clavicle or pressed thinly against the side of a rib, too crafty to be caught in its own habitat.

I spent a good 45 minutes going over the pictures with a fine-toothed comb before the sun finally checked out. I'd have to wait until Friday night when I could show them to Martha.

# CHAPTER 15

In the weeks and months that followed my first week with the Cat, days that had once been straight lines began to take on new shapes and dimensions, endless now in a way they'd never been before, the way purple was an endless color, breathless, a premonition of something bound to happen that couldn't be stopped no matter how hard you wished it away. Some days were heart-shaped, some were squares, some felt like the closing distances of circles, inevitable loops that threaded the hours into complex knots that couldn't be undone no matter how hard they were pulled or cursed at, no matter how many times you tried to tell yourself that patience was a virtue. What they had in common, though, despite their seemingly incongruous dimensions, was a beginning and an end. It was the space in between that didn't add up in my head anymore, the getting from point A to point B.

Before the Cat came along, I never thought of the length of a day as anything more than just that, a span of time that could be measured in minutes and hours, every tick of the clock a foregone conclusion, an engine of sorts that was always moving forward. The Cat, though, was not about straight lines. The Cat paced and pounced, it stopped to pull its black lips back and flash its primordial fangs, a mouth that promised dowries of blood and so much more, or to swish its lazy tail at flies or to just lie down and take a nap wherever a stain of shade happened to darken its path. Everything and nothing were reasons for it to pace out the contours of an afternoon, and in these wanderings, it created new pools of time, widening and spreading the hours as it went, forming spaces wide, narrow and otherwise that were easier than it would seem to become lost in.

I navigated these days as best I could, but it was hard, because I never knew when the Cat would appear. I could be in a meeting, or grabbing a new notebook from the supply closet, or just sitting in my office and I'd suddenly feel it swagger into view, its head moving slowly left to right as it measured distances in its mind, angles of pursuit, and without even realizing I was doing it, I would crouch down behind a chair or clap my hands, using whatever means I had at my disposal to keep out of its line of sight. I got lots of strange looks around the office, but I was thankfully given plenty of leeway as word of my "attack" spread far and wide. The partners even sent me a gift basket full of expensive champagne and caviar, which Deedee and I destroyed one afternoon sitting on the floor of my office. We turned the lights down low and she put The Carpenters on the cloud and we laughed as we sang along to "Close To You," licking our fingers so we got every last bit of the salty fish eggs. The basket had been accompanied by a note that said *Take as much time as you need,* and I think this made us laugh harder than anything else.

For her part, Deedee, who'd taken to calling me "Kitty" (a nickname I pretended to hate, but secretly loved), did her part by embellishing the story both for her own amusement as well as when it suited her needs. She convinced HR that she needed unlimited personal days in order to cope with a boss who was suffering from PTSD, and she once told Dutch that the reason I acted so strangely around him was because the cat that had attacked me had a tinge of red fur, and it would help me if he would only whisper in my presence until I could move past my trauma. Dutch, who now seemed a shoo-in for the promotion, was only too happy to comply, and it took everything in my power not to laugh whenever he came around, practically walking on eggshells as though I was a sleeping baby who would wake up screaming should he make one false move.

It wasn't all fun and games, though. I could tell that some of my behavior worried Deedee, who I'd sometimes catch watching me out of the corner of her eye and sending me frequent texts that often just included a tiger emoji with a question mark after it.

On the whole, though, things were probably better for me at work than they'd ever before. I was suddenly interesting to people in a way that was impossible to cultivate. You could climb Everest or collect sports cars, but at the end of the day, those things were hobbies at best and affectations at their worst. Anyone with money and no imagination could do either of them. But to be attacked by a mountain lion? I was honestly surprised that none of the guys in the group ever asked me where exactly I'd been attacked and gone up there themselves to see if they could get one to take a swipe at them as well.

The only person in the office, in fact, who seemed to want nothing to do with me was Les. Even though it hadn't been made official yet, he knew that things were not looking good for him as far as getting the promotion went and, although he never said as much to me, I'm sure he blamed me at least to some degree for his snubbing. I tried to be nice to him, stopping at his office whenever I passed by, but stopped even doing that when one day I went in to see that he'd decorated it with a dizzying mish-mash of international souvenirs I could only guess he had done in a last ditch effort to try and impress the powers that be. African masks adorned one whole wall and Tibetan prayer flags hung in an arc under the window sill. All of it looked brand new and I wondered if he was planning on using "cultural appropriation" as an expense code for them or if he'd taken a shortcut and held up a Cost Plus World Market.

I could tell that he was avoiding me, so one day I knocked on his door and poked my head in before he had a chance to tell me he was too busy to chat.

"Hey Les," I said in a voice I hoped sounded friendly and not horrified, because when he looked up, I saw that he was wearing some kind of long African robe type thing. Some kind of tribal drum music bobbed and weaved in the air between us. "Nice drums. Hey, it's been a while since we got lunch together. Wanna…" I jerked my thumb behind me, indicating the world was his oyster.

"Oh, hey Duncan. Just relaxing in my dashiki. Helps me think."

"I can see why," I said. "The colors are just…wow."

"Thanks. I got it when I was living in Nigeria."

"Cool," I said for lack of anything better to say. The odor of some god-awful smelling incense hit me and I was suddenly desperate to get out of there. "So, wanna get some lunch? My treat."

"I don't think so, Duncan. I've gotta work. Well, I've gotta be seen to be working. You know how it is."

"Yeah. Of course. But…"

"We can't all fall back on our mountain lion attacks, Duncan. Some of us have to work for a living. Impressions to cultivate, et cetera."

He actually said "et cetera."

"Listen, Les, I know you're mad at me about the thing with the peer evaluation and all that, but it was a weird day for me. You know, getting mauled etcetera, etcetera." Two could play at that game. "I'd really like to make it up to you if you'd let me."

He sighed and pushed the screen of his laptop closed and for a second I thought he was going to smile and say something like, "Sure, I'd like that." I didn't want to be best friends with him, but I also hated to see him so isolated and unhappy, so clearly failing at every part of life he'd probably been told throughout his youth was his God-given right. A nice family. A good job. Nothing had worked out for him the way he was led to believe it should have and to make matters worse, the life he was mourning wasn't just elusive, but vindictive as well, reminding him, I thought, as I looked at the framed picture of his family that he kept on the wall just behind him, the three of them smiling forever at the camera, that it was never really his to begin with.

"I don't want to go to lunch with you, Duncan." He sounded so fucking tired. "Not today. Not tomorrow. Please, just…" He ran out of words the way I'd run out of them so many times before, the tip of his tongue finally worn out from doing all the work his body no longer could. "Just go, okay?"

And because I knew he was going to say that as much as I knew anything, I did.

While the shapes of these days were dictated by the Cat's curiosity and whims, Fridays were another story altogether. Because while they started out in much the same vein as the rest of the week, Friday nights, which was when I had my standing date with Lydia, were a bottomless hole that we gladly fell into together, shapeless and endless, the way love always was at the beginning. This void scared the Cat, and although I sometimes saw its paw prints circling the edge of the hole on these nights, sometimes even coming right up to the edge of the chasm, it never followed us down and, as we fell, me and Lydia and *only* me and Lydia, I would watch its yellow eyes at the top, two pinpricks of fire, hunting us as we went down, down, down, until we were so far into our love they disappeared completely.

That first Friday back after my run in with the Cat, Mrs. Kim opened the door to the apartment. She still had her medical mask on, but I could tell she was smiling at me by the way the skin around her eyes suddenly stretched tight, and I smiled back reflexively, hoping she'd let up before something ripped. She made a couple of quick little bows and then shuffled off down the hallway toward the TV room.

"Come, come," she muttered, waving her hand at me like I should know better.

I followed her down the hallway glancing at the bathroom as I went, noticing with some sadness that the door was open and the lights were off. Some part of me had hoped that Martha would be in the tub again, the way she'd been last week, and I'd be called to go in again and sit with her, to hold her hand while she told me more about her cat and what it wanted, if want was even a thing for animals, or if it was only ever need. I stopped for a second in front of her closed bedroom door and put my ear against it, not knowing exactly what it was I was hoping to hear, but doing it anyway, a tithing of sorts, a nominal act of contrition after a faithless week. The wood of the door was unfinished and when I put the side of my head against it, I blushed, imagining for a moment that I was standing cheek to cheek with someone's unshaven face. Inside the room I heard nothing, and then, after a few seconds, a low murmur trickled out, a private sort of run-on sentence that, it occurred to me, might be her praying, and I drew my head back immediately, worried that my listening would somehow cancel its effects.

"Come, come," Mrs. Kim said again, and I could see that she was still smiling as she ducked into the TV room and sat on the old rose-patterned sofa, patting the seat next to her. One of those home improvement shows was on. A handsome pair of twin brothers was explaining the cost of adding a rumpus room to a suburban couple, the husband looking like he was about to puke at hearing the $17,000 price tag. "Sexy. Men. Together." Mrs. Kim said, pointing at the two handymen.

"No," I said, chalking her assumption up to some sort of cavernous cultural divide. "I think they're brothers. Twins, in fact."

"No brothers," she told me, her tone firm. "They sexy men. To-gether." And then she mushed her hands together in that universal way that indicated sex and started chuckling.

"Okay," I said, laughing along with her, because what did I know? "Sexy men."

"HAHAHAHAHA!" She shook with laughter and I leaned back

into the heavy cushions and joined her, feeling as free as I'd felt in a long long time.

Suddenly, she stopped laughing and grabbed my hand, making me jump a little. She looked at my scarred-up knuckles and then started searching the rest of me for other injuries. She quickly found the wound on my head, and then unbidden, I raised my pant leg and showed her the long red scabs lacquering my calves.

"Tsk tsk tsk," she muttered like some matron from a Dickens novel. "Bad cat."

I sat up when she mentioned the Cat, but she put her hand on my shoulder and gently pushed me back. It was humiliating to feel that transparent, not vulnerable exactly, because that at least had its charms. Predictability, though, which is what I suddenly felt like, had no charm. As she began dabbing something cool and medicinal smelling I hadn't even noticed her going to get on my ragged leg, I tried to capture one of the thousands of questions fluttering around in my mind, but none of them would be still long enough for me to grab on to. Or, it could have been that between what I wanted to do to Lydia, and what I wanted to say to Martha, there was simply no room left for questions.

For its part, the Cat never moved a muscle.

"Dun-can, oh Duncan!" Lydia's voice flowed into the room. "I'm ready for you."

"Okay okay," Mrs. Kim said. Her smile was back as she put the finishing touches on my leg.

"How do I look?" I asked.

She gave me a thumb's up. "Like sexy man."

"Thanks," I told her, because what else was there I could possibly ask for?

It took me a minute, after I walked into her room, to realize what it was she'd done to the place, but when she came out of the bathroom in what had to be her mom's old Pan Am stewardess outfit, I caught on right away. Laid down along the floor were two rows of white party lights I followed to where a chair was waiting for me, a dinner tray clipped to its arm. A Pan Am doily hung down over the headrest and a small stack of trashy magazines awaited my perusal.

"Welcome aboard, sir," she said and when she came over to check my ticket she shuffled, barely able to move her legs from within the stiff confines of her royal blue, polyester skirt. "I believe this is your seat."

I took a second to gather my thoughts. She looked absolutely beautiful, like a sixties version of herself, with her hair pinned up in a bun beneath one of those tiny pill-box hats and her face shiny with just the right amount of make-up; a touch of rogue and a dollop of lipstick was all it took to gild the lily of first impressions. Last Friday night's date didn't count, I reminded myself, smiling at her and taking my seat.

"Complimentary champagne?" Without waiting for an answer she put the drink on the tray.

"Thank you," I said, taking a small sip. The bubbles tickled my nose, and I stifled a sneeze. "When do we take off?"

"Whenever you're ready, sir." She tucked the drink tray under her arm and smiled at me in a way that that made me feel complicit and helpless at the same time, a suicide pact of a grin. "Do you think you're ready?" Without waiting for an answer, she bent down and kissed me on the lips, keeping them there for what felt like eons, as if she was searching for something within me, an answer to her question, or maybe even a better question, a breeze that was the same shape and size as a sigh that could blow away the veil between the ache of want and the anguish of need. And speaking of breezes...

A gust of wind came in through an open window and stumbled around the room, scattering papers and lifting the curtains as it lurched drunkenly from place to place. A piece of paper lifted off her desk, and, mesmerized, we watched it as hung, suspended in space, for a few seconds, and then just as suddenly, as if it remembered it belonged to gravity, too, floated back down, gently seesawing through the air until it landed at my feet. I picked it up and looked at it; it was a job application for Banana Republic. I turned to hand it to her, and when I looked into her eyes, I could see right away that she was no longer the friendly stewardess who was about to take me on a trip around the world, but that she was Lydia once again, and whatever game we had just been playing was over now. There was a fine line between make-believe and a crime scene reenactment, I thought, realizing a moment too late that what we'd been doing wasn't a game to her at all. To her this was a matter of life and death, and I was probably a stand-in for something or someone the way the Cat was my stand-in now, but I was totally unbothered by that, because, I told myself, the first part of falling in love was that you reminded the other person of someone else, or some other time in their lives when love was still a possibility and not just a prayer you uttered as you fell asleep where, if you were lucky, it became a dream that you could barely remember in the morning.

"Can I have that, please?" She held out her hand for the application.

*I can save you from this*, I thought, as I handed it over, but I didn't say it. That was another role-playing game, my game, and we were past that point. Besides, promises seemed like crossing the line, somehow. Too intimate. If there was such a thing.

She put the piece of paper on her desk, unbuttoned her jacket, and sat down with a sigh on the edge of her bed. I walked over and sat down next to her. Her hands were clasped together in her lap, and when I tried to take one, she wouldn't let me.

"No," she said, "no, no, no," the way you would if you dropped something valuable and had to watch it shatter into a million pieces.

"Lydia," she looked up at me, and her eyes, which were big and brown with flecks of green moving along the edges, were movies I wanted to watch again and again. She wanted me to say something, to make the moment right, but the words I knew couldn't do that. Words like that existed, whole empires were built with them, syllables that were stronger than bricks, honest sounds that could etch certain days in stone. I wished I knew them. I wished they were mine to give. "I want to make love to you for the next 50 years." It seemed like the thing to say when what you really wanted to say was *Do whatever you want to me*, but you weren't yours to give. Not entirely.

"Straight?" She lit a cigarette, took a glamorous drag, and blew the smoke over my head where it lingered for a moment like an illegible aura and then dispersed.

"What do you mean?"

"Like, are you going to fuck me for the next 50 years straight, or do I get any breaks in between? What if I have to powder my nose, for instance?"

She smiled at me, a smile that told me she was all in, ready to get her hands bloody, a willing accomplice to whatever shitty idea I might cook up. I leaned in and kissed her, our lips making a seal so there was nothing between us, just her breath in mine and mine flowing back into hers, a magnificent engine that needed no other fuel but the space between our heartbeats. We made love slowly, and when we were done, sleep came over us like a drug, one of those count-backwards-from-ten lullabies the doctor sang before the knife came down, when a pool of blackness the size of the world was all you wanted.

I don't know how long we'd been asleep, or maybe it wasn't sleep at all, maybe it was still the edge of that moment, hovering between worlds of grace, when she opened her eyes and mumbled, "This still doesn't count as a first date. Is that okay?"

Oceans of blackness before I said, "Of course."

In the next breath, she was asleep again, and in the razor-sharp stillness that followed, it was as if she'd never even existed, that she'd been a dream of mine, a confession I'd made to myself in the numb, dead-skin part of night when nothing but the faceless dark was supposed to be listening. Had I dreamt her? If it was even remotely possible that the Cat had dreamt me into being, then wasn't it possible that I'd done the same to her? But then she moved again, just a sleepy little stretch that pulled the crinkly white sheet down and uncovered a tiny brown mole beneath her left breast that I hadn't seen before. It was just a speck, but it left me rattled that there were parts of her I still didn't know, that there were volumes left to learn, and since it was impossible to dream what you didn't know, I deduced that she had to be real.

I pulled the sheet all the way off her, slowly, as if I was taking the very skin from her bones, and there she lay, a white outline of herself colored in with smoky space, the way the pre-dawn sky etched contours into the earth, too weak still to give it its warmth and light, just a dark purple dream of distance and time. She stirred, sighed and turned on her side, and I saw another mole, this one larger and raised, on the small of her back. There were more on her thighs, one on her toe, another in her armpit. She wasn't a person; she was a connect-the-dots drawing. I only hoped that meant she wasn't already done, because there were acres yet to know.

"What are you doing?" Her voice was small and tender, and when I looked up at her, she was smiling back at me. I kissed her leg gently, and she closed her eyes again. I kissed the other leg, and I could tell by the way her breathing slowed and deepened that she had fallen asleep.

*My kisses did that*, I thought.

I gave her one last kiss, this one on her forehead, my personal favorite place to be kissed because that's where the skin felt the thinnest, papery and warm. I got up, put on my underwear and t-shirt that I found in the tumbleweed of clothes on the floor, and headed down the hallway.

Outside Martha's room, I stopped and listened for signs she might still be awake. More than not wanting to wake her, I wanted to be sure she wasn't still praying or whatever it was she'd been muttering in the dark.

All mothers prayed. All day, every day. It was what mothers did. It was why women had kids in the first place, so that they'd have someone to pray for, a place to put their love so it wouldn't be so much to bear. I thought of my mother and those phone calls we used to have, the long drawn-out games of 20 questions I used to think of as her lame excuse for reaching out to me. All that time, I played along because I thought I was doing her a favor, making a gift of my time and attention, making her feel like she could still give me something, when really it was me who would need to give her everything for the rest of her life. I hated those calls, but I indulged them, because I thought it was just another thing she needed from me, to be a pious yes-man who could provide her an alibi as to how she spent her days, that she'd spent them well and that they were full of friends and love and laughter. But that wasn't it at all, I realized now, clutching the X-rays from my visit to Dr. Ibrahim's which I'd brought along with me but had hidden from Lydia. Those calls had been her way of praying for me, her way of wishing all of those diseases and accidents that were taking her friends out one by one would never touch me.

Martha's bedroom was exactly how I imagined it would be when I thought about this moment. I opened the door to the over-whelming odor of eucalyptus, which was what I always thought of as the scent of last resort. She looked to be asleep, lying on her side and facing away from the door, but she'd left a reading lamp on, low wattage, and she was positioned in such a way that I could see right down to her scalp, all the age spots there, through hair that was brittle as dry straw. *That's what's left of her*, I thought. *That's all that's left.* And I hated myself for it.

"Martha," I said her name gently, not wanting to alarm her. This was a woman who'd been attacked by a mountain lion, after all. If anyone was entitled to a little PTSD R&R it was her. "Martha, it's me. Duncan."

With great effort, I saw her roll over, pull her tattered nightgown down to cover her legs, and prop herself up on her elbows. Her eyelids did a Morse Code routine as they worked their way back to this version of reality.

"Duncan? Is that you?"

I smiled. "It's me, Martha. I'm sorry I woke you, but I've been waiting to talk to you all week."

"You didn't wake me," she pulled the nightgown lower still as she wiggled her eyes some more, trying to bring me into focus. I looked around the room for glasses I could hand her but couldn't locate any. "Old people don't really sleep," she smiled. "We just kind of lie around until the sun comes up and then complain about how tired we are." I didn't realize she had a sense of humor, but I was glad, because it would make what I was about to tell her that much easier to say. "Where's Lydia? Is she asleep?" I nodded. "That's good. I worry about her. I really do. I just…"

"What? You just what?"

"I worry about her. That's all. We don't talk much anymore. I'm sure she told you that. So I like to hear that she's taking care of herself. Getting a good night's sleep. Hanging out with nice boys." She smiled and put a bony hand over mine. I looked away as a shyness I didn't know I was still capable of rose in me, filling me with a warm jet stream of awkwardness that spread from the tips of my toes to the top of my head.

"I need to ask you something," I said, still not daring to look at her, my eyes wandering instead to the little tiger-shaped night light that was plugged in across the room. I wondered if someone had given it to her as some sort of sick joke or if it was something she had from before she was attacked. "When you said that you had a cat inside of you…"

"Mountain lion," she interrupted. "There is a mountain lion living inside of me."

"How do you know?"

She reached for the glass of water by her bedside and took a long sip. Her throat bobbed up and down as she swallowed, and I could hear the water splashing into her stomach, a hollow sound that made it hard to believe there was anything at all inside of her, let alone a wild animal. "I know because Mrs. Kim told me that if you're attacked and almost killed by an animal, it stays inside of you until it finishes the job."

"Can you do anything to get it out?"

She smiled. "There's things you can do."

"What about Lydia? The last time I saw you…" I was careful not to bring the bathtub. Having her get all bashful on me now was the last thing I wanted, "…you mentioned that sometimes you wanted to tear her apart. Do you remember that?" Just saying the words made me feel slightly dizzy.

"Of course, I do," she said. "Every day, it takes a little more of her away from me. Every day pieces of her float away and one day, in the not-too-distant future, there'll be nothing left of her for me. There's already so little of her...," she took her hand off mine and pulled it up to her head, "...here."

I could feel the presence of strange creatures lurking in the corners of the room where they'd been incubating for years, glued to the floor by shadows, hungry for fresh blood and a change of scenery. If I wandered too far, they'd have me in a second, rip my fucking head off, all that jazz. I scooted a little closer to Martha and heard them moan a faint groan of disappointment, felt their bones rattle in their twisted shriveled bodies.

"Are you talking about memory?"

"It's memory, but that happens to everyone. We all learn to forget. It's the last lesson our bodies teach us." My breath, which was already floundering in the shallows, snagged on the sentiment, and I forced myself to swallow the sob that ballooned within me. "What I'm talking about is love. It's making me forget how to love her. Bit by bit and day by day, I'm losing the things that made her matter the most. Can you understand the difference? The difference between forgetting and forgetting how to love? It's subtle, I know, but..."

"I do!" I said and sort of let myself slip off the bed to my knees. I took out the X-rays and hurriedly began to lay them out in the correct order on her bed. I must have scared her, because she pulled the covers up to her neck, her eyes ovaling in fright. "No, no, don't worry," I told her, careful now where I put my hands. I didn't want her thinking she was about to have a repeat of her mountain lion encounter, although I did feel the Cat begin to stalk the narrow space we shared, and then, for the first time, let out a roar that traveled through my central nervous system and ended up in my skull, a white hot sensation that made me clutch the sides of my head to keep it from imploding the way a building slated for de-molition and laced with dynamite might.

"Are you okay?" she asked.

"Just a second," I replied, putting up an index finger to let her know that I wasn't stroking out, that all I needed was a second to collect myself, that the pieces she saw scattered all around weren't the real me. The real me was back in bed with Lydia, I wanted to explain, dreaming a dream about stewardesses and Steely Dan, ev-ery perfect moment I'd ever known soaked up with a sponge and wrung out dry over my sleepy head.

And then, I don't know if the sound somehow leaked out of me, or if she could just sense how near the Cat was, if she felt the heavy sway of its impatience and how it resented being trapped, but she asked me, "You have something trapped in you, too. Don't you?" The smile that accompanied the question was one of those old women smiles that proved she could tell the future if she wanted to, that it was the past that was the real lost cause.

My eyes flew open, and I stared at her for a few merciful sec-onds, or what added up to an eternity in real life.

"I do!" I said, putting my hands on the X-rays. "It's a cat! Do you see it? Where is it? I thought it might be hiding behind my sternum…see that piece there that looks a little like a head? It's not a tumor. My doctor, who'd really love your bedroom, by the way, told me that everything was normal, but he didn't know what he was looking…"

"Duncan," she said, putting a quieting hand on my arm, "I be-lieve you. You don't have to prove anything to me."

Unashamed, I began to cry, softly at first, and then it built up steam, and pretty soon I was a regular locomotive of salty tears and snot.

"Only sometimes," I charged ahead. Nothing sounded crazy anymore. "I can't help thinking that it's dreaming me. Like what you were saying about it taking the pieces of Lydia away from you that you knew how to love. It's not teaching you a new way to love her, it's just being cruel. I feel the same way with mine. That it's dreaming me and that's what's making me whole. And if it went away…"

She looked at me expectantly, "What? If it went away what?"

"That if it went away," I went on reluctantly, afraid that my words would make it truer than it already felt, "she'd go away, too, and there's nothing worse than that. There's nothing worse than being alone."

For my trouble, I got a pitying look from her. Not a bad bargain, considering, but then she slowly turned her body around, the bedsprings shrieking their great outdoor sounds, and pulled her nightgown down, as though she was unpeeling herself to reveal the part that mattered most, the flesh and the blood, the bruised innards that proved she was still alive. Her wounds looked the same as when I'd seen them a week earlier, raised red scabs and deep claw marks that raced up and down the length of her body, swollen paths I felt the urge to reach out and trace with the tips of my fingers, an atlas of sorts, that spoke of journeys without end.

She turned back to me, smiled, and yawned, a combination of signals that told me it was nearly dawn and she was ready to get back to capturing what little there was left of the night.

"I'm going to let you get some sleep," I said, collecting my X-rays and getting slowly up off the floor.

"Thank you, Duncan."

"For what?" I asked, my hand was reaching for the doorknob, and my mind was already back in bed with Lydia, curled up next to her beneath the cool lick of the sheets, dozing in a shallow grave for lovers.

"For talking to me. For telling me about your cat."

I smiled into the dark. I wasn't sure if she could see me or not, but it felt like it was the best I had to offer.

# CHAPTER 16

Months passed. Long, luxurious months, lascivious stretches of time I imagined lay beneath us like a maze of fault lines, the very blueprints of the earth. Individual days didn't matter anymore; they were neutered and passionless, and sounded, to my ear, like the slow steady drip of last night's rain against a tinny gutter. Years, too, were monsters, a mass grave of memories and plans bulldozed together into an unmarked grave, waiting to be accidentally discovered 50 years from now by intrepid campers, fossilized and unidentifiable, a tragic relic from a regrettable past. I wrapped myself in months.

We settled into a rhythm, Lydia and I, an ocean that stretched for months and months, and with it, I felt a peace and a steadiness that moved me almost as deeply as the romance itself. During the week, we talked almost every day, by text during office hours and on the phone at night. We asked each other a million questions about our families and our pasts, the great loves of our lives and what we were like as children. She told me about her cousin that came to LA from Chicago because he thought he could prove that OJ was set up and how he'd made her drive back and forth from the Brentwood restaurant where Ron Goldman worked to his apartment on Barrington, back and forth they drove for what felt like hours.

"He sounds nuts," I said.

"I kind of liked it," she told me. "He paid me $15 an hour. It might have been the best job I've ever had."

She asked me about my work, and when I tried to explain to her what I did, I found that I couldn't in a way that satisfied either of us.

"So, let me get this straight," she tried to summarize after I'd stumbled through an explanation of what investment banking was. "You use money to make more money. But what's the thing?"

"What do you mean?"

"There has to be a thing where the money comes from, right? Something someone made. You can't just make money from money. Where did the money start?"

"Nowhere," I told her, sipping a cocktail I didn't realize I needed until I started drinking it.

"It didn't just come out of thin air! You have to make something to make money, right?"

I laughed. "Nope. You just need to move it around. And you need to believe that what you're doing is making something. That's the real trick."

"Do you believe it?" she asked, and I could tell by the way her voice was doing that steep climbing thing that she'd gone straight from confusion to indignation, as if she was climbing Everest and had neglected to stop at base camp to let herself get acclimated to the thinning air. She wasn't the first person I'd tried to explain this to and failed, which made sense, because there was really nothing rational about it.

"No," I said, taking another sip of my drink and swishing it around so it numbed my tongue. I knew this had something to do with blood vessels either expanding or contracting; I just wasn't sure which. *But that was the trick, wasn't it?* I thought, knowing which things made your blood flow faster and which things slowed it down. "But the people I work with…" There were thousands of ways I could have ended the sentence, and I chose what I thought was the most diplomatic of them, "they're a different breed."

"What's that supposed to mean?"

"They don't exactly function from the same baseline as normal people."

I realized how cryptic I was sounding and rushed to cover my tracks. "No one ever talks about their lives before coming to the firm, and no one asks each other questions. It's pretty eerie."

There was silence on the other end of the phone, and I wondered what she was thinking, what she was doing. I didn't have a girlfriend in high school, but I used to fantasize about conversations like this; her laying on her bed, staring up and finding patterns in the cottage cheese ceiling while she twisted the phone cord around her hand, pulling it tight, tighter, watching the blood drain from her fingertips and then, just when the pain stopped feeling good and started feeling a little too much like real life, letting it go and watching the blood rush back into them, amazed at all the parts of the body that could blush.

"It's like if the social contract was an NDA. Sounds okay to me," she said, and then I heard the grainy whoosh of a lighter as she lit a cigarette, that first desperate inhale. "Actually, it sounds kind of dreamy."

The only thing we never talked about with one another were our Friday nights. Not because they had no name, but because to talk about them would make them real, somehow, and to us they were a dream, always starting at about 10:00 at night or so and not ending until well into Saturday afternoon. We got to know one another during those 12-hour chunks we spent together every week, huge blocks of information and emotion coming in like transmissions from another planet. I'd never gotten to know anyone else in this way before; instead of a learning curve, it was a saturation, and there was very little room for error. Anything and everything was possible during those months, and our love felt like a run-on sentence, words kept coming to us, ideas about what we wanted to be, things we'd always wanted to feel but never had, and as we continued to fall, deeper and deeper into blackness, the Cat was right there with me, though it was not always so existential.

One night, I bought her a bird.

There was nothing like walking around the streets of Hollywood in the dead-center middle of the night. Not late at night, when drunken assholes and party boys roamed around, everyone on a mission to do anything to keep the evening going for just a few minutes more, but in the hours after that, when those people had given up and gone home to have come-to-Jesus meetings with their gag reflexes. The cold and clotted air made certain that every noise sounded like a gunshot, and when a car backfired, her hand captured mine and squeezed. She was wearing an old sweater of mine and a burgundy, mid-length, denim skirt with black leggings. A pair of Mary Janes rounded out the outfit, and I couldn't tell if she was going for sly coquette or sister wife, but whichever it was, I wanted to be in her gang.

Cars, which until just an hour before had been prowling the streets in great feral gangs, were now few and far between, just the occasional orphaned Uber forlornly trolling the asphalt as though searching for its long-gone mother, which, if those nature films from our youth taught us anything, it would never find.

"What happens when there are only Ubers on the road and there's no one left to pick up? Don't you worry about things like that?" Her paranoia and spiraling anxiety were intoxicating; I pulled her in closer and gave her a tight squeeze. Leaning down I whispered into her ear:

"What you're talking about is a gig singularity. Universe-ending stuff. Ancient prophecies in limited edition boxes of General Mills cereal kind of stuff. Highly classified carbs. You shouldn't talk about such things in public, though." I motioned to a middle-aged homeless man who was sitting in the alcove of a faux Spanish apartment building. A bright white cockatoo sat on his shoulder, bobbing its head up and down as though keeping beat to a count-down clock only it could hear, marking time until the end of the world, perhaps, or maybe it was just enjoying a tune I hadn't honed in on yet, music at a higher frequency than I belonged to. "They have ears everywhere."

She looked, and when she saw the bird, her face lit up, as big and bright as the moon, and she pulled away from me and ran towards the man. I caught up to her, and she was already on her knees in front of the guy making kissing noises at the bird. Part of her charm was how easily she fell in love, and before I could say anything, she popped back up and turned to face me.

"I want that bird," she said, and I understood it instantly as a challenge.

"What? That thing?"

"It's adorable, and I want it. Please, Duncan," she flapped her eyelashes so that I could almost feel the breeze coming off them. "Have I ever asked you for anything?"

I nodded and looked down at the guy.

"How much for the bird?" I asked him, and I could already see the wheels turning in his head, making ludicrous calculations based on the clothes Lydia and I were wearing, her jewelry, the shine of our shoes.

"Five hundred," he said in a stodgy voice with his finger in the air, which he did, I guessed, to sound academic, like he was coughing up the answer to a long sought-after math problem and would like someone to please fetch him his Nobel Prize now, thank you very much. I was sure that part of his calculations were that I needed the bird to give to Lydia if I was hoping to get laid later on, but what he didn't know was the we'd already performed our own version of the Salem Witch Trials back at her apartment, an immoral game of see-if-she-floats in which there were no winners, only penitents.

"No way," I said, "that bird isn't worth more than 20 bucks. Look at its legs. They're so skinny. And those feathers. Mottled!" Now my finger was up in the air, too, and I was worried that we'd soon be dueling. I shouted out the bird's flaws so they floated away down the vacant street, and then I felt bad, because who was I to judge? If I had feathers, they'd probably be falling out all over the place, and my beak...Oh, my beak!

"Yeah, but mister," he went on. There was still some salesman left in him yet, it turned out, and I was excited to see how he'd counter. "This bird cusses like a sailor. Not every bird can do that. Not every bird has been trained to be obscene."

"Show me," Lydia started clapping like a little girl whose most fundamental human right was being delighted.

The guy held the bird up in front of his face, and, in his best bird accent, started tossing out every profanity that'd ever been invented, and to our amazement, the bird repeated every cursed syllable. "Cunt. Bitch. Fuckface."

"Enough!" I pleaded with the bird. Out of the corner of my eye I saw that the old son-of-a-bitch was wall-to-wall teeth. We were as good as reeled in. "You've won us over. This bird's command of the vilest depths of the English language fruit cellar will protect us from intruders, relatives, and ever hoping to one day meet God. I'll take it. But I don't have $500."

"How much you got?" he asked, and I took his sudden lack of bonhomie to be slightly elitist, as though I was suddenly a piece of shit because I didn't walk around with five hundred bucks in my wallet.

"I'll tell you what," I said, still feeling the residual effects of sex and fresh air, "I'll give you all the money I have on me. I'm not sure how much it is exactly, but I know it's at least 40 bucks."

When he asked me, "What do you do for a living?" I had the nauseating sense that I was being interviewed and didn't like it one bit.

"Investment banking."

"Okay, it's a deal," he said, and rubbed his hands together like a miserly sweatshop owner.

I opened the wallet, blew the cobwebs away in a way I hoped he'd find amusing, and took out the modest wad from within. Then I made a big show of counting it into his trembling palm, "That's $20, $25, $27…" stopping only to lick my fingers once in awhile, all of which delighted the ever living fuck out of him.

"Yes yes yes!" He cried in an ascending scale so perfectly pitched it might have made a castrati cry, but then again it might not have been him at all, because inside of me the Cat was purring like a cozy little heart attack, not to mention I could have sworn I thought I heard the buildings weeping, just a little, swooning in time to the bird owner's cataclysmic ecstasy. In the end, it cost me $189 for that bird, and I paid happily. Lydia was as tickled as she could be, kissing me all over my face, then kissing the bird, then even kissing the homeless guy who got all coy and blushed beneath his sooty façade.

We'd got about 30 feet from him when Lydia suddenly stopped, turned, and shouted down the street, "I forgot to ask. What's his name?"

"Dr. Nuts," came the answer, bouncing all over the place like a little rubber ball.

And that was perfect, too.

Back at her place we made a nice little pillow fort in the corner of the living room for Dr. Nuts. We talked about going to Petco later to get a proper cage, and before I knew it, the whole thing started to feel a little domestic to me, all this chatter about cage sizes, diets and deworming pills.

She had her face down close to him and was trying to get him to repeat her name. Over and over she kept saying, "Lydia. Pretty girl. Lydia. Pretty girl." But he wasn't having it. He was bobbing his head all around and walking back and forth along the carpet, from one end of his fort to the other, and every once in awhile, he'd stop and hold real still, and it looked like maybe he was about to say something, but then he'd just start bobbing and weaving again, and I could tell that it was really bumming her out.

"Maybe he's broken," she said, sitting back on her heels and sticking out her lower lip.

"This bird? No way," I attempted to reassure her. " Just give him time. He's not used to his new digs yet. He's from the streets. All this luxury is unsettling."

"You think so?" she said, and I could see a smile beginning to crack the surface of her lips, like a shark's fin.

"Ab-so-lutely." I told her. "I've never been surer of anything in my life."

"You're right," she said. "Our son, the genius."

"Cunt," croaked Dr. Nuts. "Fucker."

"What in the hell is that?" Martha stood in the hallway. She wore a long and fraying floral housecoat and leaned on one of those canes that had four prongs at the end. Her gray hair was an unruly wad of steel wool, and her skin, where it was visible, hung down like bunting off a float. I'd never seen her standing up and was shocked to see how crooked she was, bent over the cane at an almost 45 degree angle, the crooked loop of her spine barely keeping her large frame upright.

"Mom," Lydia rushed over to her, "you're not supposed to be out of bed without someone with you. What if you fall?"

"Mrs. Kim knows what to do."

I saw some of the light go out of Lydia as she tried to take her mom by the elbow. Martha snatched it away with a deftness that surprised me.

"What is this thing supposed to be? Does he talk?"

"It's a…" Lydia started to say, but I interrupted her.

"His name is Dr. Nuts," I said. And then, as if on cue, Dr. Nuts hopped onto the edge of one of the pillows, flapped his wings a few times, and before any of us knew what was happening, flew over to Martha and perched himself on the handle of her cane. He bobbed his head a few times and then blurted, "Does he talk? Does he talk?"

Lydia and I stood dumbstruck while Martha, a smile spreading across her doughy face, began to giggle.

"Adorable!" she shrieked, and Dr. Nuts swayed his head enthusiastically, as though Martha's voice was a song. "What a sweet boy!"

"Sweet boy. Sweet boy," he echoed.

Lydia made a strangled noise, the rather intense and panic-inducing gurgle of someone choking. I tried to hug her, but she pushed me away, and inside me the Cat gave a worried roar, its binary brain deliberating between fight or flight, the only two emotions that were ever worth a damn. *Not now*, I willed it, but I didn't know if I had it in me to stop it when I didn't even know what exactly it wanted to do. *She's not choking*, I told myself and the Cat. *If she were choking, there'd be no sound and she'd be getting blue in the face. This is anger,* I thought, *and anger like this is always the end of something.*

"Lydia, Lyd…" was as far as I got when she looked at me, her eyes swimming in tears, sobs of breaths coming over her like a relentless set of waves, giving her just the briefest pause for lucidity before the next one and the next one.

"No!" She screamed, as if she could read my mind and was going to spare me the long and winding road of trying to make peace between countries that hadn't seen eye to eye since before the white man came. "I am leaving, Duncan! I don't know where I'm going to go, but I can't be here anymore! If I stay here I'm going to… to…"

"Oh, stop being so dramatic." Martha waved her hand Lydia's way — the same gesture you used when you wanted to keep a fire going.

"Lydia…" I tried to stop her before she really got going, but it was already too late. All the things I wanted to say to her in that moment trailed off into a fuzzy horizon of ellipses. I had her name and that was all. The rest of it was…

"Sometimes, Mom," she began in a dry monotone that sounded like it'd been scraped off the floor, "I lie awake at night thinking about what happened that day, the mountain lion, and I can't but think that it might have been better if it had just killed you. Because, you've been dying slowly ever since, and it's the kind of illness that spreads and it's killing me, too. It's here, all the time. It's there when I go into the kitchen late at night, sitting at the table, dunking biscuits into tea, it's sitting on the couch with the TV on and the volume all the way down, and the color is pouring over its face, greens and reds and blues, electric and sick looking. The worst, though, is when it's in the bathroom, stuck in the tub, and I can't tell if it's alive or dead for a minute, but then its eyes move, and I know it's alive, but barely. It twitches, just a little, and I know there's just enough life left in it to pull me in there with it and hold me down under the water until there's nothing left. It's everywhere I look."

A sob bobbed up within her, a squirming creature she'd had her knee on that had finally managed to wriggle its way free. It rattled her body almost an imperceptible amount, and I closed my eyes, just wanting it all to be over. "It scares me to death," she went on, half begging and half resigned, "and then I think to myself. 'Isn't a parent supposed to sacrifice everything for a child?' Shouldn't a parent want to do that? Isn't that what being a parent is all about? Some people," she went on, the sharp edge of her voice dropping in volume and suddenly dulled, as though she'd spent decades trying to saw her way through something that was impossible to cut, "might even say that that kind of self-sacrifice is a privilege." I looked from Lydia to Martha and back to Lydia again, their eyes tangled in a knotted stare. "You don't see it that way, though, do you? You never have."

The apartment was sewn up in a tight corset of silence, all the air and sound had been squeezed out to make room for something massive and unbudging, a tension dense with history that had an atomic structure all its own.

"Wait, you're not joking?" Martha asked.

Lydia drew in a giant breath, as though something humongous was sitting on her chest, "Jesus, Mom…" But before she could finish what she was saying, Martha pulled her lips back, opened her mouth as wide as it would go, and *growled* at her, a guttural noise that was as startling and bone-chilling as it was ridiculous, a killer who laughs while you're dying, who could barely finish the job because the whole thing was just too damn funny.

Lydia and I were both frozen, and where Lydia's eyes went wide with fright, I felt the Cat suddenly sit up and throw its full weight against my rib cage. The wind went out of me, and I had to dig my fingernails into my hands to keep myself from doing what exactly, I wasn't quite sure. Of course, there were a million things I could have said to defuse the situation, but then there was another whole part of me that wanted to drop to my hands and knees and roar back at Martha, snarl at her and sink my teeth into the fat flesh of her calves, pick her apart piece by piece, at first out of hunger, but then just because it felt too good to stop.

Lydia stormed away, and the bedroom door slammed shut. I imagined her inside her mother's old room where over the past few months we'd played out our courtship like it was a game of charades. I pictured her choosing a suitcase and then the clothes and knick-knacks with which to fill it, objects with lives of their own, with souls filled with as much memory and longing as any person who ever lived.

Martha looked at me and jerked a thumb towards where Lydia ran off to. "What got into her?"

I couldn't tell if she was joking or if in her mind it was just another spat, another misunderstanding in a lifetime filled with mixed signals and slamming doors.

"Martha…" I thought about how best to explain it and opted for the version where I would treat her like a child. "She needs you."

"She wishes I was dead. You heard her."

"No," I told her. "She just wants you to be alive in a different way."

She snorted. "That's ridiculous. That's not even splitting hairs. It's just stupid."

I had an idea. "Martha, what if she came home with me and, as she starts to open up to me, I bring some of the stuff to you that has to do with you and her. Little pieces here and there. Enough to help you two get back to where you were before."

She froze and considered me carefully. "You'd do that for me? You'd be my spy, Duncan?"

"I wouldn't call it spying."

"What would you call it then?"

"Helping?"

"Ok, Mr. Helper," she stuck out her wrinkled hand, "it's a deal."

I hesitated taking her hand for a moment, not because I didn't want to touch her, but because I hadn't really intended or thought about this thing as a deal, per se. But when I looked down to my side and saw Dr. Nuts staring at us, his head still and cocked to the side as though his only function was to be a witness, I realized that was exactly what we were doing. She shook my hand.

"You know what today is?" she asked, pushing the *LA Times* over to me.

I grabbed the paper, and when I touched it the dense ink coated my fingers in a way that made it feel like I was holding something toxic, something that, if I didn't let it go soon, would seep in through my pores and merge with my blood.

"Free ice cream day?" I asked, dropping the paper.

"No, silly, below that."

I looked again and saw an article about it being Saint Francis Day and that people were invited to bring their pets down to the archdiocese in Downtown to have them blessed by the Archbishop of Los Angeles.

"He was the patron saint of animals," Martha told me.

"I see that," I said, pointing at the article, "but Lydia and I haven't talked yet about whether or not we want to get Dr. Nuts baptized. I feel like it's a decision we should probably make together."

"I didn't mean the bird." She groped for the paper, and I handed it to her with the tips of two fingers. "I was talking about us. Our cats."

"Oh…" I hadn't understood what she was talking about, but my first reaction was that there were easier paths to absolution, more direct ones, too. Lydia's bedroom was 15 feet from where we sat. How much easier would it be for her to make that walk and to have a conversation? But there were hazards, I understood, the unpredictability of wild animals being chief among them. I didn't want to be a total buzzkill, so I pretended to consider it for a moment and then started puzzling the practicalities of getting her Downtown, of parking, helping her walk through the throng of slap-happy boa owners, turtle wranglers and every other animal kook who wanted nothing more than for their beloved submissive to join them in the afterlife for everlasting games of fetch and treats made from the sweetest ambrosia and mana, all of it naturally gluten free. And then I thought about finally getting to the front of the line and having to explain to the Archbishop that, *No, your Eminence. We* ARE *the animals. Forget these crazies with the soft look in their eyes and the dented skulls, we're the filthy subhuman beasts that need saving.* "I suppose we could take an Uber…"

She started laughing, and I became instantly morose thinking that I was the butt of some joke of hers about me being capable of salvation.

"I don't want to go down there," she explained. "Olvera Street? Are you kidding me? I once chaperoned a field trip for Lydia's class, and I had to confiscate bags full of fireworks and butterfly knives on the bus on the way home. I felt like a survivalist when it was all said and done. I can only imagine what they have down there now. Huh…" her face became a dreamy blur as she went somewhere else for a moment and it surprised me when the Cat suddenly sat up, alert and restored, and I knew that it was thinking the same thing as me, wondering if we should follow her down the spiny path she was headed, towards the memories that waited for her there, the ones that had been there all along and the ones that were there to greet her like long lost friends.

"What is it?"

"Oh, nothing," she said lazily, smiling to herself and at the softness of kind recollections. "It's just that the memories are already starting to come back to me. Little by little. It's a wonder, Duncan. It really is. Now we really have to pray." She let herself slip off the couch, and I rushed over to her, afraid that she was about to topple over in a fit of religious ecstasy. "I'm okay. I'm okay," she said, fending off my hands. "I never realized how flexible you had to be to be a true penitent." She groaned and patted the ground next to her. "Can you kneel with me?"

I didn't want to. Lord knows, better than anyone, I didn't want to. She began, "Dear Lord, I know that I'm not a Catholic, and you certainly know that I'm no Catholic, but I do want to offer up a prayer today. I may not know all the right words, but if you could, and if you wouldn't mind terribly, would you please bless all the animals. I know they're not as important as the humans, or that's what people say, but sometimes it feels like there's a fine line, dear Lord. A fine line between them and us. So fine, in fact, it's sometimes hard to know where one stops and the other begins, and I hope that's not blasphemous, or whatever, dear Lord, but that's just the way it seems to me sometimes." It felt like she was getting a little bit haughty, but I didn't want to interrupt her. "Anyway, dear Lord, to make a long story short, please keep an eye on us and on the things we have inside of us. They're probably not supposed to feel this different, but that's how you made me, so I guess that's the way it's got to be. Amen."

An eerie silence followed, and I couldn't help but feel like some space had been created, that new rooms in the apartment had suddenly opened up, hallways stretching out towards distances that hadn't been there seconds ago, provinces of sincerity, landlocked until now, accessible in just the twinkling of an eye.

"Well?" Her voice came at me as though out of the twilight.

"Good," I said, but it struck me just as I said it that there was something missing from her prayer. She hadn't asked for protection from the animals. It could be that she was beyond that; not too good for it, exactly, but too far gone. I wasn't.

"No, silly. What do you say?"

I looked at her blankly. I wanted her help. I wanted her to tell me what came next.

"Aaa…"

"Oh," I said, finally realizing what it was she wanted. "Amen."

# CHAPTER 17

"It's really not a problem for me to go to my friend's place in the desert," Lydia said for what felt like the fifth or sixth time, and it was starting to feel like a threat.

"Oh no you don't!" I said firmly, trying in vain to exercise some kind of manly decisiveness. I smacked the steering wheel with both palms at once to emphasize my point, but it felt like a sham, and I could tell by the way she turned her back on me that she felt the same. "I don't like that idea at all," I said, going on regardless. "You disappearing into the desert. Going to some place. There's probably not even a physical address. You'd just disappear into a vortex, and I'd never see you again. I know what happens out there..."

I knew full well that I was sounding like one of those government conspiracy guys who started frothing at the mouth whenever anyone tried to equate liberty with responsibility, but I was on a roll and self-pity had a trajectory that was hard to contain, let alone rationalize.

"Latitude and longitude become abstract concepts out there, no cell reception, nothing but white noise for eons, and then next thing you know...POOF! You're a goner. Disappeared. Off the fucking map. Oh, no. I'm not going to give you up that easy. No sir-e-bob. Not on my watch." We sped north on Crenshaw to where it T-boned Wilshire, a no man's land of lost commerce he'd never quite got his head around.

"What are you talking about?" She turned back toward me. "You sound like a crazy person, you know that?"

*Crazy person* was one of my favorite expressions and I did every-thing I could to keep from smiling.

"It is what it is," I said, stamping on the accelerator to make it through an orange light that was just beginning to change.

"Creep," she said, turning away again, but I could see the gentle pulse of a smile forming on her lips.

"Who's this 'friend,' anyway?" I took my hands off the wheel to make air quotes and almost hit a bicyclist who was trying to overtake me on the right. She rang her little bell and then deciding that wasn't enough flipped me the bird.

"Watch where you're going!" Lydia shouted, grabbing the wheel and steering us back on course just in the nick of time. "And don't wave those things around at me." I wasn't sure what she was talk-ing about for a second, but then I understood she meant the air quotes.

"Look," I said, "I want you to come live with me. How do I make you see that?"

She made a kind of grunting noise as she folded her arms across her chest. I peeked at her out of the corner of my eye to see if the assault was working. At this point, I'd settle for nothing less than grinding her all the way down into tiny bite-sized servings, but not even stopping there, but pushing down harder, crushing her with my need until all that was left was a pile of dust I could scoop into a locket and wear around my neck.

"What're you looking at?" She spat at me. But I could see that, despite trying to hide it from me by turning her head even more to the right, her smile was hardening, and that if she wasn't careful, it might stay that way forever, become ingrained in her the way a scar became a story about yourself and not a wound at all.

It was 3:45 in the afternoon and the sun was doing that homi-cidal maniac thing it did in the late afternoon, slashing at her face with straight razors of sunshine through the window of the car. We kept driving north on Crenshaw, away from Koreatown, and the dense omnibus of graffiti that annotated her neighborhood began to abate, giving way to an only occasional outburst of indecipherable fealty as we neared my place. We continued on, palm trees that were denuded along her streets suddenly gained their leaves back as though they were saved souls, and I resisted the urge to point it all out to her, how much nicer it was here, but I knew that she would take it the wrong way, so I stopped myself before I could get started. I turned left onto Wilshire, a right onto Arden and then wormed my way over to Larchmont Boulevard, a two-block gentrified shopping district that constituted the weakly beating heart of the neighborhood, the last stretch of road before we got to my place.

I started pointing things out to her, shops and parks where we might spend our time in the weeks and months ahead. I was trying like hell to make it all seem interesting. "That's the bagel shop, and we have a Jamba Juice, and oh," I said, a little too excitedly, "that's the spin place. Have you ever spun? Maybe we could do it together." I wanted her to feel that the possibilities were endless when I knew deep down it was more of the same.

She was stone silent as I blathered on, and it occurred to me that none of it was really that interesting. Did I really think she'd never had a bagel before? Or a Jamba Juice? I met her at a fucking Starbucks, after all. It only stood to reason that Jamba Juice wasn't beyond her grasp. I didn't want to jar her, though, that was the thing. I wanted it all to seem nice and easy, that this move wasn't settling. We could have fun here. There were lives here, lives that worked. "There's other places, too. Thai. Greek. Mexican. You name it. And…"

Nothing. She said nothing, and I'd officially run out of sights to show her. I wasn't sure what to do next. I could point out the three ice cream places, but that seemed like more of a strike against the place than a bonus. It was just a few more short blocks to my place, and I'd yet to win her over. A young couple walked arm-in-arm together down the sidewalk, trailing closely behind their daughter who was riding a new yellow bike. Pigtails flopped lazily down the sides of the little girl's face, and her tongue lolled from the side of her mouth as she struggled to peddle up a small rise in the road. Her parents didn't help her, but I knew they'd be there in a second if she needed them.

"And what?" she asked, her body tense, as though she was just seconds away from throwing herself out of the moving car.

"And...I love you," I said, making the last turn on my block. "I love you. That's it." It was officially the last stop on our tour. I pulled into my parking spot and stopped the motor, nervous as hell to look at her. But when I did finally glance back at her she was watching me with this weird look on her face. It was an expression I couldn't quite place, but it felt so familiar, like a place I'd been to once or something I tasted a long time ago in one of my grandmother's kitchens. She poked her tongue around the inside of her cheek and narrowed her eyes. "What?" I asked.

"That bird *is* a little fucking asshole, isn't he?"

It took me a second to figure out what it was she was talking about, but once I did, I knew we were in the clear.

"Absolutely," I said, "he's the devil. We were set up. I'm sure of it."

She leaned into me and squeezed my arm. My heart started beating...

"What else?"

"What else what?"

"What else do you have around here? Is there a coffee place?" She smiled.

"Oh, you bet," I said, as proud as if I'd invented the drink myself. "Coffee and tea. Both. In one place. I have points. I don't want to get ahead of myself here, but they could be *our* points."

"Your generosity is sickening."

"Thank you."

"Do we have to go straight home?"

"No," I said, "we can do anything you want."

"Let's get a drink." She unfastened her seatbelt and checked her hair in the rearview. It was perfect. "I could really use a drink."

We left her bag in the car and walked the two blocks over to the Tennis Club. It felt empty with just one court in action, a game of doubles between four retirees in matching tennis whites who half-shuffled, half-ran as they struggled to keep the ball in play. Every swing of the racket produced an anguished groan that echoed across the unused courts.

"That sound," Lydia said grabbing my hand, "it's like a Civil War hospital."

I laughed. "You know, if everything goes really well — I mean, really, super, no fuck-up's well — that could be us in 40 years."

"You say the sweetest things," she cooed and stood on her tiptoes to give me a long wet kiss. I held her around the waist, and when she was done kissing me, I wouldn't let go. "Duncan," she slapped me playfully, and I let out my own groan, the likes of which would have me crowned king of the seniors division, sight unseen.

I prayed silently that the old ladies who were my usual company at the bar wouldn't be there yet, and when I opened the door I was relieved as hell to find the place empty. Only Ned, the bartender, was there, decanting something yellowish and frothy from one carafe to another, more meth chef than mixologist.

"Look who's here," he said when he saw me, and then noticing that I wasn't alone, stopped himself from adding on whatever smartass comment I was sure was dancing on the tip of his tongue.

"This place is ah-mazing," Lydia squealed, running her hand over the old oak bar and glancing up at the pictures on the wall of the old-timey players in their long skirts and pants.

"That's the Mt. Rushmore of mediocre tennis players," I said, following her eyes. "The Depression couldn't stop them. Polio couldn't stop them. It wasn't until they started letting Jews and Blacks into this place that the good times finally ended."

Ned snorted as he pushed a couple of cocktail napkins in front of us.

"Not sure if Duncan's mentioned it to you or not, but the Lady Killer," he said, nodding at the menu, "is named after him."

Lydia raised an eyebrow.

"Do I want to know?"

"God, no," he said and they both laughed.

"In that case," she said, hoisting herself onto one of the wicker backed stools, "two Lady Killers please."

She put her chin in her palm and leaned an elbow on the bar. Tom Waits was on the stereo, crooning something in that voice of his that had no bottom, a bittersweet tune about leaving home and last chances. Lydia seemed lost in the music, and when our drinks came, she stirred hers slowly, humming a little song that had nothing to do with what we were listening to.

"What's up?" I asked her.

"I'm just thinking," she said, and I knew it wasn't bullshit, because her eyes weren't in some faraway place. They were clear and present, busy making calculations, predictions; they were a super computer of love, working a million miles a second all in the name of world peace.

"Thinking about what?"

"I don't want you to take this the wrong way," she started, still eyeing me up and down "but I'm thinking about you dying. You know…how, when, where."

"Oh," I replied dully, not sure how to respond. "That's…"

She interrupted me before I could go on.

"It's something I always do with people I adore. I have to picture them dying, over and over, and help myself get used to it in case it happens in real life."

"And that's what you're doing right now? Picturing me dying and then picturing your reaction?"

"Yes. I know it seems a little weird and maybe even vaguely narcissistic," she reached her hand beneath her shirt and scratched absent-mindedly at her belly-button, an unconscious acknowledgment of navel gazing perhaps, "but it's a form of aversion therapy my shrink taught me a long time ago. Expose yourself to something you're worried about or fear enough times, and it eventually loses its meaning. Isn't that amazing? I mean, it makes sense, but still…it's got to be the brain's best trick."

I thought about my brain, and wondered what its best trick was. Deep within me, the Cat, which had been oddly quiet all day, stood up, yawned widely and then smacked its lips before winding itself back up into a coil of sleep, all in the name of intimating *Do you really need to ask?*

"So that's what you're doing now?" I couldn't keep my eyes off her. I was mesmerized, I had to keep watching her, to learn all my possible fates from the look in her eyes and the tiny circles she drew on her stomach with the tip of her finger. Everything was explosively possible, but it was a fleeting feeling, gone before I could name it.

"That's what I'm doing now."

"Okay," I prodded her, "don't keep me in suspense. How am I currently dying?"

"Well," she leaned forward, put her hands in her lap, and studied me, "I'm walking home from getting a cup of coffee and I see a black plume of smoke rising from a few blocks away, and even though I can't see the building, I know it's mine. There's black ash coming down everywhere and, in a way, it's beautiful to me, and I get lost in it for a second. Some of it lands in my coffee so I throw it out. I'm starting to move quickly now, but also I stop to watch the firetrucks pulling up when I get there. I watch the firemen unspool their hoses and pull on their gear and I want to shout at them to hurry up, but I don't do it, because…you know."

I knew. "Because I'm already dead."

"Yeah, you're already dead."

"Then what?"

"Then I wait for them to bring you out. I'm in a small crowd of gawkers, but the firemen know I live there and they've let me cross the yellow tape and walk up to the front of the building. That's where you are." She stopped, her mind working, I supposed, to put into words what words could never do justice. "You're on a stretcher, and there's a sheet over you, and whatever's underneath it is still smoldering. Little puddles of smoke are oozing out and up like you're in a cauldron…you know, a witch's cauldron…instead of a stretcher. And then the fireman asks me if I want to see the body, but before I can answer," she takes a swig of her drink, maybe to steel herself or maybe just because she was thirsty, "he pulls the sheet back, and there's what's left of you." Her face morphed into a grimace, and I understood that she was seeing this as she described it, that she was only transcribing something she was being told. "It's this wretched puddle of red and skin and bits of clothes and bone, and I cover my mouth, because I'm about to scream, when the fireman takes off his helmet and grabs my hand. 'Don't be upset,' he says to me, and his voice is so kind, so reassuring, 'it's not only about what gets destroyed. Sometimes,' he says, as he covers you back up, 'when a thing burns all the way up, you get to see what it becomes.'"

She drank a few more swallows of her Lady Killer and then, realizing she was down to the ice, motioned for another.

"I hope that didn't upset you," she said compassionately. It wasn't a test or her way of letting me know she didn't really need me; it was her way of continuing to ease me into the world she inhabited, of letting me know that she loved me, too.

I was about to tell her that, no, it didn't bother me at all, when the door opened, and without turning around, I knew it was the old ladies I hoped we wouldn't run into.

I tried to sign my tab before they saw us, but it was a small bar and still light out, so despite the bad eyesight they were on us within moments. Dolores hugged me first and murmured "naughty boy" into my ear as she pulled away. When she spoke she breathed a fine mist into my ear that smelled a lot like Big Red gum and iodine and I wondered how soon until it traveled to my brain and left me paralyzed or blind or one of those things that only happened to people in the Bible. People who had tried to do good but had offended God anyway. Gladys was next and she winked at me as she came in close, her dry leathery lips brushing against mine, stealing a kiss. Hazel was last. She had mercy and only pinched my cheek, but it was a hard pinch, a pinch that said, *There's more where that came from.* All three were widows, and they were possessive of me, this youngish guy who got drunk with them, flirted with them, indulged innuendos that belonged in the Catskills 50 years ago.

"Who's this?" Hazel wanted to know, a little too aggressively for my taste.

"My girlfriend," I said. "We were just leaving."

"Do you have to?" She batted her fake eyelashes at me.

"Yeah, well," I patted my pockets as though I was already looking for my car keys, "she's moving in today and we've got a lot to do before the day runs out on us."

"That's a big step," Hazel said, not bothering to even look at Lydia. "Are you sure she's ready?"

Lydia's hackles were up. She hopped off the stool and stood a little bit too close to Hazel for my taste. I deplored physical violence, and besides, she might have, buried somewhere deep within her, her own version of a cat. Like any dirty secret or thousand-year curse, it was the kind of fate I could see stagnating in the standing water part of family gene pools, the shallow half where new diseases were the latest step in evolution. "What's that supposed to mean?"

"Just that Duncan is a catch, dear," Hazel said, making a show of plopping down her expensive Louis Vuitton purse, "and you…you don't look like a serious girl."

"And what's that mean exactly?" Lydia wanted to know. "What's a *serious* girl?"

I would have done anything to leave.

"Well for one thing, a serious girl doesn't wear children's clothes." Hazel's voice was condescendingly patient. She'd clearly played this game before where women whittled one another down to sawdust without ever breaking their cold smiles or smudging their makeup, and by the way she casually pushed a peanut into her mouth, taking a moment to run her tongue along her perfectly made-up lips to catch the stray salt crystals, she was evidently used to winning.

"That's it?" Lydia seemed genuinely relieved. "That's why I'm not a serious girl? Why don't you tell me what a serious girl does then? You know, when they're not spending three hours getting ready to drink the day away with their corpse friends."

The insult didn't register on Hazel's face one bit. "A serious girl can get a man to marry her. You think anyone is going to marry a girl like you? You're temporary to a guy like him. A rental car. A pet."

"How do you know I've never been married?"

"Have you?" Hazel asked the question before I had the chance to.

Without hesitation, Lydia said, "Yes."

Without asking for it, Ned pushed me my bar bill, which I hurriedly scribbled my name on, took Lydia by the elbow, and walked quickly out the door. Walking back to my place we were quiet. I picked a leaf off a eucalyptus tree, rubbed it between my palms and held them out toward Lydia.

"Smell," I said.

"I don't want to," she said as I unlocked the door to the lobby. It was a modern building. Clean. Completely opposite from what she'd just come from. We waited silently for the elevator, and when it finally arrived and dinged, she said, "I suppose you want to talk about the fact that I was married?"

"Well," I said, pushing the button for the fourth floor. The doors slid shut with a quiet whoosh, like the doors on spaceships in TV shows, "now that you mention…"

But she cut me off. "I don't want to talk about it."

"Fine by me," I said, as the doors opened a few seconds later. It felt like we hadn't moved at all. We walked down the sterile gray hallway to my door. 419. "Whatever you want to do is fine by me."

I unlocked the door and invited her in.

Lydia was wary at first when she came into the apartment, walking around slowly, on tiptoes, checking out every corner of every room as though she were a new pet trying to figure out where to make its mark. I didn't point anything out to her, but I trailed her as she made her way around, watched her and tried to imagine it through her eyes. Minimal furnishings, a sterile neatness, the X-rays from Dr. Ibrahim's office that were spread all over the dining room table. I wouldn't have been surprised if she ran screaming from the building.

"This picture…" she began, pointing an accusing finger at it. "Where did you get it?"

"Vegas," I said as if that explained everything. "I know it doesn't really fit in here, but I have a soft spot for it. I don't know…might have just been what was going on the day I got it. It doesn't have to stay. I'm not married to it. Actually," I went on quickly, desperate to skate past the Freudian slip, "I thought I might give it to your mom. Might look good in the bedroom. What do you think?"

I didn't know what I was thinking by mentioning Martha, but before I had a chance to take it back, she was on me like a flash.

"My mother? My mother? You're thinking about my mother? What is wrong with you, Duncan? That woman is evil. I shouldn't have to explain it to you. You should just take my word for it. Haven't we gotten to the point where if I tell you someone is a blood-sucking piece of shit, you just say, 'Okay. Piece of shit it is.' Because if we're not at that point, then I don't know what the fuck I'm doing here!"

She was hyperventilating and her face was starting to turn red. I felt the Cat get up and start to slowly pace around in small, agitated circles. It didn't take a genius to see that what it sensed was vulnerability, a weakness that was as appetizing as it was invigorating. I poured her a glass of the only thing I had in the fridge, Mr. & Mrs. T's Bloody Mary mix, and handed it over. I didn't want her passing out the way I had; that was when I'd run into real trouble with it, I remembered sullenly, passing a lightly trembling hand over the scab on the back of my head that marked my last big run in with the Cat. If she hit the deck now there was no telling…

Before I could react, though, she slapped the glass out of my hand. It fell to the linoleum where it exploded in a mess of bits of shattered glass, ice cubes, and, running through it all, the thick red liquid. The whole thing was reminiscent of a car accident, and I immediately became nauseous with the looming sense that there was a body laying just out of sight, a casualty of this collision, its lifeless face tattooed with bits of broken glass, its eyes still damp with the life recently gone.

"What else did she say to you, Duncan? Did she tell you that a mountain lion attacked her? That we were hiking and she jumped in front of me to protect me from it? Did she show you the scars on her back?" She was shrieking, but I couldn't look at her face. My gaze was still snagged on the mess on the floor. "Did she describe it to you in detail? The glint of the claws and the size of the teeth. It's her favorite story, and it gets better and better every time she tells it."

The Cat roared ,and I closed my eyes. I tried to take a couple of deep breaths, but all I could manage were a few jagged cuts of air as a patch of heat ignited on the back of my neck, singing the small hairs there, and below that, the skin. The smell of burning flesh warped the air around me as I struggled to stay on my feet, and it was not a good smell. Nothing chicken-like about it. The air around me grew hot, and then a sound began, nowhere and everywhere at once, a whisper at first, just the ghost of a sound, but it was getting louder by the second, billowing outwards until I heard what sounded like the sharp crackle of a growing fire. Behind my eyes, the Cat was going crazy. It was trapped on the top of its rock, and all around it the hillside burned; trees and bushes were devoured in seconds and even the ground began eroding under its jittery feet.

The Cat bellowed again and again, but I could barely hear it over the noise of the fire, a ravishing pulse of chemical reactions that was starting to sound to me a lot like laughter. I looked into its eyes and saw a wildness there that was God's own wrath, but then it was gone as we were pressed into darkness; the sun's grave had been shoveled over with ten tons of the blackest smoke the world ever coughed up. I put my hands over my ears and pushed as hard as I could to keep from going deaf. If it was her voice that had done this, then we were going to have some problems. We might even have to go to couples counseling, which thrilled me a little to think about, because it meant that we were a thing worth saving. And if this was her trick instead of having a cat of her own, it was a good one, I thought, as the fire grew around us, another reminder that everything in my life was flammable.

I must have been screaming when she slammed the door because my throat felt like I'd swallowed a lit cigarette, and when I opened my eyes, instead of the smoldering ruins of my condo, which is what I expected to find, I was right back in my kitchen, shaken but physically fine.

"You're crazy!" She screamed from the bedroom. "I'm going to fucking Eileen's. I don't care what…"

I wanted to beg her not to leave, but I couldn't make my tongue and lips work. The muscles that controlled them felt too small all of a sudden, and the very idea that I could will those tiny strands of flesh inside my mouth to move how I wanted them to seemed utterly absurd. The door clicked open, just a crack at first, and then slowly swung open the rest of the way. Lydia walked towards me tentatively and then threw her arms around my neck.

"I'm sorry," she said, giving me a peck on the cheek. "I just don't…can't…talk about her anymore. Martha. I don't want to pretend like she's dead, because that hurts too much, but while we're together, I need us to pretend like she doesn't exist. Like you never met her. Like…"

"Fine," I said, happy that that was all she wanted. "It's done."

Her arms still around my neck, she tilted her head, and her eyes went all soft and round.

"Promise?"

"I promise," I said, knowing full well that I couldn't do that. But in the moment it felt so good to swear an oath to her.

"Good," she went on. "Now, the other thing I want to say is…"

I braced myself for whatever it was she was going to say, worried the Cat and I wouldn't make it through another one of her grand gestures.

"Why didn't you ever tell me you had a water-bed?"

"Oh, I guess…"

But she didn't let me finish. Instead, she squealed and grabbed me by the hand, dragging me with a surprising amount of strength into my room and then flung me onto my bed. She quickly pulled her shorts and panties off and then slung-shot herself out of the old Poison t-shirt she was wearing. Totally naked, she jumped onto the edge of the bed and put an unknown quantity of fingers up to her forehead in the approximation of a salute.

"Permission to come aboard, sir."

And before I could answer, we were sailing.

# CHAPTER 18

Wet pillows of early morning fog hung lazily in the air as I stood on the corner in front of Martha's building watching a small girl as she played happily on a toy scooter. There was no holiday or special circumstances I could think of, but she had on an immaculate white dress, ruffles running up the back and down the short sleeves, that would have served her well at any black-tie affair. The smile on her face was electric, and she burned through the fog like a beacon on that gray morning, her black hair pulled back into an expert ponytail held fast with a bit of red ribbon. Back and forth she went without a care in the world, and I moved a little closer to watch her mouth move, eager to catch even a snippet of whatever song danced at her lips.

My city, in the perfect months since Lydia had come to live with me, was there, too. That morning, like every morning, the last thing I'd done before leaving for the day was to kiss Lydia goodbye as she lay tangled in the loose folds of sleep that still hung off her. There wasn't a day when I didn't want to get back into bed with her, back beneath the clinging warmth of the covers and the slightly stale smell of her sleeping breath, to fold myself next to her and dissolve back into whatever dream held her still. But I only let myself entertain that fantasy for a moment or two, enough time to feel sleep starting to make its persuasive case, before moving on to pick myself up a large black coffee, a mocha with extra whipped cream for Mrs. Kim and a black tea for Martha.

Now though, watching the little girl peddling and running, still wondrously exploring her world within a world, I saw a car start to come along. It wasn't any different than any of the other cars out on the street that morning; it was some type of Toyota, some shade of silver, but there was something about it that made me sit up, all nerves in top gear, and really zero in. Maybe it was the way it started picking up speed, slowly but steadily, or the driver who had his phone in his lap and I could see the light from the screen splashing up into his face, all those pixels acting as an exfoliant on his third eye, or simply the soupçon of window tint garnished with a Lakers flag, but I saw it coming and I just knew, more than anything I'd ever know, that it was going to hit her. For all those reasons, I dropped the tray, screamed, and...absolutely froze. I couldn't move a muscle. I tried to run and grab her, but I couldn't. I was experiencing a fast-acting variant of Locked-in Syndrome and no matter how hard I tried to move my feet I was rooted to the spot. I could do nothing but watch as time slowed down, as the layers of cities finally rose up and converged; I saw the car come into the intersection aiming right for the girl and at the very last microsecond, the girl walked casually out of the way. And the amazing thing was, nobody noticed it. Not the guy in the Toyota, who, by all rights, should have been a quivering mess of nerves, nor the little girl, who should have been experiencing a little kid's version of a nervous breakdown, no fucking pedestrians, no homeless people, no gig-economy hustlers. No one. *Who would bear witness!!* I raged inwardly, at first for effect and because it just felt good, but then for real. It was for real rage and I think I said something like, "What the fuck!" or "Oh my God!" But I can't remember for sure, and there was no one around to see it, so I couldn't ask, and as soon as I said it, that very nanosecond, I saw the cities quietly separate themselves from one another once again, resolving into incrementally different versions of the same thing.

Upstairs, the apartment was airy and light, and laying all across the floor of the living room were these perfect geometric sprays of light coming through the window, and it made me think of those IQ tests where you had to orient all these different kinds of shapes so that they could fit within a certain space.

"I'm making breakfast! Go in the TV room and sit with Mrs. Kim!" Martha hollered from the kitchen, and it surprised me because I don't think I'd ever seen her cooking anything before. These days, she barely came out of her room at all.

"Ok," I shouted back and wandered into the TV room, where I plunked myself down on the couch next to Mrs. Kim who was deep into her late morning programming. In the afternoon, if I was still there, we watched the *Property Brothers*, but in the morning it was always infomercials advertising class action lawsuits. Once she understood what substandard pelvic mesh and fibromyalgia and asbestos all had in common, she wanted in on it like nobody's business, so she waited there, day after day, for her lucky number to come up, and though it hadn't yet (she'd once gotten close on a talcum powder situation), she refused to throw in the towel.

"What do we have today?" I asked her, trying to focus on the screen. "Oh! Roundup. This one's a classic. You're gonna love how it ends. I don't want to spoil it, but I'll give you a hint..." I shrunk my voice down to a low whisper. "Cancer."

"Shhh." She put a finger to her lips and, realizing that probably wouldn't do the job, slapped me lightly across the face.

Martha called for me to help her with the dishes, which I did, and we all sat around the table eating English Muffins and fried eggs. It was such a lovely morning and I didn't want to ruin things, but the situation with the little girl almost getting hit by the car and nobody seeing it was eating at me, and I felt like I had to tell someone what had just happened.

I cleared my throat. "I don't know how to say this, but a little while ago, down on the street, I saw a little girl..."

She didn't let me finish my sentence before she started screaming.

"No, Martha," I said, and I joined Mrs. Kim in putting our hands on her arms to gently hold her down. "You didn't let me finish. I was going to say 'I saw a little girl almost get hit.' It didn't happen, but it was so close. It really shook me up."

"Oh, my. That is terrible," she said, calming down slightly. "But it's not nearly as bad as…"

"Don't even say it," I waved a hand in her direction. "Why bother, you know?"

"You're right," she said.

Mrs. Kim, who I hadn't even noticed had left the room, came into the kitchen with a heating pad which she plugged in and shoved under Martha's ass. She turned the thing on, gave me a double thumbs up, smiled, and went back to the TV.

"The state pays her $14 an hour to be here, but…do you think she would do it for free?" I followed the length of the cord from Martha's ass to the wall and thought how much it looked like it was Martha that was plugged straight into the wall, and how funny Lydia would think that was if she were here, or if I could tell her, which I couldn't do on account of her not knowing that this was how I spent most workdays. "Anyway," she said, not waiting for an answer, "either way, it doesn't really matter. Does it, Duncan?"

"No, I guess not."

We stayed sitting like that at the table for a few minutes, not talking, but feeling okay in the silence because it was just a little pause in a longer conversation that carried over day after day. Little noises percolated here and there; the sound of the TV carrying on its indignant monologue from the other room and the never-ending drone of cars moving down on the street punctuated now and again by a horn that, like a body on life support, let you know the patient wasn't quite done for yet. And although I could hear all of it, all that tumult and what felt like a million other little noises besides, none of it reached me when I was in this apartment. There was a stillness for me here that didn't exist anywhere else, not even with Lydia, and even though I had a sense that there was something vaguely parasitic about it, that it was sapping me of some kind of essential energy that would never replenish itself, I wanted nothing more than to bask in it until the end of time.

From the other room, Dr. Nuts let out an ascending squawk. I went in and gave him a little pat on the head, remembered that was a dog thing and stuck him on my shoulder before returning to the kitchen.

"I don't feel well," Martha said, nervously playing with the buttons on her nightgown. "I feel," she ran her fingers through gray hair that was starting to get frizzier and frizzier by the day, "and don't take this the wrong way, Duncan, but I feel like I'm not getting any better. Everyone else is doing great and I can't help but feel a little like a sacrificial lamb."

"What do you mean?" I asked her, pushing a crumb of English Muffin into the bird's beak.

"Look at all of you. From everything you tell me, Lydia couldn't be happier playing little miss housewife at your place, getting up late every day and hanging out at your tennis club."

"Little miss!" Dr. Nuts interjected.

"Arrgh!" Martha put her hands over her ears. "It's enough to make me want to wring his little neck!"

"Do you want me to take him out of here?"

"And you," she went on, ignoring my question. Her eyes fell on me, and in them I saw, for the first time, hate and violence, "you've got it all. The job. The girl. Money in your pocket. What about your cat? What happened to it? Because Duncan, I've got to tell you," her voice dropped into a low register, one that I'd have to lean close to her to hear really well, but I wasn't going to fall for that. She was on the verge of springing, all but salivating, "mine is right here. Right at the surface just about bursting to get out."

"BURSTING!" Dr. Nuts suddenly squawked, and thank God, because the tension was getting to be unbearable. She glanced at the thing, and I worried she would choke it to death.

Still, I felt for her. How could you not? She was all of our mothers, in a way, and maybe that was why I felt so compelled to spend time with her, that leaving her alone would eventually kill her the way it killed all old people. When she suffered, she really made you believe she was suffering for you. Just for you.

But I tried not to think about that and just hoped the moment would pass, because anything I said was just going to make her angrier, and then I suddenly remembered my mother and her sins. Not the ones she committed, but the ones to which she dedicated her life, the transgressions she invented all on her own and sent out in a secret code of disapproval shared by all mothers everywhere, a language more ancient than guilt itself. For my mother it was a sin to throw away a book (even if it was booger-smeared and chocolate milk-stained), it was a sin to throw away money, which was why we were awash in pennies, the milk jug in the corner of the kitchen filled with copper I was sure had irradiated all of us to within an inch of our lives. Lastly, it was a sin to go to bed with a wet head. I'm not sure why that one really set her off, maybe more than any of the others, but I probably spent a thousand hours underneath her hairdryer, my scalp on the verge of peeling off from the heat, all so I wouldn't...what? Catch pneumonia and die in a matter of minutes?

Martha and I sat staring at one another, silently, until I folded my hands and, in a conciliatory tone, began. "Say, have I told you about Lydia's first time at the Tennis Club? The old ladies and the branded cocktails?"

I wasn't sure at first that she'd heard me, but she eventually looked up at me and said timidly, "No. Tell me."

I told her everything about that night. About the old men playing tennis, and the ladies at the Club, and then going home with Lydia for the first time and how much she hated my Big Sur picture. I left out a bunch of stuff I didn't think she'd want to hear about, all the ultimatums and then the swan dive onto my waterbed, but I told her most of it, and I could see that it was making her happy. I normally didn't like to go on like that, usually only giving her little pieces at a time, little anecdotes about Lydia, stories from our lives together to keep her content, because I only had so much material, and then what? I didn't want to get into the business of making up stories to tell her. Somehow, I felt like she'd know I was lying to her.

"That sounds nice." She was lost in a little bit of a trance, like she was recovering from something exhausting and was maybe only dreaming this entire conversation. "I'd like a picture like that."

"Huh?" And then I realized she was talking about the Big Sur photo, the part of the story that, to me, had seemed extraneous. "Fine," I said, without thinking first. "I'll bring it by this week."

She turned to look at me and I saw some of her focus return, as though it was color rising in her cheeks after a near death experience. "We have nice talks, don't we? I mean, like really..." her whole face sunk as she tried to pin down the floundering word, "great talks."

Back outside, it had become a Fertility Goddess of a day. Mother Nature had finally squeezed her child-rearing hips through the layers of fog, and the street was washed in sunshine, scrubbed down to its gleaming bones. I took out my phone and started searching through Amazon for black and white pictures of Big Sur. I couldn't find the exact photo, but I did find one of the Cliffs of Moher in Ireland that looked a lot like it, and when I looked down at the comments and saw that someone named *DiligentHipster501* had left a review saying, *Bespoke as fuck*, I knew it would do the trick. It wouldn't solve all of Martha's problems, and maybe it wasn't even a start, but I knew how important it was to have little things to keep looking forward to. Some of us worked very hard for our distractions, which, I realized with no little sense of irony, was a distraction all its own.

Speaking of work, I called the office. It rang and rang and just as I was about to hang up Deedee came on the line mid-laugh as though I'd caught her at the tail end of a joke.

"Deedee..."

"You don't have to come in," she said before I could say anything else.

"Hello to you, too."

"Oh." She made her voice sound official. "Hello, Duncan. Sir. Mr. Beldon. Sir."

I heard Les in the background chime in with his huge, unmistakable, A-bomb of a laugh.

"Tell Les 'Hi.'"

"Mr. Beldon says, 'Hi', Mr. McCabe. Would you like me to take a memo?"

Another round of laughter. Les had been a changed man lately. He'd taken down all the Semester at Sea ephemera out of his office and started wearing normal clothes again. We went for drinks occasionally and one night, in a fit of gin-fueled honesty, I'd confessed to him that I'd made the whole thing up about being attacked by a mountain lion. I wasn't sure how he'd take it, if he'd use it as leverage against me in the endless spasms of office politics, but to my surprise he'd immediately started laughing and congratulated me.

"Kitty," she said, trying to soothe me, "relax. Everything is fine. Seriously. Everyone thinks you're at physical therapy. Besides," she went on, "what is it you think you're missing? It's not like you were doing that much work when you were here. I'm not trying to be mean, but, you know, life goes on. Just enjoy your time, okay. Can you do that?"

She hung up without waiting for an answer and I stayed where I was for a moment, trying to let myself ease into the slow current of contentment that eddied around me. It was Friday, and I knew Lydia would want us to take a nap together so we could get up and go out late at night, a tradition we'd kept up from those odd first few dates we'd had at the beginning.

It was about six by the time I finally got home, and as always, Lydia was waiting there with a drink for me. Every week it was something new, a libation of her own making to bring in the weekend, and they always had the best names.

"I call this the *Napalm Sour*," she said, presenting it to me with a fake little bow like she was the subservient one.

I took a sip, and it instantly burned everything inside of me, starting with my teeth, and worked its way along my circulatory system until every inch of me was a chemical fire.

"I'll say!" I gasped. I knew better than to ask her what was in it. She liked her secrets, and I liked that she had them. Some guys wanted to know everything that their girlfriends did and thought, but that Big Brother shit wasn't for me. I felt safe knowing she knew things I didn't, that maybe our collective knowledge would get us through the worst of it.

"How was work?"

"Work was work." I stuck my finger between my shirt collar and the skin of my neck. It'd be worth having a tie on just to have the feeling of loosening it.

"You always say that." She stuck her bottom lip out in a display of what I liked to call 'fake pouting.' We both knew it was fake, but when I called her out on it, it would sometimes set her off so I held my tongue. She was a true thespian in those instances, only too happy to go down with the ship, even if she knew it wasn't seaworthy to begin with. "I hate it. My question demands an adjective and you give me bullshit."

"Fine," I said. "Hectic."

"Nope. Try again."

"Fulfilling?"

"Uh-uh," she stamped her feet and I smiled. "They're adjectives, but barely. They're bullshit adjectives. I want something real. Emote a little," she whined as she twisted a loose strand of hair around her index finger.

We sat opposite one another in the living room, nursing our drinks and staring at each other over the new modern coffee table she'd recently purchased. Spread across it were art books and design magazines, all evidence that pointed to plans for something bigger than the both of us. I put my feet up on it and she scowled.

"Don't do that," she said.

"Don't do what?"

She walked to the bar cart and threw a couple of ice cubes into the bottom of her glass. The clink sounded like money. "Do you want another drink?"

"Of course," I said. "What kind of question is that?"

She poured my drink, handed it to me, and took her chair again. She put her feet up on the coffee table, leaned back, and drank half the cocktail in a single desperate swallow.

"I thought we weren't putting our feet on the coffee table," I said, wondering what kind of game she was getting ready to play this weekend.

She shrugged. "What's for dinner?"

"I don't know." From my phone I picked an Alice Coltrane record and sent it to the speakers. A harp carefully picked the notes of a perfect melody out of the silence, as though it were selecting the best pieces of fruit from the bunch. A coven of low voices chimed in next. They were chanting some kind of meditative mantra, and all I could think of was how good it would be for Martha to hear this. "How about soup?"

She lowered her drink and squinted her eyes at me. "Soup is not dinner, and just so you know, couples have split up for less."

"True, but chowder..." I said, dipping a finger into my drink and sucking the booze off it, "...chowder is the real home-wrecker."

She laughed, came over to my side of the table, and plunked herself down in my lap. Her arms snaked around my neck and slithered up the back of my head like a vine attaching itself carnivorously to a garden trellis. We kissed for what must have been a while, because when I looked out the window, it was dark, and my lips tingled as though I'd been poisoned.

The weekend had officially begun, and schemes were being hatched from a thousand directions at once. It was getting louder and louder outside, as it always did on the precipice of the weekend, not so much a joyous resounding of voices, but something more desperate than that, a collective rupturing of people's integrity up and down the sidewalks and through the air of an early fall evening fattened with humidity. Joining them were their commuter brothers-in-arms, cooked stress freaks who honked their horns and applied too much pressure to their brakes as they made their own getaway plans that, truth be told, were always going to be longshots.

Lydia must have felt it too, because she turned my head back to hers and pressed her lips against mine. Without breaking our kiss, I lifted her and carried her into our room and dropped her on the bed. Our weekend was still hours away from beginning.

We made love, quickly at first, but then we slowed it down, finding a cloying rhythm that suited our appreciation for wasting hours lost in one another, because we knew we had all the time in the world, and when you knew you had nothing but giant fistfuls of time, so much time that when you squeezed it in your hands it ran through your fingers and down your arms, minutes and hours like rotten fruit, you knew there was nothing you couldn't get to eventually.

When we were done, out of breath and slick with sweat like

something larval, she set the alarm on her phone for midnight, and we fell asleep almost instantly, the same dreams brewing in both our heads, or so I thought, until we woke up what felt like only moments later to the sound of fireworks exploding across the city, a bombardment of loud pops and colors detonating across the parts of the sky that sheltered sections of town we'd never be intrepid enough to visit. It reminded me how vast Los Angeles was, or maybe never-ending was a better way of thinking about it, tribal in its way, a limitless landscape with nuanced ethics on a good day. Talking about it with neighbors the next day, you might get a "I think it was to the east" or "Maybe south of us" (we sounded like old explorers), but no one was ever sure. Part of that had to do with the sheer size of the place, its sprawling confines included what felt like 12 climatic zones, warring principalities that had no intention of ever suing for peace; the concept of "take no prisoners" was sewn into our very DNA.

"What do you think they're celebrating?" She asked me after we'd done the middle-aged relay race to the bathroom thing we did sometimes.

"Celebrating?" I was groggy and groping for reality, wanting nothing more than to be back asleep. "I don't think they're celebrating anything."

"What is it then?"

"I don't know. A warning?"

"What about?"

"That they can burn the whole thing down anytime they want to." I felt her looking at me in the dark, her eyes were like that, slightly unholy in that you could feel them on you sometimes, the weight of them, two stern stones that would drag you down to the bottom of the ocean and keep you there if they had a mind to.

To change the subject, I tried to find other sounds to pull out of the night, something truer, less obtuse, but all I could get was my old familiar heartbeat, thud after dull thud, and the crackly interference of her worrying the dry skin on her lower lip, a scraping sound, something she always did when she was thinking too hard about something.

"What are you worried about?"

"Worried?" She sat up, fully awake now, flush with defensiveness. "Who said I was worried?"

"I can hear you doing that thing with your lip. You don't have to get indignant about it." I don't know why I said it, because shit like that never went down well. It was like telling someone who was in the middle of having a full-fledged temper tantrum that they should try calming down.

"Indignant...Who the hell...What are you saying?"

"Nothing, okay?" I yawned and stretched. I knew I should just stop, but something was pulling me along down this road of inevitability. Maybe it had something to do with what Martha said earlier, about how everyone but her was somehow thriving. It had let a little sliver of light into the place where the Cat had been all this time, asleep on its dreamless sea, lost but in no way presumed dead. "It's just you always do this scraping thing when you're worried or upset. It's your tell."

"Huh," she said after a few moments of contemplation.

"What?"

"Just..."

"Just what?"

"Just...fuck you, is all."

"Great," I said, hoisting myself out of bed and grabbing a blanket and pillow on my way to the sofa.

"Where're you going?" She wasn't done with me yet. Not by a long shot. She wanted to keep on fighting, but I wasn't interested in a land war in Asia when a little border skirmish would do the trick nicely enough. I liked to just exercise the muscle a little, but she was in it for blood, oblivion or bust, and I knew I wouldn't survive. I wasn't cut out for the long haul the way she was. It was probably why she told me, way back when we first started getting together, never to need her too much. It hadn't been an idle threat, I realized now, but a war cry, the thing she'd scream before slamming her plane into the side of an aircraft carrier.

I was almost asleep when she came out and shook me. I looked at the clock. It was a little after 2 a.m., and there was a chill in the air, the kind you only felt in the dead of night when there weren't enough covers in the world to keep you warm and only body heat would do. Well, I'd fucked that up, but when I was finally able to focus my eyes on her, thinking that maybe she was here for some good old fashion detente as foreplay, I saw that she was fully dressed, her face shimmering with just the right amount of makeup on it.

"I want you to take me dancing," she said, crossing her arms.

"But…"

"Now."

"It's after 2," I said, trying to find the words that would make her come to her senses. "Nothing's open. Do you want me to take you dancing at a 7-11?"

But she wasn't having any of it. "Now, Duncan. I want to go now. It's Friday night, and I want to dance."

I grabbed her arm and tried to pull her down onto the sofa with me, but she was strong, and she shook me off like I was a child. I knew that this was my punishment for not finishing the fight earlier, and I also knew that, come hell or high water, I was going to need to find a place to take her dancing.

"I don't even know where to start." I wandered into the bedroom and slowly pulled on a pair of jeans and a shirt.

"What about the guy at work you hate? The one with the weird office furniture…the redhead."

"Dutch?"

"Yeah. Dutch."

"Where'd you pull his name from?" He and Lydia had never met, but I guessed I complained about him a lot more than I realized.

"All the shit you've said about him makes me think that he's the type of person who'd know where to find an after-hours dance place. Narcissistic, abusive…Jesus, even that name. Dutch. It all reeks of entitlement and colonialism. I wouldn't be surprised if his astrological sign was bottle service."

"Fine, I'll call him," I said, "but if he doesn't answer, can we do what we always do on Friday night?"

"What's that?" She pretended to look at her nails.

"Wander the streets and pretend like we're the last two people on earth."

That caught her off guard. She laughed, put her hands around my throat, and pretended to throttle me. "Just call him. Please."

I dialed the number, nervous that I was going to rouse him out of some specific sleep schedule he was on that maximized his earning potential or some other shit like that, put it on speaker, and was shocked when Dutch answered on the first ring.

"Duncan, my man!" He screamed. In the background was a cacophony of sounds that were hard to pull apart. I definitely heard a scream and then the sound of breaking glass. Maybe some laughing. It wasn't clear if he was at a party or a slaughterhouse. "What the fuck is happening, bro?"

Lydia's eyes went wide, and she pressed her hand over her mouth to keep from laughing. "He's on coke!" she mouthed to me once she'd regained control of herself.

"Hope I'm not bothering you, Dutch, but I was just wondering…"

"Bothering me? Bothering me?" Each time he said it, his voice went higher and higher, inflating with incredulity until it sounded about ready to float away. "Hell no, my brother. I'm at a party in

Malibu! You remember that guy from Goldman we did the Mac-Graw deal with, right? I'm at his crib. It's so sick here. He's got a Bugatti in his living room. I'm sitting in the front seat of his Bugatti drinking a beer and looking out over the ocean at…" he paused as he asked someone nearby, "What island is that?" PAUSE. "No, that's an island. Fuck yeah, it's an island. Doesn't matter." He returned to our conversation. "It's an island. Doesn't matter. Could be fucking Fantasy Island for all I fucking care. That's how dope this party is. You know? Entire land masses are, like, irrelevant." Either him or someone sitting next to him snorted what sounded like a yardstick worth of cocaine. "By the way, man, for the record; I don't like cocaine. I just like the way it smells." Loud giggling erupted.

"Oh, yeah. Good one, dude. Totally," I said, shrugging helplessly at Lydia. "That's so…rad. Dutch. Hey, Dutch…"

"You know I'd invite you, right, but it's kind of a small thing. Someone said the guy who owns this place's sister was here, so it might just be family and close friends."

"I totally get it. Actually…"

Lydia was making a churning motion with her hands. She wanted me to hurry up and get to it already, but I knew Dutch and understood that there were certain formalities you had to endure when you needed to ask him for something. Finally, though, she came to the end of her patience and grabbed the phone out of my hand. She clicked it off speaker and held the thing up to her ear.

"Hi, Dutch. This is Lydia, Duncan's girlfriend…Uh huh, he does. Listen, we're really sorry to bother you, but we were wondering if you could maybe…Yeah, I'm real…Oh, he hasn't?" She glanced at me without much expression, turned, and headed down the hall toward the bedroom. A couple of times along the way she'd peek back at me from over her shoulder as though she was confirming something Dutch was saying and then she'd bark out a laugh, each one landing like a vicious blow to my exposed midsection. I followed her at a distance, pretending to straighten a picture of Lydia's father that hung in the hallway, when she slid into the bedroom and closed the door behind her, which proved to be, even more than the laughing, the knockout blow that connected solidly with my glass jaw.

I tried to listen at the door, but all I could hear was the rise and fall of the sound of her voice, peaks and valleys of breathlessness and giggling that had me writhing with jealousy on the smooth wood floor. And then just like clockwork, I felt the Cat nearby, not just stirring, but fully awake and pacing the length of its den; hungry, sure, but also stoked with a bloodlust that had a velocity all its own.

I pressed my ear indelicately against the door and felt a bubble of suction form. If she suddenly opened the door too quickly, I had no doubt that it would suck my eardrum out and whatever that was attached to as well. The brain? The limbic system (whatever that was)? At the very least, it'd leave me deaf and dumb, and when people asked me what had happened, I'd have a stock sign-language answer in my repertoire that would explain to them something along the lines of 'I'm a jealous cunt-snake who got what he deserved,' and then I'd offer to show them the vile tunnel that used to be my ear canal through which they could now look straight through to my brain, consider it for a minute or two (if they could stand the stench), and then rest easy knowing I'd gotten everything I had coming to me. Despite knowing all this, though, I couldn't help myself. I had to know what was being said, even if it meant my complete evisceration. At least there'd be something for the Cat to feast on when he made his terrible appearance, because I couldn't see him sitting still for this, either, and his methods would be profoundly more overt than mine. Lydia laughed, and I pressed the side of my head even harder against the door, willing my molecules to fuse with the atomic structure of the wood. I wouldn't rest until we were one thing, a new kind of portal for pettiness.

"Wait," I heard her say, the tone of her voice bright with amusement, "the drug dealer is named Thor? Thor? I think I'm ruined for life for other drug dealers." And then peals of laughter, a storm of laughter. I'd never heard her laugh so fucking hard in my life.

I pulled my head away from the door and tried to control my breathing, which I could feel backing up in my chest like a clogged smokestack. In retrospect, I was probably having what could generously be called an out-of-body experience but was probably more along the lines of a panic attack. Nothing was getting through to me. No feelings, no sounds, no truth. All I had was the sense that everything inside of me was being sectioned off from every other part so that there was no more "me", per se, only isolated pieces of what used to be me that had nothing in particular to do with one another. I tried pinching the skin on my arm but couldn't feel it at all. I pinched harder and then slapped myself. Nothing. I was numb. I had a new superpower I had to try out immediately, and without really thinking about what I was doing, I reared back and smashed my head against the door.

I hit the floor, lost for a few moments in a calming darkness, and when I finally opened my eyes, the lights in the hallway had shattered and had become a universe of shimmering stars in whose shyster depths I could make out various constellations. In my hazy imagination I picked out a number of dubious astral configurations, each one a bigger sham than the next, tricks of the light like those visions people had of the Virgin Mary or UFOs tumbling through the sky.

I shut my eyes again and shook my head, trying to shake off the visions, and when I opened them, the stars were gone, and this time I was face to face with a different kind of eternity. The Cat was looming over me, his face hovering an inch above mine. His mouth was open wide, and his rank breath rained down upon me. I saw the saliva coating his yellowing teeth and the serpentine blood vessels in his eyes that traced a path to wanting and a hunger that could never be sated. I was frozen, completely at the will of this enormous creature, and I knew full well that the heat from its body alone could snuff me out in a second. The look in its eye was surprisingly calm, though, and I understood this was what it looked like to have no judgment, to hear no voices, no moral commentary except for nature's own yawning need. A line of slobber descended from the Cat's lips, and I looked away as I felt it splat on my head and proceed to trickle down the side of my face. I closed my eyes, touched the wetness and, when I opened them again, the Cat was gone, and my fingers were coated with my own blood from where I'd just collided with the door.

I got up slowly, walked to the kitchen and began to take clean cups out of the cabinet and wash them, one by one, giving my hands something to do that wasn't in the service of self-destruction.

Fifteen minutes after she'd gone in the bedroom, I heard the door finally open and then the soft rainfall of her footsteps as she joined me in the kitchen. I pretended like I didn't see her when she handed me my phone, my hands busily scrubbing a Split Pea Andersen's coffee mug we'd bought on a trip up north to see strawberries or garlic or wine or some other thing that grew from the ground that was supposedly holier than us.

"Doing the dishes?" she asked, holding my phone out to me.

"Oh," I acted surprised, "didn't see you there." I wiped my hands off, and put the phone in my pocket.

"What'd you do to your head, Duncan?"

"Huh?" I asked nonchalantly.

"Your head is bleeding," she said, pointing at the place.

"So how'd it go with Dutch? Did he know of a place?" I tried to smile, but it felt all wrong, my lips were two pieces of barbed wire drawn tight across my face.

"Yup," she said. "You bet. You ready to go?"

We left the house and waited outside in silence for our Uber.

I felt her eyes on me, the slight line of a smile flowing along her otherwise expressionless face, but I pretended to notice none of it. When the car came, we got in, and she immediately turned toward me while I glanced nonchalantly out the window.

"Look," I said, pointing at a coyote whose eyes shined back electric blue at us, just as the car's headlights slid across its worried face. "Ever since the drought started, they've been coming down out of the hills at night to drink out of people's swimming pools. That might have been what happened to your mom...with the..."

She pretended not to hear. "I was trying to make you jealous."

I turned to face her. She had on the pair of dangling green peridot earrings I'd given her for our six-month anniversary, and I felt myself getting hypnotized as they swayed ever so slightly as the car descended deeper and deeper into the depths of downtown, past warehouses and strip bars and the neon desperation of all-night liquor stores.

"Why?"

"Oh, because you haven't told anyone at work about me. And because you didn't want to finish our fight earlier. But most of all, what was the thing I told you never to do when we first got together. Do you remember?"

"No," I murmured softly. Of course I remembered, I just didn't want to say it. Saying it would be worse than smashing my head or being face-to-face with the Cat. Meanwhile, there was a low ringing in my ear which I'm sure was brought on from my earlier outburst, and I opened my mouth as wide as it would go and clicked my jaw back and forth, hoping that would somehow knock it out. It didn't.

"I told you to never need me too much. Don't you remember that? It was during our first night together."

"Oh, yeah," I said, and smiled wanly at her.

"I meant it."

"I know you did. I remember now."

"Are you mad at me?"

"Yes."

"How long will you be mad at me for?"

I glanced at the ETA on the driver's phone. "Eight more minutes."

"Okay," she said, taking my hand and putting it in her lap. She stroked it softly with the back of her fingers, and for eight minutes, I knew only softness. But something nagged at me still, something at the base of my skull that wasn't a concussion or an irrational thought I could explain away as though it were a superstition from the old country. It was this feeling that all was not well, and I can still point to it, as though it were a spot on a map, as the exact moment that it all started to change with us.

Funny that it should also turn out to be our wedding night.

It turned out not to be a nightclub or a bar where the Uber driver let us out, but a medium-sized Craftsman house on a quiet residential street just east of downtown. From the outside, nothing about it indicated nocturnal hijinks other than the presence of an enormous man standing just outside the front door, who, from the looks of him, was born and bred to be a bouncer. He wore a floor-length trench coat, under which his muscles bulged, and when he saw us open the front gate and walk up the pathway to the entrance, he stood up from the stool he'd been sitting on, and for a minute there, it wasn't clear that his lengthening would ever end.

"Jesus," Lydia whispered to me out of the side of her mouth, "would you look at that guy? He's got the physique of a run-on sentence." It was so easy to love her when she said things like that, and I reached down and grabbed her hand.

"Good evening, folks," he said to us as we approached, his deep voice was a geological event. "Password please."

We both froze.

"Did Dutch happen to say anything about a password when you talked to him?" I asked her, keeping a friendly grin on my face.

"No," she said. She sounded worried. "Um, sir, I'm so sorry, but we don't know the password."

"I'm just kidding, guys. There's no password. I just get lonely out here sometimes." His voice gave off vibrations I could feel in my bones. "Go on in and have a good time."

I held the door for Lydia and saw, out of the corner of my eye, a raccoon at the other end of the porch. It was standing on its hind legs with its arms straight up in the air, like it was surrendering to some unseen bandit. At first, I thought it was a child's toy, but when I looked again, I noticed a cut on its leg half-buried under a patch of matted fur. It was real.

"What's with the raccoon?" I asked him, jerking my head at the pitiful animal.

"Oh, that's just Junior," he said, turning to look at the thing. "He got a hold of someone's edibles last week and hasn't moved a muscle since."

"Is he alive?" I asked.

He stopped smiling, thought about it for a moment, and then shrugged. "Are you?"

The rich and earthy smell of pot hit us as soon as we stepped inside, providing an almost instant contact high. The room we walked into was wall-to-wall people all swaying as one, like a field of giant poppies being brushed gently by a benevolent wind, and the music they languished in slow ecstasy to was an old reggae song I'd never heard before but with which I instantly fell in love. It was a hymn of sorts, heavy on the organ and bass, that extolled the virtues of weed and Jah with a sincerity I'd always found lacking in organized religion. The music billowed outward from a pair of tall speakers, above which, at the DJ table, an old Rastafarian was bent over the turntables.

Lydia squealed with excitement and was pulling me on to the dance floor before I had a chance to get a better lay of the land, and then we were dancing. She wound herself around me slowly and it was an agony of want I felt as a bank of different colored lights washed over us every few seconds, providing us with new perspectives on one another as they slid and spun, showing us, in their infinite wisdom, everything a body could be. I put my arms around her waist, and we danced, barely moving, so close together you'd be hard pressed to fit a dime between us. She edged closer, and then there wasn't space for a piece of paper. Closer still and not even the tiniest of particles. It was only us.

"Do me a favor," she said as I passed her a joint that someone had just passed me, "if I die before you, don't let anyone say 'she lived life on her terms', okay?"

"Why?" I whispered back, and it reminded me of the old game, Operator, only in this case there was no chance of fucking up the message because I could feel the words burrowing into me as soon as they left her lips.

"Because," she said, as we slow-danced our way into early graves, "that doesn't sound like much of a compliment to me at all. Does it to you?"

We got higher and higher and, I can't remember if it was me or her, but someone asked the other one to marry them. Assent was given, and we started walking around, tapping people on the shoulder and asking them if they were a minister or rabbi or ship captain who might be so kind as to guide us into safe harbor. There was no question that we wouldn't do it here and now. To wait felt like an atrocity, somehow. Word filtered through the crowd that there was a wedding in the offing, and in a few minutes, a space had been made for us on the dance floor, and we were standing before Trevor, the national monument of a bouncer, who, it turned out, was also a minister.

"You sure you're legal?" Lydia scrutinized him as though she were about to make an ascent and was looking for safe toeholds.

"In every state but Nevada," he said proudly.

"Why not Nevada?" I asked, purely out of morbid curiosity, but he just patted me on the shoulder, smiling, and took a small Bible out of his jacket pocket.

"Now," he said in that low voice of his, "who's ready to see a wedding?"

# CHAPTER 19

Because we didn't get married under the most normal of circumstances, we didn't have any of the regular ephemera most married couples were left with after a wedding. There were no truckloads of kitchen gadgets, no linens, not even an invitation we could frame and hang on the wall.

On a lark one day, we registered at Bed, Bath and Beyond and acted like a couple of gunfighters as we went around zapping everything in sight. Six of these, a dozen of those, we were indiscriminate in our generosity toward ourselves as we took up flanking positions in the bathroom section and anyone who got in our way was going to be the collateral damage of our love. I leveled my price scanning gun at a Sonicare just as a little kid got in the way.

"Blammo!" I shouted at him and he started to cry. I put the barrel of the gun to my lips and blew as his mother came by and saw what was happening. She grabbed his hand and they ran for the register, an area of the store we'd agreed upon as a no-man's-land. I laughed. I was at the peak of some sort of ecstatic revelation, and no little kid was going to get me down. Besides, his mother knew what she was getting into when she brought him to Hollywood in the middle of the day.

My laugh must have given away my location, because in the next second Lydia was right behind me, firing away until there was nothing left to do but grab her and body slam her onto one of the show beds. We tussled for a few minutes and when I started tickling her, she began to shout so loud that several employees, a security guard, and the manager rushed over to see what was happening. The manager was aghast.

She checked our progress on the gift registration front. "What are you going to do with four ice cream makers?" she asked, raising her eyebrow to unbelievably dizzying heights of condescension.

Before I could defend our battle tactics, though, Lydia jumped up on the bed and started bouncing around. "We're bourgeois pigs and waste makes us horny!" She screamed it like it was some sort of old union rallying cry, and I thought I heard one of the stock boys answer back, in a meek voice, "Si se puede!" in solidarity. We were asked to leave — without even a parking validation for our troubles.

There was no piece of wedding cake in the freezer for us to defrost when we hit our first anniversary, no wedding dress preserved in a big box that was pushed to the back of a closet along with ski equipment and camping gear, the building blocks of all future familial disappointment. There weren't even any pictures except for a few hazy cell phone shots; one of me with my arm around Junior, the permanently stoned raccoon, and a great one of Lydia standing on top of the bar where I had vague but persistent memories of her dancing. In the picture, her arms were raised above her head and her hair whipping around in a sensuous blur amidst a fog of lights that weren't any one color, but a riot of all of them, an entire spectrum built just for her. We had the pictures framed, and I wanted to put them up in the living room, give them some place of honor, but Lydia insisted that we put them up in the bathroom. "When I get mad at you," she explained, "that's where I'll go, and if there's a picture of you in there maybe my madness won't last so long."

"That's a different kind of madness," I started to tell her, but it was no use, she was already hammering the first nail into the wall.

"It's a shame we only get to die once," she said, once pictures were both up. She stood back to admire her work, crossing her arms like an old world craftsman.

"Why's that?"

"Wouldn't it be amazing if after a night like that," she nodded at the photos, "we died, like spectacularly, and then, the next morning, we were alive again and we could tell people about what an amazing night it was, and if they doubted it at all, we could say, 'Yeah, but at the end a car hopped the curb and smashed into the bar and it was like a slaughterhouse in there with body parts and Red Bull all over the place and the only thing that still worked was the sound system, and there was like, Reggaeton blasting out everywhere, covering up the screams and stuff, but not totally. You could still hear the screams. Until you died.' Then they couldn't doubt it, could they?"

"Dutch wants to see you," Deedee said to me one morning.

I'd been coming into the office in the mornings lately, skipping my regular visits to see Martha, because I was starting to find them depressing, and because Dutch got the promotion (like everyone thought he would), and I wanted to see how things would shake out before I started ducking out again. I knew spending time with Martha was wrong, but her depression was unrelenting and there was little I felt I could do to alleviate it. I guess my presence was helpful to her, in a way, and I'm sure Mrs. Kim liked having me there so she could work on her lawsuits and prepare the vegetables that she unfailingly turned into the most delicious stews and rice dishes I'd ever eaten. It was just that, with the Cat in perpetual hibernation now, there was little I was getting out of our visits anymore. She was draining me, slowly but surely, and Lydia's old admonition about not wanting me to need her too much had rubbed off, and I was feeling like if I didn't start backing away soon there'd be little left of me for Lydia.

"What did he say exactly?" I sat on the edge of Deedee's desk trying to appear nonchalant, but it was an awkward pose for me. I wasn't a "sit on the corner of someone's desk" kind of guy, and no one knew that better than Deedee.

She laughed. "Why are you so worried, Kitty? Have you done something you shouldn't have? Did you meow when you should have purred?"

Her relentlessly upbeat mood was beginning to be a pain in my ass. It was hard to get a straight answer out of her anymore about anything, buoyed as she was by a new kind of confidence and optimism she didn't used to possess, and that made her sort of invincible against bullshit and innuendo, the carbon and oxygen of corporate America. I wanted to know her secret, but I didn't dare ask.

"I'm not worried. I'm just being..." I thought back to business school for one of those words they taught us that meant nothing but inferred everything, "...tactical."

"Ha!" Her face lit up when she laughed, forcing a blush of color to rise into her pale cheeks, and it was wonderful to watch her body brighten like that, centimeter by centimeter, a crude but accurate measure of joy. "I hope you're not scared of him just because he's your boss now. That's not like you, Duncan. Remember the good old days when you didn't care?"

"Hey," I said, feeling indignant, "I can still not care with the best of them! It's just that new regimes call for new ways of not caring, whole new modalities of apathy."

Her eyes widened in bemusement. She was mocking me, and I deserved it. I wouldn't say I was afraid of Dutch. Not in so many words, anyway. But I also couldn't deny that life had become a different kind of thing in the past couple of months, a slower, more regular rhythm that was as much a comfort as it was a source of anxiety. Lydia and I had gone through the honeymoon phase of our marriage and had settled into a kind of inevitable status quo, and I could feel her restlessness at times, reverberating through the apartment and next to me as we slept, a tinny kind of vibration that resonated with cosmic frequencies I couldn't hope to tap into.

She wasn't materialistic, but she was greedy for the stability of our new life and for the distance it afforded her from Martha and the rest of her past, just as I was greedy for her protection from what I'd been before her (whatever that was — I couldn't even remember it now) and from the Cat that was flesh and bone and need and, worst of all, had the patience of a saint.

Okay, and if I had to be honest, of course I was afraid of Dutch. He had my future in his hands, and he was unpredictable as fuck. Also, his name…it would never stop bothering me. And that hair. No, no, no, he was frightful to the core. Then there was the whole thing he had about obliterating the past and crushing the bones of his enemies and making a kind of soup out of them.

Deedee poked the tip of a pen between her teeth and narrowed her eyes at me.

"Remind me what that was like again," I asked her, rubbing my temples to forestall the migraine I felt building behind my eyes.

"Are you getting a migraine?" she asked, and I forced myself to smile and moved my hands away from my head.

"No. I don't know. Maybe. It's…" I didn't know what to say that wouldn't sound like I was complaining, "…been a tough week."

"Why don't you go lie down." Her face brightened when she was being compassionate. She wore it better than anyone I'd ever known, and it made her beautiful. "I'll get a washcloth real hot and put it on your head. My dad used to do that for my mom whenever she had headaches. I don't know if it really worked or if it just made her happy to have someone doing something nice for her, but we could try it."

"But Dutch…"

"Ach," she pushed back her chair and stood up. Suddenly she was all old country. "He can wait another ten minutes. It's not going to kill him." She started down the hall toward the bathroom. "If you don't tell HR, maybe I'll even try to find that pressure point in your hand people are always talking about. The one that makes frigid housewives instantly orgasm and can cure gout."

"You'd do that for me?" I feigned a debutante's gratitude.

"Yup," she yelled back down the hall, "everything but the orgasm. You're on your own there."

The muffled sounds of ringing phones and frantic conversations chased me as I slipped into my office, but I slammed the door on them and quickly dialed up some music on the cloud to keep them at bay. My office was simmering with light, so I angrily closed the shades, kicked off my shoes and threw myself onto the couch. Deedee came in a few minutes later, and when she opened the door, those sounds tried to rush by her to get at me again.

"Close the door! Hurry!" I had to raise my voice so she could hear me above the keening jazz I'd chosen, something old and blurry but with an undercurrent of a tempo that put me in the mood to sit on the toilet with a cigarette and the Sunday New York Times until my ass got sore and it became dark outside, the way my Uncle Bill had done to get away from his wife and five kids on the weekends, whole Sundays spent in the basement john, with only that dark puddle of moody music and all the bad news that was fit to print to keep him company.

"Oh, calm down, would you?" she shot back, having none of it, but was all kindness when she laid the cloth on my face and took my hand in hers and started gently pressing it, probing it for knots and ribbons of tension. The cloud gave a little thunderous growl of appreciation, and everything felt right for a moment, until the door opened again and Les walked in.

"Close it!" Deedee and I both shouted at once and then started laughing.

"Sor-ry," Les muttered back, not sure of what transgression he'd committed but getting the impression it was probably up there in the faux pas hall-of-fame.

"It's all right," I said, sitting up. Deedee was still holding my hand but she was looking up at Les with fawning eyes and he looked back at her with the same. They exchanged cultish smiles with one another, the kind usually reserved for members of the same pyramid scheme who were still at that stage when they thought they were on to something great and not ignorant hayseeds who were being taken for the ride of their lives. Something was definitely up with these two, but I didn't have the energy to start any heavy-duty probing. Besides, I still had to go see Dutch.

"This isn't what you think, by the way," I said, taking my hand back from Deedee's. "We're just friends."

Les forced a honking laugh but didn't seem to care one way or the other. "Deedee, I was wondering if I could have a moment alone with Duncan." He stood with his hands clasped together at his waist, and I had the strangest idea he was about to ask me for her hand in marriage.

When Deedee was gone, I sat up and patted the seat on the sofa next to me. "Better make this quick. Dutch wants to see me. How're you feeling about all this?"

"About what?"

"Him getting the promotion. He's going to be after you, you know?"

He laughed a little and scratched the back of his head. "You know what, I honestly haven't thought about it at all."

I relaxed into the couch and looked at him carefully, not knowing exactly what I was looking for, but sure that it was there somewhere, some crack or dent in his façade that might not mean so much now but could be the sign of bigger problems to come.

Les looked back at me with a goofy smile dangling haphazardly off his face. His tie was loose, and he smelled like women's deodorant, flowers and clean laundry, the scent of soft nights and long days sprawled out under the shade of a leafy tree. He hadn't woken up at home this morning. I didn't know if what he was telling me about not worrying about Dutch was the truth or not, but it was the truth as he saw it, that much was clear.

The room was still dark from my session with Deedee, but when I went to open the shades, he stopped me.

"Wait," he said, "leave it dark for a minute. I want to play you something." He pointed up at the cloud. "Can we hook my phone up to that thing?"

"What is it?"

"When Tina and I were first dating, we were long distance for the first year, and we used to send each other these tapes all the time, romantic stuff, sometimes sex talk. It kept us going during that time, and there was one tape in particular…" he stopped himself as he looked down at his phone, "that I could never bring myself to erase. Can I play it for you?"

I sat back down. "You sure?"

But he was already connecting to my speaker, and without even answering, he hit play.

It started without fanfare, just the old familiar hiss of a cassette recording that took me instantly back to high school, to mixtapes and bad radio reception, the worse the quality of the music, the more undying the love it expressed. And then, slowly, other sounds started to manifest, simple truths that patiently explained that she was at a park, and it was a beautiful day. Not too far from where she was sitting could be heard the solemn work of kids laughing and playing, their happiness a palpable thing, as solid as any element on the periodic table. And beneath that, like a geological relic, was a Greek chorus of small birds, shamelessly gossiping the day away, and the distant warbling music of an ice cream truck whose slightly out-of-tune song never failed to charm my sweet tooth. Most audible, though, were the sounds that weren't there but that I heard all the same, louder almost than the ones spilling out of the speaker. The tintinnabulation of sunshine splashing against the scalding metal of a children's playground and, up above, a cloudless sky, a blue that if you peered into it too long, you'd see wasn't so much a color as it was infinity trying to explain itself. I knew that sky well, and I knew the heat of the slide and of the swing-set. I knew it all as well as I knew the Cat was nearby, suddenly, just behind my shoulder, sitting as patiently as a pet, waiting for the story to begin. Out of the speaker came the sound of an airplane roaring overhead, and then she started to speak.

"Leslie," said the voice in a whisper, as though she was afraid someone might hear her, exposing her as some weak little girl and drag her into the sandbox for a game of tag, "I miss you." She cleared her throat. "And I love you." And then her voice became a little bit louder, the preamble out of the way. "I'm on my lunch break," she went on, "and I'm sitting in the park by the office, and I have my little brown lunch bag open next to me. There's a tuna sandwich and a bag of chips…yes, they're boring old Lays, the yellow ones. I know you think it's funny that those are my favorite, but maybe I'm just a plain girl, did you ever think of that? Maybe you should be grateful that I am." All the while, the cloud was doing its flashing color thing, tipping drunkenly into blue, then purple, red, and then back again, its low dense thundering making it seem like it was chuckling along with her corny joke.

I stole a look at his eyes as they danced in place beneath the changing colors, and I wondered where he'd gone and how I might follow him.

"Anyway, I'm going to send this tape out to you today, so you should get it by Friday. Isn't that weird? It's Tuesday now. What if I don't feel the same way now as I do when you're listening to this? To you, it'll seem like I'm telling you all this in real time, but in reality, it's how I felt three days ago. A lot can happen in three days, Les. More than in an entire lifetime, when you think about it."

Suddenly, she started laughing and the cloud picked up its pace, churning happy sparks of lightning out from somewhere deep within its digital guts. "But of course I'm going to feel the same way in three days as I feel now. That's the beauty of what we have. That it doesn't change. That whatever I say today I could say in a week, or a month, or a year. And the funny thing is," she popped a chip in her mouth and crunched lightly, "it's been that way since the beginning. I know I've told you the story a million times, about the first time I saw you, but I want to tell it to you again, because love at first sight stories are not that common. People think they are," she said, her voice ascending into a knowing stratosphere, "but they're not. Not like ours."

I snuck another look at Les who was now leaning back on the couch. He had his hands folded on his stomach and he was staring up at the cloud. A huge grin warped his face and I wondered what he was thinking. Was this painful for him? Was it a happy memory? Or was he simply trying to prove to me that at one time, not that long ago in the analog age, he'd been loved unconditionally by a pretty woman who sat on a park bench pining for him, making love tapes that told their story again and again like a piece of wartime propaganda that became truer every time you said it.

"We were at that party," she said with a twinkle to her voice, wind chimes rustling in the breeze of recollection, "Remember? Neither of us knew whose house it was or how we wound up there, but there was this massive lawn out back and what felt like a hundred people all laughing at once. That's such a great sound, isn't it? I miss that…" She paused, and I imagined her looking at a group of kids at that long-ago park as they chased one another around in tight looping circles that had no end, the promise of forever always just an arm's length away. "Anyway, there was a big pool, and I was sitting in the shallow end with my legs hanging down into the water. I had lost my friends, and I was wondering how I was going to get home, whether I should start walking or call a cab. I was gnawing on the lip of one of those red plastic keg cups, trying to decide which would be worse; spending money I didn't have on a taxi or risking getting attacked walking home by myself, when suddenly, I felt the cup crack and the edge of it slice right into my bottom lip. At first, I tried to catch the blood by cupping my hand underneath my chin, because that's what you do, right? Try to hold on to the parts of you that are slipping away? But then I just let it start pouring out onto the side of the pool and no matter which way I turned my head I was getting everything all bloody. The grass, the pool, my arms and legs. It looked like a mass murder. That's what you said later. Remember? 'Who got killed?'"

She laughed at the private joke, and out of the corner of my eye, I saw that Les was still smiling. Whatever the memory meant to him, he seemed to be at peace with it now, those rivers of blood a part of some distant past, a metaphor for something that had once meant everything to him but that he could now barely even recall.

The Cat's curiosity, though, was piqued. All this talk of blood and murder had moved it to slowly stand and stretch with its giant paws straight out in front of it. Still in that downward position, it opened its enormous mouth and yawned, teeth and tongue out there for the world to see; only the world wasn't looking, it was just me. It was a series of movements meant to look casual, like it wasn't really paying any attention, but I knew that wasn't the case. It sensed something weak and vulnerable, and it was laying a trap.

"I was just sitting there," she went on, "I didn't know what to do. I didn't know if I should go into the house and use the bathroom or just…I don't know…bleed out? Is that a thing? I think it is." More laughter. "Anyway, I was staring into the pool, mesmerized a little, I guess, how people get sometimes when they're looking at water move and try to follow it with their eyes. You get dizzy, but it's a good kind of dizzy, like you're being hypnotized or falling asleep in the middle of the day. I didn't realize anyone was swimming, when all of a sudden I see this person moving toward me, quickly, but also like he was hardly moving at all. It was like you were frozen in ice or something, and the ice was moving, not you. I remembered being totally transfixed. It was the most beautiful thing I'd ever seen in my life, and I couldn't take my eyes off of you. You were swimming the whole way across the pool underwater, just this green and white streak, and I had this moment of panic that when you broke the surface you'd pop, like a bubble, and be gone, and I'd never get to see what had been underneath. How sad that would be, I remembered thinking, you gone, or maybe it'd be me that would die before you got to the end, and how romantic it all seemed, how doomed. You got closer and closer, you were headed right toward me, and I told myself that when you finally came up, I'd be in love. Sometimes you say things like that to yourself because you want them to be true, but in this case, it was more than a wish, you know," I wanted to answer her, to scream out "yes", but then I remembered that she wasn't asking me. "It was an answer. Or maybe a truth. Are they the same thing? In any case, you finally got to me, and I sucked my breath in, as much as I could swallow, and maybe it was all the blood I'd lost, or maybe it was the beer, but whatever it was…" Her voice cracked and trailed off, like she was just as dazed as she'd been on that day, "Then you were breaking the surface of the water, and it was like you being born. It seemed like it took forever, and you were in this, like, sleeve of water, and all your features were carved in crystal, and I wanted you to stay like that forever, because you were perfect. It was perfect…"

The room was plunged into silence as Les suddenly hit 'stop' on the recording. The Cat growled, and I sat up quickly, needing to hear the end of the story but also knowing that what he'd already played for me was more than I'd deserved to hear. The cloud, too, was silent. Not a color. Not a spark. I looked over at Les, and he was looking down at the phone, a smile still stretched across his face despite it all.

"What now?" I asked him, wondering for my sake just as much as his.

"This," he said, and without thinking twice about it, he slid his finger across the recording and clicked the 'delete' button. Gone forever.

"Is that it? You don't have that recorded anywhere else?"

"Nope."

"And you wanted me to…what? Watch?"

"It sounds so perverted when you say it like that," he laughed, "but yeah. I knew you'd understand, because of..." he waved vaguely at me from head to toe, "...everything you've been going through."

Subconsciously, I put a hand on my chest and started to move it around. I didn't know if I was searching for a heartbeat, some trace of the Cat, or what, but whatever it was, I wasn't finding it. They were both in there, of course, both things carrying out functions that were integral to my staying alive, but no matter where I moved my hand, I felt nothing.

Les laughed and rubbed his face in his hands. His hair was standing up like he'd just stuck his finger in a light socket, but when he lowered his hands his face was serene.

"Is there something you'd like me to listen to?"

"Huh?" I heard him, but wasn't processing the words.

"Your chest," he nodded at me, "it looked like you were searching for something. Is there something you want me to listen to?"

"I'm not going to spy on Les for you."

Dutch was already in his new office, a corner affair with slightly more square footage and a better view than his old one, a window that looked out onto the courtyard where fall was breathing a heavy sigh of gold and orange across the tops of trees, a nod at serenity to which you were reminded on an almost daily basis that you were in no way entitled to enjoy.

"Why not?" he asked, genuinely confused.

"Because," I started to explain, and I could already feel myself getting frustrated because he was never going to understand, "it

195

has nothing to do with work. It's just vindictive and mean. Why can't you just leave him alone?"

Slowly, Dutch leaned back in his chair and tented his palms together in front of his face. He was already adopting the body language of upper management, a patronizing posture that suggested patience had its limits, and he was nearing his.

"How are you feeling, Duncan?"

"Huh?" I sat back down in the chair not even realizing that I'd stood up. "What do you…"

"Your head and your leg," he moved his finger around the back of his head and then his leg, identifying on his own body where my injuries were, "the mountain lion attack. You've been doing physical therapy for a long time now, missing a lot of work, and I'm just wondering," he joined his hands together in front of his face once more, palm-to-palm, as though he was holding a prayer vigil for my well-being, "if you're better."

I sat back in the chair, and without any other existential warnings, felt my stomach drop through the bottom of my pelvis, down my legs and into my feet, and, in the empty hole that was left, the Cat once again appeared. It walked forward slowly, sleekly, pacing itself and its hunger for what I suspected it saw as easy meat.

Luckily, Dutch wasn't really looking for me to answer, because he was at that stage in his power trip where he was more than happy to answer his own questions.

"Because," he went on, tapping the spacebar on his computer and glancing casually at the refreshed screen, "we want to keep you, Duncan. We really do. We like you. We know you bring a lot to the company. It'd be a shame…know what I mean? Can you help me? Can you help me help you, Duncan?"

I eked out the slightest of nods.

"Great!" Dutch slapped his desk with the palms of his hands suddenly, which evidently was what was needed to thaw me out, because I jumped. "I knew this was going to be great. I knew we'd do some good work here today, pivoting and whatnot." He stood and I took it as my cue to leave.

Before I left, I considered for a moment telling him about what had just happened in my office, how Les' happiness didn't seem to have anything to do to him, that it wasn't a power play or part of some Machiavellian ploy to unseat him and, if anything, Dutch should be happy that Les seemed content. It was one less person he had to worry about now. One less obstacle to clear out of the way. But I knew that would never be the case. With or without my help, Dutch was going to finish him, and if I didn't get him some kind of death blow, I'd be as good as dead, like Les.

"I'll think about it," I murmured.

"What's that?" he asked, pretending he hadn't heard, as he showed me the door.

Walking back to my office, I already knew I was going to have to do what Dutch asked me. He'd made it seem like I had a choice, a gracious gesture on his part, but it wasn't real. Nothing about my life was the same as it had been just six months ago. There was Lydia now to provide for, and in recent months I had felt her interest starting to wane, not in me exactly, but certainly in our marriage. The little drinks she used to have waiting for me when I got home, the ones with cute names like Tight Squeeze or Spooning, had started taking on a more cynical tone, and in recent weeks I pretended to enjoy the Pre-nup and the Stockades, vile potions laced with unspeakable liqueurs I imagined she had to go deep into the most ethnic of neighborhoods to procure. Maybe that's what she did with her days. I was curious about what she did all day, but I never asked her, afraid she'd misconstrue my curiosity for jealousy or mistrust, in short needing her too much, the only caveat she'd ever place on our relationship. I knew that with these little warning shots, she was testing the waters, baiting me into retaliating so she could fly off the handle again like she did the night we got married, a reason to doubt the happiness she never felt she was entitled to, I guessed, but I choked it all down with a smile, refusing to give her an excuse.

I chalked her passive aggressiveness up to boredom and suggested she take up a hobby or enroll in classes. "Like what?" she asked me one particularly tense evening.

"Maybe jewelry making?" I shrugged as I said it, knowing how stupid it sounded as soon as the words left my lips. She'd been working on a hangnail with her teeth when the words came out, and she stopped suddenly and glared at me. "Go fuck yourself, Duncan." A few minutes later I heard the front door slam.

I waited up for her in bed, and when she finally came home, I pretended to be asleep as she slid in under the covers next to me, reeking of booze and cigarettes. She cuddled up to my back, for the heat, I supposed, and soon I felt hot tears blotting my bare skin. I turned over and gathered her into my arms, and that's when she really started to cry. "I thought…[sniffle]…you were…[sob]… sleeping, you liar."

"Shh," I tried to console her, but she only cried louder and harder. "Where were you? You smell like a Freemason."

She laughed and sniffled at the same time. The sound, like a vacuum being plunged underwater, made us both giggle.

"I went to the Tennis Club. That old bitch who told me I wasn't a serious girl was there and she kept mad-dogging me."

"Don't mistake antagonism for dementia," I said. "She probably thought you were Eleanor Roosevelt."

Lydia started laughing again, and it made me feel like I'd won something or that I'd overcome some terrible bureaucratic hurdle. We kissed some more, and I felt myself dissolve on her lips, not completely, but to the point where all that was left of me was vapor, stippled dots of condensation that swirled languidly as our tongues worked against one another and coalesced around her mouth. I could get used to this state of matter, this in-between thing that was neither liquid nor solid, but the waiting as one became the other.

"Your kisses…" she pulled away, and I could feel her eyes on me, trying to see past the dark, into the mist I was slowly becoming.

"What about them?"

"Sorry if this isn't nice, but they're very anxious."

I stroked her hair, then gathered a handful of it and tugged lightly, playfully, but enough so that I heard her draw in a quick breath, like what came next might hurt, but in a good way. "In the old days, the Romantics would have called that sorrow. Try thinking of it that way."

"Oh, brother!" she cackled, eviscerating the moment. "Pity? Is that what you're after?"

"No," I said, wanting to get back to what we were just a few seconds ago, back when I was just a puff of air she might inhale, the last gasp of almost knowing. Pity would have been nice, but I knew better than to start down that road with her. She'd warned me where it led, and I had no interest in testing her resolve, because I knew that it was strong, that in the face of it I would be reduced to a tragic pile of rubble.

Her smile disappeared as suddenly as it had arrived, and she started crying again, a thin, drunken mewling that pulled a tight band of worry across my chest.

"What is it?" I asked her.

"I…I…" she started to stutter, and for a brief moment I thought she was going to say, "I miss my mother" and it would have scared me more than anything else she could have said. Deep down, I knew that it was always going to be one or the other of us, me or Martha, and that the Cat might step out of nowhere to remind me how close I was to disappearing inside myself and that Lydia was the only thing standing in its way. I also knew I was going to have to tell Dutch something about Les, some morsel he could make a meal of, because the job was all part of it, part of keeping Lydia happy and giving her a reason to stay. Each of these little dangling ends were part of a tapestry that, if you just stepped back from it now and again, looked a lot like life.

I kissed Lydia's shoulder, swept the hair back from her face, took her tiny hand in my sweaty palm. "You what?" I asked, holding my breath for whatever came next.

"I lied to you about being married before. I just didn't want those old ladies to think they knew me." She let go of my hand and turned on her side so that we were facing each other. "They don't. No matter what they say, they have no idea. You understand that don't you, Duncan? That people think they know but no one really does? Not really."

Some questions were like shrapnel, I thought, and all bodies are bombs.

# CHAPTER 20

Except for the light spreading out from under the bathroom door, the apartment was in almost total darkness as I waited for Lydia so we could leave for Dutch's promotion celebration, which some of the other VP's had planned for him at the office. I'd chipped in my hundred bucks but had no part in the planning of it, feigning a hectic time with the closing on a deal I'd actually already closed a week earlier. It was supposed to be just a small affair, something from the guys for Dutch, who until only recently had been one of us. But I feared it was going to turn into a gross spectacle, not only an excuse to get drunk in the office, but a master class in one-upmanship as they tried to subtly outdo one another in kissing Dutch's ass now that he was our better.

I warned Lydia that she probably didn't want to come, that it was going to be repulsive and sad, but that only piqued her interest.

"That sounds like something I've got to see," she said.

"Yeah, I know it sounds funny, but in reality…uh…it's not. It's one of those things that's actually worse in person that it is on paper. You'll hate them. Trust me. Dutch has flaming red hair and all these freckles…" I pointed furiously every which way, "A lot of people get nauseous the first time they see him because they don't know where to look first, and their eyes start going all over the place, and pretty soon, it's like you're in a jet fighter pulling five G's. I've seen people puke their guts out just for laying eyes on him."

We had the conversation on a Sunday, as she was hiding behind the Arts section of the New York Times, reading an article about art forgeries. "Fine. Whatever," she said, not putting it down, "It sounds to me like you just don't want me to be there, if I have to be honest."

*No*, I thought to myself, *you don't have to be honest. That's the beauty of being married. Little deceits don't break the bank anymore. It takes a whopper to kill the vibe.*

"Not at all," I said way too emphatically. "I actually really do want you there. I just don't know if this is the right time. There's this other guy who's going to be there. Bradley Tupor. He's an analyst. One of these number cruncher types who never leaves his desk. Total sociopath. Really. I don't want to subject you to it. If an FBI profiler could see the way this guy eats pigs in a blanket…"

"Forget it!" she said, folding the paper and slamming it down on the couch next to her.

She stormed off into the bathroom and turned the sink on full blast for the next three hours, a solid stream of white noise that was meant to drive me crazy wondering what she was doing in there. We'd been arguing like that for weeks now, passive aggressively chipping away at one another's façades, doing surface damage, which, over time, would eventually spell the end of one or the other of us. And if we timed it right, it would be both of us at the same time, two crumbling mounds of dirt and dust where a family unit once stood. When she finally came out, I did the only thing I knew how to do, which was to apologize and beg her to come.

The night had finally come, and we were running late. I fidgeted in my pale gray suit, lifted myself off the couch and pulled the ends of my coat out from under my ass. It helped a little, but there was nothing I was going to be able to do that would make me feel good about this evening.

"You almost ready?" I shouted into the void, trying not to sound as impatient as I felt. We were finally wrapping up the fight about whether or not she should come with me, and I knew the slightest edge to my tone would be misconstrued as sonic warfare and we'd be right back where we started.

I checked my watch. We were already ten minutes late. In the morning it took around 20 minutes to get to the office, but how long it would take at 7:30 p.m. was anybody's guess. Streets in Los Angeles had a way of lengthening and shifting depending on the time of day, and a drive that took 20 minutes in the morning might take five minutes or two hours at 7:00 at night.

"Lydia..." Just as I said her name, I heard the hairdryer come on, and sighed. It was hard to know at what stage of getting ready the hairdryer was brought to bear, but it didn't bode well. I took out my phone and thought about watching a YouTube video by a poster who called himself Mr. Video, a middle-aged black guy from Dayton who filmed himself listening to classic rock songs for the first time. Zeppelin, Floyd, the Beatles...he'd heard none of it growing up, and it brought me no end of pleasure watching his eyes light up as he listened to 'Dazed and Confused' or 'Comfortably Numb' for the first time. I doubted it at first, I just couldn't believe someone could go through 40 some-odd years of living in America without ever hearing 'Here Comes the Sun,' but the look on his face when George started in with that perfect riff, and then John and Paul came in with the harmonies, that wasn't something you could fake. No one could fake melting away like that. I was about to fire up 'Ironman', because I knew it was going to blow his mind, when she suddenly switched off the hair dryer, shut out the bathroom light, and opened the door.

"Are you ready?" The apartment was almost completely dark, but I could hear the clackety-clack of high heels. "Why are you sitting in the dark?" She flipped the light switch on and the room was suddenly awash in a white bloom of fluorescent light, and she was standing there with her hands on her sides like she was the one who'd been waiting for me the whole time, and she was stunning. Her hair was up in a bun, with just a few stray pieces sticking out, and she'd put on a ring of bright red lipstick that instantly turned the night into an evening. She had on a short black cocktail dress and high heels that cinched at the ankle with pieces of black ribbon, and altogether she looked like a flapper orphan who had just come into a vast inheritance of immorality. Even the Cat was purring.

"Wo-o-ow," I muttered, stretching the word out into a tawdry act of submission.

Driving over, I could barely keep my eyes on the road. I kept stealing glances at her out of the corner of my eye, hardly able to believe my luck. We stopped at the corner of Sunset and Vine and the neon lights from the lobby of the CNN building fell into our car, drawing inkblots on her pale thighs and kissing the soft curve of her neck. I didn't even have time to worry about being late because I was too busy trying to sneak a glance up her skirt.

She fixed her lipstick in the mirror and cracked a grin. "Are you trying to look up my dress. We're married, Duncan, in case you didn't remember," she pursed her lips, checking to see that she was all even. "That makes it somehow more perverted."

We made it to the office in under 15 minutes, and as we were waiting for the elevator in the parking garage, she nodded at the defibrillator hanging on the wall. "What's up with that?"

I dug my hands into my pockets, too scared somehow to put my arm around her waist which is where I really wanted it to be. "I don't know. I think it's to make us all feel okay about not knowing CPR. Kind of a general amnesty from any kind of thoughtful responsibility."

"Huh," she said. "Like Never Never Land."

It was unclear if she meant it as a compliment or not.

We found the party in full swing in the larger of the two conference rooms on the ninth floor, Dutch's new fiefdom. And there he was, big, strong Dutch, standing at one corner of the room, a glass of champagne held high, all eyes turned adoringly up at him. He was dressed simply, but elegantly, crisp white dress shirt tucked into a pair of slim black pants, and whatever he was in the middle of toasting, he stopped when he saw us walk in, and I could tell that he was staring at Lydia, as dazzled by her as I had been just a little while before. Everyone else in the room, 20 or so of my colleagues and their spouses and dates, turned to face us, adding to the collective awkwardness of arriving late.

But Lydia wasn't having it. She looked too good for a mere faux pas to spoil her night. "Hello," she said loudly and clearly to the room. "Sorry we're late. Duncan's such a diva, though. I practically had to burn the place down to get him out of the bathroom."

Laughter all around and Dutch's loudest of all, booming up and out of him like a geyser of black gold.

"Duncan, you missed my toast. How could you? Should I do it again?" He looked around the crowd. "Maybe I should do it again, huh? What does everyone think?"

A loud cheer went up and Dutch once again hoisted his glass, repositioned a beatific expression on his face as though it were something he'd just set aside, and cleared his throat.

The speech he went on to give was more of a rant, really, than a toast, a long-winded O. Henry-type story in which he painted himself as the perpetual underdog. If he was suffering from delusions of grandeur, they were at least well thought out, because his little words of wisdom had it all, including no less than 11 sports analogies, three vague allusions to fascism and a quote he attributed to Darwin but that I knew damn well was the lyric to a Rush song. At one point, I leaned over to whisper to Lydia what a crock of shit the whole thing was, but she "shushed" me before I could even get started. I supposed that if you weren't used to it, there was bound to be a certain natural attraction to that type of grandstanding, a fugue state of empathy that was unlike the bottomless pity her mother demanded of her. This was the spectator-sport version, and her seats were the best in the house.

I didn't see Les, but hoped that he wasn't taking it as seriously as I was and that he had the good sense to stop off at Sparkles for a lap dance and four or five tall whiskeys. I prayed that was the case, because Dutch kept making a point of saying his son's name, Coleman, over and over again, in what I knew was a dig at Les' suicide attempt and not actually a nod to the blessings of family, because, why bother?

As discreetly as possible, I bent down and looked under the table, half expecting Les to be down there, shit-housed, petting the carpet and whispering to it that it was the best dog a boy could ever hope for. It was either that, or he was in the back somewhere trying to force himself into a paper shredder dick first. He was nowhere to be seen, though, and I wondered what the long play here was, if his not showing up was some sort of delicious ploy or if he'd simply gotten lost in the golf game on his phone he loved to play so much.

"What are you doing?" Lydia mouthed at me when she saw me looking around, but I just smiled back at her and nodded as if this was the way we did things in corporate America. She snarled and put her eyes back on Dutch.

When the speech was over, there was a panic of applause.

"Wow," he said, awkwardly attempting modesty, "went over even better the second time."

After a round of back slaps and a bindle or two of cocaine being pressed into his palm by some of his admiring sycophants, he made a beeline directly for me and Lydia, just as I knew he would.

"Well, well, well," he said, taking a mighty sip of what I guessed was straight vodka, "let me guess. Is this Mrs. Beldon? In the flesh?"

When he said the word "flesh" I felt my stomach turn, but Lydia clearly wasn't as jaded as I was. She took the bait and smiled. "And I don't have to ask who you are. I know a Dutch when I see one."

He laughed too hard and too long, and we were hit by a wall of nicotine breath and the mints he'd chewed trying to cover up the smell.

"So," Lydia said, taking a swig of a drink that someone put into our hands without asking what it was first, "I've got a question I've been wanting to ask you."

The endless possibilities of what she might say next made me physically sick, and I could sense the Cat wasn't happy about it either. I felt it roar a frustrated complaint and start walking around in worrying little circles, pawing the ground as it decided whether to pounce or to start eating its young.

"Duncan tells me that you, and by you, I don't mean just you, I mean all of you," she waved her hands around like she was blessing everyone in the room, a not-so-subtle benediction that drew many pairs of eyes, "don't like to talk about your pasts all that much. He says it's a very live-in-the-moment kind of place. So tell me," she paused to take a careful sip of her drink, "is it true that you don't like to share? Or is he exaggerating? He does that sometimes. We all do, of course, but he's got a special," she paused, as if she didn't already have the word teed up and ready to go, "flair for it."

The room swam around me as I felt my stomach dodge to the left and then to the right. Dutch didn't say anything; he just kind of grinned at her and then at me, back and forth like that, and I knew he was trying to work out whether he was being flirted with or mocked (and what a fine line it was for a bastard like him), and, in the vacuum of conversation her little comment had created, a few more strays wandered over to our group, colleagues and their wives who responded to awkward silences the way normal people ran to the sound of a car crash.

I wasn't sure what game she was playing with me — if she was interested in humiliating me for not asking her to come to the party right away or if she was simply creating an awkward moment for the theater of it. Whatever the case, once I got my legs back under me, I decided to play it cool.

"I don't think I ever used the word 'share'. That doesn't really sound like me does it, Dutch?"

Dutch looked from one of us to the other and back again. "You guys are...funny. Is this your schtick? Bad cop, dumb cop?"

Lydia walked over to the large picture window that looked out over the city. Dutch joined her on one side while I took up position on the other. I wasn't too keen on the two of them spending any more unsupervised quality time together than was necessary, so the three of us looked out without speaking as below us on the streets, the late shift of commuters were having it out with one another in tense vehicular dogfights, and beyond that, at the bleeding edge of the horizon, the faint cursive ridgeline of the Santa Monica Mountains writing its closing dedication to the day against the blank page of the sky that hadn't yet started filling up with stars and moon. Lydia pointed at a lake of darkness in the middle of all that light and traffic. "What is that?"

"That?" Dutch asked, following the slender line of her finger, "That's the Brentwood Country Club. I'm a member."

"Fancy," she said, not bothering to look at him.

Unbidden, he started pointing out other worthless landmarks to her as if she were new to town and hadn't lived here her whole life. He showed her the Century City Mall and the Mormon Temple, and she just let him, nodding along like it was all so wonderful, all so new, a smile like a spark fixed on her lips, as if they were two sticks being rubbed together.

Just then, Ben Dantle, another VP in the group who I had very little to do with on the grounds that he ate with his mouth open and once told me he'd throw it all away for a night with Lady Gaga, tapped me on the shoulder and whispered, "Where's the card?"

"Huh?" I angled my body to block him out. I was trying to stay in the conversation, but Ben was insistent.

"Hey," he tapped me on the shoulder. "The card for Dutch. I left it on your desk. Didn't Deedee give it to you to sign?"

"Ben," I said, moving over again, "I'm kind of in the middle of something here. Important conversation."

"You need to get the card," he went on undeterred, his inner bureaucrat raging. "It must still be on Deedee's desk."

"I don't really think…" I made my eyes go wide and nodded at Dutch and Lydia, hoping he'd get the point that there was no way in hell I was going to leave my wife, who looked like the lead character in a movie about a young woman coming into her sexuality, but he kept prodding and nudging until I finally exploded.

"Fine! Fuck!"

Dutch and Lydia stopped talking, and they both looked at me with identical questioning glances.

"It's fine, Duncan," she said with a certain coolness I wasn't expecting, "do what you have to do."

I never realized how much I hated that sentence until she said it.

I handed her my drink to hold, so she wouldn't have a free hand to burn and hurried out of the room, skipping the elevator in favor of the stairs, which I took two at a time.

Deedee's desk was a cluttered mess. I started going through her things, coming across a treasure trove of Amazon return labels; there was one for some makeup, another for some lingerie and yet another for personal lubricant. I pawed through the papers, faster and faster, every second that went by, I imagined Dutch inching ever closer to Lydia, his fiery redness descending upon her like a meteor, until he finally ran out of municipal landmarks to show her and started pointing out my shortcomings, instead. I never should have left them alone together. I should have told Ben to go fuck himself, that Dutch didn't care about our cards and our well wishes, that what he wanted was our fealty. It was going to be total submission or bust. Our performance reviews were going to start resembling high-end S&M sessions. 'Mark my words,' I should have told him.

My phone started buzzing, and I swatted at my pocket like it was full of angry insects. I didn't even need to look to know that it was Martha again. She'd been calling and texting me non-stop for the last week or so, asking why I wasn't coming over anymore, sending little animated GIFs of mountain lions, begging me to give her more. The problem was, I didn't have any more bits of Lydia to give her. She'd used them all up. Devoured each and every one then licked the bones clean. All that was left were the things I didn't want to share, the small parts of her I liked to count in the dark and the ones that were bigger than the light of day. All the things that kept the Cat at bay.

I finally found the card. It had a drawing of an owl with spectacles on the front, and inside was the epigraph *Congratulations to a wise man.* I hastily added my sloppy signature, stuck the card in the envelope, licked and sealed it, and was about to sprint back upstairs when I noticed a faint blue light seeping out from under the door to my office. I looked around. None of the other offices had lights on in them, and although I was in a hurry to get back to Lydia, my curiosity got the better of me. It's possible I could have left the cloud on or maybe my computer monitor was still up. I was about to go in when I heard the traces of music slipping out from beneath the door. I turned the doorknob slowly, thinking that maybe one of the janitors had figured out what the cloud was for and was conducting a seance or jacking off or doing whatever people who worked the night shift did after hours, and peered in. On the couch were two fully nude bodies I quickly recognized as Deedee and Les. Les was on top of her, fucking her slowly, Deedee's pale legs were wrapped high up on his back, and I could just hear her little moans of pleasure bubble up over the sounds of Spandau Ballet's *True.*

I quickly and quietly shut the door. They hadn't seen me, thank God, and I knew I shouldn't have been surprised, but they were such an unlikely pair.

I took the elevator back up to nine, still pondering what I'd just seen and then laughing to myself about what Dutch would say if he knew why Les was missing his party. The doors opened and I hurried over to Ben and slapped the card in his hands. He was in the middle of saying "thanks," when I rushed over to the window where Dutch and Lydia were still standing together, fresh drinks decorating their hands like costume jewelry.

"I'm back," I announced, grabbing a glass of champagne from a passing waiter. "What'd I miss?"

But they didn't laugh. Actually, neither of them said a word. They just turned to face me, the same angry look on both their faces, a look that told me nothing was ever going to be the same again.

# CHAPTER 21

She didn't say a word to me for the rest of the party, and the dirty looks got dirtier and dirtier as the night wore on, until, by the time we left, I felt like she had worn a hundred holes through me. I asked her a million times what had happened. I wanted to know if it was something I'd done or if Dutch had said something untoward. Revenge fantasies began to pour through my head as I thought of the Cat cornering him in the parking garage, and then, with one small flick of its tennis racket-sized paw, eviscerating him, opening him like he was a sack of gummy bears, spraying blood and guts across his new Tesla.

But I knew from the way she snarled when I asked her if it was something Dutch had done that it wasn't. I knew intuitively that whatever had set her off was my doing. I could feel it the way you'd feel any dread, a fist in the gut clenching and unclenching, clenching and unclenching, over and over like that until it was the only heartbeat to be found.

Instead of driving us straight home, I took us the long way over one of the canyons, up the mountain on Mulholland to the views she loved, the ones she said made her feel like she knew everything about the city, like every single corner and crevice was open to her the way it wasn't when she was down below, where the streets and the people ran together in a blurry mess so that there was no way to tell them apart.

I was lost in it all and almost didn't see the little deer that had wandered out into the road. I swerved just in the nick of time and Lydia and I both screamed. That, along with the squeal of the brakes and a metal sound I couldn't place, a deep rattling that shuddered through my hands as I jerked the wheel over to the right as hard as I could turn it. The car skidded to a halt perpendicular to the road, and it was suddenly all still again but for the sounds of our ragged breathing and Steely Dan's *Kid Charlemagne* on the radio. I gripped the steering wheel as hard as I could, until it felt like my hands would shatter, because I needed some place for the tension to go, a place that was not my fist through the window, or worse, through Lydia's face.

I started the car and pulled us over on to one of the little turnouts that afforded what was usually a romantic view of the city, but which now reminded me of the glittering debris of our almost-accident.

"Are you…" I started to ask, but she cut me off with a wild-eyed stare, like she had just woken up in a bed and had no idea how she got there or where she was.

"Why did you tell all the people at your work that you were attacked by a mountain lion?"

She was shaking all over and when I tried to put a hand on her shoulder she threw it off.

"I didn't…" I stopped myself. There was no point in denying it.

"I'm not asking you if you told them. I'm asking you why."

"I'm sorry," I said, knowing it was the worst thing to say in a situation like that, but I said it anyway because this wasn't real.

"You're sorry?" The headlights from a passing car swam through the windshield and grafted themselves to her face, where I could see her eyes swimming in water and a few stray tears shimmying down her cheeks. She didn't bother trying to wipe them away, instead, she let them fall as she leaned her chin on her hand and looked out the window on her side. "When we met I told you that I didn't want to have to save anyone else. I thought about that a lot after I said it, about what a bitch I must have sounded like, how fucking unreasonable. But what I was trying to say, and I think you figured this out as we went along, was that I didn't want love to be tied to that much need anymore. That night," she turned toward me, but I still couldn't see her face, "remember? That first night. You held my mother's hand and we wore their old clothes and we both did something wonderful for one another. That wasn't need. That was love. To me anyway, it was love. I thought it was for you, too."

"It was, it still is."

"Then why," she used the back of her hand to wipe the tears away, "would you tell people that? Why would you lie and why would you use the worst moment in my mother's life — in my life — like that? Do you think it's a joke? Or was it just convenient? Like on the tip of your tongue or something?"

"No," I said, knowing I should go on, but not knowing what there was to say.

"I bet you're thinking about her even now, aren't you?" Lydia asked, the question dangling above my neck like the sharpest of blades. "Even now, that's where your mind goes when I talk about the beginning. I swooned when you first called to ask me out. Can you believe that? For the first time in my life, my feet left the floor for all the right reasons. That's the beginning for me. That's our story. But you fell in love with a story that had already been written, and I can't say I blame you," she squeezed something in her lap which I guessed was a napkin as her voice cracked under a new wave of tears, "because it's a hell of a story. It's tragic and full of despair. There's violence…but you've never heard the gory details, have you?"

"Lydia, you don't have to…" I started to say, but I didn't mean it. I didn't want her to stop. The details were exactly what I wanted to hear and the Cat, which had been pacing back and forth this whole time, wearing lines in the ground, suddenly stopped and cocked an ear.

"My dad had just died. I told you all about that. We had a small funeral for him, but that's just what we told ourselves. Small funeral…" she let out a small chuckle, "It was a small funeral because he didn't have any friends. My mother saw to that. He barely had a daughter. Right before he died I knew it was going to happen. I just had this feeling, and he did, too, because he'd stopped talking a lot. But he called me in one day when my mom wasn't around, and he asked me if I loved her. 'Yes,' I said, but it took me a second longer than it should have to answer, and we both just started cracking up. We hadn't laughed like that together since I was a little girl, and it felt so good, because even though we both knew it was the end, we were getting in the last laugh, and it was about her. It would kill her to know that." I could feel her eyes turn toward me for the first time since getting in the car.

I tried to swallow, but found that my throat had gone dry.

"When we finally stopped laughing he told me, 'You don't need to hate her, Lydia, and that's why you'll always be a better person than she is. Remember that.' He was so weak and I remembered thinking: *This is not him. This is not my father. This is a man who is about to die, who can't be my father, because my father does not have skin that sags like that. My father does not moan and go to the bathroom in his bed. My father doesn't have only sporadic moments of clarity. My father is not this man.* But it was him. That's when you know they're going to die, because you give up trying to figure out who this person, this weak, disgusting person, is in front of you, pretending to be someone you love, and finally admit to yourself that it's him."

She stopped, and I wanted to reach out and touch her face or put a hand on her shoulder, anything to show her that I loved her and that I understood, but I knew she didn't want that.

"After the funeral, there was this rain that wouldn't stop. It just kept coming and coming, not an El Niño, just a no-name rain that kept me and Martha in the apartment together, each of us in our own rooms, only meeting when we ran into one another in the kitchen or on the way to or from the bathroom. It was terrible. Awkward silences like the world before there was talking." Another sob ran through her while I tried to imagine the two of them in that tiny apartment, each trying to create a world that wouldn't impinge on the other's, while all around them toxic clouds of words not said wafted throughout, poisoning the air and destroying their spirits. It was a terrible image.

"Finally, though, after like two or three weeks, the rain stopped, and she came to my room, and she had showered and changed, and she had this smile on her face. She looked like a different person. One I'd never even imagined she might have once been. I mean, I'd seen pictures of her in her old stewardess get-up, but that was for a job. This was who she wanted to be. Truly and earnestly, and it touched me, Duncan," it startled me when she said my name. I thought she'd forgotten I was there, "because for a second I actually felt bad for her, like she'd never gotten the chance to be who she really wanted to be, and now that my dad was gone and the rain was done, she was ready. Ready to start over or whatever you want to call it. She wanted to go for a hike. It was going to be muddy, she said, but screw it. She sounded like a little kid. Like she wanted to be naughty and get dirty, and I got caught up in the moment. I admit it. I told her yes, and I remembered it feeling like I was saying yes to so much more than just her asking me to go out hiking with her. I felt like I was saying yes to loving her and letting her love me. I was saying yes to a new life together. Silly, but that's what it felt like."

As she went on, I noticed something moving outside the car, over her shoulder, a shadow that was darker than the night. I was only half listening now, trying to figure out if what I was seeing out there was real or just a trick of the night. The Cat noticed it, too, and I could feel it standing stock still but ready, nerve endings bristling, trying its hardest not be noticed as it craned its head around this way and that, trying to pick up a scent or a vibration that would tell it if what it was dealing with was prey or a threat.

I caught only stray threads of her story, "...came out of nowhere..." and "...I just started screaming..."and she was starting to cry these huge thunderclap sobs but I couldn't stop looking out there, past her, into the night, and every time I had myself convinced it was just my imagination I'd see it move again, just a little twitch, and then just as suddenly it would stop, and I'd wonder all over again if it was my imagination, or her story, or if there really was something out there, something sizing us up as a meal, or God forbid, something more sinister than that. More fragments from her story swirled around the inside of the car like a dust storm: "…raking her back…" and "…snarling…" and through it all, through this story I knew I needed to hear because it was my story now, too, even though I didn't know it, it was every part of me, I was barely hearing any of it.

Her words kept coming, falling all around me like confetti, piles of pain littering the car and making it feel that much smaller. It was getting hotter, too, and I was finding it harder to breathe as steam began to build up on the inside of the windshield, just a little to start with, but I could see that it was spreading upwards, and before we knew it we'd be fogged in, not just outside, but in there, too, lost to one another for good.

The thing outside moved again, and everything inside me tensed up at once. If she could see my face she'd accuse me of not listening, and she'd be right, but it wouldn't be by choice, I'd try to explain as the Cat's ear flicked suddenly, picking up the kind of thin vibrations I could only dream about feeling. Whatever it was, it was moving closer and closer to the car, taking its own sweet time, which I imagined was part of the fun. Lydia was weeping, and even though I couldn't focus on what she was saying, I knew that she must be getting near the end by the way her voice kept coming apart, splitting and splitting again like something cellular, an atom destined for better and bigger nuclear things. I pinched myself under the arm to try and get myself to pay attention, staring at her through the dark, trying to make out the edges of her face, the contours of her dress, the details that made life worth living.

"…and see," she went on, and I knew she could have just as well been talking to herself, "I never got a chance to love her. Not really. I had to save her, again and again, it was always me picking up the pieces, but then you came along, and you were so kind to Martha and to me. When I asked you to come in and hold her hand while she was in that tub, I remembered thinking, as I was running to get Mrs. Kim, that there was no way you'd be there when I got back. You'd be gone, and Martha would just be floating there; she'd be dead, and I'd have to try and keep a straight face when the paramedics got there and try to explain to them what had happened, and then, after they left, I'd have nothing again. Not even someone to save. But you didn't leave. You were there, and it was the nicest thing anyone has ever done for me."

And just as she finished the story, I saw it. The little deer that we had almost slammed into moments earlier was at the window behind her, just standing there, looking in at us as though it wanted to check to see if we were okay or maybe to ask just what the hell we thought we were doing driving like that. The Cat saw it at the same time as I did, and before I knew what was happening, it lunged at the deer, and I watched it dash back into the brush, and in the split second before I slammed myself into the window, I grabbed Lydia and smothered her in a massive bear hug.

"Your heart is beating like a freight train. Are you okay?" she asked me. She sounded confused.

I couldn't live like this. There wasn't room for the two of us anymore. It was the Cat or me, which meant it was me and her. It had to be me and her.

"I'm fine," I said, and I could feel tears catching in my throat.

She patted me gently and then pushed away. "Oh, my God!" she suddenly shouted, pressing her palms to the sides of her face. "I can't believe how fucking melodramatic this is getting. It's so stupid!" I couldn't see her face, so it was impossible to tell if she was weeping or laughing.

"Are we staying together?" I asked quietly, hoping the Cat

wouldn't think it was a question I was asking it. But the Cat wasn't there now. Missing the deer must have sent it back into whatever part of my body it hid in while it waited for me to fuck up again.

After a long pause. "Do you want to?"

"Of course," I said, starting up the car and carefully pulling us back on to Mulholland.

"Why?" she asked, but she didn't wait for an answer, which was good, because I wasn't sure what I would have told her. "I don't know, Duncan…"

"I want to make it up to you. I want to make things better. Do you think we can?"

"Maybe." She sounded doubtful but not impenetrable.

"How?"

She was quiet for a long time as we drove. The clouds were starting to split apart, and the lights from houses on the Hills began appearing, like they hadn't been there all along.

"I'll think about it."

Going down the mountain always seemed so much shorter than going up it.

# CHAPTER 22

After the night of the party, we tried to go back to our normal lives, but it didn't take a genius to see that things weren't right. I'd missed so much of what she'd said to me that night because of the Cat that, for all I knew, her careful avoidance of me was an overgrown pregnant pause in that conversation, and it wasn't me who was waiting for the other shoe to drop, but her who was still waiting for me to answer for something, a question posed to me in the midst of her slap-happy ultimatum that I hadn't heard because I was too busy with what was moving in the shadows outside the car, when my focus should have been inside with her.

My bed was now the couch, a modern Scandinavian thing we'd upgraded to a few months earlier, and I wasn't sleeping well at all. But even if it hadn't felt like I was about to be waterboarded every time I laid my head back, the Cat's constant pacing and sporadic howls would have been more than enough to ensure sleeplessness the rest of the time. When I did manage to finally doze off, the dreams that came to me were so vile and haunting I would have much rather skipped sleep entirely, relying on coffee and the heart-pounding dread of what Lydia was concocting in the way of retribution that she'd only hinted at that night up Mulholland.

I watched her carefully for clues and quickly ruled out the possibility of a series of charming little larcenies that barely broke the surface of antisocial behavior. She wasn't messing around; whatever she had planned was going to be huge, a Super Bowl Halftime show of torment I wouldn't soon forget. Whatever it was, I just wished she'd let 'er rip already. All the anticipation was fraying my nerves, and it took everything I had not to throw my phone across the room when I saw another call come in from Martha. I listened to the first couple of messages, demanding to know where I was and why I wasn't coming over anymore. She needed me, she said, she wanted to know how I was doing and what the latest was with the Cat. She also wanted to know how Lydia was, and that was always when the real panic seeped into her voice, building and building until by the end of the call she sounded like a garbage truck backing up, a persistent shrillness that warned you to get out of the way lest you be smashed into nothing by two tons of something that never even knew you were there.

Once, when I was expecting a work call, I accidentally answered one of her calls. She started sobbing when she heard my voice and I tried to calm her down, speaking to her in the most soothing manner I could imagine, like one of those ASMR performers who gets paid millions of dollars by lonely perverts who want to hear what it sounds like when a pretty young girl drinks milk.

"Martha," I tried to speak over her wailing, but it was like trying to stick a finger between spinning fan blades, "I've got <SOB> nothing left <WAIL> to give you. There's no more <END OF THE WORLD MOANING> of her I can share. We've <MOAN WAIL SOB> nibbled so much there's barely anything left for me." After that, I hung up and stopped answering her calls. There was only so much hunger a man could take.

My only respite became work, where Deedee and I would spend long hours sitting together on the couch in my office, the cloud storming along to the slow drudge of old reggae or whatever music Deedee had chosen to accompany the moment. Sometimes, she would open the window, which I was shocked to find out was actually an option, and she would sit on the ledge smoking a cigarette, always careful to blow the smoke outside. She'd started dressing differently since her thing with Les started, more low-cut shirts and tight jeans, and once, when she leaned over to exhale a stream of smoke out the window, I got a good look down the front of her shirt at her black lacy bra and wondered what it would be like to kiss her.

She turned, and catching me, grinned and then pursed her lips, trying not to let her smile grow into something bigger, something more deliberate.

"What're you thinking about, Kitty?" she asked me, the cigarette scissored elegantly between her middle and index finger.

A lot of the time, Les would join us, and I was always careful to give up my seat on the couch so that he could sit there. They listened as I droned on and on about my troubles with Lydia and the category five silent treatment I'd been getting from Dutch, but it wouldn't be long before I saw their fingers start to creep towards one another over the expanse of cushions that lay between them, and I'd excuse myself and wander the halls with my hands stuffed into my pockets, counting Mississippis until it felt like enough time had passed for me to go back.

One afternoon in the staff lounge, a room that was ostensibly for everyone, but in reality only used by the assistants and junior associates, I sat alone at the linoleum table drinking water from a mug. I put it down and turned it towards me so that I could read the words printed on its fuchsia side. *World's Greatest Mom.* As soon as I read it, the Cat was there. It pounced forward out of nowhere, swiping at the mug and I dropped the keepsake on the floor and watched it with a surprising amount of curiosity as it exploded into a million pieces. That was how it let me know it was never far away, that it even existed in between the long seconds I couldn't help but keep counting. One hundred and thirty-five Mississippi. One hundred and thirty-six Mississippi. How many Mississippi's did it take to fall in love? How many to fall out?

I was on my knees picking up the pieces of shattered mug when someone came around the corner, saw me, and froze. A water bottle in his hand, the guy, who I vaguely recognized as someone from the IT department, stared at me with wild eyes as though he'd caught me in the act of some unspeakable crime. From where I knelt, he looked enormous, and as the standoff continued, I felt the sleek coils of the Cat's back legs tensing up as it prepared to defend itself against this new threat, an animal that drew itself up to fairy tale heights to impress upon its foe a sense that it was bigger than it actually was and maybe more dangerous, too. But the Cat was too smart for that kind of amateur posturing. I snarled at the poor IT schlub, and he slowly backed out of the room, holding the empty water bottle out in front of him as though a little bit of plastic would be enough to stop me from separating muscle from bone. Evisceration was well within reach. I held on to the Cat with everything I had while he continued to creep backwards, and just when I felt like I couldn't hold on another second, I hissed at him: "Get out now!" I watched him turn and run, and when he was out of my line of sight, I let myself go, collapsing into an exhausted heap on top of the broken bits of pottery. It wasn't until I felt the Cat recede back into whatever shadows he rested in that I pushed myself off the floor and looked down to find the now too familiar sight of blood flowering on the arm of my white shirt where I'd landed on the broken pieces of mug. World's Greatest Mom, indeed.

I got up, brushed myself off, and ran out of the room. I couldn't go back to my office and home felt out of the question. What if Lydia was there and the Cat decided to make an appearance? There was nowhere to go so I took the elevator down to the garage, got in my car, tilted the seat all the way back and screwed my eyes shut tight. I wanted to see nothing, not even the colorful spirals of blood vessels that sometimes danced in the darkness when you tried too hard to black everything out. I squeezed my eyes shut tighter and tighter until it felt like something in the front of my head was going to burst, but even then I couldn't find the nothingness I craved, the blankness I knew was always there but never within reach when it was needed most. I squeezed harder, my temples were starting to throb now, and went down past the squiggles, past where the Cat lived, deeper even than my love for Lydia and the feeling of Martha's hand clutching mine that first night when I sat beside her, doing everything she could, I realized now, to hold her own cat back from having its way with her daughter. Further and further I went, until finally, I broke through to the place I yearned for, the place where there was nothing to see, and just as I started to relax, to feel the thing leave that had been pressing the air out of my chest as I struggled under the crushing weight of its insincerity, I heard something in the distance. It was a ticking; a bomb perhaps, or it might have been a stopwatch, the kind strict coaches used to time their runners down to the tenth of a second, because that was the level it took to get to the bottom of anything really worth knowing, but whatever it was, I knew with everything inside of me that it was counting down to something inevitable, an ending to things or the beginning of new things, which were, I knew perfectly well, not the same, but still... *Tick, tick, tick.* And without even realizing I was doing it, I found myself counting along, keeping time to the expanding seconds and the manifold universes I knew they contained.

Four hundred and twenty-two Mississippi...four hundred and twenty-three Mississippi...and so on.

As terrible and depressing as my days at work now felt, always waiting, it seemed, for either a summons from Dutch to finally discuss my six-month lie to the company about the mountain lion attack or a call from Lydia telling me yet again that what I'd done to her was worse than cheating, or yet another text from Martha trying to cajole me into visiting her, as though I owed her everything, including the pristine skin off my back she'd never have again, the nights were even worse. At least during the day I had Deedee and Les to keep me company and sympathize, and even though their barely clandestine games of kissy face made me want to puke a little at times, I appreciated their always being there for me.

When she was in the apartment, Lydia did everything she could to avoid me, going so far sometimes as to hiss at me like a feral cat when I got too close, a little too on the nose, I thought, but never said a word. When she absolutely had to communicate with me, she'd leave notes composed of terse groupings of nouns and always signed with her full name as if there was anyone else around who hated me enough to talk to me in their own invented language. She ordered all her meals in, and there was a perpetual odor of Chinese, Mexican, Thai and Greek food that hovered over everything, a multi-ethnic tribunal that sat in judgment over the place and that never let me forget that the sentencing part of the trial was still to come. Sometimes, she went out, always banging the front door shut loudly behind her that always made me jump as though the apartment was being firebombed or on the verge of collapse, and I treasured the imagined feeling of weightlessness I'd be treated to as the floors pancaked downwards, one on top of the other, as we fell into a pile of forgettable rubble, leaving in its wake a Chernobyl-shaped cloud of dust, only instead of a thousand years of cyclops offspring and tap water that looked like Mountain Dew, we would suffer through a long afternoon of traffic delays and power outages, equally as aggravating and twice as inconvenient. I never went after her when she stormed out, and when she came back, I never asked her where she'd been. Interrogatives and righteous indignation were out of my purview by that point; my scope of responsibilities had been reduced to fretting and pearl-clutching, and even that I wasn't doing particularly well.

It was getting on towards the middle of summer and the heat in LA was unbearable. Dry one day, humid the next, the human body struggled to keep up with the ever-changing acclimatizing demands, and people's tempers, everywhere, were flaring. Out on the streets, drivers honked at one another for the most minor of offenses, while inside their cars they babbled noiselessly, beseeching God to the accompaniment of obscene Eastern European hand gestures they were able to intuit in their close proximity to misery, to deliver them from this hell, and if it wasn't too much trouble, maybe see to it that the guy who cut them off one block back got decapitated by a low hanging bridge in front of his wife and kids, Amen. Air conditioning helped, but the threat of rolling blackouts made using it feel like a game of Russian Roulette. I never realized how many machines were running in the apartment until we lost power in the middle of the day, when everything that was plugged in - the coffee machine, the satellite TV box, even the cute his and hers matching Sonicare toothbrushes - would heave a sudden dying electric last gasp that was followed by a silence so total and deafening, people up and down the block would suddenly start screaming, some for the files they just lost or the bread they'd just started toasting, but when you listened closely you realized it wasn't exactly screaming, but more like a chorus of clearing throats, a collective attempt to dislodge something gristly and indigestible they just realized was caught in their veins and in their chests.

Sleep, for me, was more and more of a catch-as-catch-can proposition than it was before the heatwave hit. Lydia didn't like the A/C on at night, and rather than taking on yet another front in the domestic war by sneaking the thermostat down degree by passive aggressive degree, I suffered through it, tossing and turning out on the uncomfortable couch most nights until the early morning, when my body would finally grant me a few minutes of sleep, just enough so that when my alarm went off shortly thereafter, it always felt like I was walking around covered in hot glue for the rest of the day. I definitely wasn't dreaming a lot, but when I did have occasion to slip below the milk skin of sleep the dreams I remembered were doozies, the kind where everything seemed as normal as could be except for one massively disturbing difference that no one but me found strange. In one of them I was back in the bathroom with Martha on the first night I met her, holding her hand, keeping her safe from something I had no idea was already in me, too, when I looked down and saw that it had come detached from her arm. Her wrist was pumping out jets of blood that clouded the water, but when I looked at her, she showed no signs of noticing. Her eyes were closed and a smile was spreading over her face, a darkly growing shadow that would one day slip from her skull and devour the entire planet.

On this night, my dream had me sitting next to Les' wife on a park bench, just as I had imagined her when he played me the recording of the love letter. In the dream, I was writing out the words she was saying on massive cue cards with one hand, and my other hand was stuck up under her denim skirt, where I was fingering her. We smiled at one another occasionally as kids ran by, chasing one another on their way to and from the playground. None of them stopped to watch us, and what we were doing felt fine and normal as long as she kept explaining to Les how she knew they were going to be together forever. The smell of something roasting suddenly wafted by, and I stopped writing to look around for its source. Over by the restrooms, a vendor with a hot dog cart had set up shop, and when he could, he'd reach out with his greasy tongs and snatch one of the kids running by and chuck them into his cart, where they'd burn up in the belly of the wagon. The other kids made no attempt to run away, and when one of their friends was caught, the rest went on playing without acknowledging it. Something about the setup struck me as being not right, but I couldn't quite put my finger on it. I laid the cue cards down and took my hand out from under her skirt.

"Are you hungry?" I asked her, feeling suddenly peckish myself.

Instead of answering, she clicked off her recorder and squeezed my cheek, hard, the way a childless aunt might.

"Typical," she said, shaking her head.

But before I could ask her what she meant, I sat bolt upright on the couch and wiped the sweat from my stinging eyes. I was breathing hard, and it took me a few seconds to realize that the smell of smoke was still there. I jumped up and started running down the hall towards the bedroom, where I was having visions of finding Lydia splayed out on the bed, half eaten by flames, a forgotten cigarette dangling glamorously from the tips of her fingers, her head thrown back over one side with her soft white neck offered up to the night's highest bidders. But when I threw the door open, the room was dead silent, and there wasn't a hint of smoke or fire to be found; it was just Lydia curled up in the center of the bed in the fetal position, snoring softly, her red sleep mask pushed high up on her forehead. I wanted so badly to be curled up next to her, as close as two people could get, to seal her body up in mine like a tomb and sprinkle roses around to mark the spot, a shrine for pilgrims to visit for centuries to come, couples trying to get pregnant and lonely spinsters with soul-crushing cases of halitosis. Just a glimpse of the closed parentheses of our bodies could cure cystic acne, gout or hypertension, but then I sighed and backed out of the room. We used to glitter like that, but those days seemed lost now. Now we were barely hanging on, which was another kind of monument altogether, less a holy place and more of a car crash, an epicenter of bad vibes people walked past quickly as the real Lord's prayer dappled their grateful lips: *There but for the grace of God go I...*

I closed the door and went back to the couch, still smelling the air, wondering to myself off-handedly what use dreams were if real life could find their way in so easily, when I looked out the sliding glass door that led out to the balcony. Way out in the distance, where during the day the prematurely graying San Gabriel Mountains usually stood, a dull smudge of orange stained the smirking length of the horizon. I looked at my phone. It was 3 a.m., far too early for the sun to be rising, which meant only one thing; it had to be a fire. I slid the door open and stepped out onto the narrow balcony, where a hot wall of air hit me, followed closely by the acrid smell of smoke. I coughed once, testing the air and the quality of my lungs. Everything felt okay. I wondered how close it was and if

I should start getting some stuff together in case we had to quickly evacuate, but I couldn't think of anything I'd actually want to take with me; the bed was too big to move and I'd already taken the Big Sur picture to Martha's. Everything else I owned seemed built to be torched; the couch, my clothing, the few pathetic houseplants I neglected with the diligence of a martial artist. IKEA should start a line, I thought, the "toss a match and go" collection by Duncan. It turned out that I was alarmingly unencumbered and perhaps even more telling, completely emotionally unattached to my material possessions. How was it that I was never approached by the CIA or one of those other morally ambiguous organizations that put a premium on human go-bags?

I pocketed the two pictures of us from our wedding. *There*, I thought, as around me the city slept on unaware, people breathing fire into their own hungry dreams, adding flame and choking smoke to their unconscious yearnings, so that, at any moment, the neighborhood would collapse in on itself in an earthquake of night terrors, *ready to go*. The only good thing about being up at that hour was the occasional breeze that rose up from the street, and I gave a little shiver as it climbed up my back, running its shifty fingers through my clothes, bracing me for whatever small fortune it could get its mitts on. But it might not have been the wind at all, because the next thing I knew I felt the Cat sitting up, its eyes darting back and forth while its ears flipped around nervously, as though it was trying to pick up the immoral frequency that might tell it whether to engage its fight-or-flight muscles. It opened its mouth, and instead of the morbid howl I braced myself for, only the smallest of nervous peeps emerged, just the trace elements of its ruthless potential it didn't yet know whether or not it needed to deploy.

A fleck of something, an insect or a piece of dust, flittered by my face and I waved at it only to find it wasn't just the one fleck, but an infestation, one or two of them even landing on my lips. Carefully, I poked it with my tongue. Ash. And when I focused my eyes on the building next door I saw torrents of it falling silently, piling up on the parked cars up and down the street.

I was so focused on trying to see the individual flakes that I almost screamed when I heard the flick of a lighter from the balcony next to mine. A burly, gray-haired man in his sixties wearing nothing but a silk Mondrian dressing gown and a pair of genteel reading spectacles low down on his nose touched the flame to the point of his cigarette. He took a deep drag and blew the smoke out the side of his mouth towards me. It was a menthol, and mixed with the odor of the fire, it smelled like burning toothpaste.

"It looks like a gash," he said, gesturing at the line of fire.

"What does?" I wanted to be sure I understood him. It was a sentence that could be interpreted in many possible ways.

"The fire," he gestured again with the tip of his cigarette, as though he'd been the one to light it and was making sure he'd done a thorough job. "It looks like someone has slit open the sky and it has a wound. Or is a wound."

I hadn't thought of it in that way, but now that he mentioned it, it was hard to see it any other way. I studied it again. "Or a clock," I said.

"Huh?"

"It could be 3:15, if you want to think about it in terms of time. Like how long it's been burning and how long is left before it gets to us."

"Huh," he said, considering it. He leaned over the balcony as if to get a better look. "Nah, I don't see it that way."

I shrugged. "I've never seen you before," I tried to keep the conversation going. Small talk felt oddly attractive given the alternative, which was to go back in and tie myself into anxious knots about everything I was worried about before, but this time, I could add the fire to the list of usual suspects, *You know,* I told myself, *just to keep it fresh. "Did you just move in?"

He blew out a mouthful of smoke and grinned. "I've lived here for 16 years. I've seen you. I've seen your girlfriend. I tend to stick to the nights."

I nodded, mildly freaked out that he was keeping such close tabs on us. "What line of business are you in?" I asked, curious, but also unwilling to accept any answer other than that he was the comptroller for a company that made snuff films.

"Jewelry," he said. I wasn't sure if he was being vague on purpose or not, but he went on to clarify. "Gold mostly. I know a lot of gold people."

The image of a dozen of his friends, all wearing identical silk robes with dangling spectacles and dipped in gold sprang into my head and I suppressed a smile.

"Ah," I said, gazing back out toward the fire line. It looked to me like it was moving closer.

"Sorry," he said, noticing I wasn't looking at him, "am I boring you?"

"What?" I asked.

"You keep looking out there, and I'm just wondering if you're finding what I'm telling you boring or something."

"No, you're not boring me," I answered, trying not to sound defensive. I didn't want to get pulled into his guerrilla staging of *Godot*. "It's just…" I gestured into the distance, hoping it would be enough and I wouldn't have to elaborate for him.

"What?" he said condescendingly. "The fire? You're afraid of the fire. Let me tell you something: I've lived here for almost 20 years — I've been through earthquakes, riots, fires…" he paused for a second when he ran out of disasters. "You name it, and I've fucking been through it. Don't worry about the fire, okay? We're going to be just fine." He hocked up a wad of phlegm and, without looking, spat over the side.

"How can you be so sure?" I knew it probably wasn't such a good idea taking my cues about disaster preparedness from a guy who attended a forest fire in flammable jammies, but he had the air of a survivor about him, a robust case of *who gives a fuck?* that, in my mind, made him an expert in everything.

"Because," he said, his voice getting a little louder now, "it's way out there. It's literally hundreds of miles away. Maybe even thousands. It just looks close because we're up high. If we were down another two floors, you wouldn't even notice it."

I nodded, not really interested in getting into it with him, when I felt more flakes of ash begin to spark along my arms, putting me in mind of winter, and I shivered instinctively; my body was falling for this con and nothing I could say or do would convince it otherwise.

"I don't know," I went on, disobeying my better nature, "that seems pretty close to me. Maybe Pomona. Maybe even Pasadena. More like ten miles." I reconsidered. "Less."

He shrugged. Those places didn't matter to him. Only the nighttime mattered to him. I knew the type well from a decade of entertaining a certain kind of client who demanded the strip club and half-hourly bump of coke treatment, all-nighters that spiraled out of control in a thousand different directions and didn't end until the sun came up, and then with a brotherly hug and an invitation to "do it again sometime." After a night like that I usually needed a couple of days to recuperate. People who loved the night, though, were ready to go again 12 hours later when the sun went back into witness protection.

He pushed up his glasses and squinted into the night as though he was trying to read the same imaginary map I'd been studying. "Listen," he said, "do you mind if I change the subject?"

"No," I said, grateful I didn't have to keep going round and round with him on the finer points of LA geography.

"I've noticed your girlfriend isn't wearing an engagement ring yet. If the time comes," he went on, and for a second, I had the weirdest feeling he was about to ask me to pull the plug on him in case he even got a really bad case of heavy metal poisoning or a terrible rash from unwashed silk, "that you're thinking of proposing. Please come see me. I'll get you an amazing deal on a ring. You'll be knocked out. I'm telling you. Deep discount. Friends and family. All that shit."

A ring. I'd never thought to get her a ring. And in the midst of the fire, Martha, the cat's anxiety and whatever weird psychological suffering was headed my way, I knew beyond a shadow of a doubt that getting her a ring would fix everything.

"We're actually already married. It was a spur of the moment kind of thing. We skipped over all the formalities. I never even thought about a ring…"

"You skipped the formalities?" He flicked the cigarette over the side, and I watched it tumble, spitting out sparks as it fell, landing in one of the kumquat trees that were in front of the building.

"We just decided to do it," I went on, realizing that it was the first time I'd ever told the story to anyone. "We were having this wonderful night, one of those nights where you knew something important was going to happen before it was through, and we were at this reggae speakeasy in Boyle Heights and next thing you know…"

"Oh, that old story," he said, stopping me by putting up his hands.

I wasn't interested in finishing my own story. I needed to get to the nuts and bolts of the thing. I felt like Golem. "How much is a ring?"

"Depends," he said, "are you an Elvis kind of guy, or are you one of these…" he waved a hand out across the city, "assholes?"

"I'm an Elvis," I said with no hesitation. The Cat knew what I was up to and started snarling at me, but I ignored it as I pretended to think about his question again, just so he wouldn't think I'd answered without giving it some real thought. "Yup, definitely an Elvis."

"I need you to understand something," he went on with something like determination on his face, and I knew he was winding up for the big sales pitch, "gold is a very precious commodity. Very rare. Very precious."

"Right," I broke in, trying to move things along without getting bogged down in a history lesson about precious metals. "Which is why it's so valuable. I know. I get it."

"Oh," he said with a disgusted tone, and I got suddenly worried that I'd somehow blown it with the big galoot, "you don't know how much of an understatement it is to say something like that. Typical. Typical and ignorant."

"Sorry," I said as earnestly as I could, "I misjudged the…scarcity?"

"Let me tell you something," he pointed half an index finger at me, and I just knew the story about how he lost the other half, if he ever cared to share it with me, would change my life forever. "If you took every bit of gold there was in the world, and you melted it down, do you know that what you have wouldn't even fill an Olympic-sized swimming pool? That's how rare the stuff is. So don't come in here talking about what has value and what doesn't."

As I wondered how I'd managed to offend him so deeply, I snuck a look out to the fire and was sure now that it was getting closer. Before, it'd just been this static smear of color, but now I could see that it was throbbing with an unhealthy orange glow that made the darkness look like it had an infection. Then, revisiting reality for a hairy moment, I did a quick calculation, and I don't know what made me do it, if it was the Cat throwing itself again my rib cage, trying to get out and make a break for it before it was too late, or if it had something to do with the heat and the ash and the fact that it was 3 a.m. and the city was burning and he just got me to admit out loud that I was "an Elvis", I said to him, "Wait a second. There's no way that's possible. There's more gold than that at your average NBA game."

The look I got back, even in the charitable darkness of the hour, was pure murder, and I could almost feel his scowl coarse against my skin, like one of those shirts made of sackcloth that penitent priests wore to mortify the flesh.

"Google it," he spat at me and then turned his body away to wait while I did what he told me. He lifted the cigarette to his lips, and I saw that his fingers were all bent, as though they'd each been broken many times, and when he gripped the Kool he did it between the knuckles of his index and middle finger, making talons of his hands..

I did as he told me, and it didn't take long to discover that he was right.

"You're right," I said, holding the phone up to him, a white flag I hoped he'd accept. "I stand corrected."

He didn't say anything to me for a few seconds, and I got the sense that he was savoring the victory, that maybe they didn't come all that often to him, and he had to take them where and when he could.

"I don't know why you wouldn't believe me," he said, pulling the cigarette from his lips. I noticed he was wearing a pinky ring with an enormous stone set in it.

"It wasn't a character judgment. Don't take it personally. I'm kind of a skeptic by nature. It's how I was raised."

"Mm-hmm," he muttered.

"Listen," I went on, trying to steer the conversation back into less personal waters. "I think you're right about a ring. I need to get one for Lydia. How much is something nice?"

He shrugged. "Depends on how nice of a guy you want to be."

I did a few quick calculations in my head; Christmas bonus, mortgage payment, tennis club membership and spat out a number I thought I could afford. "Would $40,000 get me something nice? I'd wanna use your gold guy, of course."

His glasses slid down off his nose as he did a double take.

"Did you say 40 grand?"

"Four-oh," I repeated. "Does that work?"

"For 40," he declared, sounding slightly out of breath, "I can guarantee that she'll fall in love with you all over again and then some."

We made some vague plans about me getting him a down payment and even though I was intensely curious about what he meant by "and then some" I didn't ask. After we'd traded contact info, an act I found the very definition of pathological given we literally lived right next door to one another, he pitched another cigarette over the balcony as he scuttled back inside, presumably to get a hold of his "gold guy" in whatever time zone people like that existed.

I knew perfectly well that it was an absurd amount of money to spend on a piece of jewelry, but I didn't know what else I was going to spend it on. I already owned my apartment, my car worked fine, and I didn't like to travel (or "having diarrhea in different time zones," as my mother used to call it). My future had to look like something. It might as well shimmer like gold.

It felt wonderful to have made a decision, and I smiled as I looked back out at the creeping line of fire, and for the first time I started to hear fire engines in the distance, wailing like tantruming children as they raced around in what seemed like every direction at once, and then, from somewhere nearby, a pack of coyotes answered that noise with their own hysterical barking, and, inch by screaming inch, nights within nights began to open up, sealing the fate on what wasn't even yet a brand new day.

'A gash,' my neighbor the jeweler had called the fire, and now I couldn't see it any other way.

# CHAPTER 23

I awoke early the next morning feeling refreshed and hopeful despite only getting a couple hours of sleep. I whistled while I shaved and dressed, admiring the stretch of white skin on my neck as I lifted my chin to do the knot in my tie. It was a new day, I thought to myself, and all I had to do was keep everyone in a holding pattern until the ring arrived. It probably wasn't the best idea putting so much faith in graven idols, but hope, I'd come to realize, craved a container where it could be kept pure from the withering grasp of reality, and I couldn't think of anything more graven than a $40,000 piece of gold jewelry.

Before leaving, I glanced out the big sliding glass door to where the sun smoldered like a cheap cigar in the faraway sky behind a bank of murky smoke, and its dullness was a sight to behold. I stepped out onto the balcony into a hot wind that smothered my face with humid, motherly kisses and instantly turned the saliva on my lips all gummy. The air was a strange yellowish-brown color, and it shivered with sickly vibrations that, given the circumstances, passed for the light of day. There but not there, the sun bided its time, hanging patiently behind the parasitic scrim of toxic formalities for the curse to be lifted, playing a waiting game that was dear to the hearts of galaxies and ghosts.

Down on the streets, people were using their messenger bags and the sleeves of their shirts to wipe away the piles of gray ash that had accumulated on their cars overnight, and, as they worked, ash continued to flutter down over them, so that pretty soon they were covered in it. They worked until they saw the foolishness of it, and, giving up, they sped away, leaving eddies of the cancerous dust in their wake to dance briefly in the poisoned air before settling back on the street and on the lawns of neighbors, where the earth absorbed it easily, consuming it without objection.

I got in my car, and when I pulled on to Melrose, traffic immediately came to a standstill as, inside their cars, my mummified neighbors shook their heads in wonder as the black and white world around them did things it wasn't supposed to do. Anything was possible, I'd assure them if I could, that sometimes the sky burned with colors and made promises from its airy depths it had no intention of ever keeping, because Mother Nature had a funny way of never keeping her word.

My phone dinged, and I picked it up, flipped to my emails and saw something there from my neighbor, the jeweler. It was hard for me to picture him now and that it hadn't all been a dream, and when I tried to conjure him, all that came to mind was a shadowy mass on the balcony next to mine with nothing to confirm his substance but a cloud of menthol smoke and a neon squiggle of glow-in-the-dark gin blossoms.

The email read like a Western Union Telegram:

> *Neighbor! Good news — money order has been received. Gold guy very happy. Initial design concepts attached. If you pick one by noon, I can have this candle lit for you in a week. You will thank me later. — Bud*

I quickly scanned through the designs. The first was a pharaoh's head, the second was the Mercedes logo, and, though I shouldn't have been surprised, the third was a lion. All three were held next to a pencil for scale and each one was more massive and garish than the next. I emailed him back a one-word response. *Lion.*

Still frozen in the unmoving line of cars, I looked to my left and saw a long line of workmen lined up at the window of a lunch truck, and I suddenly realized that I was as hungry as I'd ever been in my life. My stomach growled, and I inched my way in front of the car to my left and then cut off two more lines of traffic to get to the other side of the street. Either move would usually earn me the middle finger or worse, but on this morning, it was the least of anyone's problems, and I barely got a sideways glance.

Parking my car, I got into the line and touched my growling stomach. Hunger roiled through me, and it was the kind of hunger I imagined someone felt after a long day's work, an appetite that was only ever earned. I expected strange looks from my fellow patrons; a white guy in a black suit on a day like this? But no one gave me a second glance.

I got to the front of the line and looked up at the menu. I had no idea what to order. A kind looking older woman poked her head out and waited for me to speak.

"What's the heartiest thing you have?"

Without answering me, she ducked her head back in, spoke quickly to the chef, and then poked her head back out.

"El menudo," she said.

Menudo…

I felt a tap on my shoulder and turned around to see a short Mexican man with dark skin and a pencil thin mustache who was wearing white overalls. He held a folded ten-dollar bill in his hand.

"Do you know what is menudo?" he asked me kindly.

"No," I admitted.

"Hmmm…" He thought about how best to describe it to me. "This is like the guts of the animal," he began in broken English, and then he rubbed his stomach to show me the general area to which he was referring.

"Oh," I said, getting it now. "Yes," I turned back to the woman, "uno menudo por favor."

I watched as she dipped an enormous ladle into a steaming vat, poured it into a bowl, and then handed it through the window to me. I paid and thanked her, then stood near a clump of other men quietly devouring their own bowls. I tasted a little bit of it;

hot, rich, and salty, it was everything I could have asked for, and I ate without stopping until there was nothing left at the bottom of the bowl except for some gristle and clumps of fat, and I took a moment to read my fortune in that viscera before tilting my head back and swallowing that, too, haunted by a bone-deep need for sustenance I'd never known before.

Sated for the moment, I nodded reverently to the men around me as though we'd just completed some noble task, and I was about to get back in my car when I noticed that traffic on both sides of Vine Street had stopped. I looked across the street where all the attention seemed to be focused, and in the parking lot between the Yum Yum Donuts and a place that covered car seats in sheepskin, a baby deer, probably driven from the hills by the fire, stood motionless as the world around it waited breathlessly to see what kind of omen it would show itself to be. Everything was perfectly still around us except for waves of heat shimmering above the sidewalk and the almost constant sound of sirens moaning in the distance, maternal and eternally remorseful, and it was from within that relative stillness that I understood that it wasn't just the baby deer; the world was full of signs whose only provenance was to remind us how uncomplicated we really were.

Cars idled in the street, and the men at the food truck put their spoons in their bowls, and around us, flakes of ash blizzarded noiselessly as we all waited to see what the deer would do. And at the height of the stillness, our representative emerged; a bent old woman came out of the donut store with a bag in her hand, and, seeing the deer but not realizing that it was the current center of the universe, broke off a piece of donut, tossed it to the animal and then walked on up the street without giving a second thought to anything or anyone. The deer dipped its head, gobbled up the offering and then bounded away into an alley behind the stores, and when it was gone, it was like a spell had been broken. Motorists resumed their commutes, and menudo went back to being devoured, and giant clouds of smoke pilloried the gem-blue sky imprisoned behind it.

I thought I'd bought myself a few hours reprieve from the Cat by shooing it into a food coma with that enormous bowl of menudo, so I was shocked when I felt it suddenly lurch after the disappearing deer. I staggered forward a couple of steps and clutched my stomach as shooting currents of pain lanced through my guts. The guys around the food truck put their spoons down and watched as I doubled over, struggling to catch my breath. But after a few seconds, it began to subside, and just when I thought I was in the clear and started to straighten up, the Cat pounced again, and I was driven down to the sidewalk on my hands and knees. I started retching as my stomach sparkled with dazzling facets of pain, and I was impressed that I had the presence of mind to trace the random whorls of concrete and ash with my eyes as I pulled madly at the strands of saliva hanging off my lip. I was incredibly embarrassed by the noises coming out of me, but there was nothing I could do about it except try not to laugh when I caught a glimpse of my menu translator dump his bowl into the garbage and make the sign of the cross over himself.

When I finally threw up it came in torrents, three or four massive purges and then nothing but the sound of my blood swimming through my ears. After it was over, I slowly made my way to my feet, smiled meekly at anyone who was still in the vicinity and got in my car.

When I finally made it into work I staggered past Deedee's desk and collapsed on the couch in my office. I was still having trouble catching my breath, and there was something trying to claw its way out of my stomach, so when Deedee came in and asked me if everything was okay, it was all I could do to groan at her.

She lit a cigarette and sat on the windowsill. "Pull your knees to your chest."

I assumed the fetal position without hesitation. Becoming ball-like seemed as good a strategy as any, but after a minute or so, I still wasn't feeling any better. "What's this supposed to do?"

"It pushes the gas out. It was my mom's cure for everything. She had thousands of ways to make us fart."

"Did it work?"

She smiled. "I'm still standing here, aren't I?"

I laughed, and a new inkblot of agony flashed in front of my eyes.

"Stop making me laugh," I begged.

"Wait a minute," she tapped her cigarette out the window, and the ash fell and gently mingled with the ash that was still coming down outside, "does it hurt on the left side or the right side? Because if it's the right side it could be appendicitis."

"What if it's the left side?" I clutched at my stomach, and it felt like I was holding my guts in, like if I moved my hands, they'd come shooting out of my mouth, nose, ass and ears, all at once.

"The left side?" She faked a horrified expression, "If it hurts on the left side, it means you're...you're..." her voice became a cursed whisper, "...*bi*."

I moaned, and a little fart broke loose. We both started cackling. "You're a medical professional. You're not supposed to laugh at pain."

"What else do I have?" she grinned.

I told her about my morning, eating the bowl of menudo at the roach coach and then the Cat going after the deer. She nodded like it all made perfect sense.

"I was just reading something online about that when you came in. Apparently the fires are driving animals out of the hills, and there've been sightings of critters all over the city. Coyotes drinking out of pools in Brentwood, hawks feasting from hummingbird feeders…some poor clerk at the Prada store in Beverly Hills almost got his face chewed off by a bear on his way to the dumpster. It's a jungle out there, Kitty."

My phone buzzed for what felt like the fiftieth time that morning. I ignored it, but it was clearly agitating Deedee.

"Who the hell keeps texting you?"

"Speaking of wild animals," I said, sitting up and fumbling for the cloud remote that was sitting six inches away on the coffee table. It felt like a million miles. "It's Lydia's mom. She won't stop calling and texting. I've been trying to ignore her," I explained without going into all the details, "but she won't take benign indifference for an answer."

I finally got the remote and dialed up an old Mikey Dread album. The song, *SWALK,* came overflowing out of the cloud, all bubbly and spacious, and I closed my eyes as the bass went to work on my nerves. It didn't last long, though, because a few seconds later, the phone on Deedee's desk started ringing, and after three or four bursts of it, I opened my eyes and looked at her.

"Far be it from me to tell you how to do your job, but…are you going to do your job?"

"Do I have to?" She smiled and batted her lashes, which I just noticed for the first time were as white as the rest of her.

"It'd be nice," I said, giving her my phoniest smile.

"Fii-iine," she fake whined and then pitched the cigarette out the window.

"You shouldn't do that, Deedee."

"You worried I'm going to start a fire?"

Nothing got by Deedee. "Fair point," I said, closing my eyes again as she went to grab the phone. I was almost asleep when I heard her voice suddenly brighten.

"It's nice to meet you, too. I can't believe it's taken this long." My eyes clicked open as I waited for her to speak again. "Yes, he's here. Working away as usual. Always working." God I loved Deedee. "Hold on one second…Mm-hmm, I hope to meet you one day soon, too. You betcha…Okay, buh-bye." I heard her put the phone down as I struggled to sit up.

"Oh, God," Deedee said when she walked in and saw me. "You look terrible again. A new kind of terrible this time. More complete."

"Is that Martha?" I whispered to her.

"No, and you don't have to whisper. It's your wife. We were just saying how weird it is that we've never met." She smirked. "Are you hiding me from her?" She went back to her place in front of the window, and, backlit by the flickering lines of ash falling behind her, she looked like a TV channel that wasn't coming in clearly.

"Don't joke," I tried to sound uptight, but I didn't really have the energy to muster any kind of authentic indignation, and the words kind of just died as they came off my lips. "What did she want?"

"I don't know," she lit another cigarette and smiled. "Why don't you ask her? She's on hold."

I glanced at the phone on my desk and then back at Deedee. The optimism I'd woken with was leaving my body, calamity forcing it out of me in a great migration of ruffled feathers, matted fur and a skin-and-bones appetite that was second to none. I shooed Deedee outside, closed the door and sat at my desk. I gingerly picked up the receiver with just my thumb and forefinger, being extra careful with it, as though it were a loaded gun, and placed it snugly against the side of my head.

"Hello?"

The call with Lydia was quick and to the point. She gave me the address of a marriage counselor in Beverly Hills and told me I should be there in 45 minutes if I wanted to try to "save this thing." I tore out of the office, got in my car and sped the whole way to a medical high rise on Rexford, where, in the elevator on my way up to the 17th floor, I was crowded in with half a dozen women, all in various states of recovery from different types of plastic surgery. One had a heavily bandaged nose with thick, plum-colored bruising rimming her eyes and another was gently pressing on her swollen lips, as if to remind herself again and again that they were a part of her body. We were all careful to avoid one another's eyes, not out of any sense of embarrassment, but what I hoped was a mutual respect for self-improvement, and when I did accidentally lock gazes with one of them, a middle-aged housewife type with her ears pinned back, she gave me a little smile and a shrug as if to say, *We do what we can.* When we hit the 15th floor, they got off en masse and started meandering to the oasis of rhinoplasty that awaited them at the end of the hall.

The therapist's waiting room was empty and dark, but it was cozy, with accountants' lamps and an assortment of well-read magazines spanning back a decade or more fanned out on the end table next to the couch. I sat and started to peruse an article in *Details* about how Splenda was going to be the next big thing when a tall, skinny, bald man with oval glasses and blue corduroy pants poked his head in, and with a smile that was too big for his face, invited me to "come on back."

Lydia was already there waiting for me and Dr. Mark started in right away by acknowledging that this wasn't the way he usually liked to start seeing couples. He'd already been seeing Lydia for about a month and wanted to try something new with us, something, he said, lots of "his couples" were benefiting from. He didn't want me to feel ambushed, though, he said, and his voice had that mental health professional lightness that made me want to yell at him to speak up, but I said, "I don't feel ambushed. I feel fine."

But I actually did feel a little ambushed, and I could already feel the Cat, energized by its hearty breakfast, pacing the length of my rib cage and pawing the warm wet ground of my guts.

"Lydia has something she wants to tell you, and we both decided it would be best if she did it here in this safe space."

Lydia sniffed the air and wrinkled her face. "You smell like throw up, Duncan. Have you been drinking?"

I shot a look at Dr. Mark. "Is that it? Is that what she wanted to tell me?"

My eyes slid past him to his bookshelves, where a tribunal of foreboding tomes promised to diagnose any malfunction, real, or, preferably, imagined. I wondered if any of them had anything to say about weaponized spirit animals, and I laughed, just a chuckle, but it was enough to make Lydia "tsk" and turn to Dr. Mark.

"See, I told you this wouldn't work. I told you he wouldn't take it seriously."

"Sorry," I said, aiming my gaze at the doctor, but clearly addressing Lydia, "I missed the part where I became an irredeemable piece of shit. Can we…"

"Now, now," the Q-Tip-shaped medical professional held up his hands, "this process isn't about blame. We're not here so anyone can get retribution. This is a place for healing…"

I checked out after that as he rambled on and on. He said some more stuff about "safe spaces" and then about "centering ourselves," and I was about to ask him for the key to the bathroom, where I had visions of flushing myself down the toilet or scarfing down a urinal cake, any easy way out of this nightmare, when he said something that shifted my attention back front and center.

"Did you say 'Ecstasy'?"

He smiled and folded his immense hands on his lap. He knew he had me now.

"Yes," he went on. "In a minute, if you're willing, I'm going to give you each 120mg of MDMA. We'll talk for a little while, and after the medicine starts working," I suppressed a smile when he said 'medicine', "we'll do some intimacy exercises, and then," he looked at Lydia, "I think Lydia made a reservation for you at a hotel nearby where you two will spend some time alone. Does that sound good to you, Duncan?"

We each got a can of La Croix and a hit of Ecstasy. To cut the tension in the room, I made a little joke about insurance reimbursements, but no one laughed. Dr. Mark's gaze felt sticky on my skin as I tried to figure out a comfortable way to sit on his postmodern loveseat.

"Why don't you go over and join Duncan, Lydia."

Wordlessly, she got up and plunked herself down in the narrow space next to me. Her face made a grimace as she landed in the uncomfortable groove.

"We have the matching couch at home," I told Dr. Mark, and then turning to Lydia, I said, "You should try sleeping on it sometime."

Lydia looked away from me, but Dr. Mark, not one to let a passive aggressive remark go by unacknowledged, said to me, "Is that how you want to start, Duncan?"

"I don't know," I picked at an imaginary thread off the arm of the sofa. "How does one usually start?"

"How do you want to start?" He turned the question back on me as a million possible starting points materialized in my head, a tangled mess of memories and feelings I knew somehow added up to the truth, each as good a place as any to begin, but the problem was that nothing was clear anymore, and whenever I tried to imagine particular moments from my childhood, or even things that happened just a couple of months ago, it all became a blur. I had no doubt the Cat was somehow responsible. Even now, I could smell its stinking breath and see with perfect clarity the nauseating smear of blood around its snout. After that, it didn't feel like there was a lot of room for anything else up there.

"I don't know," I finally said after a long pause. "All I know is, I don't want to start at the beginning."

"Well, now," he sat forward and leaned his head to the side, "that's very interesting. Its own starting point in a way."

Lydia sighed in a way where I couldn't tell if she wanted to be there or not, and I was about to remind her whose idea this was but stopped myself. I wanted this to work. I needed this to work, and Dr. Mark's plan was the only one I had at the moment, and it seemed as good as any.

"When I was a kid…" I began carefully, like I was trying to remember the directions to some hidden place, but nothing materialized. I couldn't think of a thing that felt worth talking about and I started to worry that it was because there was nothing there, that it had been erased somehow, replaced by a yawning pit of need no amount of love or fear or any of the other pressure points I'd come to think of as interchangeable could ever hope to fill.

"Are you trying to remember something?" the doctor asked, trying to move this along.

I nodded as my eyes began to fill with tears. I wanted to speak, to say something that would make a difference, but I was stuck, hung up on the fear that whatever I would say would expose me as a fraud to Lydia, and maybe worse, to the Cat.

"What?" he asked in the softest of voices, barely a breath really, just a warmth that spread across my chest, a feeling that reminded me of dread but without the tightness.

"Anything," I said, hoping that one of them would help me by feeding me the next line or telling me what I needed to do to get out of this. Dr. Mark had a plan, which I was grateful for, but I understood that it might be too late for that. I'd spread myself awfully thin, I could see that now, expected too much from too many people without ever once thinking about what kind of payment plans existed to pay off debts of the mortal persuasion.

I felt a tickle on my arm and when I looked down to see if I was imagining it or not, Lydia was holding a tissue that she was trying to get me to take.

"Thanks." I took it and pressed it to my eyes, unaware that I'd started crying.

"How about this for a starting point," Dr. Mark said, sitting back in his chair. "Why do you think it is we're here today, Duncan?"

Out of the corner of my eye, I saw Lydia look up from the floor to stare at me. If she was looking for some sort of pitch perfect mea culpa performance, I'd do my best to give it to her.

"We're here because I told my colleagues at work that I was attacked by a mountain lion, even though I wasn't."

"I see," he said and then jotted something down in his notebook as though phantom animal maulings were a dime a dozen in his practice. "But that didn't happen, did it? Who did that happen to?"

"Martha."

"Okay," he scratched on. "And who is Martha?"

"My mother-in-law."

"Or…"

I cocked my head, not understanding what he was after.

"Your mother-in-law, or…"

"Oh," I said, catching on. "Lydia's mother."

"Riiight," he replied, elongating the word so it felt like I was getting a big treat for performing an extra special trick. "And in taking on one of the central traumas of Lydia's life, would you say you were trying, at least subconsciously, to alleviate some of the pain it's caused in her life?"

I searched Lydia's face for clues. If this was what she wanted to hear me say, then I was only too happy to comply. Neither one of them needed to know the truth. We were so far past that by this point it wasn't even funny.

"Yes," I said, "that sounds right. I was trying to empathize, but I guess I got carried away."

Dr. Mark's face lit up like a pinball machine. "I commend you for that, Duncan. I really do. On the one hand, that's incredibly generous of you. But on the other hand, can you also see how it might be painful for Lydia to find out from others that you did this without talking to her first? Without explaining your motivations? Can you understand how she might see it as you co-opting her grief to gain sympathy at work? Do you see how that might be painful for her? And if you can see that," his voice rose as he invited me to make a mysterious lover's leap with him, "can you understand why Lydia might want to do something to hurt you back? Something impulsive but something very very hurtful."

Not seeing what other choice I had, I nodded.

"Good," he smiled widely and looked at Lydia. "Lydia…"

Lydia smiled back at him as she took my hands in hers. She shifted in her seat so she was facing me, and she simply stared at me with the gentlest expression on her face, and for a moment I watched as the rest of the world broke away, leaving just the few deep breaths lingering between us.

"Duncan," she said, bringing the world back to life with her voice, "I want you to know that I slept with your boss. I slept with Dutch. I did it because I was mad at you and because I know how much you hate him and how bad it would make you feel. I'm sorry I did it, but I also feel…"

I lost the rest of what she said as faces came up to me out of the darkness of thought, stories thick on their lips, with smells, sounds and colors to match. The only problem was, I didn't recognize a single one of them and their stories, as wonderful and lewd and moving as they were, had nothing to do with me. Either I was suddenly living someone else's life, or...

But wait, I thought, maybe they were mine after all. I suddenly remembered running high up in the mountains through a scarlet dusk, crossing the ridgeline into snow and tall pines and finding a family of dead rabbits hidden behind a rock, a mother and two babies, a few dots of frozen blood matted on their fur as the only evidence of the violence that had visited them. I didn't remember killing them, but I knew I had, just as I knew I'd almost been killed by the speeding metal thing as I crossed the road on my way up there. I remembered the screech of an owl as the moon elbowed its way through a dense shroud of clouds, I remembered that the sky was imprinted with ancient pictures, and most of all, I remembered everywhere the smell of meat. Lydia hadn't stopped looking at me and I wanted to know if she saw in my eyes that it wasn't me anymore, that what she was staring at was all hunger and need; survival, in other words, the last dregs of my very soul.

"You're not saying anything." She sounded disappointed as she let my hands go. "And when I look in your eyes, Duncan..." My heart skipped a beat. Maybe she knew. "When I look in your eyes, I feel like you're not really feeling anything, either. Or maybe it's that you're trying to figure out what you're supposed to be feeling? Is that it? If so, that's almost worse," she said, half to herself and half to me.

Either way, I supposed Dr. Mark took my lack of a response as shock or a complete shutdown of the central nervous system, because he stood up and did an overdramatic stretch, a yoga pose I imagined was called Awkward Silence and then patted his tummy. "This might be a good time for a bathroom break," he suggested, and Lydia took the interruption as an opportunity to jump up and leave the room.

I could tell we were in a time-out after she left because Dr. Mark opened the window blinds and stood there quietly, looking out over the slate gray of it all. "It's so apocalyptic out there."

"It's so apocalyptic in here," I shot back and when he snorted a laugh, I felt an unreasonable sense of accomplishment.

"Now, now," he said calmly, as though he had five more appointments just like this one still to get through, "you guys are doing great." And then, in an attempt to sniff out the trail of small talk I'd just desecrated, he said, "Have you heard about all the wild animals people have been seeing everywhere? Crazy, isn't it?"

It was the perfect opportunity to tell him about the Cat, to confess everything, but he looked so at peace with himself, so proud with how this was all going, that I didn't want to disappoint him. Besides, I didn't see what difference telling him would make; the animals had the run of the city and now that they'd tasted the good life, how the hell would we ever convince them to go back to eating roadkill and sleeping in dirt?

"Absolutely batshit," I agreed with him out of the goodness of my heart.

When Lydia came back into the office, I could tell the Ecstasy was working its magic. She was practically vibrating as she tried to walk a straight line to the couch, and her eyes were firing buckshot glances around the room, trying in vain to focus on a single object at a time. She smiled as she plunked down in my lap, threw her arms around my neck, and leaned all the way back so her head was almost touching the carpet, making herself into an almost perfectly straight line, a human 'you are here' arrow on a map of what we used to be. She used my neck for leverage to pull herself back up, and when we were face to face, she started smothering me in kisses, quick pecks all over my face and on my lips, the most wonderful degradations given the state of things, but I loved them nonetheless. Lydia had finally dropped her bomb, we both ate Ecstasy, and then in a few minutes we'd be on our way to the Regency to screw all night. Then, in a few days, I'd give her the ring and it would be done. An exorcism for the ages and all would be holy again. Foolproof.

It was when I said "Foolproof" out loud that I realized how high I was.

We laughed our way out of the office and down to the street, our arms slung around one another in a sloppy half-embrace, merrily staggering along like we were recently-separated conjoined twins who hadn't yet learned how to move without the other. The normally tourist-thronged streets of Beverly Hills were eerily deserted because of the fires, the colorful windows in the designer boutiques no match for the breezy vandalism of ash that piled up in morbid clumps in front of Prada and Dior, so that it looked like the fancy boutiques were in the process of converting their spaces into high-end crematoriums.

On our way to the hotel, we stopped at a Starbucks, and that's where it all fell apart. At the front of the line Lydia gave the barista her order and when she was asked for her name, instead of giving it to him, she turned to face me, and I could see that she was all jumpy and nervous, kind of strung-out seeming, but with a subtle mean streak that I'd become accustomed to her snapping at me as though it were a wet towel and our life together a high school locker room.

"I'm not going to the hotel with you, Duncan. I…I just can't. I need some time away. To think. After I sober up, I'm going home to pack my stuff. I'd appreciate it if you waited until later tonight to come back."

"But why?" I wanted to know. I thought we'd hit our stride at Dr. Mark's and this part was supposed to be the reward after all the hard stuff.

"It doesn't feel right, and I need some time to figure out why that is." She sounded kind of sad when she said it, but she was resolute. I knew there would be no swaying her.

"Where are you going? To Dutch's?"

Luckily, she didn't take the bait.

"No," she said, paying for her coffee. "He's as despicable as you said he was. I think I'm going to take my friend up on her offer to use her place in the desert. I could really go for a lot of wide-openness right now." She smiled and I could see that in her mind she was already a million miles away. "The desert makes me feel sad. Did I ever tell you that? But something about all those miles and miles of nothing sounds good to me right now. No distractions."

"I feel so betrayed," I tried to say without whining, but I'm sure it sounded pitiful.

"I told you already, Dutch was…"

"I'm not talking about Dutch!" I snapped at her.

"Then what?" she asked, and I saw how tired my griping was making her, how all she wanted was an explanation. But I didn't have one, not one that was worthy of the look she was giving me out of that foxhole of a face of hers anyway. She deserved everything, but a single word was all she was looking for, a gesture, even something symbolic would suffice, and as I struggled through the waist-high fogginess of the drugs and the magnificent blue-and-red echoes of a passing police car, I tried to give it to her. I willed myself to say something, anything, and maybe I was on the verge of that when, out of nowhere, the Cat waltzed in, laid itself down, and slowly started licking its paws. I watched, transfixed, as, one by one, it dragged its long, pink tongue up and down the length of each claw, not so much a veiled threat as it was the perfect excuse, and whatever the word was I was about to give her was gone.

"Oh, Duncan," she sighed when she realized I had nothing to say and that it was truly over. She laid a hand on my shoulder which I instantly shrugged off.

I left not long after she did and drove around in circles for a while, watching the ash gray out the otherwise blue sky. When the phone rang I wasn't surprised in the slightest to see Dutch's name pop up. The timing was perfect. It was like he had a sixth sense for when it was time to hop on the top of a dog-pile.

"Hello," I tried to make my voice sound neutral, like he wasn't catching me at a bad time.

The line was silent for a good ten seconds, for effect I thought, and then he finally spoke, saying just my name which he uttered reluctantly as though it were a safe word he was ashamed of having to conjure. No, "Hello." No, "How are you?" The guy had slept with my wife and he still had no problem giving me shit. Keeping my job was more important than it had ever been, though. What if I could figure out how to get rid of the Cat and Lydia decided she wanted to come back to me? I had to have my job going for me, at the very least. *Behave,* I thought.

"Duncan," his voice was flat and the dullness was what made it sound so threatening and I felt the Cat give a snarl. "I need you to give me a reason to keep you on, because I've gotta tell you, my guy, I am running out of patience. No one has any idea what you're even working on anymore. You're like a ghost. And an unproductive one at that. Duncan, if you can't…"

"Les is sleeping with Deedee." I said it before I even realized what I was doing, a fight-or-flight kind of reaction, I rationalized to myself in the moment. But of course, I knew that was bullshit, because the regret that instantly flooded through me had nothing to do with a survival instinct. It was just another excuse; no better and no worse than the last one.

There was no sound from the other end of the line, and I imagined Dutch sitting at his desk, clear lines of drool already falling from his grinning maw, and I knew that whatever insatiable animal that lived within him was up on its hind legs, its head angled towards the thinness of the night air so that nothing was in the way between its celebratory ululations and the moon.

"That's so sick," he said, with what I imagined to be the world's shit-eatingest grin suffocating his face.

"He's not sick!" I shouted without thinking. "Why is it so hard to believe he just wants a little happiness? Why does it have to be so embarrassing to admit you want to feel better?" My hands were wrapped tight around the wheel, and I was almost out of breath from yelling so loudly.

"Don't you fucking lecture me! Don't anything me for that matter." Then a pause. "This is good, though, D. Really great work. I knew I could count on you."

I felt like I was going to puke just like I had at the lunch wagon, only this was different. It wasn't so much that I felt like puking as much as I felt like I needed to empty myself of myself, that I wanted everything out of me, a purge to end all purges, and before I had a second to think better of it, I had my index and middle fingers down my throat, and I was pushing them, down, down, down, as far as they would go. Tears ran down my cheeks and I was making these terrible retching sounds, dying noises, and somewhere in the background of it all I heard Dutch ask me if I needed him to call "nine-uno-uno" and that just made me push harder, made me want to be that much emptier.

I jammed a third finger in there and pushed some more until I started seeing spots and I kept on rooting around in my throat, willing myself to go further; I was hellbent on scooping every bit of myself out, every last organ, every last blood vessel, every last molecule. I wanted it all out and once I was empty, I thought to myself, ignoring the sporadic spurts of vomit that were burbling up and out of me, splattering my shirt and pants and even the dashboard of my car, once all this was out of me, including the Cat, and I was as hollow as a person could be, then maybe I could start filling myself up again with all of the good things in life my emptiness had made room for.

# CHAPTER 24

Lydia had done an incredibly thorough job of eliminating all traces of her ever having lived with me, scrubbing all evidence of her existence from the apartment by removing all of her things so completely that I spent the next two or three days wandering around in a kind of daze, trying to reorient myself by remembering which of her clothes used to hang in that space on the left side of the closet, and had it been her deodorant or a lotion that used to sit on the bathroom counter where there was now just a fading, sticky circle? Playing detective, I examined every inch of the place for clues, wiping my finger along bookcases, kitchen cabinets, and even in the refrigerator, where I used to love drinking off the rest of the half-drunk cans of Diet Coke she put away, optimistic that she'd return to them but knowing she never would. It was okay, though, because I loved finishing them, tasting the sticky sweetness where her lips had been, using my tongue to lick off the drops she sometimes left.

The radio in the apartment was tuned to one of those 24-hour-a-day AM news stations that repeated the same headlines every 15 minutes (sports and weather on the fives and fifteens). Today's news was all about the fires that were still blazing all around Los Angeles, how they were getting closer by the minute. The locations of evacuation centers and acreage burned were reported with icy, newsman efficiency, the numbers and locations a blur of information that didn't seem to have any correlation to real life.

A knock at the door jarred me out of my reverie and I leapt to answer it. I wasn't sure what the protocols were when it came to exes returning to the scene of the crime, if there was a state of grace or statute of limitations about knocking or whether they could just come right in, but I wasn't going to take a chance on missing her. The Cat, which was with me all the time now, growled at the door and I muttered a *Go fuck yourself* under my breath as I wrenched it open. Ignoring real people, which is what I was doing to Deedee, Les, Dutch and Martha was hard enough; ignoring imaginary friends was a 16th-degree Masonry level of negligence that I hadn't yet mastered, but one I'd have to get used to if things didn't soon change.

There was nothing in the hallway but a thin plume of minty smoke I recognized as belonging to my neighbor. I was about to close the door, when I noticed a small white jewelry box with a red ribbon tied around it sitting on the floor in front of my apartment.

"Thank you," I hollered into the void, as if the ring were a gift from the universe and not a $40,000 impulse buy. Both were omens, but only one portended good fortune, while the other foretold a long life of terrible decision-making and an over-abundance of comeuppance; not a curse, just another way that life could go. I grabbed the box and heard a muffled *You're welcome* as I closed the door, throwing the ring on the little table where we put the mail and our keys, all the things that were so easy to lose.

I looked at the box, but felt no desire to open it. I liked it the way it was, the promises it still held, the cute little ribbon I imagined my neighbor stealing out of the hair of a small child. I had the box in my hand when the radio did its *bong-bong-bong* thing, signifying not only that it was the top of the hour, but also a friendly reminder that you were indeed still listening to AM radio and, while it was cute to be quaint and bespoke and all that, the information you were getting wasn't really all that useful as news as much as it was a coping mechanism as you eased yourself into the lukewarm jetstream of chronic loneliness. The DJ, a man I pictured wearing a three-piece suit, black horn-rimmed glasses, with a well-worn copy of *Atlas Shrugged* tucked into his breast pocket so he'd have something to read later when he took his shit during weather and sports (shitting on the fives and fifteens!), began reporting, not about the fire, but about something else that froze me and the Cat where we stood.

It seemed that along with the coyotes and deer and other little critters that had migrated down out of the hills for safer surroundings, a mountain lion was spotted and tracked to the crawl space under a house in the north San Fernando Valley, in a little planned community called Glad Glenns to be exact, which I knew all too well, having grown up in that particularly scorching-hot shit hole. I barely thought about it anymore, and when people used to ask me where I grew up, I would either lie and say "in the country" or tell them the name of the place and then point out it was the stupidest development in the country. The developers accidentally spelled Glen with two n's instead of one (the name, not the place), which for some reason always conjured for me the image of a masturbating speedboat salesman, a thick coat of zinc oxide plied on his nose.

After my mom died, I inherited the house, and after a year of sitting on it, the only attention I'd given it was to have the place tented and sprayed for termites. I hadn't even taken the time yet to go and clean out her things. It would be convenient to blame it on heartbreak, that it hurt too much to go back, but the truth was, I was just lazy. At some point, I knew I'd have to get my shit together, fix it up and put it on the market, but the idea made me so tired that I kept putting it off until I simply forgot that I owned it. Deedee filed away the deed and keys for me months ago, and now, given this latest bit of news, it seemed I might have to break a thousand promises I'd made to my teenage self about never going back.

Speaking of which, I looked around quickly for the Cat, half expecting it to already be exploding down the freeway toward the Valley, but when I turned around it was still there, sitting as calmly as a house cat waiting for its dinner to be spooned into its bowl, its tail wrapped loosely around its own legs, and I sensed that for the first time, I was perfectly safe in its presence. Without any fear, I walked right up to it, closer than I'd ever been before, so close I could feel its hot breath scorch the hairs on my arm and smell the earthy dampness of its gamey fur. I looked it dead in the eyes, and we sat like that for what felt like hours, enthralled by the calm comfort we found in one another's presence, an ultimatum of sorts that had no real consequences. The Cat's eyes flicked back and forth across my face, trying to read me for a change, and I realized that it didn't know any better than I did what this piece of news meant. For the first time it was as vulnerable as I was.

The phone rang and I jumped, putting my hand to my chest. It was Martha, and I quickly answered, assuming she'd just heard the same story as me and wanted to talk about it. For the first time in many weeks I was glad to hear from her, and I hoped that she already had a plan in the offing, some brilliant battle tactic or strategy that I could just plug into, because I was fresh out of ideas.

"Martha, did you just hear…" Before I could get the rest of the sentence out, though, a scream tore through the phone. "Martha…" I ventured again, this time getting back a more muffled version of a scream along with the most horrible scratching and tearing noises I'd ever heard, flesh and bone sounds, body parts moving in directions that nature had not intended them to move, and then a new kind of scream burrowed its way into the earpiece, one I couldn't quite place, one that I wasn't even sure was human. Whatever the hell was happening over there, the one thing I knew for sure was that something or someone was dying. "Martha!" I shouted into the phone again, and it felt as useless as shouting into a deep hole. "Martha! What's going on? Are you okay?"

Finally, a voice came on, garbled and frantic, and it took a full five seconds to realize it was Mrs. Kim.

"Duncan!" She shouted my name, while in the background, the snarling changed pitch, going from frantic to a steady ripping, a rhythm amidst the chaos.

"What is it? What's happening over there?"

"Martha! You come now! Martha..." She was crying, but there was also a world-weariness to her voice, a sadness we shared like it was the last cigarette in the pack.

"Mrs. Kim, do you need me to call the police?" And then a thought crossed my mind. "Is it Lydia? Is Lydia there?" The phone disconnected before she answered me, and without hesitating, I grabbed my keys and ran down to my car.

I drove like crazy over to Koreatown, weaving in and out of traffic as I imagined what the hell might be going on over there, and although I practically begged myself to stay calm, feeding myself the bullshit line that there was probably a perfectly logical explanation for the screaming and the ripping sounds, the sounds I was sure no human could make, my animal brain knew better.

The palm trees along Wilshire weren't doing anything to help my anxiety either. The wind was shaking them into a swaying frenzy and every once in a while, a long branch plunged to the ground landing with a resounding crack, like someone had fired a cannon somewhere far behind me, and any moment, the ball was going to catch up with me, and I would be blown to smithereens.

At Martha's building I double-parked and took the stairs up two at a time, so that I was huffing and puffing when I finally threw open the door to the sixth floor. I ran down to the end of the hall, and when I got to the door of the apartment, I stopped suddenly. It was open a crack, so much more menacing than if it had been open all the way, and when I put my ear up close there wasn't a sound to be heard, including the television that I liked to think of as Mrs. Kim's life support machine.

There wasn't enough space to peer in, and for a long moment I was back to that first Friday night to pick up Lydia. If I called out her name, I had no doubt I'd hear her voice come back to me, begging me to come inside, to help her. And when I did, I'd be back in that bathroom with Martha, our hands joined together like some vertebrae-less sea creature just under the milky surface of the water, and this time, when Lydia went to find Mrs. Kim and Martha whispered her terrible secret about the mountain lion that lived inside her that sometimes wanted to tear her daughter to shreds because her love for her was so real and had nowhere else to go, I'd surprise us both by introducing her to the Cat.

"Mrs. Kim? Martha? Lydia?" I was barely whispering, barely breathing, because, truthfully, I didn't want anyone to hear me. What I wanted more than anything was for there to be no answer, so I could run back home and climb under the covers of my big waterbed and ride the half-assed waves down into a sleep for the ages; nothing less than three solid days of dreamless slumber would suffice.

I was about to turn when I heard a shrunken voice whisper my name from inside. "Duncan? Duncan?" It was Mrs. Kim.

Steeling myself, I pushed the door open slowly. At first, nothing seemed amiss; the apartment was eerily silent, and nothing moved. The air felt heavy and dense, and I searched through the ether for the hum of the fridge or the low static from the transistor radio Martha always kept tuned to the college classical station, any sign of life. But there was nothing. I was afraid to move, afraid that if I took a step or even turned my head too far one way or the other, the thing hiding in the shadows would suddenly pounce, and I'd disappear, too, and not just my body, but my sounds as well, my scent, even the memory of me. But then I heard my name again, and when I spun around, there was Mrs. Kim sitting on the couch. She had her surgical mask up and her hands were pulled into the deep pockets of her magenta puffer jacket, and I could tell from her eyes, the way they flicked from the end of the hall where Martha's room was, back to me, and then back down the hall again, that she was still seeing something that she would probably be seeing for the rest of her life. Slowly, she pulled one of the hands from her pocket and, unreeling a bony, yellowing finger, lifted her shaking arm and aimed it at the room at the end of the hall.

I didn't bother her with questions; whatever had happened was done. I understood that. Besides, I had the feeling that I didn't deserve her answers, that whatever was down the hall was something I was going to have to see for myself.

I started walking down the hall but stopped when I saw spots of something white on the ground. Feathers. It looked like someone had had a pillow fight, and the further I walked the more and more feathers I found, and then a few feet from the door to her room, I noticed that some of them were stained red. Here and there along the carpet I found more blood, not a ton, just dots and lines of it, as though someone had tried to spell something out in Gothic cursive, a sentence perhaps, a farewell note.

Holding my breath, I put my ear to the door and listened to the silence on the other side. I touched the doorknob but drew my fingers back reflexively when I felt something wet and sticky that I didn't have to look at to know what it was. More blood.

"Martha," I said as calmly as I could, "Martha, I'm coming in. Whatever it is, we can fix it. You know that, don't you? Whatever it is you've done..." I didn't quite know how to finish the thought, though, so I stopped myself and pushed the door open.

Someone had taken the tin foil and the newspaper off the window, and a gentle light was painted across the floor and ceiling of her room. Martha sat on the edge of her bed, her back towards me, staring out at the swirling storm of ash. Huge black clouds of toxic smoke still loomed in the distance, and it seemed for a stark moment that nothing would ever change again, that this was going to be how the world was from now on.

The trail of blood and feathers ended next to her, where pieces of Dr. Nuts were strewn about the bed, a queen-sized altar upon which the poor creature had been brutally sacrificed. A rank coppery smell suffused the room, and I stood next to her, trying my best to keep my distance from the pile of meat that had once been a keepsake from the best night of my life. Amidst the gore, I made out the bird's tiny feet, a wing and the pasty torso that had been plucked of its feathers so that the raised dots of gooseflesh underneath were visible. The rest was unrecognizable, a still-warm slick of flesh and bone, and I took a deep breath.

"Martha…" I laid a hand on her shoulder, and it was like touching stone. She was cold beneath the thin nightgown, and I might have mistook her for dead except for the subtle sway of her breath and the faintest of tremors that ran through her body, and it took a moment for her to respond, but when she finally did, slowly turning her head to me, I snatched my hand away when I saw her face. Smeared with blood, she wore an enormous smile, and protruding from her mouth, like a dog's plaything, was the bird's lifeless head.

"Lydia…Lydia…"

Martha kept moaning her daughter's name, and I started to believe those conjoined syllables were the only part of her that her cat hadn't yet completely obliterated. "Lydia…"

I was cleaning up the bedroom, changing the sheets and trying to scrub the blood off the carpet and the walls, while Mrs. Kim was in the bathroom giving Martha a bath. Mrs. Kim hummed as she washed Martha, and I tried to focus on the nameless melody rather than Lydia's name, which Martha kept repeating over and over.

I wasn't planning on going into the bathroom, but the Cat was back, and it wanted to see her, wanted to understand what it was that it had missed the first time. The bathroom was steamy and smelled of soaps and tinctures I couldn't place, a mixture of sweet and tangy scents that made me suddenly nostalgic for a homeland

I'd never laid eyes on. I walked in and stared down at Martha, who was sitting in the tub in exactly the same spot she'd been the first time I saw her. My breath became shaky as those smells entered me one at a time, and if I traced them back, as though they were pieces of thread, I understood they would return me to the beginning of time.

As I stared at Martha, I noticed that Mrs. Kim's song had become a river, slowly, patiently, gouging out epochal grooves into the mountainside where the Cat was sitting, and over it all, Lydia's name. Again and again...Lydia...like a holy point of reference, the first star in a new sky.

Martha reached for my hand, and we smiled at one another for what felt like generations of time. Soapy water pooled around her breasts and when she said "Lydia" again I joined her. It had never felt right before, wanting the same thing as another person, gauging the depths of my need against someone else's, but I was vanishing now, returning home, and there seemed to be little else to say.

I took a piece of paper and a pen from the kitchen drawer, sat at the table where I'd drunk so many cups of tea these past months, where I'd reminisced and conjured lives out of thin air, and wrote steadily. Mrs. Kim came by once to get a glass of water for Martha. She looked over my shoulder for a moment, but I didn't stop. She pulled her mask down to kiss my cheek, but I barely noticed; words were pouring out of me, plans, all the things I needed to make this right. When I was done, I folded the paper and stuffed it into an envelope I found in one of the kitchen drawers. I wrote Lydia's name on it and left it on the table, tilted up against the napkin holder.

It was after five by the time I got back in my car. I called the office, hoping I hadn't missed Deedee yet.

"Duncan Beldon's office," she said flatly. It took me a second to realize that it was my name she'd just said.

"Hi Deedee, glad I caught you before you left," I was speaking so quickly that I was feeling out of breath. "Can you do me a favor and leave the keys to my mother's house on my desk? You still know where they are, right?"

"Sure, but what for? Planning on having a rager? Do you need me to order you a couple of kegs and a waterproof ping-pong table?"

She giggled, utterly delighted with herself, and for the briefest of moments, I almost told her what I'd done. I wanted to come clean, tell her that I'd been a coward, that I was scared of losing Lydia forever and that by telling Dutch about her and Les, I was somehow saving the thing we might still have. Maybe she'd understand. If anyone would understand, it'd be her. But I didn't want to test it. One thing at a time.

"There's a mountain lion in my mom's old neighborhood. Maybe you heard about it? It's a refugee from the fires. Turns out it's pretty close to her place, actually. I'm going to catch it. For Martha." I changed lanes, narrowly missing some sort of hipster with huge, old-fashioned aviator goggles piloting an electric scooter.

"Kitty," she suddenly sounded worried, sober, "I don't think that's a good idea. Don't you think you've taken this too far?"

The guy on the scooter pulled next to me and shot me the middle finger. I nodded at him, perfectly at ease with his ire.

"Just a little bit further. I'm almost done."

"Well, Jesus Christ, if that isn't the most ominous thing anyone has ever said to me." I heard her swallow hard. "Do you think maybe you're having…"

"Delusions of grandeur?" I interjected.

"That's not what I was going to say. Not grandeur. I don't see much grandeur in this. I would have stopped at 'delusions'."

What she said made a lot of sense, but I was running out of time and there was still so much to do.

"Are you going to remember to leave the keys for me, Deedee?" I shot back a little impatiently.

There was a pause, and I could almost hear her thinking of ways to talk me out of this.

"Will you at least let me call my brother? He lives for this kind of a thing. The guy is a born accomplice. Also, he used to do something with animals. I can't remember what exactly."

I was glad of the offer, because I didn't really have an idea as to how I was going to do this on my own. "Won't he think this is weird?"

"No," she said, "that's the sad part. Not at all. He's the kind of guy where if you say to him, 'Dead body,' he'd automatically ask you, 'How deep?'"

"Fine. Have him meet me there tomorrow afternoon, okay? I need to get the place ready first."

"Okay. But for the record…"

"I know. I know. You don't think this is a good idea. So predictable, Deedee."

"I'd rather be predictable than mauled." I was about to hang up when she spoke again. "By the way, I didn't know you played poker."

"Huh?"

"Dutch called to make sure you were still planning on coming to the poker game at his house tomorrow night."

"Fuck!" I'd forgotten I agreed to that particularly horrifying rite of passage.

"Want me to cancel?" she asked, sounding like an assistant for the first time since I could remember.

"No, I have to go."

"You never cease to amaze me, Kitty."

I felt hot with shame thinking about how easily I'd given her up, how I'd sold her and Les down the river for nothing more than the ghost of a chance at happiness. I was pathetic.

"You too, Deedee. You too."

To my surprise, the old key still opened the front door. No one would have changed the locks, but it had been over a year since I'd stepped foot in the house. The unlocking astonished me nonetheless, almost as much as if my mother had been there waiting for me, her arms crossed in pretend annoyance that I'd kept her waiting, the beef stew long since gone cold.

I stepped into the front entryway, dusty and musty-smelling from disuse, and immediately heard my feet crunch something on the floor. When I bent down to get a closer look, I saw that it was dead bugs I was stepping on, thousands and thousands of silver-fish, termites, and God knows what else scattered everywhere. It was the aftermath of the exterminator.

I grabbed a broom and went from room to room in a daze, crunching and sweeping the brittle corpses of bugs, telling myself that it was autumn somewhere on the East Coast, and those were leaves I was walking on and not the petrified remains of everything that had once called this place home. Everything was as I remembered it. My mother had been a fastidious housekeeper in her time, but when it came to curating her life, she'd kept everything, preferring to live with her past rather than create a new life after I moved out, and then again, a couple of years later, after my father died. The banker's box with my dad's old work papers still sat right to his nightstand, and when I dug to the bottom, I found the dozen or so old dirty magazines I'd known so well as a kid. Even the seemingly random order in which they were stacked was the same, an order I'd religiously committed to memory early on, as though it were holy liturgy, afraid that if I put them back the wrong way the gods would be displeased, and my sex life would come to a wrathful and shameful end.

My head was spinning with the familiarity of it all, and I would have given anything for a moment of déjà vu, to feel a little time out of space, a little disorientation. But I just couldn't get there. Everything was so precisely the same, I found it impossible to locate the nostalgia or the sentimentality. I used to exist here, and now I existed here again. There was no déjà vu in a time machine. I checked in with the Cat to see how he was taking all this in, but instead of anxiously pacing, the way he so often did these days, I found him in his new landscape huddled under a rock, his eyes fluttering around half-mast.

I suddenly had an idea. I opened my closet, and, pushing back behind the stacks of board games and Dungeons and Dragons books, found my old bong, 'Bessie', that I'd made myself with some plastic tubing, a glue gun and that old soldering iron, my schoolboy fantasies of being an engineer disappearing in a single, stoned afternoon. I went online and ordered a gram of something called Purplish Cheesecake from a weed delivery service, because it sounded so decadent, and 45 minutes later, I was handing my bank card to a stoned 20-something co-ed who asked me as I clumsily entered my pin on her small credit card machine if people "actually lived out here."

"Not really," I said, offering her a half-smile and a ten-dollar tip for her troubles.

"Gee, thanks!" she said, the happiest drug dealer I'd ever met, skipping as she bounded down the driveway to her Vespa.

Back inside, I sat in my father's old La-Z-Boy and packed a bowl. I had never been allowed to sit in the chair when he was alive, and my ass slid comfortably into the divot his 30 years of inertia had carved into the cushion. I picked up an old Sharper Image catalog from the magazine holder next to the chair that said "Christmas Gifts for '84" on its cover. My father never let my mom throw it away because it advertised a $15,000 massage chair, and he thought that was the funniest thing in the world. Every now and then, he'd grab it and start waving it around, telling me all the things he'd do if he ever had 15 grand to play with. I flipped open the catalog and a handful of petrified silverfish slid on to my lap. Brushing them away, leafed through the pages until I found the chair. I looked at the price and laughed. In today's money, that would be around $35,000. If only he'd lived to see the day. Nothing, including grandkids, would have given him more pleasure than to see how 30 years of inflation had made the notion of the chair that much more ridiculous.

I took a giant rip off the bong and held the smoke until I felt the time space continuum start to tear apart and then held on after that. The chair was incredibly comfortable. Sensuously so. I used to always wonder what it was my dad — an English teacher with a dry wit and a terrible way with money — and I had in common, what I'd gotten from him. I searched for commonalities in sports, movies, even tried to read some of the dusty French literature he loved so much, but sitting in this chair, my ass perfectly filling in the crevices he left for me like an unexpected inheritance, I knew that this was it. Or maybe I was just already high. No, I was definitely high, there were no maybes about it. The room swum around me, and when I got up to check out the garage, which was where I was going to have Deedee's brother store the mountain lion, I forgot how to bend my knees for a minute and had to use the back of the chair to steady myself.

Other than more dead bugs, the garage wasn't in that bad of shape. I swept the flaky little carcasses out into the street and moved some boxes with my mom's things in them over to one side. A large oil stain revealed itself on the floor of the garage, and I circumambulated it as slowly as any worshipful penitent, searching for hidden messages and meanings. My stoned brain, acting as a kind of metastasizing life-coach, chided me that I'd been too picky when it came to cosmic interference, and as I circled the stain, my mind purring and warped, I first glimpsed what looked like the cover of the Eagles' *Hotel California* album cover, then, as I continued clockwise, the cover receded, and I saw the bathtub where I'd first seen Martha. And then, last, but not least, after I'd almost made a complete circle, I was looking at a perfect reproduction of Lydia's face. Her mouth was open a little bit; her expression, which struck me as simultaneously worried and judgmental, made me think she was trying to warn me of something and pissed off that I wasn't understanding her. It wasn't clear what story was being told here, but I had a feeling that if I went around counterclockwise, another universe of cryptic advice would reveal itself, and maybe that was the point, that you only got to go around once.

My mouth was dry, so I stood at the sink and drank three glasses of water without pausing, some vague worry about overdosing on electrolytes lurking at the back of my head like a gargoyle just waking up from a hundred-year sleep in stone. Ignoring my pulsating bladder, I stretched myself out on the couch and tried counting sheep, but the Cat kept chasing them all over the bucolic little pasture I'd imagined, and when I finally fell asleep, it had caught one of the somnambulant little fuckers and was tearing its guts out with relish, making sure we made eye contact while its teeth tore through the soft flesh.

I awoke some time later to the strange sound of someone spitting over and over again and debated whether or not to keep my eyes shut and let the next dream come and ferry me away from whatever waking horror was impinging on me or if I'd be better served by grabbing the bull by the horns and raw-dogging my way back into real life. In true mediocre fashion, I decided the safest bet was to split the difference and lifted one eye to see a tall, lanky man with a mullet and a Kid Rock t-shirt sitting on my father's chair spitting tobacco into the old Steve Garvey glass I got from my neighborhood Chevron in 1981, the year the Dodgers won the World Series. The well-groomed, reliable Garvey was my favorite of the crew, and I thought it ironic that this phantasmal carnie had chosen Mr. Clean to relieve himself into instead of, say, Ron Cey, who, with his bushy mustache and bow-legged batting stance, stood out to me, even as a child, as the personification of stranger danger.

"There he is," the lanky man said cheerfully, as consciousness had its ungentlemanly way with me.

I sat up, and while the world took a second to catch up to my vertical orientation, recalled not-too-fondly that I was still high as fuck. This was Deedee's brother.

"You're Pete," I pointed at him, as proud of myself as if I'd just won the Nobel Prize for physics.

He laughed and nodded at the bong. "Bessie, huh? Mine was named Helen Reddy. If anyone coughed after taking a rip we'd start singing I Am Woman." His subsequent smile showed a meteor storm of mismatched teeth and receding gumlines.

I laughed. "That's really funny."

"Life's funny," he said without even a skidmark of irony, and I had a feeling that I already liked him.

I held the bong out toward him. "Want a hit?"

He held up both his hands and nodded in polite refusal. "No thanks. Never while I'm working. Besides, I just got out of rehab. I'd like to give it more than a few days to see if it'll take this time."

"What were you in there for?" I knew it was a personal question, but my inhibitions hadn't fully returned to me, and besides, I was deeply curious.

"Nitrous oxide," he said matter of factly. "Doesn't seem like you'd need to go to rehab for a thing like that, right? But let me tell you, I've done heroin, oxy's, crack, shoebangers, doopsy-doos, devil's blowjob…you name it, but nitrous is my queen. I can't even look at a balloon without getting wet." I thought of all those drugs laid out end-to-end at a Soup Plantation-type restaurant with Pete going from station to station, filling up his plate and finishing it off with a whippet on top, like a cherry on the sundae of bad decisions. "You should definitely take another hit, though. I ordered a pizza. Should be here in about ten minutes or so."

"That is literally the nicest thing anyone has ever done for me," I told him, trying not to tear up.

He winked at me. "I got you, hoss. Deedee told me to take good care of you, and that's what I'm going to do. I draw the line at kinky shit, but anything right up to that line is fair play in my book."

"Your sister is quite the woman."

He put down the Steve Garvey glass and took his hat off, as though someone had just mentioned the passing of JFK. "That little lady has saved my life more times than I've deserved to be saved. I'd do anything for my little sister." He looked me square in the eye and said solemnly, "And she'd do anything for you."

"I know," I said, feeling sick to my stomach with the memory of what I'd done to her.

"Anyway," he said, returning his hat to his head. "Deedee tells me I'm here to catch a big cat. Is that right? I've got a cage in my van, bait, traps...I've never done anything quite like this before, but I'm excited to try. I like trying new things."

"Really?" I was suddenly a little worried about his credentials. "Deedee told me you worked with animals."

"I do. I euthanize dogs and cats for a living. This feels adjacent."

"Do you need a degree or special training for that?"

"I don't know," he looked slightly confused. "Do you?"

He told me his plan, which seemed solid enough, and when I asked what he needed me to do, he told me nothing. "Just hang out here. If everything goes okay I'll be back right after daybreak. Oh, by the way, where do you want the cage?"

I motioned behind me. "In the garage."

"Got it," he said.

"Any other questions?" It all seemed too easy, too ripe for a tragedy all the oil stains in the world couldn't predict, but when the Cat suddenly leapt into my line of sight, swiping at something in the air with that great big paw of his, I reminded myself that time and options were in short supply. Unlike Pete and his countless trips to rehab, this was my last shot.

"Just one," he said, as he held up the Sharper Image catalog, a wide smile opening across his face like a trapdoor at a funhouse. "Who the fuck would pay 15 K for a massage chair?"

After devouring the pizza, Pete flipped the Domino's box over and drew a makeshift ouija board on the back. I politely demurred, explaining that I didn't like to fuck with the afterlife on a full stomach, but he insisted, burping up a marriage of odors from which I was able to deduce pepperoni, Copenhagen chew and root beer, the combination of which spoke unexplainably to me of brotherhood, hopelessness and mortal fear, and it made me suddenly wistful for close combat or a foxhole, anywhere I could die with friends.

"That pizza was delicious," I said, sitting back and letting the couch devour me. "I don't know why I don't order Domino's more often."

"Because you're a coastal elite," he said matter-of-factly. "That's what Deedee says anyway. She's hardest on the ones she loves," he added quickly to reassure me. "If she didn't care about you, she wouldn't shit on you."

"I know," I told him.

"God, I love that girl. Kids used to be so mean to her when we were growing up. Called her all sorts of names on account of her albinism. I can't tell you how many heads I've smashed on account of that girl's complexion. I remember one girl in seventh grade told her she'd never fall in love. On account of the color of her skin. Can you believe that?" He dropped a piece of burnt crust into the box. "There's nothing I wouldn't do for that little girl."

Without a word, he peeled off his Kid Rock tour shirt to show me an enormous back piece of a python that'd been done for him by a prison cellmate.

"What do you think?"

"It's beautiful," I lied.

"I've always felt connected to pythons," he pulled the shirt back down, and I let my eyes slide around the room, trying to shake the black spot that hovered somewhere towards the upper left side of my vision, a shape, I started to realize, that looked an awful lot like the oil stain in the garage. The messages were coming in fast and furious, ripping me apart from the inside out, and I just wanted them to stop. It was so much worse being the cipher than simply being the message itself.

"Ever catch a snake?" I tried to keep the conversation going, worried that if we slipped into silence the spot would keep growing, inking its way to the outer reaches of my sight until all that was left was the sick, myopic peepshow the Cat wanted me to see.

He held out his arm to show me a silver dollar-sized scar around which was a patch of blackened necrotic skin. "What do you think?" He laughed. "You know how a lot of people say they're dead inside? Well, I'm dead outside, but inside," he smacked his stomach with an open palm, and the hollow sound bounced off every wall in the house, "alive and kicking."

The darkness continued to grow around me, and I thought it as good a time as any to get some sleep.

"I'm going to bed," I told him. "See you in the morning?"

"Not if I can help it. I hope to have this sucker all ready for you by the time you wake up. Then I'm out of here. Going to take your $2,500 and spend the week at Two Bunch Palms. Mud baths. I want the mud to go everywhere."

I was embarrassed I'd forgotten about his fee. "How do you want me to pay you, by the way?"

"Venmo's fine." He handed me a business card. *Pete DeWitt - Hypnotism, Animal Euthanasia, Carpet Cleaning — @DeWittQuitYou*

"Wow, hypnotism and carpet cleaning, too? What's that all about?"

"I help people quit things. Drugs, smoking, stubborn stains… basically, I can help you quit anything."

I stood up and yawned, and then without realizing I was doing it, got down on the ground and got into a cat pose, not the yoga one, but the stretch I sometimes caught the Cat doing when it thought I wasn't looking.

"What are you going to do with this once you have it, by the way? Normally I don't like to ask questions, but…"

"Funny thing for a guy who makes his living helping people."

"Maybe that's how I help them best. By not asking." He picked the pizza box off the floor, and started picking off the pieces of cheese that were melted into the cardboard and popping them into his mouth, an act that made me uncomfortable to watch, an intimacy I considered on par with eating hot wings or praying; two things I never wanted anyone to ever see me doing. "Anyway, how about it?"

"I don't know. I guess I just want to look at it. I want to look into its eyes. I want to smell it. I want to see what the light looks like as it bounces off its fur." Finally, I sighed. "I think I want to know what makes it real."

He nodded as he continued to push the crisp pieces of cheese past his lips. "The teeth. The teeth and the claws. That's what makes a thing real." He shrugged, not stopping his foraging for a second. "In my opinion."

"Thanks for such an entertaining evening, Pete. I haven't laughed that hard in a long time."

He winked at me. "She told me to do that, too."

I got it now; Deedee was looking out for me. I couldn't believe how badly I betrayed her, not to mention what Pete would do to me if he ever found out.

"Do you do everything she tells you to do?"

He looked around, as if to search for the person who would ask anything so stupid. "Don't you?"

True to his word, when I woke up, Pete wasn't around.

I peeked out the window, and outside, the Santa Anas were still blowing, but they were much less powerful than they had been just 12 hours earlier, and looking up I could see small spots of purple-and-orange sky poking through the retreating gasps of smoke and night.

Inside, I made a wide circle around the door to the garage and, walking into the kitchen, made myself a cup of coffee and slid a piece of bread into the toaster. The whole time I was eating my breakfast, I didn't once take my eyes off that door. When I was done, I did the dishes, looking back over my shoulder every few seconds, worried that if I took my eyes off the door for too long, the mountain lion would come charging through and have me pinned to the floor in no time.

When I was done and everything was put away exactly as it had been, I wiped my hands off on an old dish towel and stared at the door some more. I walked toward it slowly, and when I finally reached it, I laid the side of my face against the cool wood and listened - nothing. My heart was slamming against my chest, and the Cat had backed itself into a corner where it was crouched low to the ground, snarling, the roof of its pink mouth glistening like a piece of wet coral. *A million things could be behind that door*, I told myself, my breath quickening as I wrapped my hand around the knob, but as I twisted the handle, every fiber of my being screamed at me that it could only be one thing; my last chance.

As I pushed the door open, a dusty, earthy smell hit me, and I knew instantly that I wasn't alone. The garage was pitch dark, and I fumbled on the wall by the door for the light switch. Finding it, I took a deep breath and flipped on the lights.

The cage was in the dead center of the garage floor, covering up the oil stain, and sitting in it, just as still as could be, was the mountain lion. It barely flinched when the lights came on, just an automatic twitch of its ear, and as I edged closer, it sat politely, turning its head slowly to look at me. When I was only a few steps away from the cage, it registered me and turned back to stare at the closed door again. Whatever Pete had used to dull its senses it was still pumping through the mountain lion's veins. Its eyes were as big and as glassy as two snow globes, and when it opened its mouth to warn me not to come any closer, it did so only half-heartedly, emitting only the kittenest of mewls.

I walked up to the cage but stayed just out of arm's reach, in case it got a sudden burst of energy and decided it wanted to tear my face off for old time's sake. I circled the cage slowly as I examined it from every angle. The line of short black hairs that traced the outline of its ears and came down over its face, framing it in a kind of spider web of dark highlights; the way its fur lightened from tan on the top to white on its underside and even the bored look on its face were all as familiar to me as if I were looking at my own reflection.

"Do you know me?" I whispered to it after making my circle. The question hung in the air for a second, and it surprised me by opening its mouth a little as if to answer, but this time no sound came out, not even the tiniest of whimpers.

# CHAPTER 25

Before leaving the Valley, I stopped at Costco and picked up ten pounds of organic ground turkey. At checkout I noticed that Costco offered funeral packages right where they kept the other impulse items like gum, mints and those little shot glass-sized bottles of 5-Hour Energy, which I'd never tried before. I added a cherry flavor 5-Hour Energy to my cart as I examined the funeral packages, where with the titanium tier, you got a casket or urn (your choice of colors and materials), premium flower package and a premium plot at a non-denominational cemetery in Simi Valley. I had a feeling I knew what "premium flowers" meant (lilies and gladiolus, the kind of things that were too beautiful for someone to ever buy for themselves), but I wasn't sure what "premium cemetery plot" meant exactly. Regardless, I threw the tag in my cart.

The checkout lady stopped snapping her gum when she scanned it and I could tell it made her a little bit sad.

"It's not for me," I tried reassuring her. "It's for a friend."

"Oh." She smiled at me, resuming her popping and scanning, "Cool."

When I went back in the garage, the mountain lion was still laying down exactly where I left him. I watched the rise and fall of its chest for a while, a hypnotic undulation it was hard to look away from. Up and down. Up and down. But there were also these ripples of light that reflected off its barely moving body, light that looked like a flickering aura, vacillating between ways to be.

"Hi," I said finally. "I thought you might be hungry." I un-wrapped the meat, pushed it into the cage and jumped back, terrified that the scent would suddenly spark something primal within it, and, in the flicker of a second, it would grab hold of me through the bars and before I knew what was happening, I'd have my arm dangling out of its wide mouth like a turkey drumstick. "I hope you like turkey. I know it's not what you probably usually eat, but it's organic and..."

Nothing. It didn't even turn to look at the meat.

"Okay. You rest then."

I was about to leave when something in me told me to walk back to the cage. I approached it slowly, trying to make my footsteps fall as soundlessly as possible, a held breath captured in my lungs I wouldn't let go of for all the money in the world. I touched the bars of the cage. Ice cold. And then before I even knew I was do-ing it, I reached my hand out slowly toward the mountain lion. I wanted to stop, but it was like watching someone else doing it. That wasn't me. Those weren't my trembling fingers moving closer and closer to its huge, muscular flanks. Those tiny hairs standing straight up on that arm didn't belong to me. I was somewhere else entirely. I was in a movie theater with a bag of popcorn and a cold soda clutched in my hands, warning whoever it was up on the screen that this was a terrible idea, anyone could see that. *RUN, DUMMY! RUN!* But it was too late. My hand was on its fur, and I finally exhaled as the warmth of its body entered and spread through me, and for one moment, we were a thing with one heart-beat.

It never even raised its head.

I drove back to my apartment, and it wasn't until the NPR an-nouncer - one of those flat, affectless gluttons for indignancy with a name like an undiscovered star system - pointed it out that I noticed the ash had stopped falling. The fires, he said, were over 90 percent contained, and with the Santa Anas moving offshore, we could expect to have clean air and clear skies by morning. And while I couldn't quite take credit for the good news, the way my plan was coming together, it sure as hell felt like I had at least a small hand in it. I smiled to myself. I was feeling excited and hopeful for the first time in a long time. If this was what people who had their shit together felt like all the time, then sign me up.

I scanned the radio until I landed on a station playing one of those nameless DJ numbers where it was all about the moment the beat dropped, the music climbing steadily to an inevitable peak, and I readied myself by moving my head to the music, punching my fist harder and harder in time to the escalating beat until finally there was no place left for it to go, but to...DROP!! I went crazy. My limbs weren't mine anymore, they belonged to the music, and I felt like a machine whose only function was to feel happiness. No, fuck that. I was blessed. This was what it felt like to be really and truly blessed. Not just hashtag blessed, but for-real, supernova fucking stoked. I had the overwhelming urge to give an acceptance speech to someone, to effuse, to emote, to spontaneously combust if only God would point me in the right direction, and when a couple of teenage girls pulled up next to me in their Kia and started laughing and pointing at the old man who was emphatically letting the music fucking take him over, really wash through him, I rolled down my window, smiled, and shot them a finger gun. I may have even winked, but it was hard to know for certain. They tore out of there faster than quicksilver. I belonged to the drop.

Back at my building, my neighbors had wasted no time at all in assuming their familiar positions, half-dressed, prostrate on plastic chaise lounges as the sun mercilessly inscribed its hopes and dreams on their exposed and already deeply tan backs and chests.

I was still nodding my head to the drop when I got into my apartment and slid under the covers of my bed. I was exhausted. I set my alarm so I wouldn't miss the poker game and tried to calm myself down but couldn't; I was too jacked up. I tried masturbating, but it was hard to focus because I couldn't stop nodding, couldn't stop feeling great. Finally, I did a body scan, a technique an old girlfriend would talk me through whenever I was on the verge of a panic attack, where you focused on each part of your body individually, acknowledging the tension and then willing it to leave. When I was through, I felt like a wet noodle, and as sleep slowly crept over me, I realized that in my scan I hadn't seen the Cat once, not even a hint of its frizzy tail sticking out from behind a rock, or, at the very least, its glowing eyes I had become so used to seeing, set deep in the face of the darkness that was the backdrop to all my internal dialogues. If it worked for me, I told myself, then it would work for Martha, and as I slowly started to drift off, it was the thought that she'd soon be in my garage seeing what I'd done for her – done for us – bringing everything as close to normal as it ever had been, that finally let me fall asleep.

Later, after I'd woken, showered and dressed, I grabbed the little box with the ring in it and shoved it in my pocket. It felt good there, heavy and serious the way a fait accompli was supposed to feel.

The poker game was in full swing when I got up to Dutch's house. He lived on one of the Bird streets above the Sunset Strip, and I had to step hard on the accelerator to pass a double-decker bus that was parked in the middle of the road so its top-heavy load of tourists could snap pictures of some celebrity's wrought iron fence and dream the dream that all flightless birds shared, the one where you were anyone but who you really were.

Dutch's wife Heather answered the door.

"Duuuuuncan!" She screamed my name at me in a descending tone that made it sound like she was falling off the side of a cliff. I wondered if certain death was her usual modality and, based on her overall appearance, guessed that it probably was. Her smile was an enormous boomerang of emotion, and before I knew what the fuck was happening I was swallowed up in a desperate embrace. She didn't want to let go, and I finally just went limp, hoping it would work the way it did when you were caught in a pit of quicksand. She finally released me, and her smile slipped for a second.

"Wait, you are Duncan, right? You're not the Mr. Chow's guy?"

"Nope. Sorry to disappoint. Just Duncan."

She'd had so much filler that, even this close-up, I couldn't find one pore on her stiff mask of a face. Her blonde hair, recently colored and cut, was perfect, as were her nails, and she was wearing one of those deceptively expensive sister-wife sack dresses that were so in fashion these days and made her look like she was into *Little House on the Prairie* cosplay. I didn't quite see the point of dressing like that when you were just going to spend a small fortune on the hair and the fillers and the pilates that kept the whole thing tight as a wire, just so you could cover it all up again, but I went with it, giving her back my winningest grin.

"And you must be Heather, right? I've heard a lot about you. I love that picture he has of you in his office..." and at the same time we said, "...Rounding error." She laughed, coquettishly biting her lower lip, and I got suddenly stressed that it was going to burst and whatever it was they used to plump them up would start running down her chin and stain her dress. For some reason, I pictured sweet 'n sour sauce. "That's a nice dress, by the way."

"You like it? Really?" Her voice definitely had some weird modulation thing going on and I looked for neck scars, wondering if her vocal chords had ever been crushed. "Dutch says it makes me look like a cult member."

"Nah," I said, waving away the suggestion as though it were a pesky fly, "and besides, if it were a cult then that's some Kool-Aid I might not mind drinking." I didn't know why I was flirting exactly, but I couldn't resist. Knowing what the next 24 hours held in store had me feeling confident and a bit playful, and it felt good to spread it around. She blushed, I think, just as a wiry, strung-out looking terrier mix padded up to stand at her side.

"Is that the Mr. Chow's guy?" Dutch screamed from somewhere out of sight. Her hand dropped off my arm, and I saw the dog stiffen with terror at the sound of his voice and instantly start to shake and whine. I knew exactly how it felt, and I bent to pet it in a show of solidarity, but Heather warned me off.

"Better not," her voice warbled. "Dutch had some ex-Green Beret train poor Ziggy to within an inch of her life. She's not used to affection. It might make her head explode."

I knew that feeling, too, and I looked down at the poor animal as it gave another little whine, begging for a mercy killing the way most dogs begged for a treat.

"Right," I said, watching the pitiful animal trot back inside.

Taking his place at her side, as though it had been pre-arranged, came Coleman, their four-year old son. Snot bubbled out of his nose, and there was a smattering of the thick green sludge running down his Spongebob shirt. To my horror, Heather reached down and wiped it away with her bare hand without even thinking twice about it.

I smiled at the little shit, who ironically looked a hell of a lot like a 70-something year old Walter Matthau.

"Hey buddy," I said, "how are you?"

In response, he shoved a finger up his nose almost to the second knuckle and asked me, "Have you ever been in love?"

Heather knocked the finger out of his nose. "Coleman R. De-Witt! I told you to never ask anyone that. It's a vile question." She looked up at me. "I'm sorry. They're learning about love in TK. Really pushing the empathy agenda on these kids. He's been asking everyone if they're in love. He made the checkout girl at Whole Foods cry the other day."

"I don't mind," I said, turning back to the boy. "I have been in love, and I am in love. It's a really nice feeling, Coleman, and I'm sure one day you'll be in love, too."

"I already love my Mommy," he said, and I watched as Heather melted a little, her hands falling on his chest as she pulled him toward her.

"And how about your Daddy?" I asked, knowing that I probably shouldn't.

Coleman was thoughtful for a moment before saying judiciously, "He's surrounded by idiots."

I laughed as Heather gave him a playful spank on the tush.

"Coleman!" Then to me she explained, "That's what Dutch says when he comes home every day. We're working on his empathy. Isn't that right, Coleman?"

"Right!" he said, before suddenly dashing off to infect more surfaces with his germy hands.

"Duncan, is that you?" Dutch's voice bellowed at me from out of the depths of the split-level modernist house. "If it is, get your dumb ass in here and lose some money already. And if it's the Mr. Chow's guy, you can have my wife as your tip."

There was a chorus of laughter, and I watched as the smile disappeared from Heather's face. She didn't say anything, so I gave her a weak smile as I walked uncomfortably past her into the house.

"It was nice meeting you," I said, but the bonhomie had drained from her body, and she kind of half-mumbled a pleasantry at me before turning away and disappearing up the stairs.

There was a poker table set up in the living room with seven guys, including Dutch, well into a game of Hold 'Em. Dutch nodded at the only empty chair as he broke down the chip values, a huge cigar clamped between his teeth. I nodded at the guys I knew from work and shook hands with the ones I didn't, took a few hundred dollars out of my wallet, and tossed it on the table. I got my chips and anted as the dealer button passed to the guy sitting on my right who was the spitting image of Burt Reynolds. He had the corporate logo of a rival investment firm — Blank, Kaplan & Doozy — tattooed on his bicep, and if I had to guess, Dutch had invited him either to pump him for insider information or because it would be funny later to talk about his bushy mustache or how every time he said the phrase "data mining," which he did often, he'd unconsciously pick his nose. A boxing match, muted, played on the giant flatscreen, and from an Alexa came what else but *The Eagles Greatest Hits*. My goal was to lose as quickly as possible so I could get out of there and head over to Martha's place, and when I folded at the end of the hand with three nine's, I slammed the table pretending to be pissed at my bad luck.

"Take it easy, Chief," the look-alike Burt said, handing me the deck to make.

I shuffled and dealt. After the flop, I was already working an ace-high straight and chuckled at how even good luck knew how to fuck you sometimes. When it came around to him, Burt threw his cards disgustedly into the center of the table.

"What's the deal with this creep, Dutch? You told me it was only going to be real players."

"Duncan's as real as they come," Dutch said, taking a giant drag off his cigar. He held the smoke in his puffed-out cheeks as his eyes landed on me. It came out in a slow trickle, and through the pungent fog I could see in that stare that he knew that I knew about him and Lydia and that it didn't bother him a bit. In fact, I thought, as I waved thoughtlessly at the air, he probably preferred it that way. "Isn't that right, Duncan?" he added, as though he'd been reading my mind.

I threw my ante into the pot and leaned back. "Whatever you say, Dutch."

"Hey," Burt said, interrupting what had just become an awkward silence, "what was the name of the thing that guy used to try and off himself with again. I want to see if you can get it from Alexa."

"It's called a Suicide Bag," Evan Anguilla, a colleague from work said, without looking up from his cards. "Apparently, some old woman makes them and sells them online. Not sure you can buy it from Amazon, though." He looked up. "You should try."

"Hey, Alexa," Burt shouted at the machine, cutting Witchy Woman off mid-song, "I want to order a Suicide Bag. You got that?"

I looked over at Evan. "What's he talking about?" Evan suppressed a grin and looked at Dutch. "What?" I asked again, feeling something deep down inside my stomach start to tighten.

"Sorry," Alexa piped up, "I didn't quite get that. Did you say, 'Beautified Bag'?"

Everyone laughed, Burt especially, and when he pounded my shoulder it felt like someone had hit me with a baseball bat.

"What's so funny?" I asked again through a forced smile, as the tight feeling started to spread to my arms and legs, weighing them down with a molten dread that would soon make it hard to move.

"You need to start reading the company intranet postings," Dutch said, glancing over his shoulder at the fight. It was in the late rounds, and the two young Latino boxers were trading exhausted blows, head shot for head shot, both of them in it until the end.

I fumbled with my phone and went on the company intranet, which I hadn't looked at in years. It took me a few seconds to remember my password, but when I finally got in, I saw the post they'd been referring to almost immediately - a Quicktime video with the title "HR Violation?" that had been posted last night by an anonymous employee.

I swallowed hard and hit play. It took me a moment to understand what it was I was watching, but after a couple of seconds of squinting and head tilting, I understood that I was looking at my office. The lights were low, and the cloud was on, shoveling handfuls of dank, earthy dub around the room as it sparked and stormed in time to the music. Filling up most of the frame, though, was my couch, which meant that someone had probably left their phone running on the bookshelf until they got what they'd been looking for. Two naked bodies wriggled on the couch; the one on top was extremely pale, and after watching them have sex for a few minutes, the occasional grunt and moan articulating just what a wonderful time they were having, I began to hope that we'd never see their faces and Deedee and Les could at least have some semblance of plausible deniability. But several minutes later, when they were done, the camera caught Deedee climbing off him and turning directly into view as she put her hair up, her white face framed dead center in the middle of the screen. Beads of sweat flecked off her smiling face, and behind her Les sat up, rubbed his eyes and made a playful grab at her. She laughed as she slapped him away, and, as they got dressed, they began making plans for the weekend, movies they would watch, meals they would eat. She wanted red wine. He wanted Marvel. It sounded like a match made in heaven.

The video ended, and I looked across the table at Dutch who was still turned around watching the fighters pound one another into oblivion.

"Dutch…" I said to him, but he didn't hear me, or at least he was pretending not to. "Where's Les?"

"Read your emails," he said, still not turning around. I wanted to imagine it was shame that prevented him from facing me, but I knew better. "Gonna have to get better with staying up with current events if you're going to want to survive the new regime. Isn't that right, boys?"

"All the news that's fit to print," Evan said with a smirk.

I opened my emails up and saw an ALL STAFF - URGENT note from old man Loam, one of the firm's founders whose email account was only ever invoked when a somber tone was needed — a death or layoffs. The last time I remembered seeing an email from him was when the Market crashed in '08. At the time, his tone had been apocryphal and ministerial, encouraging us to not lose faith while at the same time admonishing us to stand fast in the face of our enemies. He'd conjured up a war for us to be soldiers in, a fight that we could call our own, but now, as I read this piece of shit out-of-office condolence email, I thought I might be sick.

*It is with a heavy heart that I convey to you that our colleague, Les McCann, tried to take his own life early this morning. He is in a coma at Cedars-Sinai, and it is not known whether or not he will survive. Our thoughts and prayers are with Les and his ex-wife and son at this difficult time. For any questions about the Young-Jorgeson Merger, please see Dutch DeWitt. — Stan Loam, Chairman Emerita*

"What did you do?" I asked Dutch, who finally turned to me. He took a Tammany Hall-sized puff off his cigar and blew the smoke at the center of the room.

"I hope you're not serious right now," he said without even a trace of anger in his tone. "I hope you're not forgetting how this piece of information came to me, Duncan. And I hope you're not fool enough to think, when you gave it to me, that I wouldn't use it. That doesn't sound like me," he went on, turning back to the TV, "does it?"

Dazed and feeling like I was about to be sick, I got to my feet and walked into the kitchen. I tried to call Deedee but couldn't find a signal and started wandering from room to room, my body trembling with anger, but the whole place seemed to be one big dead zone until I went upstairs and into the master bedroom. I sat on the edge of their bed and looked around as I waited for Deedee to pick up; family and wedding pictures on the dresser, a CPAP machine next to Dutch's side of the bed along with copies of *The Art of War* and Walter Isaacson's biography of Steve Jobs, and a can of something called "Loki-scented Axe Body Spray," whatever the hell that meant. On her side of the bed was a tower of self-help books and a package of pot mints. Domestic bliss. I was about to hang up and head over to Cedars when Deedee finally picked up.

"Why?" was how she answered, simply, her voice shrunken almost to the point of annihilation.

"Deedee..." I started to say, but she wasn't interested in my cheap excuses, my sympathies even less.

"Whhhyyy?" She repeated the word, slower this time, stretching it out so it had the tempo of a dirge.

One of the things I admired most about Deedee was her directness, her fearlessness when she asked a question, as though there was nothing that was none of her business. But now, sitting on the receiving end of that openness, there was none of that. Instead, all I found in that single word was a child's earnestness, a little kid who wanted to know why the world had to sometimes be such a bad place.

"Because I was scared," I admitted, touching the spines of the books on Dutch's nightstand.

"Why?" she asked again, and I couldn't tell if she was going to keep asking until we got to the answer that made the most sense to her or if this was a cumulative exercise, my faults being tallied up into its egregious sum. In either case, I felt certain that if I admitted to much more, the Cat would be making a return appearance. But that was probably just a rationalization, too, another way to fool myself into believing that it hadn't always just been a matter of time.

"Because I was selfish."

"Why?"

"Because I didn't want to be lonely."

"Ahhh..." She alighted on that sad little flower of an answer like a bee landing on something it might conceivably pollinate. A silence followed, and I wasn't sure whether or not it was my turn or hers, but the machine that I assumed was keeping Les alive suddenly beeped somewhere in the background with what sounded like only the vaguest of efforts. A doctor was paged over the loudspeaker, and I tried to imagine the scene; the sterile room, maybe just the one machine because it was that bad, tubes down his throat and up his cock, and Deedee sitting by his bedside, her hand covering his, staring at the eyelids she'd give anything to see flutter. "Let me ask you something, Duncan. How many more chances do you think I'll get? How many more times do you estimate someone like me will get to fall in love in their life? Care to work the numbers out on that?"

"I'm so sorry, Deedee." I didn't want to say it, but it kind of just slipped out.

"You should have seen him, Duncan. He had a bag over his head hooked up to a tank of helium. I guess he bought it a long time ago, just to have around, for like, special occasions. The housekeeper found him, and by the time 911 got there, he was almost dead. His face is all puffy, and his lips are blue. He looks like…" She stopped herself before veering off into cliche territory as a sudden burst of tears overtook her.

"Is he going to live?"

She ignored the question, but the machine answered for her, beeping only once, code for, *Don't ask stupid questions.*

I looked around the bedroom again, and everything suddenly got blurry as tears began to pool in my eyes.

"If I could trade places with him, I would." I wasn't too proud to use cliches. If she'd only stay on the phone with me long enough, I'd try them all like a custodian's keyring until I found the one that worked.

Deedee, though, didn't have that problem. "What's stopping you?" She found the right one right away.

She hung up first, and when I looked back at the door Dutch's wife, Heather, was just coming into the room. She didn't seem surprised to see me there as she closed the door behind her, locking it softly. I wiped the tears from my eyes, about to explain that I wasn't snooping, that I had just been trying to make a call, when she surprised me by striding quickly over to me, pulling her dress up and her panties down in a singular feat of Fellini-esque gymnastics, and straddled me. She immediately began kissing my face and neck, not even stopping to ask me about the tears covering my cheeks.

"Wait," I said, trying to hold her back. "What are you doing?"

In response, she leaned in harder, and I felt her thighs and pelvis tighten around me as she secured her grip.

"I want you to fuck me," she moaned, clutching my face in her hands.

"Yes, I can see that. It's not a great time for me, though," I could feel the Cat coming back suddenly, walking slowly over a hill that wasn't too far away, pacing itself as it approached, spurned and vibrating with malice. "My friend is in the hospital and…"

"Yeah, yeah," she said, dropping her hands so she could get to work on my belt, "I heard about all that. Don't worry, though. This will make it better."

"I don't think so," I said, trying again to lift her off me. She had a way of making herself feel like dead weight, though. I'd sooner move a mountain.

"Listen," she said, stopping her strip-mining of my face long enough to speak, "I hate to break it to you, but my husband fucked your wife, and now you're going to fuck me so that I can have a little balance in my life. Do you understand that?" Instead of waiting for an answer, though, she started to try and force me back onto the bed. She was strong, but just as I was about to tip backwards, I used the leverage of us falling over to spin her around and, once I was on top, quickly backed away from her. She mistook the judo as foreplay and laid back, wiggling out of the rest of her clothes as she inched her way back up towards the headboard. "You know what would be hot?" she asked, eyeing me up and down like I was a Peloton. "I want you to wear his CPAP machine while you're fucking me. I want you to sound like a congested Darth Vader when you call me a dirty slut."

I backed away from her slowly, and even the Cat seemed confused by what was going on. When she realized that I meant to escape she jumped up and grabbed me by the wrists, trying to bring me back to the bed with her. I shook my hands loose and yelled at her to stop.

"Lydia left me," I tried to reason with her. "I know they had an affair, but I've done some things that I'm not proud of either. Things with her mom..." That came out wrong. "I'm going for a clean slate. I want to start over. This is not how that's going to happen for me. I hope you're not going to take this personally. You're an incredibly beautiful woman, Heather, and your husband's an absolute bastard, and if you cheated on him or poured protein shakes down his CPAP while he slept or whatever else you could cook up, you'd still be on the morally justified side of the ledger, but I can't do this." I was yelling by the end, but I had to talk over the Cat's booming roars, and I guessed it was registering with her, because she stopped coming at me finally and started to slowly and embarrassedly put her clothes back on. She grabbed the can of Axe off the nightstand and walked over to where I was standing. I braced myself for another carnal blitzkrieg, but the fire had gone out of her eyes.

"Wait a minute," she said, shaking the can slowly, "let me get something straight."

"What?" I asked.

"You knew about Dutch and your wife?"

"Yes," I said, glad that she was finally getting it.

"And you didn't do anything about it?"

"No..." I said, and just as I was about to explain myself again she lifted the can and sprayed it directly into my face. The stuff went straight into my left eye and burned worse than anything I'd ever felt in my life, like a tunnel was being dug out from the front of my head to the back, with hot lava poured in for good measure.

"Aaaaah!" I screamed and ran into the bathroom, where I began to shovel handfuls of cold water into what I was sure was the campfire taking place on my face. Heather followed me in, berating me all the way. She told me that her husband always said I was a weak pushover, and then she called me a pussy for not doing anything about the affair when I found out about it. As I continued to scream and splash cold water in my face she summed up: "I'm glad it hurts." She started to leave and then stopped herself. I was terrified that she'd found another beauty product to cripple me with, but it was just a last thought she wanted to share. "Oh, and I heard about the thing with the mountain lion. Pretending you'd been mauled or something to get out of doing work. What a pathetic fucking liar. I hope your dick rots off, you asshole."

I knew I had a lot of strikes against me, but I'd never thought of myself as a liar, per se, until now. Might as well add it to the list.

When the pain was a little more manageable, I pulled my hand away from my face and looked in the mirror. The eye was a red, swollen mess. There was some pus coming out of it and the white part had turned a thick, solid red. I could barely see and wondered blithely if I was going to be blind in that eye for the rest of my life. Sighing, I used some KT Tape and a washcloth to create a makeshift eyepatch, and when I was done with that, I sniffed the air. Something smelled funny. I inhaled, thinking for a minute that it might be an infection I was smelling, the odor of my own body giving up on itself, when I realized all of a sudden what it was. Loki, it turned out, smelled like sandalwood and new car.

By the time I got downstairs, I was strung out on bloodlust for Dutch, but he wasn't at the table.

"Where is he?" I growled, and I could tell the Cat liked this by the way it arched its back and the little hairs along its spine raised and stiffened.

The guys around the table were laughing, but when they saw my face they clammed right up and their faces grew worried. I could only imagine what I looked like to them, but as long as it stopped their stupid grins and got them to listen, I didn't care one little bit. The only one who didn't see me was Burt who had his back turned toward me. He was still having a grand old time with the news about Les, even though he had no idea who the hell it was who was sitting on life support over at Cedars. *He only gets one machine,* I thought as Burt cheerfully hollered out again like he was choosing a child bride from a line-up of farmer's daughters. "Alexa, su-i-cide bag." He enunciated each syllable distinctly, like he was trying to teach a foreigner the juiciest swear words.

I came up right behind him, the pain in my eye subsiding as adrenaline filled in all the mortal gaps, and kicked the chair legs right out from under him. They snapped with a soft and satisfying *crack* and he went down in a burly heap, smashing his chin on the table as he went. On the floor he went right into the fetal position, and I straightened him out so I could get a good look at his long body, locate the softest spots, and leaned my knee on his windpipe. His groans of pain were immediately replaced by the sounds of him struggling to get enough air, and his eyes were wide and staring up at me, confused too, and maybe even a little bit outraged, like this was the first moment of real clarity he'd ever experienced in his long and miserable life.

"Where did Dutch go?" I asked my colleagues who were staring between me and Burt, their faces smeared with pure panic like a group of toddlers who'd just eaten their fill of hot fudge sundaes.

"He got a call. Emergency at work." Evan said finally, realizing the trouble they were in, that I meant to kill this man, and there probably wasn't going to be anything they could do to stop me. "That guy looks really bad, Duncan," he added, almost as an afterthought.

I looked down. Burt's face was turning a very satisfying scarlet, and his mouth was bobbing open and closed like he was trying to say something but kept forgetting what it was. I realized that his name wasn't actually Burt and I started to laugh that he might very well die a Burt.

"What kind of emergency?" I asked. I felt remarkably calm. I was in total control and the Cat growled its appreciation, its not-too-subtle way of saying *I've been trying to tell you it could be like this.*

Evan looked at Burt's face, the features of which were deepening to a rich purple. Usually a fickle color, he wore it well, I thought.

"I'm not sure. He got a call and his face got really pale," Evan looked quickly at Burt again.

"The opposite of this," I nodded at Burt's full burst of violet complexion. "Got it. Keep going."

"He said something about Helen Reddy," said Gary, another colleague who looked like Evan but was quieter. "That's it. Duncan," he nodded at Burt, "I think you're killing that guy."

I looked down at Burt. His eyes were closed now and his tongue was sticking out of his mouth. The Cat was telling me to finish him off, that his corpse would make a nice meal or, at the very least, would prove a pretty unbeatable conversation piece. I took my knee off his throat, and the life rushed back into him, igniting a combustion of the senses that made him cough, yell, sputter and go bug-eyed all at once. I was already out the door, running at a full sprint to my car, when his shouting threats reached my ears.

I raced west along Wilshire toward the office. Mercifully, traffic was light, and with the windows down and the wind rushing through the car, a vivid jet of fresh air that slipped beneath my clothes and ran up and down the length of my heated skin, I could almost imagine myself running, alive with speed the way the Cat might be on the brightest of nights, vivid and inevitable.

The parking garage at the building was nearly empty. There were just a few cars by the entrance that I knew belonged to the security and custodial staff. Everyone else was gone for the weekend, which was how it should be at 9 p.m. on a Friday.

I slowly cruised the aisles looking for Dutch's car, and I could sense the Cat looking, too, peering left and right with quick moves of its giant head. It was on full alert, hunting mode, every one of its senses attuned to frequencies I could neither see nor hear. We both deserved our pound of flesh, but I wasn't interested in that kind of revenge. I didn't know what punishment I'd pick for Dutch, but it wouldn't be violence. He had so many tender spots he'd covered up over the years with humiliation and bullying; it would be nothing to strip those away and expose him. But that was part of the problem; I was the only one thinking in terms of punishment, the Cat was all hunger.

Dutch had at least a 15-minute head start on me, and I knew that it was probably too late to help him. Last night, Pete told me again and again there wasn't anything he wouldn't do for his sister and I believed him. It wouldn't have been a stretch for Deedee to figure out that Dutch was the one who posted the video, and I could imagine how quickly after that Pete's impulses went to murder. He said he helped people get rid of things. Why should any of this be surprising?

I curved my car slowly down the ramp to the third floor of the parking structure, and in the far distance, beneath the yellow sodium lights that made everything look like the recreation of a crime scene, I could see Dutch's car. Driving slowly toward it, I glanced around, having to move my whole head because of the one eye issue, looking for signs of Dutch or Pete. I saw nothing, and for a moment I tried to make myself believe that I'd misjudged this whole thing. Maybe Pete wasn't as raving a psycho as I thought he was, or maybe Deedee never called him, and the thing about Helen Reddy was just a code word from a mistress. But then I saw Dutch's Tesla, and when I was about 30 feet away from it, I suddenly hit the brakes as I saw something on the ground by the driver's side of his car begin to move. It was hard to tell what it was at first and even the Cat strained its neck to get a better view. My heart clacked unsteadily in my chest.

I put the car in park, and even though I knew it was a bad idea to get out, I also knew I couldn't just sit there. I closed the door softly, scared that a loud slam would bring the whole building down on my head, and walked toward the car with careful, measured steps. Between the low light and my eye that felt like I had a piece of hot metal stuck in my face, all I could see were shapes, and whatever was next to Dutch's car started to slowly stir again, this time with a low and long moan that creased the distance between us with a declaration of pain that opened up a wellspring of pity in me I hadn't known was there. It was a primal noise, moreso because of the desperation that suffused it, but most of all, it sounded like the end. It was clear that whatever it was that had made that noise didn't have long left.

I sped up and was only two or three steps away from it when the massive roar of a mountain lion suddenly washed through the garage. I stopped myself to make sure it hadn't come from me, and once I'd been exonerated, I listened to it echo outwards to every level and corner of the structure, dissolving slowly after what felt like an eternity or whatever the hell the half-life of true menace was. I froze and looked around. Nothing moved. Even the air was still. The only movement was the occasional and terrible oozing of the shape by the car.

"Dutch?" I called out to the thing. I was trying to be as quiet as possible, afraid that my voice would give away my location, and, in an instant, it would be on me. But who was I kidding? It already knew I was here. It probably smelled the rotting flesh behind the

homemade eyepatch before I even got out of the car. I was petrified, but I forced myself to take a couple of more steps, cheering
myself along with the memory of Lydia standing naked at the foot
of the waterbed, saluting me and asking for permission to come
aboard. All I'd ever wanted was to say yes to her.

"Dutch?" I said again, and this time the shape moaned back.

I took the last couple of big steps toward the car, knelt down,
and used the flashlight on my phone to light up what was left of
Dutch. Half of his face had been ripped off and I could see straight
into his mouth where his tongue tried to make words that had
never failed him before. He was probably firing me, I thought, and
let him. I deserved it. In a way, it was all my fault. I'd had a plan
for fixing everything, for getting rid of all the animals, but I saw
now that it didn't work that way.

My knee slid on the floor that was sticky with his blood, and,
looking more closely at him, I saw that pieces of his flesh had been
peeled off in straight, precise strips down his chest, arms and legs.
It almost looked like someone was getting ready to re-wallpaper
him.

"Dutch," I said again, and I held his head up, because it appeared that he was choking on something that probably used to
be attached to him. His eyes were closed in tight fists of purple
bruises, and he was groping around, I realized, not in pain, but
because at the end he just wanted to touch something real. I took
his hand in mine, and I was surprised by the strength of his grip.

"That's quite a grip you have there," I said to him, trying to
come up with something, anything, to say. I knew it was wrong
to make jokes, but it didn't matter. His grip relaxed bit by bit, and
after a couple of more ragged seconds, he stopped breathing, and
then it was just me holding him.

The Cat let out an excited roar, almost like a war cry, and I
ground my teeth and hissed at it to stop. It didn't listen though,
it just kept on roaring, rubbing it in my face now, so I started

hunting for it, slapping myself in the face, pinching my gut, and I was just about to start working on pulling out my hair when the other mountain lion, the real one, roared again. I looked up quickly, my good eye struggling to focus on whatever wasn't a shadow, and there it was, nestled amidst the latticework of pipes that crisscrossed the ceiling of the parking structure.

I shined my light up at it, and for the briefest of moments, all I could see of it were its two eyes shining down on me, yellow circles of electricity that didn't even need a body. I moved the light away from its face, and then I could see the rest of it, so different looking now than it had been this morning when it was a drugged-out, rag-doll version of itself. Sleek and long, it watched me warily, and then started licking its paws, red now, rich with Dutch's blood. I backed away from it slowly and watched with a kind of fascination as it leapt down, first onto the roof of the Tesla and then onto the concrete ground, where it stood for a moment over Dutch's body, never once taking its eyes off me. We watched one another for a few breathless seconds, and I wondered what it wanted, if what we needed were the same things, if we were really as different as all that. My heart slammed against my chest as I waited for it to decide what it wanted to do with me, if there was even enough left to bother with. And then, without a sound, as if answering my question, it turned and ran with a speed I found breathtaking and beautiful, across the length of the parking structure, up the ramp and out of sight.

Long gone, and Martha still had her cat in her, and I still wanted Lydia. It felt like I was right back at the beginning. The Cat started to howl, and I gripped my head in my hands and staggered to my feet. I didn't know what it wanted, and then I started thinking that maybe it didn't want anything. Maybe this was going to be the way it was from now on. My head spinning, I made my way over to the elevator, where there was a little more light, and hit the 'up' button. The elevator cars moved slowly, and, as I waited, I took my hands away from my head for a minute, when my eye caught on the defibrillator hanging on the wall between the two closed doors. An idea suddenly struck me, and I took the thing down and tucked it beneath my arm. When the elevator finally arrived, I pushed the button for my floor and rode up, thinking about how this would work exactly.

On nine, I walked quickly down the long hallway to my office, ignoring the Cat's running back and forth, its swiping at thin air with its monstrous mitts, the way it gnashed its teeth as though it were some sort of monster and not just another idea I once had about what love was supposed to be.

Stopping at Deedee's desk, I took the box with the ring out of my pocket, wrote her name on it, and leaned it up against her brick wall of a monitor. She deserved this. She deserved more than everything I had, and I could only hope that this might be a start.

In my office, I turned on the cloud and dialed up that Mikey Dread album I loved so much, the one that made time stretch out in all directions at once, including backwards, the way any good map was supposed to do. I'd need a good map where I was going. Uncharted territory and all that. The great unknown. I didn't want to get all woo woo about it, but if there was ever a time...

I laid down on my couch and soaked it all in for a minute — the music, the throbbing in my eye, lights in the distance from houses in the Hills. All bliss. It was all bliss, and it was all right. I fished the phone from my pocket, called Lydia on speaker, and laid it down on the floor next to me. While I waited for her to answer I put the defibrillator's paddles on my chest and hit the charge button, starting a ten-second timer until the machine would be warmed up and ready for blast-off.

"Hello," She answered.

"Lydia?"

"Duncan? Is that you? You sound weird. What's that music playing in the background? Where the hell are you?"

There was so much I wanted to say, but I didn't have a lot of time left. The charge was already down to three. I pressed it again and it went back to ten. "I'm sorry, Lydia"

"Sorry about what?" she asked. "Listen," she went on, all businesslike, "I'm at my mother's. I'm moving back in." And then, a shameful coda: "Temporarily. By the way, I saw this note you left for me. What the fuck are you talking about, asking me to bring my mom out to your mother's place in the Valley? I didn't even know you had a house in the Valley. That's weird, Duncan. You've gotta admit that's weird, right?"

In the background, I heard the sound of the bathtub filling up, and it calmed me down. I could picture it all so clearly; Mrs. Kim tutting around with her veggies and her manifest-destiny hypochondria, Martha serenely soaking, a fragile Queen Mother, and Lydia in the kitchen with her Mötley Crüe shirt on, fretting over everything.

"It is weird," I agreed with her, "but you can throw it away. That plan isn't happening anymore. I have a new plan now."

"Oh," she said, ignoring the bit about the plan. "I just noticed the Big Sur poster is here. What's that about, Duncan? Were you coming over here when I asked you not to? I still haven't figured out what's going on with you two, but I know it can't be good. And definitely not healthy. This break is going to be good for us. I hope you can see that now."

"I do," I said, trying to ignore the Cat. It was trying to stop me by throwing itself against my insides, but I ignored it, despite the bruising pain in my ribs. I made myself focus. "And then after the break…" I started to say, but she interrupted me.

Her voice was resolute, but I sensed there were breaking points in it, soft spots where it might one day splinter if the right kind of pressure was patiently applied. "I'm not making any promises about what comes after. That's not what a break is. A break is a break. From thinking about it, especially."

"I wasn't going to say that," I explained patiently. I wanted everything to be crystal clear. "I was going to say that I had a plan I thought was going to help us all, but it got kind of ruined."

She was quiet for a few seconds, and I couldn't tell if she was busy helping Martha or if she was thinking about what I'd just said. "I'm not sure what you're talking about."

"Deedee's brother caught that mountain lion the paper's been reporting on," I started to explain, keeping my eye on the counter. "It was in a cage in my mother's garage, and I was going to have your mother come see it, because I thought if she…"

"What?" She screamed. "Are you fucking crazy, Duncan? If she what? What exactly? Saw it and had a heart attack? Is that how you were going to help her? By fucking killing her?"

The machine hit zero, and a long loud beep spread around the room.

"What's that?" She asked. "Are you playing video games or something?"

I laughed. "No." I hit the charge button again, and another ten seconds appeared on the counter. If only the rest of life was like this, I thought, ten extra seconds whenever you needed it just by pushing a button. "I wasn't trying to give Martha a heart attack. I just thought if she could see it, or talk to it, or pray with it…I don't know. I wanted her to get to look in its eyes and I thought if she could do that it would help her. I thought it would maybe free her somehow. But I know now, that's not how it works."

"That's literally the craziest thing I've ever heard in my life. You understand how this sounds, right? You understand how crazy you're sounding right now, don't you?"

One of the paddles slipped a little, and I caught it before it fell off my chest. I put it back on top of me and clicked the charge button again, just as the counter was rounding 'two.'

"I do," I said. "That's why I have a new plan now. I know how to get rid of the Cat and when I do I think everything will be different. For us and for Martha. It's going to be great, Lydia. Really."

"I don't know what you're talking about," she said, and I could hear sadness catching up to the frustration in her tone. She moved the phone away from her mouth and spoke softly to Martha. "No," she said to her mother, "it's Duncan. He says 'hi.'" I laughed. "I don't know what you're talking about," she was talking to me again, repeating what she'd just said to make sure I hadn't missed a word, "but you do what you have to do."

"And if this works," I said, pushing the charge button once again right as it was about to hit zero, "we can try again? All of us?"

She was silent, and I heard the water turn off, imagined the tendrils of steam reaching up to the ceiling, the soap and the toilet paper cover, all those wonderful woman smells. Promises of perfect homes and perfect lives. "I don't know," was all she could give me.

"Can you at least say that you never know what will happen? Would you give me that at least?"

Silence, and then, "Would that make you feel better?"

The buzzer hit zero, and I pushed the charge button again.

"It would," I said. The Cat was looking around crazily, doing that animal thing where they sensed danger but couldn't tell yet exactly how bad the thing coming was going to be.

"Ok then," she made her voice do a phone sex operator Disney princess thing. "*You never know what the future might bring.* How was that?" she asked, switching back to normal Lydia mode.

"Perfect," I said, and I meant it. I looked at the timer. 4 seconds…"Goodbye, Lydia."

"Goodbye?" She sounded kind of surprised. "That sounds awfully final. After what I just said to you? Let's not be so final, okay? I like this leaving it open thing we have going on. Let's leave it at the part where we were before the goodbye. At the 'you never know' part. Okay?"

One…and then the loud beep again like a long hallway, only

there was something there at the end, wasn't there? Was it a door? Or a person? Or was it the shape of a dream? Whatever. It didn't really matter. Because with the push of a button, we were off.

# ACKNOWLEDGMENTS

I wrote *Mountain Lion Blues* during the pandemic, an extremely isolating time for me and everybody else. Writing and sharing pieces of this book with my friends helped ground me and connect me to a world I sometimes forgot still existed, but was so happy to be reminded, in my interactions, was still there. Thank you to Monica Corcoran, Gene Morgan, Tim Adams, Chuckles and Adam Bregman for reading and encouraging. Thanks to Chelsea Hodson and Chris Compton for the edits, especially to Chelsea, who may just very well be a lumberjack. Thanks to Brad Listi for your support and for giving book people a place to be. Thanks to Miles and everyone at Chevalier's for the recommendations and support. My sincerest gratitude to Abby Weintraub for the magical artwork that makes a book feel like a thing. To Mark Givens, my publisher, who, when he said, after reading the manuscript, "Fuck it, let's do it" made my heart sing. And last but not least, my thanks to Ellen, Harper and Sasah whose love is what makes it all make sense.

# ABOUT THE AUTHOR

Adam Greenfield was born and grew up in Los Angeles, which he sees as a blessing and a curse. The ocean has paralyzed him emotionally in many ways. In his waking life he works for a national social impact communications firm. He is married and has two daughters who like to bake and watch old movies with him. His kids are 16 and 13 and he recently read that as a parent about 80% of all the time you're ever going to spend with your children is before they're 12. He feels that that's a lot to reckon with. *Mountain Lion Blues* is his second novel.

112 Harvard Ave #65
Claremont, CA 91711 USA

pelekinesis@gmail.com
www.pelekinesis.com

Pelekinesis titles are available through Small Press Distribution,
Ingram, Gardners, and directly from the publisher's website.

Milton Keynes UK
Ingram Content Group UK Ltd.
UKHW040652120923
428521UK00004B/253